Everything I Know

About Zombies,

I Learned in

Kindergarten

BY

Kevin Wayne Williams

Most of the locations in this book are real, but, with one exception, the people are not. In particular, no student or staff member of the PS43 depicted in this novel represents any student or staff member of the actual PS43.

Mary Mallon (aka "Typhoid Mary") was a real person and actually was quarantined on North Brother Island.

This book is set in Goudy Bookletter 1911, created by the League of Movable Type. The titles are in Bonaventure Condensed, created by Greater Albion Typefounders.

Heartfelt thanks go to my brother, Robert Franklin Williams, who sorted through the typos and punctuation errors.

PUBLISHED OCTOBER, 2014 BY MOTT HAVEN BOOKS

The work of three preachers inspired this story.
They probably would not be pleased.

In 1741, Jonathon Edwards, A.M., wrote the sermon SINNERS IN THE
HANDS OF AN ANGRY GOD and unwittingly created horror as a genre.

In 1906, the Reverend Charles S. Wing wrote the
STORY OF THE ENGINE THAT THOUGHT IT COULD.

In 1988, Reverend Robert Fulghum wrote ALL I REALLY NEED TO
KNOW I LEARNED IN KINDERGARTEN. Amidst all the platitudes and
reassuring heartwarming stories, there were fifteen rules. Rule 15 read:

*"Goldfish and hamster and white mice and even the little seed in
the styrofoam cup — they all die. So do we."*

Everything I Know About Zombies, I Learned in Kindergarten

BY

KEVIN WAYNE WILLIAMS

The Fall of PS 43	1
The Hall	9
Señor Jesús to the Rescue	16
Inside the Cafeteria	21
A Plan	24
An Auspicious Beginning	27
Look Both Ways	30
In the Garden	32
The Alleyway	33
Dinner, then off to Bed	36
Candy for Breakfast	40
Hey, Mom! I'm Home!	43
Burning Your Bridges	45
To the River	46
Bedtime	50
Lost Pup	53
On the Roof	61
Now I Lay Me Down to Sleep	66
Yo' Mama Is So Fat ...	68
North Brother Island	70
Coloring Book Day	74
A Treasure Trove	76
Practice Makes Perfect	79
The Night the Lights Went Out	81
A Flotilla Launches	84
The Hospital	86
Setting Up Camp	89
Teach a Man to Fish	93
The Notebook	96
Window Day	99
Hair and Sharpening Stones	100
Laying in Supplies	102
Slim Pickings	104
Prayers for Little Criminals	107
Fishing Trip	108
Fun and Games	110
Shooting Practice	111
As Ye Sow, So Shall Ye Reap	112
Barbeque	115
To Mills Rock and Back Again	117
Days of Summer	119
Emergency 911	121
Helpless	123

The Clinic	125	Corner Office with a View	208
Snack Time	127	Back on the Roof	210
What Happened, Anyway?	128	Escape Attempt	211
Overnight Camp	131	Between Brothers	214
Late Night Awakenings	133	Astoria	215
New Arrivals	134	Conflagration	217
Out and About	137	Flotsam and Jetsam	219
Me and My Shadow	139	In the Clinic	221
Organizing	141	What Next?	223
Typhoid Mary	143	Gossip	225
Neighbors	147	Speeding Through the Night	227
The News	148	Regrouping	229
Dormitory Days	149	Breakfast	230
A Prayer for the Prisoners (silent)	151	Preparing for a Visit	232
Where There's Smoke...	152	Setting Up House	234
Back Across the River	154	Under a Flag of Truce	236
Settling In	156	A Boat Ride Home	239
Cliff	158	Cleaning up the Mess	243
Dessert	162	Now It's Time to Say "Goodnight"	245
The Pile Grows	164	A Funeral	246
New Skills	166	Remodeling	248
The Nursery	169	Route Planning	249
A Prayer for Babies	171	The Secret Pages	251
A Lazy Afternoon	172	Warehousing	252
The Burial	175	Target Practice	253
A Prayer for Catalina	176	Scouting Trips	254
The Great Guinea Pig Roundup	177	I-95	257
Theology	181	Another Notebook Page	258
Cold Snap	182	Thanksgiving	259
Third Avenue	184	Christmas	261
On the Beach	185	The Children's Table	264
The Man in the Green Shirt	188	Ice Fishing	266
Special Treatment	190	Springtime in New York City	267
A Prayer for Marie	191	Sneak Attack	271
Plumbing	192	In the Dormitory	273
Maternity Ward	194	Unleashing the Horde	275
Be Prepared	195	Tactical Support	278
One is the Loneliest Number	197	Roof of the Otis Bantum Center	280
Roosevelt Island	199	Noisemakers	284
Being Useful	201	Back Home	288
Resistance	202	Hunting Party	290
On the Roof	204	Pancakes for Breakfast	292
Cold Storage	205	A Journey of a Thousand Miles	
The Container Yard	207	Begins with a Single Step	293

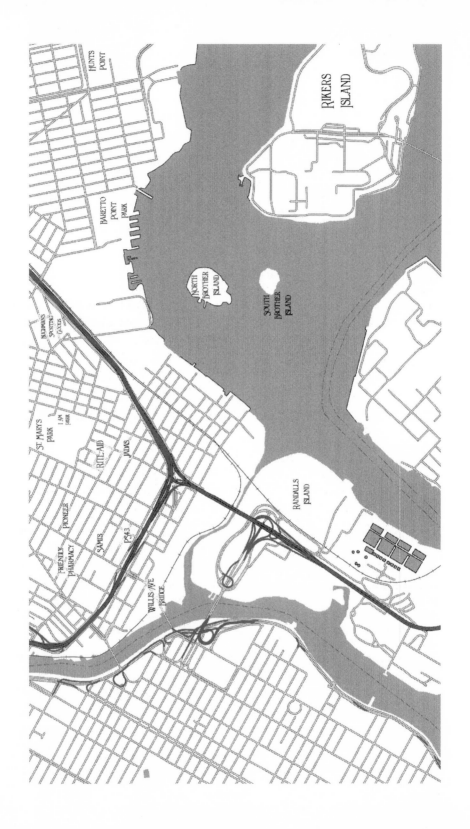

CHAPTER 1
THE FALL OF PS 43

The morning of the apocalypse opened, as most mornings did, with Letitia on her hands and knees searching in vain for something Jahayra had lost.

"Found it!" came Jahayra's voice from atop the bed. "I put it under my pillow last night so I don' lose it!" Letitia pulled her head out from under the bed and stood up, wiping the dust off the knees of her pants while Jahayra slid the once-lost yellow bead bracelet on her wrist.

"When you goin' to stop bein' this way?" asked Letitia. "Every morning it like this. Can't find your own stuff. Can't comb your own hair."

Letitia stopped for a moment and adjusted Jahayra's shirt. "You *five* now. It time to be learnin' how to do stuff. How we ever goin' to make someone want to keep us if you be like this? Who goin' to want to be our mama if that mean she goin' have to follow you around all the time?"

She stepped back and inspected Jahayra. At least Jahayra had her backpack on. Some mornings, she even managed to lose *that*. "I mean it, you know. What goin' to happen to you if they split us up again like they did last year?"

She looked at the clock. 8:20. "Look at that. No time for breakfast *again*."

Letitia pulled Jahayra's arm, dragging her towards the door. "G'bye, Mrs. Brown," she called as she grabbed a foil envelope of Pop-Tarts from the box on the kitchen counter, "we goin' to school now."

Letitia continued to grumble as she chewed on the cold pastry during the walk to school. They weren't even real Pop-Tarts. She liked a nice, toasted, strawberry Pop-Tart, the kind with frosting on the outside, the frosting with the little colored sprinkles pressed in. DCFS money wasn't enough to get Mrs. Brown to buy real Pop-Tarts, so these were some kind of fake store-brand things that tasted funny even when you toasted them. Jahayra being so slow all the time meant that she never got a chance to toast them. Every day it was something. Today, the bracelet. Yesterday, the pink shirt. Who knew what it would be tomorrow?

Jahayra chattered as they walked. "I hope I get the good crayons today!"

Letitia raised her eyebrow and swallowed the bite she had in her mouth. "*Good* crayons?" she asked. "What make a crayon a *good* crayon? Ain't they all the same?"

"No. We got some special crayons now. They really bright. It nearly like they glow. But Rosarita takes 'em every morning. She so big, she think she can have everything."

"Don' Mr. Domacasse do nothin' about it? She ain't bigger than Mr. Domacasse, is she?"

"He just say to share, but she don' know how to share. She barely know how to *talk*. Always sayin' 'see' when she mean 'yes' and 'no' when she mean 'not' and things like that. He say the next time we fight over 'em, he just goin' to take 'em away."

"Be nice," said Letitia, "lots of people talk kind of funny. Lot of people think that *we* talk funny." She knew she didn't talk right and worked hard at sounding like her friends. Kids didn't hear the Trinidad and Jamaica from her parents in her voice so much anymore, so they didn't laugh as much as they used to.

Letitia walked Jahayra right to the kindergarten door. Jahayra didn't even say goodbye: she just ran into class, made a quick detour on the way to her desk to pick up a box of crayons, and left Letitia behind. Letitia walked back three doors down to reach the fourth-grade classroom.

A couple of hours later, Social Studies class found Letitia staring grumpily at a page in the workbook for *Communities: Near and Far*. Inuit? What kind of name for people was "Inuit"? How was she supposed to care about some kind of people she can't even say?

"Is something wrong, Letitia?" Mrs. Robinson asked.

"No," replied Letitia.

"Then why isn't anything getting done in your workbook?"

"It just these stories 'bout people that I ain't never going to meet ..." Letitia began to complain. She saw the look on Mrs. Robinson's face and groaned inside.

"It *is* just these stories about people that I ain't never ... *am* never going to meet," she continued. Talking like that made her even grumpier. She wanted to talk like her *friends*, not Mrs. Robinson.

She didn't try to sound like Mrs. Robinson unless she had to. *Nobody* talked like Mrs. Robinson, with all her rules about double negatives and 'Don't say 'ain't' "and " 'I am' not 'I be' " and on and on forever. She had long ago decided that Mrs. Robinson must have taken special classes in how to talk like an old white lady because there was no way she could have come up with it by herself.

Loud pounding sounds came from the hallway. Mrs. Robinson started paying attention to them and stopped paying attention to Letitia, so whatever they were, they couldn't be *all* bad.

"Children, stay in your seats! I'll go see what's happening." Mrs. Robinson left the room, pausing once she got into the hallway, then closing the door with a sudden slam, her high heels clicking on the floor as she ran towards the entrance.

The pounding sounds got louder, and Deon, the boy sitting next to Letitia, couldn't contain himself. He got out of his seat and opened the door a crack, peering out.

Letitia couldn't help but follow. She half-hid behind Deon, staring over his shoulder, making it clear to anyone watching that *he* had opened the door, not her. A broom handle, wedged into the door handles of the main entrance, was bending under the strain of someone trying to force their way in. Some of the teachers were leaning on the doors, holding them closed, while others were trying to get a metal bar forced into the handles. Hands pressed against the outside of the windows next to the doorway, leaving red smears all over the frosted glass.

Letitia tried her best to make sense of this. If it was a movie, it would be some kind of monster or something. Vampires, maybe, or werewolves. When she lived with the Freemans, Mr. Freeman was always shouting about terrorists when he watched the news. Every bad thing that ever happened was because of terrorists. She had never heard of terrorists in an elementary school, though: she thought they did all their stuff in airports. Robbers? There's nothing in a school worth stealing. Why would they pound on the window? Why would they cut their hands?

Mr. Domacasse ran past, a box of fluorescent crayons in his hand, then ran back towards Jahayra's class. Letitia pushed her door open further, poked her head out, and watched him. He threw the crayons down by the fire box, smashed the glass and took the ax out of the case. Letitia stared. An *ax*? Mr. Domacasse must *really* want to scare those people if he was going to pretend he was going to hit them with an ax.

"Stay in here!" Mr. Domacasse shouted into Jahayra's class. "Keep this door closed and *don't* come out in the hall!" He slammed the door and came running back for the entrance.

Now the fire alarms were going, making it hard to hear the pounding at the entrance. The sound made the people outside even crazier: they pounded harder, making the glass start to crumble. The wire mesh inside the windows started to show. When Mr. Domacasse reached the front entrance, he began swinging the ax at the intruding arms and heads that were pressing their way through what was left of the windows.

Mr. Domacasse reared back and swung the ax with full force. A severed hand bounced off the linoleum. Deon ran from the doorway, pushing her out of the way and ran to the window. Other kids followed him, opening the windows and climbing out. Others ran down the hallway or tried to hide under their desks.

Letitia didn't know what to do. She pressed herself against the wall of the classroom, not looking out the door, just trying to be as small and flat as she could. The window didn't seem smart: if somebody was outside trying to get in to hurt little kids, wouldn't running outside be just like running right up to them? It would be better to hide somewhere and hope they couldn't find you. There was a supply cabinet ... maybe she could get in there. She started to open the cabinet when it hit her: Jahayra!

Whatever the smartest thing to do was, Jahayra wasn't going to do it without someone to help her, and if Mr. Domacasse was at the front door, he wasn't in Jahayra's class to help her. She crept back towards the door and peeked out. Nothing had changed, except there were more hands lying on the floor. She took a deep breath, squeezed through the cracked door, and ran down the hall, away from whatever was going on at the entrance and towards Jahayra's kindergarten class. She hoped she was wrong, that she would find a teacher's aide or something, helping with the kids.

She burst into the kindergarten, surprising a line of small children that all scrambled for their seats and tried to pretend that they hadn't been about to open the door. Letitia's heart fell. Mr. Domacasse really had left these kids alone.

Letitia was the biggest person in the room. Might as well go with it.

"I don' know what up," she started, "but Mr. Domacasse, he tell me to take care of you," she lied. "Somebody bad trying really hard to get in here. The teachers, they stoppin' 'em. Well, they *tryin'* to stop 'em."

Letitia poked her head out the door and took a fresh look back down the hallway. Mr. Domacasse was still swinging the ax as hard as he could. Mrs. Robinson's feet protruded through the window opening, jerking back and forth as something was dragging her outside. Letitia very nearly just grabbed Jahayra and ran for it, but there were twenty little kids in here. She couldn't just leave them, and there was no place to run, anyway.

Letitia came back inside. The kindergarten had its own small bathroom built in. There was a supply closet and a small sink with a cabinet under it for cleaning up on art days. A row of windows lined the wall, but the sounds of screaming coming from outside now were frightening, and she wasn't about to try to get this group of kids to leap out the windows. Besides, the screams outside meant she was right: the kids that ran outside must be getting caught. She was stuck here now, and there was nothing to do but hide.

"Jahayra!" she shouted over the fire alarm. "You and your friends get to emptying that closet. Just throw that stuff on the ground, make some room in there!

"You!" She pointed at one of the larger boys. "Help me with this!" She and the boy began pushing the desk towards the doorway. Some of the other children joined in, eager to see something that they could do to feel safe, while others just looked on terrified. Within a few minutes, the doorway was blocked with the desk and a couple of file cabinets. She felt a little calmer: at least no one could just walk right in anymore.

The windows were still a problem. She couldn't block them, but she could at least keep people from seeing in. Grabbing a stack of construction paper from the heap that had come out of the supply closet, she set children to taping and gluing paper over the windows.

The clock said it had only been fifteen minutes, but they had accomplished a lot. The room was closed and hard to see into. She couldn't tell what was going on outside, but the screams continued, along with loud chewing and swallowing noises.

They were trapped now. The popping sound of gunfire came in from the street, and sirens were wailing everywhere. The siren inside the building had finally stopped, but that just made it easier to hear all the noise coming from outside. Fearful tears welled up in her eyes as she thought about what would have happened if she had tried to get the kids to jump out the windows. She fought them back. Some of the little ones were already crying, and if she started, everybody would start.

She wiped her face dry with her sleeve and looked at the crowd of little ones around her. "Only be three places to hide in here," she said. "Under that sink, in that closet, and in that bathroom. I don' know who out there or when they going away, but I *know* they be bad. We got to hide. We get to hidin', and everybody got to be quiet till I tell you come on out. Remember, *quiet*! Pretend it be hide-and-seek or something, but *no noise!*"

No one argued. Letitia could barely keep them from running to the hiding places, trying to get away from the gunfire, screams, and sirens and helicopters that surrounded the school.

Letitia opened the doors under the arts-and-crafts sink. It was little, but big enough for four of the littlest girls. The closet wasn't much bigger, holding just five little boys. She grabbed Jahayra and pulled her into the bathroom with her.

"Everybody else, in here," she said, "pack in tight, 'cause there a bunch of us."

From here, the sounds from inside the school were muffled, but they were coming from everywhere now. Adults shouted orders at children until they started screaming, a sound that was always followed by waves of high-pitched screams and running feet. She hoped they were getting somewhere, but she couldn't think of anyplace *to* go.

One of the little ones near her, a pudgy little Dominican girl, began to wail. Letitia clamped a hand tightly over the child's mouth.

"You got to stop that," she said in a fierce whisper, "you just got to stop. Can't let anybody know we here."

The tears kept coming, complete with snot oozing over her fingers, when there was a loud *thump* at the door to the classroom. The child she was holding choked back her tears. The others all held their breath.

The noise came again, accompanied by a slight squeak as the desk slid a bit under the impact. The noise kept up for hours, the only change coming when the door started to crack and splinter. No one cried anymore. They made no noise, trying hard to just disappear.

Sounds came from other places in the room. A low crying, snuffling sound came from one of the other hiding places. Letitia couldn't tell whether it was the girls under the sink or the boys in the closet. She could tell the effect it had on whoever was at the door, though. The crying would get louder, and the thumping and squeaking would get more furious. Something would distract the thumpers, and the thumps would stop for a while. The crying would stop, then start, and the thumpers would start again. Over and over until she heard one long squeak.

Footsteps shuffled into the room, and the pounding sounds moved to the cabinet under the sink. The wooden cabinet doors cracked. The girls under the sink screamed, cried, then went silent as wet ripping and chewing sounds filled the room.

The sounds proved too much for the boys in the closet. The closet door squeaked open and the running footsteps sounded as the boys tried to make a run for it. The sounds in the room subsided as slower footsteps followed them out the door. The screams from the hallway didn't provide her with any hope for the boys.

The sounds from inside the building slowly faded away as the hours went by. The children grabbed fearful sleep, more a case of succumbing to shock than resting. Finally, it was quiet enough that Letitia dared open the bathroom door. She wasn't sure how long they had been in there. Two days? Three? Four? It was hard to tell time when you worried about dying. Two days, probably.

"You guys stay in here. I'm goin' out, goin' to see if it safe out there," she said as she cracked the bathroom door open. Leaving the bathroom and seeing the girls, she quickly slammed it shut again behind her before any of the little ones could see. She remembered how Mrs. Robinson slammed the door behind her that first day. She hadn't thought she would *ever* act like Mrs. Robinson.

She knew what she had to do today, though. Maybe acting like Mrs. Robinson wasn't a bad idea: she had to *look* calm. It didn't matter if she wanted to crap her pants, she had to look calm. If she lost it, all these little kids would start running around screaming and get everybody killed.

She walked over to the bodies of the four girls that had been in the closet. Bile rose in her throat. She scanned around the room a moment. There wasn't anything here that would let her move the bodies without having to touch them.

She steeled herself inside. This wasn't going to be the first dead body she had to touch. It wasn't like it had been with her mom: she didn't know them or anything. They were just bodies. Not even bodies anymore, really: mainly bones.

The bones were easy. She stacked them in the closet. The soft parts were far worse: she could barely make herself touch them. She grabbed the trash can and carried it over so that she could do it quickly. She picked up the bits of loose meat and threw them away. One head was left. When she picked it up, it looked like the face was still moving. She closed her eyes and pushed it deep into the sack. She'd heard that you could have dreams while you were still awake if you stayed awake long enough. She dragged the trash can to the closet and set some play mats on the floor to cover the stain. It wasn't perfect, but it should keep the little ones from freaking out.

The sounds from inside the building were nearly gone. Outside was different: the helicopters were still flying over, the gunfire continued, and there were explosions in the distance.

The nasty sights taken care of, she opened the bathroom door. "Come on," she said, "I need you to help me get the door closed up again." They quickly slid the desk in place and pushed the file cabinets back to try to hold it there.

The smell out here was horrible, with the smell of rotten flesh making it so she wanted to choke. It wasn't enough to cover the smell of the children, though: none of the small children had kept their toilet training. Fixing that was the first thing she could do to start making things normal again.

"You guys got PE clothes or anything? Somethin' you can get changed into?"

The children pointed at a rack of cubbyholes on one wall. "Go get 'em," she said, and each of her charges found a bag of PE clothes. She washed each of the children in the arts-and-crafts sink, wadding up the soiled clothes. Soon she was surrounded by clean, fresh young five-year-olds all dressed as if it were time to go play volleyball.

"Get back over by the windows," Letitia said. "Look away." She went over to the closet where she had stuffed the dead girls and threw the piles of soiled clothing in there with them.

"The school make you guys sack lunches, don' it?" Little heads nodded: Mr. Domacasse always put the lunches from the free lunch program in each child's cubby every morning. The lunches were still there, waiting. She waited for everyone to grab a lunch and then took one of the ones that was left. They sat at the little desks and wolfed them down.

"Roll call," she said. "Jahayra the only person I know here."

The twin boys revealed themselves to be Jorge and Diego. Malik was the largest of the bunch and the hyperactive little boy proved to be Trevon. The runt of the litter, Jose, was barely half the size of the other boys. The little clique of friends over in the corner was Kiara, Tiara, and Jada, while the taller, aloof girl was Rosarita. Lucia and Maria rounded out the group.

Letitia still didn't know what was going on, but she was certain that help wasn't coming. If help had already come, it had missed them. She needed to find out what was going on.

"Malik, Rosarita, you two be biggest. Rosarita, you the boss of the girls, Malik, you the boss of the boys. Open the door a crack. I'm goin' out. Close it up after me. Don't be opening it till I'm back."

CHAPTER 2
THE HALL

The hallway floor was covered in blood, torn clothing, and body parts. Letitia knew this wasn't from bombs or guns because it looked more like the leftovers on her plate the one time she had gone to Ponderosa: everything on the floor was bits of bone and gristle, with all the softer pieces gone. There was a big pile of bodies outside the fifth-grade class: little kids lying in an enormous heap in front of the door, their heads smashed in with baseball bats or sticks. Letitia peeked carefully inside the room and saw the school janitors sitting inside. The baseball bats lay at their feet, and there were bodies everywhere. The janitors looked asleep, their hands resting on great big bellies like it was right after Thanksgiving or something. They didn't look right at all, though, with bluish, waxy skin covered in great big rips and cuts, like the zombies she saw sometimes in movie ads.

Zombies. She'd figured zombies were like vampires or werewolves, something that didn't really exist. She didn't really know exactly what she had been expecting instead.

Letitia kept walking towards the front entrance, where everything had begun. It was blocked by another large pile of bodies: bodies that had been mainly eaten mixed with bodies with the head smashed in or, sometimes, with a big thing like a screwdriver sticking out of its head. Anything that wasn't moving had something wrong with its head.

There were a number of heads that were still alive: the body was gone, but the head still looked alive. Maybe she hadn't been dreaming when she saw the head in the class move. Mr. Domacasse was still there, his clothing, jewelry, and wallet scattered all over as his head helplessly watched. He gnashed his teeth, but couldn't do much of anything.

Letitia went over to examine Mr. Domacasse more carefully. The eyes blinked and watched her, the teeth snapped at her as she approached. No sound, though: without lungs, he couldn't make a sound. She crouched in front of him. He *had* to be dead. There was no body. No lungs, no heart, nothing that could keep him alive. She wasn't dreaming this, though: that mouth was moving.

She had to find a way that she could make things like this stop moving. Those janitors would wake up sometime, and they still had arms and legs.

She turned back to Mr. Domacasse. He was already dead, wasn't he? It wouldn't be like killing him, would it? She had never liked Mr. Domacasse much anyway. She found the ax he had been using in the first place and brought it down on his skull. It split open and his face stopped moving. She pulled the ax free and wiped it off with a piece of his shirt.

Maybe those movies had gotten parts of this right.

Those little kids weren't going to be able to do it this way, she realized. *She* could barely do it this way, because it took most of her strength to swing and control something the size of the fire ax.

"Got to find something the kids can use," she began to mutter to herself before closing her own mouth with her hand. That didn't mean she was wrong, though: she had to find something a kindergartener could handle that could do some good. Since the janitors were all in the fifth-grade classroom, she made her way to the janitorial closet.

Letitia opened the closet door. There was all kinds of junk in here: cleaning bottles, mops, brooms. Not much good unless there was a way to clean a zombie to death. She searched the shelves, eventually finding a set of garden stakes buried underneath the clutter: eighteen inches long, metal, and sharp. Not much, but all a five-year-old was going to be able to handle anyway.

Letitia went back to class. She knocked very quietly on the door. The reply was the sound of dozens of tiny little feet running away.

She knocked again and whispered "It me! I need back in!"

She heard murmured discussion and then the sound of filing cabinets being moved and the desk sliding a little bit. The door opened about an inch, and childish eyes peeked though the gap. She whispered again. "It really me. Let me in!" More noises, and then the gap widened enough that she could squeeze sideways through the crack. She helped push things back in place, then started the task of trying to explain things to the kids.

"How many of you know 'bout zombies?" she started.

Just as in class, the little hands popped up. Just as in class, Trevon couldn't restrain himself.

"It a dead person that be walkin' 'round eating people. My brother has movies about them, but they just made up things. They ain't real!"

"That what I thought," said Letitia. "Not no more. There be zombies out there."

The children broke out in an excited argument. Most of them decided that Letitia had to be wrong, but they had seen through the crack in the door and had spent so much time so scared of so many noises that they knew *something* scary was out there. Letitia finally shut it down: "I just saw some. Killed some. You want to stay alive, you goin' to have to help me kill them. I can't do it by myself."

With that, she gave each of the children a garden stake.

"I think it like the movies," said Letitia. "Look like all of them that be dead got that way by someone hittin' em on the head." She decided it wasn't the right time to mention Mr. Domacasse. "You guys too little to be beating they heads in with axes or nothin'. I think it work if you poke that in their head, through an eye or an ear or somethin'. We gotta try, or we ain't goin' nowhere."

A quick expedition into the hallway later, Letitia came back with the upper portions of Mr. Brahms and Ms. Beasley. The children backed against the wall, holding their stakes out in front of them, not as weapons, but more like the crosses from vampire movies, as if they thought the stake would scare the zombies away.

"If you goin' to learn to kill 'em, you gotta get close to 'em." Letitia pointed at the remains of the teachers. "Look at 'em. They still kinda alive, but it ain't really them no more. No arms, so they can't grab you. No legs, so they can't come runnin' after you, neither."

The children slowly came forward to take a closer look. They had all seen dead things before: mainly dogs and cats that had been run over by cars. This wasn't too much different. Mr. Brahms had been decapitated by something sharp, his head ending cleanly at the neck, but Ms. Beasley had been more or less ripped asunder and still possessed a large flapping structure of skin and shoulder.

The boys all found Ms. Beasley fascinating. Trevon pointed at the flap of skin. "I think that piece there is one of her boobies!" he declared. Jorge nodded, and soon all the boys agreed.

Letitia cut the discussion off. "OK, Rosarita, right?"

"*Si,*" responded the tallest girl.

"Take that stake you got and push it in her eye. Hard as you can. Let's see if you can kill her."

"*Que* ... what?"

"Push it in her eye till she stop floppin' 'round like that."

"*Ay, no.* I no can do that. *Es imposible.*"

Letitia persisted. "What you goin' to do if one of them come after you? Shout 'S imposiblay' at it? There a bunch of these things out there. Some got arms and legs."

Rosarita couldn't. Letitia looked at the rest of the little ones, and not a one looked up to it.

" 'kay, come with me," she said, and walked over to the closet. She opened the door. "Look in there. See what happen to your friends? You wanna be like that?"

The children ran. Jose was the first to run back into the bathroom, but once he did, the other eleven all followed and closed the door, leaving Letitia alone in the classroom.

Snuffling sounds came through the door, followed by full-on tears. There was a quick rustle of motion, then the sound of tiny hands being clamped over a crying mouth came through the door. Letitia sighed. At least they had learned not to cry out loud.

This was a lot like outwaiting one of Jahayra's tantrums. It didn't do any good to yell or push, you just had to wait. She poked around the classroom and scanned the little bookshelf. She remembered most of these books: *Where the Wild Things Are*, *Green Eggs and Ham*, *The Little Engine That Could*. She paged her way through *The Cat in the Hat Comes Back*, waiting for the murmured discussion in the bathroom to stop. The doorknob turned, and Jahayra's head poked out of the bathroom door.

"Letitia?"

"Yeah?"

"Everybody want to know why we got to do it. You the biggest. Why can't you do it?"

"I ain't no Wonder Woman!" Letitia answered. "There a lot of these things. Can't do everything by myself."

The door closed again. More murmurs leaked out. The doorway opened again, and Jahayra's head popped out.

"You sure the ones you brought in can't hurt us?"

"Don' think they can. They just sittin' over there where they were when I brought 'em in. Can't chase you with no legs. Can't grab you with no arms."

The door closed again. More murmuring.

Jahayra poked her head out once more. "OK, we try."

The troop came out of the bathroom. "C'mon, Rosarita," said Letitia, "you still the biggest. You first."

Rosarita took her stake in her hands and pressed it up against Ms. Beasley's eye. Ms. Beasley didn't react: she just continued moving her mouth up and down.

"Press it!" said Letitia. "She ain't goin' to pop like a balloon or nothin'. You got to press hard." Rosarita closed her eyes and pushed as hard as she could. The stake went in the eye, but Ms. Beasley continued to move. Fluid slowly dripped down her cheek, leaving a small puddle on the floor.

"Try movin' it back and forth. See what happen."

Rosarita gritted her teeth and wiggled the stake. After a bit, Ms. Beasley suddenly stopped moving. Rosarita pulled the stake out with a soft *sflup* sound. She looked like she wanted to be sick, but she walked back to the end of the line.

Malik went next. He didn't make the same mistakes that Rosarita did and quickly pressed his stake through Mr. Brahms's eye and wiggled it until Mr. Brahms stopped moving.

Letitia needed to get more heads. The girl in the closet would be easy to get, but that would probably make the kids freak out again.

They pushed the file cabinets and desk back one more time, and Letitia walked back out into the hall once more. The smell was getting worse out here. She looked closely at the heads in the hallway: she hadn't noticed on the first trip out, but a lot of these were still moving. That was easy to figure out: when people ate animals, they didn't usually eat the head. Zombies did the same thing when eating people. The eyes and mouth wouldn't stop moving until something smashed the brain.

Little kid heads would be hard for everybody, so she looked for adults. She found a secretary, a librarian, and a few teacher's aides. She carried them back, one by one, to the doorway.

"It me again," she whispered, and, after a few noises, the door cracked open again.

"I ain't got one for everybody. Probably better if you guys do it with a buddy, anyway. Just like when you go on field trips.

"Jahayra, Kiara, you two next."

Jahayra and Kiara walked up to a teacher's assistant. Jahayra pressed against one eye, Kiara pressed against the other. They each leaned in and wiggled the stake. With two working together, it went quickly. Each pair of kindergarteners got a chance to push and wiggle a stake.

Doing it in a crowd and not having to be first made it easier. Everyone managed one kill as Letitia watched. They wouldn't be very use*ful*, Letitia thought, but at least they wouldn't be use*less*.

The sun was setting as Letitia walked over to the row of cubbyholes. Eight sack lunches left. She piled them on a low table.

"We can't eat those!" Jorge whispered harshly. "Mr. Domacasse always say that we can't eat nobody else's lunch. Just our own." All of the other children nodded vigorously.

"This different," said Letitia.

"Why?"

"You ain't supposed to eat the other kid's lunch because he get hungry with no food, right?"

The children nodded.

"They can't get hungry no more, can they? They don't *need* their lunch no more."

The kids thought. "We ain't seen Bobby! Or LeVar, or Pedro, or Juan..." Jorge protested.

"If they still alive out there somewhere, they got to find something to eat by themselves. We the only ones here, and we got to eat," declared Letitia. She opened the sacks and did her best to split eight lunches thirteen ways.

It was dark in the room now. She kept the teacher's lamp on, but decided not to turn the big lights in the ceiling on. "Get your mats," she said. "Time for sleep."

The children placed the mats in a circle. Letitia went to the bookshelf and scanned the titles, quickly finding the one she was looking for.

" *The Little Engine That Could*," she began, reading in a whisper. "*A little railroad engine was employed about a station yard for such work as it was built for, pulling a few cars on and off the switches ...*"

When story time was over, eleven of the children were asleep. Jose tossed and fidgeted. Letitia was about to go over and talk to him when he got up and carried his mat with him into the bathroom.

Letitia waited, but no noises came out: no running water, no flushing, nothing. She finally went over and cracked the door open. Jose lay curled up on his mat, next to the toilet, fast asleep.

Letitia sat in the dim room, listening and watching for sounds of trouble, worried about having eaten all the food. If help hadn't come by morning, they were going to have to try to get food from the cafeteria. She crossed her fingers.

It didn't sound like people were going to be ready to come get them yet. The sound of gunfire continued all around, and the sounds of helicopters never seemed to stop. There were frequent crashes and bangs, like people dropping great big pots and pans.

She didn't have to wake Malik for him to take his turn. He awoke on his own, roused by the familiar and uncomfortable sensation of being cold and wet. He laid awake and ashamed in the dusky room, a room illuminated only by one small lamp acting as a nightlight. He hadn't wet the bed for over a year and now he had done it when everybody would know.

Finally, he stood up and walked over to Letitia.

"I need to change," he said.

"Change? Why?"

Malik shuffled a little bit, eyes downcast. "Wet myself," he murmured.

Letitia felt irritated but tried not to let it show. She'd shared enough foster homes with enough bedwetters to know that if you made a big deal out of it, it just got worse. At least he hadn't peed all over *her*.

"No big deal," she said. "You just a little scared. Everybody a little scared, I think." She thought a moment. "Still got some gym shorts over there, don't we?"

Malik nodded.

" 'kay, go wipe things up with some paper towels. Throw your mat in that closet. Long as you clean up after yourself, I ain't worryin' about it."

Malik got to work and got the area next to his mat dry. He didn't like opening the closet full of dead girls, but it was better than letting everyone see his wet mat. He found Robert's gym shorts and put them on. He hoped Robert got away that first night, but he didn't think so. He knew that Robert wouldn't need his gym shorts anymore, though.

CHAPTER 3
SEÑOR JESÚS TO THE RESCUE

"*¿Dónde? ... ¿Escuela?*" Rosarita woke up, struggling for a moment to remember where she was before realizing she was still at school. Jahayra's sister said she couldn't go home until the noises were gone or someone came to get her. She wanted to go home *now*. Mama was going to be angry that she hadn't gone home on the bus, and maybe Mama wouldn't even *believe* her about the scary dead things. Then she'd be in big trouble, like the time she ran away. Mama wouldn't let her play outside for a week after that.

Abuela would believe her, though. Abuela always warned her that if she wasn't good, *el Diablo* would send the *cucos* after her. When Abuela talked about them, the cucos were always big: great big things that hid in dark shadows until you were bad, when they would chase you down and eat you. She hoped that Abuela would be there when she got home. Mama might not believe her, but Abuela would, and Abuela would make Mama believe her. She was Mama's mama, after all, and Mama still did what Abuela said, at least most of the time.

Nobody else was awake. Malik was sitting at the table, but he was asleep. Rosarita walked to the bathroom and went inside. Jose was lying on the floor, sleeping. "*Es no habitación, es baño,*" she said, kicking Jose lightly on the side. Jose picked up and left.

Rosarita nearly flushed when she was done, but remembered just in time not to. Señor Domacasse always made a big fuss about flushing, but Jahayra's sister said to only flush if it smells really bad so we don't make too much noise. She had had to ask Lucia about that, because she didn't believe she had understood right. Not *flush*? Everybody always got mad at her when she didn't flush.

She washed her hands anyway. Nobody told her not to wash her hands, and that was another thing Señor Domacasse always made a big fuss over. She was in enough trouble already for not going home.

She went back out in the room, where everyone else was starting to get up. She was hungry. Even on days when there wasn't any meat, Mama could give her enough rice or beans so that her stomach didn't feel like this, and the school always gave her a big lunch that she didn't have to share. That was another thing Señor Domacasse always said, that everybody should eat their own lunch. Eating somebody else's lunch was another thing Jahayra's sister said was OK to do last night. She hoped she didn't get in trouble for that, too.

Jahayra's sister was talking again. Señor Domacasse always said everything twice: once in English, and then again in Spanish, but Jahayra's sister didn't speak any Spanish, so she was really hard to understand. It was something about waiting for help. Something about it being safe in here. She listened hard for words like "food" and "breakfast." She didn't hear any. Sometimes people would use words she didn't know, though. She missed out on lots of things because she didn't know the words.

Her stomach rumbled harder. She walked up to Jahayra's sister. Rosarita tugged on her sleeve. "*Hermana de Jaha...*"

She cut her off. "My name ain't 'Herman', it 'Letitia.' *Letitia.*"

"We have food for *desayuno* ... for breakfast, *Letícia*?" Rosarita asked.

"No, there ain't no more food," Letícia said, "them sack lunches last night was it."

Rosarita's stomach grumbled and hurt even more. Everybody started to whine. Letícia looked angry. "You want me to go back out there?"

Everybody nodded.

"It ain't happenin'. Just ain't."

Rosarita promised herself that she wasn't going to whine like the littler kids, but some of them even started to cry. Lucia didn't just cry a little, either, it was loud. Letícia put her hand over Lucia's mouth. "You can't cry that way. You *can't*. Them things hear us, they come for us. You gotta stay quiet." She shook her head and looked like she was going to cry too.

"If I go get us food, you guys promise to stay quiet? No more cryin'?"

Everybody nodded again.

Letícia looked the way Mama did when she'd been up all night taking care of the baby but still had to go to work. Mama really *did* cry, sometimes, but Letícia just covered her face with her hands for a moment.

"'kay," she said, pointing at Rosarita and Malik, "you two biggest, so you got to come help. There got to be somethin' to eat in the cafeteria."

Rosarita felt like crying, too. She hadn't been outside the room yet, but she had looked through the door when Letícia came in and out. She had seen the blood and smelled the smell. She didn't want to go out there.

She wasn't going to be a crybaby, though. This Letícia was smarter than Señor Domacasse about one thing: Letícia knew that it was important that Rosarita was the biggest girl in the class. Señor Domacasse never acted like her being the biggest was important, but Letícia knew better. She couldn't act like a baby now, not when it was her chance to show everybody how big she was.

She ran and got her stake from her cubby, then helped push the file cabinet and desk out of the way. Letícia opened the door and the stink came in from the hall. It was a lot worse than yesterday. Rosarita gulped and tried not to breathe any more than she had to. Nearly everybody gagged, and she heard some run for the bathroom.

She couldn't run for the bathroom: being the biggest meant she had to pretend not to be bothered by the smell.

Letícia started out the door. Rosarita started to follow her, but Jahayra pushed right past her, running right out the door. She was only gone a few seconds and came back in with the box of special bright crayons in her hand. She stuck her tongue out at Rosarita and ran to the table.

Rosarita didn't have time to fight over crayons. She followed Letícia out the door. It was really messy out here, with little bits of dried-up meat and bone all over. There were bugs everywhere, buzzing flies and little white worms that were eating the specks of meat. The door closed behind her. She wanted to run back in before they could move the desk in place, but acting the biggest meant she had to pretend not to be scared. She crossed herself. Mama always said that Señor Jesús would help you if you crossed yourself and asked for it, so she asked for help.

She moved her stake into her left hand and grabbed Malik's hand with her right one. He squeezed back, and they started to follow the big girl down the hall. She hoped she didn't look as scared as Malik did. Letícia's ax made her feel a little better. She wished she was big enough to have an ax.

They kept walking by piles of bodies, and she had to keep asking Señor Jesús for help. Nothing came out of the piles, so he must be helping. He even helped her not to fall when she slipped on that puddle of brown stuff by the third-grade class.

Letícia and Malik kept looking ahead, but she was afraid something was going to come up behind them, so she kept looking over her shoulder. They got to the big square spot in the hall, the place that had the library doors on the left side and the cafeteria doors on the right. Letícia started to push on the cafeteria door. It was a good thing that Rosarita kept looking backwards, because another girl nearly the same size as Letícia came out of the library. She looked scary, because her left arm was gone and her skin was blue, a blue you could nearly see through. The skin looked like the candles that Mama lit on special days. She didn't have any of the things Abuela had warned her about. She wasn't tall. She wasn't wearing a robe. Still, she looked like something *el Diablo* would send. Maybe Abuela had been wrong about some parts, but this had to be a cuco.

"*¡Vamonos!*" cried Rosarita as she pulled Malik towards the cafeteria. Letícia stopped a moment and said "Leonie?" and then her face looked all scared.

They ran in the cafeteria and stood in front of the double doors, holding them closed. The lock was way up high, past where any of them could reach. She kept asking Señor Jesús to lock the door, but the lock stayed where it was. The door kept bumping her against her back because the cuco kept pounding on it.

"Do you two think you can keep these shut? Just for a few seconds?" Letícia asked. Malik asked her what she was going to do.

"I run up there and get ready with this ax. When I tell you to, you come up behind me. Think you can do that?"

Rosarita looked over at Malik. Malik looked back at her, and they both nodded at each other. "OK, we try," Rosarita said.

Letícia ran up, turned around, and lifted her ax way over her head. Rosarita asked Señor Jesus for help again when Letícia shouted "GO!" She ran up and stood behind Letícia. The big doors came open and the girl with the blue waxy skin came through. Letícia let the ax drop. It bounced off the cuco's head and got stuck in her shoulder, right above the arm that was gone. Letícia pulled on the ax, but it didn't come loose. The cuco kept moving her arm and trying to get Letícia, but Letícia kept her hands on the ax, and that kept the cuco away. Letícia kept wiggling and pulling, but the ax stayed stuck. Rosarita and Malik stayed behind Letícia's legs.

"You two gotta do *somethin'*!" Letícia said.

Rosarita thought about running back to class and getting everybody, but she wouldn't have Letícia and the ax with her. She didn't want to be out in the hall with cucos without Letícia and the ax.

"Rosarita," Malik said, "that side with no arm? She can't get us on that side."

Rosarita looked. This wasn't like yesterday. Yesterday was just a head, a head that didn't have arms or legs. This cuco didn't have *both* her arms, though, so Malik was right: they should be able to poke her with the sticks.

She hoped that Señor Jesús didn't get mad at little girls that asked for help too many times. "Is true, we try," she said.

Rosarita ran towards the cuco and pushed her stake into an eye, and Malik ran and did it too. The stakes didn't go deep enough.

"*¡Por favor, Señor Jesús!*"

They pushed the stakes again. This time the cuco fell over like she was supposed to. Rosarita squeezed Malik's hand tightly. Her heart pounded, she wanted to vomit, but it was nice to know that Malik and Señor Jesús were going to help with things.

CHAPTER 4
INSIDE THE CAFETERIA

Letitia looked down at the ground. Rosarita and Malik pulled on their stakes, withdrawing them from Leonie's eyes with a pair of satisfying *sflup* noises that made Letitia confident that Leonie wasn't getting back up.

Letitia stood on Leonie's chest and used the leverage to withdraw her ax. This hurt. Leonie wasn't any different from her, except that Leonie used to cheat off of people's papers in class and Letitia didn't. That wasn't a big enough difference to make this feel good. Saying she was sorry wasn't going to make any difference.

"Sorry," she said anyway. She rolled Leonie over so she didn't have to look at her face and the three of them dragged Leonie away from the door.

They sat for a few minutes, catching their breath and letting their hearts slow back down. Letitia felt a tug on her arm again. "Letitia? Is that goin' to happen to us?"

"I don' know, exactly," answered Letitia. She tried to think of a way to answer without making things worse. "In the movies, you only get like that if one of 'em kill you. I got my ax. You two got your sticks. Long as we take care of each other and kill them first, we don' have to worry."

Letitia went over to the kitchen and pushed on the steel door. It didn't move. The locks were these great big security locks that needed keys, and she wasn't going to go to the office to search for keys. This ax would just break. That left the vending machines.

These weren't good vending machines like you saw in stores, the kind that were full of good stuff. These only had the kind of food that the school thought was good stuff and that wasn't very good. It was full of flavored water, mushy overripe bananas, bags of dried fruit chips, and rice cakes. The entire contents of the vending machine was barely a meal for them.

Still, it was something, and they were hungry.

"We gotta figure out a way to carry this stuff before I smash up the machine," she said. "Once I smash it, them things be hearin' it and comin' in here. We got to be fast."

Rosarita and Malik took off, over towards the dish return, holding hands the entire way. It was hard not to be a little jealous of having someone that made you feel safer. They found one trolley that hadn't been locked away and rolled it over by the machine.

"Watch the door," Letitia said, raising her ax and swinging. The safety glass on the front of the machine crumbled and didn't make a lot of noise. Maybe nothing would notice.

They looked nervously at the doorway anyway, half-afraid of a zombie horde and half-afraid that a teacher was going to walk in and catch them messing with the vending machines. Neither happened, so they loaded the cart with snacks.

They pushed the cart towards the double doors, and Letitia wished she could see through them. She settled for standing a few feet in front of them, ax at the ready, while Rosarita and Malik each pulled on a door handle. The doors opened wide, and nothing came through. She waited a few seconds and then walked forward, pulling the cart behind her. The little ones quickly followed her.

When they got back to class, Letitia knocked softly. A little voice came out from behind the door: "That you, Letitia?"

"Of course it me. You think zombies be knockin' on doors?"

The sounds of the desk and file cabinets being moved came through the door, and the door opened once more. Letitia rolled the cart into the room. The kids descended on the cart, and Letitia shushed them away.

"This got to last us a while. There ain't no more in the cafeteria, and we ain't goin' looking for more. Let me get it counted."

Letitia counted out some snacks for later, handed out some snacks to each child, and they all sat down to lunch.

Rosarita sat next to the other Spanish speakers. Letitia couldn't tell exactly what they were talking about, but whatever Rosarita was saying, the others didn't look like they believed it. They kept giggling and Rosarita kept getting madder.

Lucia ran over. "Rosarita, she *really* save you from a monster? Is true?"

"Yeah, it true. Malik and Rosarita, they kill one." Letitia looked around the room. Everyone was listening. She continued in a low voice.

"Rosarita and Malik, they do good today. They work together, they kill one of them things. Kept me from gettin' hurt. Everybody goin' to have to learn to do that, but they the first, and they done good." Rosarita and Malik beamed.

After lunch, Jahayra tugged Letitia's sleeve. "Look at the picture I drew!"

The drawing of Letitia, Rosarita, and Malik walking down the hall was brightly colored in fluorescent crayons. Letitia had to admit that the choice of "Radical Red" for the bloodstains worked pretty well, and even Rosarita smiled broadly when she saw it. She was still a bit angry about the crayons, but Jahayra had made her nearly as big as Letitia in the drawing. She liked that.

CHAPTER 5
A PLAN

Nobody could get to sleep that night. The guns outside were louder and closer, the explosions were bigger, the helicopters were lower. Jose crept off to the bathroom to sleep like he had the night before. Jada and Tiara joined him, curling up in little balls in the place that had kept them safe the first night.

The whole building shook for a while at midnight, then the noise began to subside. They got to sleep, and, when they woke up, everything was quiet.

The silence was somehow scarier than the fighting. It felt like it meant things should have changed, but there still wasn't anyone there to help them.

Letitia gave out bags of apple chips, the last of the vending machine snacks, and began to make plans to leave the school. They couldn't wait forever, and, since it was quiet outside, they might be able to get somewhere.

She went over to the windows and carefully peeled back a sheet of paper so that she could take a good look. There was nothing moving in the street. It was cleaner than the hallway was, without the big piles of bodies.

When everyone was done with the apple chips, she went around the room and talked to each child, getting everybody's address. She got a box of crayons and the biggest sheet of construction paper she could find and tried to draw a map. She really wished she was in a different classroom: it was hard to be neat with crayons and construction paper.

A lot of the kids rode a bus, so they weren't all right by the school. On a good day, the furthest one would be a twenty-minute walk. She didn't think today would be a good day. She didn't think that really mattered, anyway, because she didn't think they were going to be able to find anybody. It was *quiet* out there, a kind of quiet she had never heard before. There were always noises in the Bronx: people talking, cars, subways, buses, airplanes, but today there was nothing. She peeled the sheet of paper back again and looked outside. There wasn't *anybody* out there.

Trevon was the first to ask about the quiet. He came over to the table where Letitia was working. "It all quiet outside now. Can we go home now?" he asked.

Letitia didn't want to answer that, but every kid in the class was standing in a crowd now, waiting to hear what she said.

She thought fast. "This afternoon," she said. "It only been quiet outside for a little bit. We don' know what going on. Maybe your mamas need to get permission or somethin' to come get you now. If nobody come this morning, we go out this afternoon."

The kids all started making excited noises. "Hush!" she hissed, but it was too late. There was a thump at the door and the squeak of the desk shifting. They all became quiet again.

The latch on the door was broken now, so that first thump had pushed the door open about an inch. There was another pounding sound, and the desk shifted a bit again.

The little ones all ran for the bathroom. Letitia ran to follow, but stopped short of the door. It's *too quiet,* she realized. The kids were the only things making any noise at all anymore, so there wasn't anything to distract it. It would keep pounding, it would get in, and they would have to fight it anyway. All the noise of the thumping was going to bring more of them. She had to get the noise to stop.

She turned back towards the door. The crack was wider, but not wide enough for the zombie to get in. Letitia ran to the desk and pushed as hard as she could, trying to hold the door closed. The next thump moved the desk, but she was able to move it back a bit.

"Help me!" she shouted. "You gotta come help!" She hadn't spoken out loud for four days and it felt strange.

The little ones stayed in the bathroom. A low murmur of talking and crying came through the bathroom door. Finally, Rosarita and Malik came out of the door and stood beside Letitia, pushing the desk back.

"Pull back on the desk a little bit. When it get it head in, push. We trap it there so we can stab it."

The zombie thumped the door again and poked its head through the doorway. They pushed the desk as hard as they could, trapping it there, its head still poking into the room.

Now that it was trapped, Jahayra and Kiara left the bathroom, ran to their cubbies, and got their stakes. Jahayra ran up to the door and stopped, a couple of feet too far away to reach anything. Kiara joined her there.

"C'mon," said Letitia, "you guys can do it. We holding it there. All you gotta do is poke through the eyes. Just like the other day."

The little ones got closer. Jahayra grabbed her stake with both hands and pushed it towards an eye. The zombie jerked and her stake missed, poking into the zombie's cheek. Kiara tried and scratched its forehead. It was harder for them when there was a whole body attached and everything kept moving. The two kept stabbing ... they started to cry, but they didn't stop stabbing. They finally hit home and the zombie slumped. Letitia pulled on the desk, and they pushed the zombie back out into the hall. Everybody looked nervous and sick. Everyone but Jose came out when it was clear that they had won.

Letitia was more convinced than ever. They could get out of here. It may be hard, but they could do it. First, though, she had to get the kids calmed down one more time.

Everyone was giving Jahayra and Kiara hugs. They were calming down, their tears turning into smiles. Letitia walked over to the bathroom.

"C'mon, Jose," she said, "it gone now. Won't hurt you. You can come back out here with the rest of us."

Jose stood up. Letitia wiped his tears away with a little bit of toilet paper. "C'mon out."

Jose followed closely behind her. "OK, kids. Get your mats. Sit in a circle. Quiet 'bout it!" she said.

They scurried, dragged their mats together, and sat down in the center of the room, each in their own spot. The familiar pattern calmed them down, despite the nine visible holes in the circle.

"Can you read a story?" said a voice from one side. Maybe Diego, but maybe Jorge. She wasn't good with the twins, and the identical little PE outfits didn't help.

It would probably be the best way to get them calm again. "You got to be super quiet so I can stay quiet while I read, 'kay? Then it time for a nap, then it time to go."

Everybody nodded. Letitia went over to the bookshelf, where she spotted the one she wanted. Returning to the circle of mats, she had them all scoot their mats closer so that she could keep it down to a whisper. She sat in a small chair in the center of the circle. "*The Little Engine That Could*," she began ...

CHAPTER 6
AN AUSPICIOUS BEGINNING

Letitia checked out the line of children. Each had a little school backpack with a water bottle tucked inside and held a sharp garden stake in one hand. She held back a giggle. With their identical little PE outfits on, they looked like they were in uniform.

"We goin' to see if we can get you home. First, we go to Sami's though, and get some food. Remember, everybody stay with your buddy, just like when you go on a field trip. Hold hands. Girls, Rosarita your boss. Boys, Malik your boss. Me, I everybody's boss. Hide if you can, run if you got to. If you got to kill one, do it with your buddy."

Letitia had decided that Sami's Minimarket would be her first stop. They had a phone, the man that ran it was nice to kids, and even if it was bad there too, there would be something to eat. They could get out the back of the school, head down the alley, and be right there. She still hoped that somehow, someway, once they got away from the school everything would be all right. She didn't believe it: if it was all right out there, people would be in here helping her. Since they weren't, it wasn't.

First, they had to scoot the desk back. They did it a little at a time. Jahayra and Kiara stood watch at the crack in the door, looking for anything that came for the noise. Nothing did. The door was open a foot wide. Hard for an adult to get through, but easy enough for a small child.

Letitia went out and did a quick survey up the hallway. Nothing in sight. A quick peek down the next hall showed nothing between her and the exit to the playground.

She returned to class. "Follow me. Quiet, though!"

Except for the pointy stakes they were carrying and the body parts strewn in the hallway, it was just like a trip to the museum: holding hands with a buddy, in a line, with someone in the lead to follow. The heads lying in the hall snapped and chattered as the class passed by but couldn't chase anybody or hurt them. Letitia wondered if something without a stomach could still be hungry, but she decided not to try and find out.

In a couple of minutes, they arrived at the rear door. Letitia peered out the window. Nothing on the playground. They opened the door and were outside for the first time in days. Their eyes blinked in the bright April sunlight, their noses tingled as the fresh air rinsed out the smell of rotting meat.

They walked towards the basketball court. A few dozen zombies roamed the field on the other side of the hurricane fence. They came up when they saw the kids, pressing themselves against the fence. The kids backed up. Lucia and Maria bolted, running back towards the school.

"Stop that!" cried Letitia. "Stick with us. We *ain't* goin' back in there now that we out."

Lucia and Maria turned and nervously rejoined the group.

"Get ready to run ... I'm goin' to try somethin'." Letitia walked a few feet towards the fence. The zombies got excited and started to shake it, but none even tried to climb it, or go around, or anything: they just pushed up against the wires. She swallowed hard and walked closer. A few feet more didn't make any difference. All pressing, no climbing.

"Don' look like they smart enough to climb it." She walked up to a few inches from the fence. The zombies on the other side pressed harder and shook harder, but still didn't do anything that would actually get them through it. She sat down and they bent over to reach her, bringing their eyes within easy reach of a kindergartener.

"Rosarita, Malik, you two gettin' good at this, so you go first. I think you can get the eyes through those big holes." They ran right up and did it, managing to stab hard enough the first time, much better than they had done with Leonie. Rosarita even looked proud this time, not sick like she had the time before. Kiara and Jahayra did well. It was the first time against a complete zombie for Jada and Tiara and they froze. Jada started to cry.

"C'mon," Letitia said. "You guys can do it, too. Them four all did it. Jahayra and Kiara ain't no bigger than you. If they can do it, you can."

Jada stopped crying, but didn't move.

"It just like the little train in the story. He all scared and worried, right?" Jada nodded.

"Once he try, though, he able to do it, right?"

Jada nodded a little harder.

"So go on, try. We all here. If somethin' go wrong, we here to help."

Jada and Tiara gripped their stakes and walked towards the fence. They pushed the stakes through the gaps into a pair of eye sockets and wiggled them back and forth. The zombie fell. They looked an inch taller on the way back to the end of the line.

Two by two, each buddy pair came to the fence, staked a zombie in the eye sockets, watched it fall, then went back to the end of the line to wait for their next turn.

"*Sflup*," went the stakes coming out of the eye sockets.

"What you say?" asked Letitia.

"I think I can!" came the replies.

CHAPTER 7
LOOK BOTH WAYS

This wasn't working out as well as Letitia wanted. The kids were getting better and better at it. None of them were crying anymore, and even Jose was able to get right up to the fence and stab. This kind of easy practice helped a lot. Still, for every zombie they killed another took its place, and zombies that hadn't even been in the field were coming over. She didn't know how many of them there were in the Bronx, but she knew they couldn't keep this up for long. The kids would get tired long before the Bronx ran out of zombies, and it wouldn't be that long before there were so many of them that they could push the fence over. They weren't all that strong, but a hundred of them would be strong enough.

136th St lay ahead, just on the other end of the basketball court. A line of cars sat along the curb in front of the community garden. She fantasized about stealing one and driving everyone away, but she knew that she'd just get herself killed.

Still, the garden looked empty. The fence would slow down anything that came after them, even if it couldn't hold forever.

"Think you can climb a fence like this?" she asked each pair. At first they thought she meant climbing right into the zombies, so she pointed towards the empty garden. "Not here, there!"

Everyone agreed after that.

She led them away from the basketball court a bit, drawing the creatures away from the path to the garden. She stopped the children there, nervously watching as the zombies began to make the fence sag. Still, if the zombies were all here, they weren't in the basketball court and weren't in the street. Best to make a game of it.

"You all sure you can climb a fence?"

"Yes," they answered.

" 'kay, then. When I say 'Go!' run to that fence and climb. Fast as you can, all right? We see who get there the fastest."

They seemed excited. She'd been right: making them kill some when it was easy had them excited. Instead of crying and snuffling, they were acting big, proud, and fierce.

"Go!"

The little swarm of five-year-olds took off hell bent for leather, across the basketball court and onto the sidewalk. When they got to the street, two of the buddy pairs stopped dead, while the rest completed the mad scramble over the street, past the cars, and over the fence.

"Go!" Letitia shouted again.

"We can't. You gotta hold our hands."

Letitia stopped in frustration "Just go!"

"We can't."

Letitia tried to figure out how to get four pairs of hands, four sharp stakes, a fire ax, and herself across the street in one pass. It reminded her of one of those stupid questions they asked on those intelligence tests. Those problems always had wolves and sheep, though: never little kids and axes and zombies. She never had figured out what those stupid questions had to do with being intelligent anyway.

Finally, one pair of children holding hands holding one of her hands, a sharp stake and a fire ax in the other, she made her way across the street. Up the fence the little ones went. Turning to go back for the other two, she was in time to see a stiff, cold hand making a reach for Jose. That was enough. Jose no longer cared if he would be in trouble with his mother, his aunt, his brother, or God himself, he crossed that street with Trevon close behind. Up and over, and everyone was behind a fence again, the creature shaking the wire from the other side. From here, though, they knew what to do. Trevon laid down. When the creature bent down, Jose poked and poked until it fell over. Get *him* in trouble with his mom? No way.

CHAPTER 8
IN THE GARDEN

These gardens were worse than the school vending machines. There wasn't anything she would call food here. Unripe bean pods, some kind of green leaves, hard little apples, nasty green tomatoes. All this food and not a thing to eat. She wanted something with a wrapper. All good food came in wrappers. All you had to do was unwrap it and eat. Why couldn't they grow something like *that* in a place like this?

The little ones were restless, too. It was past time for lunch, they were all hungry, and there wasn't anything here. She tried to figure out how to get to the minimarket from here. They'd have *real* food there.

She walked towards 137th St. There was a parking lot and and alleyway that would get them nearly all the way to Willis Ave, where Sami's was. Harder for things to see them than if they went down either 136th or 137th. It was like the time she tried to chase that mouse out of the apartment and it kept trying to get in little cracks so she couldn't get it. She'd felt kind of sorry for the mouse then, and she felt kind of sorry for herself now.

She assembled the children at the fence next to the parking lot. "You guys stay here a few seconds, let me go take a look," she said.

She climbed over the fence. There were still a dozen cars in the lot, but nothing else in sight. She ran up the parking lot and saw that she got right to the alley behind Sami's. She ran back to the fence to get them over. She didn't want another one grabbing a kid like that one had grabbed Jose.

" 'kay, you guys come over with your buddy. One pair at a time. When you get over, go hide under one of them cars till I get everybody over."

Jose and Trevon came first, climbing the fence and scooting under an old pickup truck. While she was getting Jahayra and Kiara over the fence, she heard a scuffle behind her. As she turned, there was the soft, wet *sflup* of a garden stake coming out of an eye socket. The creature that had tried to reach under the car Jorge and Diego were under went still.

"I thought I could!" came the small voice from underneath.

CHAPTER 9
THE ALLEYWAY

The troop made its way down the parking lot. Letitia hated being in the open. She'd try to be in the front, but then she'd worry about whether the ones in back were keeping up. She'd go to the back, but worry that they were walking into something she couldn't see. It was only a few hundred yards to the alley, but it felt like miles. By the time they got to the alley, she had settled on walking to the front, letting the group pass her, walking to the front, letting the group pass her, over and over again.

"Hold up!" she said as they reached the alley. It was clear to 136th St, but the corners of the buildings blocked the view of the street. This was just like one of Mr. Freeman's war movies: they always had scenes with little groups of guys caught behind enemy lines, trying to get through, with traps ahead. It was a lot harder to do in real life. She had to figure out just what one of those little groups of guys would do. Probably, they'd send a scout ahead.

There was a dumpster set just a little away from the wall, right at the corner. She called Jose over. He was a skinny, tiny little thing. Must have been a crack baby, with one of those mothers that never bothered to eat while he was growing and never bothered to feed him when he was little. Not very bright, either. Still, she didn't need much. Sneak, look, come back. Those were things even a crack baby could do.

"Jose, see that dumpster? See how it about a foot from the wall there?"

"Uh huh," came the reply.

"Think you can get in that crack and see what up the street?"

His face brightened at the familiar phrasing. "I think I can!" he said proudly. Jose always liked it when he had the right answer. It always made the teacher happy. He could see it made Letitia happy, too.

Jose scurried up to the corner and got behind the dumpster. He crawled forward, poked his head out from behind the dumpster, and looked. He could see pretty well. There was a store with a picture of scissors in the window and a striped pole, and next to it was a building full of washing machines. One of the bad things was pretty far away, down towards the school, but there wasn't anything the other way. He looked again. It felt good when bigger kids gave him things to do, so he didn't want to mess it up.

He ran back to the group.

"Only one bad thing. Is that way." He pointed back towards the school.

Letitia was encouraged and brought the group forward to the street. Jose was right. Not only was the thing pretty far away, it was facing away and walking away. If they were quiet, things would be OK. She turned towards Willis Ave. The awning on the front of Sami's was there, just like it always was.

Sami's took up the ground floor of a four-story brick building, with apartments on the upper floors. There was a fire escape on the side of the building, right next to another dumpster, and, next to it, a spiked fence surrounding a cellar doorway. The spiked fence looked like a good thing to hide behind, and being up on the fire escape would be safe, too.

She handed her ax to Malik and climbed up on the dumpster. "Hand me that back," she said, and hooked the ax into the bottom rung of the escape ladder. She held the handle, jumped, and hung there in the air, a few feet off the ground. Unless she could get the release operated, this wasn't going to help. She let go and dropped to the ground.

" 'kay, Malik, you comin' up with me," she said. They climbed on the dumpster and she boosted him up to the platform. Wriggling his way up, he got on the platform and pulled the release lever. The ladder moved a bit. She grabbed the ax handle again, and the ladder slowly slid down to the ground.

They crept forward to Sami's, past the "*Open 25 hours a day!*" sign. The man that ran the place was nice enough, even if he couldn't count. It would be nice if he was still inside the store. He'd help a bunch of kids in trouble.

There wasn't anyone coming in and out of the store, though, and there was *always* someone coming in and out of Sami's. She pushed the door open. There were dark red stains and piles of food on the floor. The cage around the cash register was empty. Her heart dropped into her stomach. She was disgusted with herself for having hoped so hard when she knew better.

The kids started to break out with the snuffles again.

"C'mon," said Letitia. "Ain't that bad. There lots of food still here, and stuff to drink, and nothing that want to hurt us. We eat, and then we figure out what to do."

"We supposed to wash our hands before we eat. Mr. Domacasse always say we got to wash our hands," said Malik. Everyone nodded. Letitia winced, but she found a little bathroom in the back.

" 'kay, everybody get in line and take turns. While your buddy inside, you stand by the door and guard it." It seemed like the best idea: she couldn't watch all of them all of the time, so she had to get them used to watching each other. They were going to be doing this for a long time. She'd been right about it being too quiet: everybody was gone. All that was left was those things.

She stood at the door to the shop with her ax as the children waited in line to use the toilet, each buddy proudly guarding the door with a pointy stake while the other went. It seemed like it was working: the little ones weren't calm, but they weren't running around screaming, either.

Jahayra set her stake down on the ground. Letitia walked over and gave her a light swat on the behind. "Pick that up. Hold onto it. Who take care of Kiara if you ain't doin' it?"

She crouched down a little bit. "That the rule now. You *always* got to hold onto your stake. You *always* gotta guard your buddy." She stepped back. "Everybody hear me? I mean it. Until we find out where everybody went, we gotta watch out for each other. Don' be setting your stakes down or getting too far away from each other."

She walked back to the entryway to keep an eye on the street. It seemed like most of the old rules were going away and she was having to make up new ones. Things like "*i before e except after c*" and "*when two vowels go walking, the first one does the talking*" just didn't fit with "*always guard your buddy*" and "*always hold on to your stake.*" She knew which rules were more important, though.

CHAPTER 10
DINNER, THEN OFF TO BED

Having everybody in Sami's made Letitia nervous. Too much glass, too easy to see into, and no good places to hide. They needed to get out of there quickly.

"C'mon, everybody, eat one of these while I get your backpacks packed." She grabbed a box of Snickers off the candy rack and handed everyone a bar.

Letitia decided she loved school backpacks. The ones these kids wore weren't big, but they were big enough. Every backpack got a little carton of milk, a wrapped sandwich, and enough candy bars to fill it up. She worried about getting some vitamins and stuff like that into everybody. There's some in milk, and there's probably some in a sandwich. A candy bar keeps you from being hungry, but there aren't any vitamins in candy bars. Every teacher and foster mom she'd ever had said that.

She didn't know how long it takes to die from not getting enough vitamins. No one had ever taught her *that* in school, either. She hoped it was more than a few days.

She double-checked the backpacks and decided it was time to get someplace safe to eat and maybe sleep for the night. She had been right: it may only be a twenty-minute walk to the kids' homes on a good day, but this wasn't a good day.

Maybe it *was* a good day, though. She had started the day with twelve kids and she still had twelve kids. They weren't trapped in a kindergarten classroom anymore. She had food. She had an ax. The kids were getting better at doing the things they needed to do. Just like the things they should be teaching in school had changed, maybe what made a day *good* had changed, too.

Out they went, in pairs, just like in one of Mr. Freeman's movies. She guarded the door with the ax and sent a pair to the fire escape. One kid would scurry up to the first landing while the other stood at the bottom, then the second one would climb up. Once Letitia saw they were up, out went the next pair. Another little rhythm, another little feeling of comfort, like she was learning to do something right. Maybe they wouldn't all die.

Finally, they were all up and she followed. Once on the landing, she pulled the release and brought the ladder back up. She didn't think that zombies could climb fire escapes, but she wasn't sure. They climbed to the fourth floor. None of the zombies spent a lot of time looking up, so no one noticed them.

They got out sandwiches, milk, and candy bars for dinner and began to eat. From here, she could see way down 136th St and southwest down Willis. There weren't any adults that she could see. She didn't see *anything* that looked normal. No cars driving down the street, no one walking. There were creatures meandering up and down the roadways.

It wasn't like everyone had turned into one of those things, though. The streets would be packed with them if they had. It looked like everybody had gotten away. That was a nice thought. If everyone else had gotten away, then all they had to do was catch up. It was kind of like being lost in a crowd. It was scary, but sooner or later, you caught up with the adults and everything was OK again. She liked the sound of that.

The little ones murmured while they ate. Jada and Tiara were busy whispering with Jahayra. Jahayra was whispering back. Others started to get in on it.

"What's the problem?" asked Letitia. "What is it you don' want me to know about?"

Jada gave Jahayra a light shove. "Go ahead, ask her!"

"Everybody just want to know whose apartment we goin' to first," Jahayra said.

Letitia winced. Couldn't these kids figure this stuff out? They think everybody run away but their mamas?

"We ain't goin' to nobody's apartment tonight. Took too long to get here, and there weren't nobody at Sami's that could help us. I ain't goin' to walk around in the dark, neither. We try to get into one of these apartments. Maybe there a phone in there, we can try to call somebody's mama to come help us."

She tried the door into the fourth floor, but it was locked: trying to keep burglars out, she guessed. She went down a floor and tried again. No luck. She swung her ax and the glass shattered. It made way too much noise, and some of the creatures started to walk towards them. Still, she remembered that first night: if she was right, once they got out of sight and stopped making noise, the creatures would lose interest. Pair by pair, the little ones were brought down stairs and into the third-floor hallway.

She walked down the hallway, checking doors until she found one that had been left open. Letitia may not have paid enough attention to war movies, but she loved cop shows. She kicked the door open and stayed back, waiting to see if anything came out. They went in as a group.

"Rosarita, Malik, stay here. Make sure nothing sneak up on us." She went into the kitchen, leaving Jahayra and Kiara there, then the bedroom, dropping off Lucia and Maria, and then the bathroom. Nothing. She had the children look under the beds, under the furniture, and behind each door. It was all clear.

She closed the door to the apartment, and the group of them moved the couch in front of the door. Then a chair, and then a dresser. She thought it would be enough to slow down anything that might be kind of alive in the building. The electricity and water still worked, which was comforting.

There was an old-fashioned phone on the wall of the kitchen, the kind with a tangled wire that hooked onto it. She picked it up and listened to the reassuring buzzing sound.

"It sound like it still workin'," she said. "Let me try my foster place first." She was right: it worked, but there was no answer. She shook her head disappointedly.

"How many of you know your phone numbers?" They all acted excited. All of them had a phone number memorized for emergencies.

"OK, we take turns. Rosarita, you first."

"*Ocho seis siete* ..." began Rosarita. "Eight six seven..." she tried again. Letitia dialed. No answer.

Jorge and Diego's number reached voicemail. "This is Letitia Johnson. I got Jorge and Diego with me. We need help. Lots of help. We in an apartment over Sami's Market. Number here is 867-5309. Call us, please!"

She tried nine more times, leaving more messages, but no one answered. She looked at the phone again and pressed 911. It rang and rang, with no answer.

Bathtime became a strange mix of old and new rituals. Everyone got cleaned and scrubbed, a buddy standing guard over the bathroom door during the process. Letitia kissed the little nicks and scratches that had been acquired during the day and put symbolic bandaids on everything. Rosarita and Malik kept guard over the front door, with other buddy pairs keeping an eye on everything. Finally, they all piled into the bedroom. It was a king bed, so all of them were able to pile on at once. Another dresser got pushed up against the bedroom door. Letitia had to modify the "*always hold on to your stake*" rule and permit them to all be neatly stacked by the bed. She did make sure that there were six stakes on one side and six on the other, with her ax lying neatly at the foot of the bed.

Some of her foster parents had tried to teach her about church and stuff. She wasn't all that certain about it. Not many things she had seen growing up made her think there was someone watching her that wanted good things to happen. Still, it didn't seem like a good idea to piss God off if he really was watching her. She'd be getting special attention now, since there weren't very many people left for him to watch.

"Be quiet, everyone. Bow your heads.

"God, I hope you watching us. I know you don't like us to kill nobody, but please forgive us, because I don't think we could've done different today. Or yesterday. I'm sorry I didn't talk to you yesterday, but we been busy and tired and scared.

"I don't know if you think these things are still people, so maybe it's all right with you if we kill them. I hope so.

"Please have somebody's mama call us back.

"Please make it so it ain't so scary when we wake up.

"Amen."

After all were settled in, Letitia pulled out the book.

"*A little railroad engine was employed about a station yard for such work as it was built for, pulling a few cars on and off the switches ...*"

CHAPTER 11
CANDY FOR BREAKFAST

There was some snuffling and crying during the night, but the warmth and coziness of being surrounded by friends got everyone through it. It was so much better than that first night in the bathroom or the nights on the floor of the kindergarten that it kind of felt like a camping trip or a slumber party. Malik stayed dry the entire night, and Jose didn't hide in the bathroom.

Leaving the bedroom was the reverse of entering: everyone grabbed their stake and buddied up. Rosarita and Malik led the assault on the living room, stakes pointed menacingly ahead. Once the group discovered the sofa still blocking the door, they relaxed a bit.

There wasn't much food in the house: mainly beer and frozen Lean Cuisines, so they ate candy bars from their backpacks. The vitamin situation still worried her, but she thought they should be able to make it to lunch without vitamins. She didn't know how much longer than that they could go without. Fortunately, there was a drugstore on 138th St that should have some. They would have to go there first, before trying to find anybody's mama.

She went down the list of phone numbers while everyone used the bathroom. There was no change from last night.

Getting clear of the apartment and back to the fire escape was easy, but getting back down the fire escape was not. The zombies that had heard the glass smashing last night were still there. They weren't paying attention to the window, but nothing else had caught their interest. There was a group of six of them very near the ladder and a few across the street. She didn't feel like going anywhere that nine zombies would notice. It was a big building, so there would be other ways out.

They made their way to the stairway in the center of the building. One landing at a time, they descended, keeping watch for anything that might attack. Nothing popped out at them. The empty building was spooky, but being empty was better than being full of these things.

There was something trying to push its way through one of the doors on the second floor: too dumb to turn a doorknob, it just kept pushing. It would make it someday and she didn't want to be around when it did. A lot of these buildings probably had zombies in them. Opening a door could be very dangerous, but it wouldn't be too hard to outsmart something with a dead brain. Even crack baby Jose could probably outsmart them.

The door on the street was solid, with no window. She stood to the side with the ax, Rosarita and Malik stood at the ready to do what they could, with everyone else far back. Jahayra pulled the door open and Letitia crept cautiously forward. There was one creature in the direction of the pharmacy, but there was no way that they could go anywhere if they stopped every time they saw one. She'd just have to outsmart it.

They walked down Willis, towards 138th St. A lot of the little shops here had been looted, their windows smashed in and things taken. They'd done that too, though, to Sami's. She rolled that around in her head: "*Letitia Johnson, Girl Looter.*" No, that wasn't right. She may be taking things, but it wasn't for money. She didn't know what to call herself, but "looter" wasn't it. She was only taking things that she absolutely needed: food, water. She was going to take some vitamins, but that was only to keep everyone from dying. She was going to keep an eye out for a clothing store, too. The little PE outfits not only looked funny, but they were starting to stink. She knew these zombies couldn't smell too well, but there was no reason to push it.

The zombie she'd spotted earlier finally spotted them and came closer. She climbed into a nearby car, leaving the door open. Slowly, he reached inside. Letitia inched away slowly. The zombie came further in, Letitia inched further away. Once he was in, Letitia jumped out and closed the door. Malik and Rosarita rapidly shut the other door. The zombie began pounding on the door and the glass. He'd get out someday, but not until everyone was safely past.

Letitia heard some low barking and then heard a girl's voice cry out. "*¡Perritos!*" It sounded like one of the two Dominican girls, but she didn't have time to figure out which one before she felt Lucia and Maria rush past her.

Letitia quickly looked behind her. Everyone else stayed in formation.

"Come on," she said. "We better catch up with 'em."

They marched rapidly up to the remains of the window of Willis Ave Pets. Lucia and Maria were staring through the broken glass at the cages inside. Several zombies stood inside, trying to get their fingers through the wires as the puppies cowered and whimpered.

Letitia was angry, but knew that she couldn't get in a shouting match here and attract the attention of the zombies inside and she couldn't try to rescue a puppy if the kids might get hurt. What was she going to do with a puppy, anyway? These kids were trouble enough.

"You two! Back in the line!" she half-shouted, half-whispered. "We come back for 'em, but we got stuff to do first! Rosarita, you supposed to be watching the girls!"

Rosarita stood up a little bigger and taller. She was a good three inches taller than either Lucia or Maria anyway, but she liked being told she was supposed to boss them around. She and Malik brought up the end of the line, so she put Lucia and Maria right in front of her where she could grab them if she needed to.

Lucia and Maria fidgeted, but they stayed in place all the way to the Friendly Pharmacy. Looters had gone after it hard and empty pill bottles were scattered everywhere. In the middle of the mess was one shelf that had just what she was looking for: Flintstone chewable vitamins. Boxes and boxes of them, with one bottle inside each box. She put two boxes inside each backpack. Maybe they would all die from zombie bites, but not because they didn't eat their vitamins.

She wondered about the Flintstones. She'd seen one of the cartoons once, and it was pretty weird. A bunch of cavemen and cavewomen, and all the cavewomen were crazy about some guy named Cary Granite. Her foster dad at the time acted like kids should like the show, but she didn't think it was very funny. She always had the idea that they were making fun of something that she didn't know about in the first place. She remembered the weird word, though. As she passed down the line of children, she'd take out a pill, put in the child's mouth, and murmur "Yabba Dabba Doo." It seemed appropriate, somehow, like a magic chant that would make everything outside go away.

When she took her own pill, she closed her eyes, swallowed the pill, and said "Yabba Dabba Doo" as loud as she dared. She opened her eyes again. Nope. Didn't work.

CHAPTER 12
HEY, MOM! I'M HOME!

"Puppies now?" asked Lucia. Maria grasped Lucia's hand as both looked pleadingly at Letitia. Letitia was frustrated. The kids had been doing what she told them, but she wasn't going to be able to put this off forever.

"One more thing first," Letitia said. "We right by Jorge and Diego's apartment. Maybe their mama be home." She paused a moment. "Maybe she got a place for puppies," she stalled.

Letitia didn't think there was any hope of Jorge and Diego's mother being home, but she had to at least try to get the kids home. At least she had to let them *see* that there weren't homes for them anymore. She'd love to be wrong. She'd love to find out that their mother was sitting on the couch waiting for them to get home from school and that she just loved puppies. The pleasant thought floated through her head for a moment.

She snapped back to reality and turned to the boys. "Where your apartment be, anyway?"

They pointed at the Rinconcito restaurant. "Right over there, over the restaurant," said Jorge.

Jorge and Diego had a key, so there wasn't any need to smash things to get in. Letitia liked that. As long as they stayed quiet, nothing bad happened. Letitia guarded the opening with her ax as Jorge pulled open the street-level door and Diego guarded Jorge with his stake. Nothing came out.

The electricity here was out, so they climbed the narrow staircase in the dark. They kept formation, the line of children bristling with pointy stakes ready to jab out at anything. When they reached the apartment, it was cop-show time again. Jorge opened the door and Malik and Rosarita ran in, brandishing stakes. Pair after pair of children ran in, established position, scanning for any enemies. If anyone had been home, they would have laughed at the sight of a midget volleyball team taking over the territory. At least they would have laughed if their eyeballs hadn't accidentally been removed by a frightened child. They hadn't seen a living person in so long, Letitia was worried that they'd accidentally kill the first one they met.

Nobody was home. Jorge and Diego took it hard. The troop blocked the doorway and prepared to stay for a bit while they calmed down.

"Maybe she just went shopping," protested Jorge.

"Or to get her hair done," said Diego. "She loves to get her hair done."

That sounded pretty silly to Letitia, but she couldn't just come out and say it. As she sat in the kitchen trying to think of what to say, she saw a piece of paper on the table. "EVACUATION NOTICE," it said on the top. Reading, she saw that everyone was supposed to go to Randall's Island Park. She knew where that was. "NO VEHICLES! PEDESTRIAN TRAFFIC ONLY!" it said beneath. Well, that explained it! Everyone had walked to the park and that's why they weren't here. All she had to do was get everyone to the park and everything would be fine.

The troop went back to Willis Ave and began to walk towards the Harlem River. Walking this direction, she noticed something she hadn't noticed coming the other way: big blue signs that said "Evacuation Route" with arrows on them. The arrow pointed right down Willis Ave towards the Willis Ave Bridge. She wasn't sure exactly what the difference was between "evacuation" and "running away." It would take hours (maybe days, at this rate), but Letitia knew where to go.

Letitia stayed on the far side of the street as they passed Willis Avenue Pets and wouldn't let anyone go across the street. "We goin' to catch up with the adults. We tell them about the puppies and they come back with us. They bigger than us, it easier for them to kill those things," Letitia explained. The kids were crestfallen, and not just Lucia and Maria. Letitia hoped she wasn't lying: sooner or later, one of these kids would run over to the puppies.

They passed by Sami's Minimarket again and they stopped to refill their backpacks. Letitia finally felt like the day may actually turn out well. She knew where everyone had gone, she knew how to get there. They were getting pretty practiced with the zombies, too. They saw a few and got past them all. When they could, they just locked them up in cars. No one felt really good about killing them, but they could when they had to.

At Highway 87, they found out what happened to people's cars when they didn't obey the "NO VEHICLES! PEDESTRIAN TRAFFIC ONLY!" warnings. Big bulldozers were parked clear across Willis Ave. There were cars covering everything they could see from Willis Ave to the Harlem River. It looked like they had tried to park them at first, but then gave up and just stacked them, nine and ten high in spots. Letitia could hear the story problems in her head again: "*If three bulldozers could stack ten cars a minute and four million people are all trying to run away at the same time, how long would it take to fill the Bruckner Expressway?*"

She didn't know the exact answer, but she could tell someone had tried to find out.

CHAPTER 13
BURNING YOUR BRIDGES

They walked around the bulldozers and stood at the foot of the Willis Avenue Bridge. The pavement was cracked and the air smelled like cold ashes. They walked out a little way and could see the blackened edge of the crater in the middle of the bridge.

Letitia led them out as far as she dared. She looked towards the RFK Expressway and the 3rd Ave bridges. Both were the same. Huge sections were missing and what was left was blackened and scorched. Not only had the grownups run, they'd made very sure that nothing could follow.

Not even their kids.

CHAPTER 14
TO THE RIVER

Letitia still hadn't quite given up. The river between the Bronx and Randall's Island got pretty small for a while close to PS43. It was still too big to cross, but she might be able to get an adult to notice them and come get them. It was still early in the afternoon: they'd have time.

They walked down the other leg of the bridge and down to Bruckner Ave, towards the big postal station. It looked pretty strange to Letitia with no one inside, just hundreds and hundreds of little white trucks, all decked out with "US MAIL" in red and blue. It was surrounded by hurricane fence, and that was OK, but it had that razor wire on top. There was no way they were going to make it past razor wire, and that meant they could only get in and out through the gate. It was cracked open, so they could hide there if they had to. Zombies that can't climb fences weren't going to get through razor wire, either.

They scouted for a bit and found a little path through a field that took them to the railroad yard.

The railroad yard was impressive. If things didn't work out, maybe they could be hobos, she thought. She'd read about them, but wasn't sure that there were still hobos anymore. All she really knew about them was that they rode in train cars and carried stuff in a little sack on the end of a stick. She was pretty sure that if there still were hobos, they would use backpacks now, just like they did.

She didn't like crossing the rail yard. There were just too many places for things to hide. It made her nervous. Despite her fear, nothing happened as they walked to the edge of the river. There, not thirty feet away, was Randall's Island, but the narrow river was full. She was disappointed: sometimes this stretch of water went so low that a person could walk across, but this wasn't one of those times.

She wasn't certain what to do. She'd been expecting to see someone, but they didn't see anyone. They didn't see any zombies, either, on either side.

Finally, she decided to risk shouting to try to get someone's attention.

"Hey! It Letitia Johnson, and I got a bunch of little kids with me! We need help!"

She waited patiently and tried again. If everyone was supposed to be here, why weren't they coming?

Finally, she saw someone. She shouted again, and he started over towards them. A few more followed him. They were walking a little funny, kind of like they were stiff. Hundreds more came over the ridge. She couldn't breathe looking at them. No one that had run to Randall's Island was still alive.

She made herself pull air into her lungs. "Run! Them ain't people. Run for the trains!"

The narrow river here slowed the zombies down, but didn't stop them. By the time the kids got back to the railway cars, hundreds of zombies had plunged into the river trying to follow them, and the river didn't wash them away quite as fast as they were coming. She didn't want that many zombies following them back to the apartment over Sami's. They were going to have to get rid of them down here.

She spied an open boxcar. "That one!" she cried, pointing. She had to break the buddy pairs up to get them on board, lifting them one at a time onto her shoulders. The separation made the panic worse, but it was brief. Separate, one up, second one up, back holding hands. Thirty seconds, tops.

Not quite fast enough, though. By the time Letitia got the last pair up into the car, the first of the wave of zombies was upon her.

She ducked under the car. Excited little feet ran back and forth above her. She got a grip on her ax. She swung out at the zombie's ankles, but couldn't get a good impact on anything. She could tell she was breaking some ankle bones, but all that did with a zombie was slow it down. She needed to kill them, not slow them down.

Up above, the kids took position by the door. The *sflup* of stakes being pulled out of eye sockets began, and limp bodies began to pile in front of her. She moved back away from the horde and got out from under the car on the other side. The door on this side was closed, and she couldn't signal the kids to open it. Several cars down, she found one open on both sides and managed to climb in.

She looked over at the other car. The kids were doing great: buddies together, they were efficiently killing every zombie whose head appeared in the doorway. As that zombie fell, though, it created a small pedestal, making the next zombie a bit higher when it got to the door. That one made the ramp a bit bigger, so the next one was a bit higher, and the next one higher. Occasionally, it would backslide, as the weight of the top zombie would cause the body parts below to slip and slide. Still, the pile built.

Finally, one of them got a good grip on Diego's ankle and pulled him off the boxcar platform. Jorge dutifully held onto his brother and was swept away into the crowd. It became like a pack of wild dogs arguing over a piece of meat, with Jorge and Diego being ripped apart on the ground. The defense faltered, and the fighting at the front stopped. The wave of zombies was nearly high enough for some to walk in.

Letitia finally dared to shout instructions. "Look for the little door in the back! Get it open! Get out of there!"

She leapt out the back of her own car and ran back towards the children's car, just as the rear door was getting open. Panicky blood-covered kindergarteners began leaping out.

"Run! Get to the Post Office yard! Behind the fence!"

The remaining children ran, still paired together, limbs flailing, bodies bouncing, little balls of nervous energy that should be getting expended chasing a ball. The little yard, filled with its array of little white trucks, lay just ahead.

Running in through the front gate, they rolled the driveway gate shut. Letitia immediately ran back to the other side of the yard. She was counting on the zombies to try to aim straight for her and didn't want to be near the gate opening.

This time, they had learned a lesson. Just as in the schoolyard, Letitia would lay at the base of the fence, then the little ones would take care of the zombies: *sflup, sflup...sflup, sflup ... sflup, sflup*. When the pile started to build, Letitia would walk down the fence a bit and lie down again in a fresh place.

When it was over, Letitia looked at the pile. This was a lot more than a hundred zombies. Maybe three hundred of the zombies had made it across. She didn't know where the ones that hadn't made it across were. Some had probably washed back up on the island, some on the Bronx side, and some washed out to sea. She wasn't going to go near Randall's Island again. Just no reason to stir things up.

They sat together, catching their breath. Lucia was crying again, and Maria had her arms wrapped around her friend.

"Shouldn't we go get Jorge and Diego?" Trevon asked.

"Go get 'em?" asked Letitia.

"Yeah. Bury them or somethin'. We can't just leave them out in the field."

Ten little heads nodded. Even Lucia stopped crying long enough to nod.

They went back over to the box car and found Jorge and Diego, still snapping and trying to bite.

"We can't bury 'em if they still movin'," said Letitia. "You want to bury 'em, you gotta stop 'em from moving first."

Trevon and Jose volunteered.

"Goodbye," said Letitia.

"Goodbye," said each child in turn.

"*Sflup sflup*," said Jorge and Diego.

They didn't have a shovel to dig a hole with. They finally settled for a spot underneath a large tree next to the postal yard, a tree with gaps between large roots that were filled with soft leaves and soil. They used their stakes to scoop out a hole for the heads and covered them again with dirt. They made a little cross from sticks and put it in front of the tree.

"Shouldn't there be some kind of thing with their names on it?" asked Trevon.

"Ain't got nothing to write with," answered Letitia.

Jahayra dug in her backpack for the box of crayons she was still smuggling around and handed a black one to Letitia. Letitia found two flat rocks, wrote "Jorge" and "Diego" on them, and placed them on the hole.

She made them all stop and bow their heads before walking back to Sami's.

CHAPTER 15
BEDTIME

The journey back to Sami's was uneventful. Even the zombies that had been hanging around the fire escape had wandered off, distracted by something. Letitia was grateful for that. She was tired and sad, not feeling the energy to fight. The children held onto their stakes more tightly and looked around more alertly, but didn't look as confident as they had earlier.

Climbing back up the fire escape, they reentered the apartment from last night. As the troop swept the room for invading zombies, Letitia remembered one chore left over from this morning.

"Rosarita, Malik, c'mon down with me. I don't want to be sleeping on top of that thing thumpin' on the door downstairs."

They went down two flights of stairs and stood in front of the door. The pounding noises continued. Letitia turned the doorknob, but it was locked. She swung her ax at the doorknob, knocking it away from the door. That kind of thing always worked in the movies, but it didn't work for her here. The deadbolt was still engaged and the door remained closed.

Finally, she whacked the door itself several times with the ax. Each *whack* of the ax was greeted by a stronger *thump* from inside.

Eventually, the *thumps* started to win. The door began to splinter around the cuts from the ax and damaged blue hands began to poke through the doorway, followed by a blue face. Rosarita and Malik staked it and it became still. Letitia pushed on the head with her ax and it fell back inside. The trio stopped and listened. No more sounds.

Climbing back up the stairs, they reentered the apartment. Once again, time for dinner, bath, and bed. She went through the phone list again and left messages again. She was glad the electricity was still on here, but she wasn't sure how long that would last. She didn't even understand how it worked. She knew it got turned off if you didn't pay the bill, but did that still happen if the guy that switched it off had run away? She was going to use it while she had it.

They all got hot baths, scrubbing the blood, muck, and gore off themselves. Their t-shirts and shorts got rinsed out in the sink and scattered all over the apartment to dry. Once again, the eleven of them lay down in the king bed in a great big cozy heap, ready to sleep.

"Be quiet, everyone. Bow your heads.

"God,

"Please take care of Jorge and Diego.

"I don' know if we was supposed to kill them, too.

"I really tried to save them. We all did.

"Please take care of them in heaven.

"Please make it so it ain't so scary down here when we wake up.

"Amen."

"Amen," came a whispered chorus of voices.

Then she pulled out the book and began, as she had the night before and probably would every night for a long time: "*A little railroad engine was employed about a station yard for such work as it was built for, pulling a few cars on and off the switches ...*" One by one, the ten little faces became peaceful, drifting off to sleep.

Letitia stared at the ceiling, her brain too busy sorting out the day to let her sleep. The adults were *gone*, and that was scary. She wasn't going to catch up with them and have everyone be happy. Nobody was going to show up and rescue anyone. Everybody had gone over those bridges, blown them up, and left them alone.

On the good side, Randall's Island nearly worked for holding zombies. She had seen the zombies try to cross the river. Most hadn't made it, even though that was just a little bit of water. Nothing like the whole East River or anything. She remembered the history shows Mr. Freeman watched in between his war movies. There was one about an island in the East River that had been abandoned for fifty years. She didn't like most of the things he watched, but she'd liked that show, mainly because it was about something right next to her. It had turned out that you could see the island from the Freemans' apartment window.

She missed Mr. Freeman.

Mr. Freeman had taken the time to stand and look out the window with her. He pointed out the three islands right next to each other. The big one was Rikers Island. She knew that one from the cop shows. Whenever somebody did something bad, they went to Rikers Island. The one next to it was North Brother Island, with the abandoned hospital and things. The smallest one was South Brother Island, and it didn't have anything on it.

She was pretty sure she could find them again, but that wouldn't matter unless she could figure out how to get across the water. She knew that zombies couldn't swim a mile, but she couldn't either. She caught herself. That wasn't the right attitude.

"I think I can!" she said firmly to herself, scrunching her eyes tightly shut, trying to get to sleep before any new thoughts showed up.

CHAPTER 16
LOST PUP

Letitia woke up because someone was bouncing on her. Maria was on the bed, her hands on Letitia's chest, bouncing up and down, making Letitia sink deep into the mattress and spring back out.

"Lucia! Lucia is no here! She no here!" The words came blubbering out of Maria.

"Not here? What do you mean, 'no here'? You check the bathroom?" asked Letitia.

"No in bathroom, no in kitchen. No here at all. She keep talking about those puppies."

The puppies. With everything that had happened in the railroad yard, Letitia had forgotten about the puppies. Lucia hadn't, though.

"What did I say about you being buddies?" snapped Letitia. "I say you stay with her. I say you watch out for her. I say you keep each other safe. How you let her sneak out?"

When Letitia saw Maria's reaction, she regretted saying it. A little. Not for long, either. If Maria had kept Lucia here, that would have been best. If Maria had gone out with Lucia, *maybe* Lucia would stand a chance. Either way would have been better than this. Out there by herself, trying to rescue puppies? Letitia shuddered.

"Everybody up! Fast! We going now!" It took a few minutes, but the children were assembled. Letitia grabbed the buddieless Maria and they set off down the stairs.

She could see and hear the problem from blocks away. The puppies were howling, and zombies were moving towards the pet shop from all directions.

"We have to keep going. Don' let one catch you, but don't try to kill one here on the street. Rosarita, Malik, you at the back. Make sure everybody keep goin', yell if there a problem."

Letitia aimed for gaps, moving as quickly as she could without losing the little ones behind her. It wasn't crowded here, but ahead, a crowd was visible around the pet shop.

A high-rise apartment building with a wrought-iron fence stood across the street from the pet shop. The fence was lower than a hurricane fence and harder for kids to climb, but it was the only thing in sight. Letitia pointed.

"Run for it. Get over that fence!"

The children scrambled, sprinting to the fence and clambering their way over it. The zombies that couldn't make it in the pet shop turned towards the yard, pressing against the fence. The front row of zombies became pinned in the spikes at the top of the fence. The ones behind them kept pressing, and the ones behind those kept pressing them.

Just as the first zombies were getting pushed over the crowd and into the yard, Letitia smashed one of the windows with an ax. She boosted each of the smaller ones inside and then climbed in herself.

They were in an apartment, a little larger than the one over Sami's. The window was set high enough that the zombies couldn't walk in, but they would pile up under the window and get crushed into a ramp for the ones behind them.

Letitia thought for a moment. " 'kay, let's get up a floor," she said. "They won't be able to get in there." She led the group up to the third floor. Trying to pound the doorknob off hadn't worked yesterday, so she pounded a hole in the plaster next to the doorknob and lifted Jose to the hole. He reached in and turned the doorknob from the inside.

They made their way to the window. The crowd was growing, but wasn't as focused as it had been. The sound of puppies barking and Lucia crying was enough to keep the attention on the pet store. A few were still interested in the window they had broken into and some were still trying to get over the fence, but most were turning back towards the noise.

Letitia spotted a fire escape that went to the roof on the building next to the pet store. Letitia knew they could get away if they could get to the rooftops, and she thought she would be able to get Lucia to the ladder safely.

"We goin' to open this window, and you guys gotta be *noisy*. So loud these things try to climb up the building to get you. Think you can do that?"

The children looked nervous, but finally Rosarita nodded. "*Si*. Yes. We can do that." She opened the window. "*¡Oye tú, imbécil!*" she shouted.

The effect was immediate, as the things down on the ground turned towards her. The few in the courtyard immediately below the windows started scrabbling at the wall. The other children saw this and liked it. It felt good to make fun of these things, and it felt good to feel safe because they were up so high. Little kids leaned out the windows and started to shout insults.

Letitia gave it a few minutes. "Rosarita, block this door after I leave. C'mon, Maria. You lost your buddy, so you with me." She turned and left, Maria close behind.

The pair went back to the ground-floor apartment they had broken into. The little courtyard was clear, with all the zombies trying to get into the pet shop or climb the wall in the next courtyard to reach the kids.

"We run for that ladder. We get there, we get up on that little planter garden thing in the sidewalk. I boost you up, you climb up on the platform and kick the release. 'kay?"

Maria put on her best brave face. "OK. I climb up, I kick the lever until the ladder go down."

They ran across the street and climbed up on the planter. Letitia lifted Maria up. Maria could barely reach the ladder, but got her hands on it. She pulled herself up and managed to get on the platform. Letitia was getting nervous: across the street, the mound under the third-floor window was growing. The first-floor window under it was covered with them and new ones kept arriving. A couple of them noticed her and Maria.

A voice came from above. "Letitia! It no work! I kick and kick and nothing happen. *¡Nada!*"

"Just keep kicking! You got to get it loose!" Letitia grabbed her ax tightly and prepared herself as zombies in the crowd noticed her. The little garden planter made her two feet taller: she could reach their heads without as much trouble. Maria kept kicking and Letitia kept swinging. She focused on teeth: good solid whacks to the jaw so that nothing could bite her. Then she would take the time to pound on the skull. That took time and effort, but with the zombie being toothless she could take the time and effort.

Finally, she heard a "*¡Bien!*" from above, followed by the squeak of a ladder extending.

"Can you make it drop?"

Maria put her weight on it, and the ladder slowly lowered.

"You stay up there. Wait for me."

Letitia swallowed hard. The sidewalk in front of the shop was clear: everything that wasn't inside was busy trying to get into the apartment across the street. A row of cages lined one of the walls of the shop, with all kinds of small animals inside. Lucia had climbed on top of the cages to escape. Curled in a little ball, crying, she was wedged into the gap between the top cage and the ceiling. Zombies filled the store, zombies that were too stupid to get out of each other's way and pull on the cages. They were crowded in so tightly they could barely move and their bodies were holding the cages up. They couldn't get in them, they couldn't climb them, but the cages couldn't collapse into the crowd either.

Letitia climbed in through the broken window and stood on the ledge inside, ankle deep in strips of newspaper stained with yellow, brown, and red. The zombies were so packed they couldn't rush her or climb on the platform. She swung her ax at arms and jaws. With no teeth and broken arms, the ones surrounding her were frightening, but they kept the ones behind them from reaching her without being able to hurt her themselves.

That didn't help Lucia, though. She couldn't get down, because to climb down meant climbing onto a zombie's head. She couldn't stand, so she couldn't leap back to the window where Letitia was. She was stuck.

"Lucia! Can you get one of the cages loose? Throw it to me?"

"I think so," came the reply. Lucia backed up, further into the corner, and worked on a cage full of hamsters. The little hooks tying it to the wall were too tight for her to remove.

"Pound on it! Get it loose!"

Lucia began whacking the top of the cage with her fists. It bent, coming free of the hooks.

"You want me to throw it? At you?"

"*To* me, yeah."

Lucia grabbed it and swung it over. It landed halfway between the window display and the cages, floating on the zombie mosh pit. The crowd went wild, struggling to grab the cage. Letitia hadn't realized that hamsters could scream.

"You have to do better than that. What in the cage you on top of now?"

Lucia looked through the wire mesh under her feet. "Is *cuyes*. Guinea pigs? Something like that? My neighbor, she cook them."

"OK. Don't throw the cage at me. Get a guinea pig out. Throw it out the door. Give it a chance to run away."

Letitia didn't think the guinea pig would stand a chance, but she didn't think Lucia would throw it if what happened was what Letitia thought would happen, no matter whether her neighbor ate them. Lucia reached down, opened the door, and was promptly nipped. She grabbed the one that bit her and chucked it overhand through the door.

Letitia smiled when she saw what happened. As she hoped, the squealing guinea pig went running as soon as it hit the sidewalk, a dozen zombies shuffling after it in pursuit.

"Another one!" she shouted. Three tosses later, four guinea pigs went scurrying down the street, taking a large group of zombies with them. Letitia used her ax to hook the cage of hamsters that was still floating on the crowd of zombies and set them loose on the floor. It was a zombie pandemonium, each of them struggling to reach the live food and getting in each other's way. Letitia lashed out with the ax, working on slicing jaws and hands off.

The puppies in the lower cages began to howl. With more room to move, the zombies trying to reach the puppies were able to shake the teetering wall of cages. With the top cage unhooked, the column in front of Lucia toppled. The cages, no longer supported and boxed in, became fragile. Zombies were able to get a grip on all sides, squeezing and pushing them until they broke, spilling their contents into the crowd.

As the zombies feasted on beagle puppies, Siamese kittens, chinchillas, and little white mice, Letitia shouted at Lucia. "Get down and run! Now!"

Lucia made her way through to the window. She and Letitia leapt outside, running for the fire escape and joining Maria on the first platform. The two buddies hugged and spoke to each other in rapid Spanglish. Letitia didn't follow it, but she was pretty certain that this buddy pair wasn't going to get split up again. It kept sounding to her like they were talking about cuckoos, though. She was going to have to ask about that.

Later, though. Right now, she had to get the group back together. The others were still shouting out the windows. The pile of zombies across the street was up nearly to the second floor, nearly filling the courtyard on that side.

Letitia waved and gestured to be quiet. It took a while, but the kids finally got the hint. She risked shouting from the platform. "Trevon, Jose, get over here. Everybody else make noise while they be running!"

A minute later, Trevon and Jose popped out of the first-floor window. Letitia dropped the ladder so they could scoot up onto the platform.

"Up on the roof, everybody," Letitia said. "Don' need to be making a lot of noise right here, and don' need them be seeing lots of meat, neither."

The little ones scampered up. Letitia gestured, and Tiara and Jada came for the next trip. Next was Jahayra and Kiara.

That left Rosarita and Malik. The fire escape was attracting attention, and there wouldn't be anyone left shouting to attract the zombies to the apartment building. Letitia couldn't help but think of those story problems with the wolves and sheep again. She gestured for quiet.

"You keep makin' noise. We go look for another way up and down from here. OK?"

The two talked. "Yeah, we do that," shouted Malik.

"OK, then. Don' do nothin' stupid!" She climbed the escape. The roof was flat and broad, covered in tar paper and gravel.

"Be careful, but go find another way up here. Got to be more than one ladder."

The buddy pairs scattered. In a couple of minutes, Jahayra and Kiara came back and pointed north. "There another ladder over there. Nothing around it," said Jahayra.

They reassembled and went over to the ladder. Letitia scooted down on her own and checked the release lever. She was able to get it to move, and the ladder moved freely.

She climbed back up to the top and got Lucia and Maria. "You two started this mess, so you the ones be waitin' over there. When you see them on the street, drop the ladder. Don't go down till you see 'em, though."

The rest went back to the front fire escape and climbed down to the bottom platform. She gestured for quiet, then began to shout herself.

"There another ladder over on that side." Letitia gestured. "We make noise here. You two, run that way, come up the other ladder. 'kay?"

Rosarita and Malik shouted that they understood.

Letitia started to shout insults at the zombies across the street. It *was* kind of fun. It felt good to feel like you were bigger and stronger than these things. Everyone got into it, shouting nasty things about hairstyles, clothing, anything that came to mind.

Malik was scared to death. Letitia was so much bigger than him that he always felt safer when she was around. Rosarita was a little bigger than him, but not that big. Her mama held her back in school, just like his did, so she was seven like him. That made them bigger than everyone else, but it didn't make them *big*. Not big enough to be alone in a room that a whole mountain of zombies was trying to climb into. He fought back tears. Rosarita wasn't going to be able to call him a crybaby.

"They keep trying to climb in this window," said Malik.

Rosarita nodded. "We go watch from other place," she said. "We see from there."

They climbed the central stairs and peeked carefully out the stairwell window on the fourth floor. The top layer of the mound of zombies wasn't trying to get in the room they had been in anymore. They were all starting towards the fire escape across the street, but a lot of the pile couldn't move very fast anymore. The zombies on the bottom had broken bones and were just wiggling and flopping their way across the road.

They kept watching, peeking out the window every few minutes. "Time to go?" asked Malik, after half an hour had gone by.

Rosarita looked out the window. The street was nearly clear. All the whole zombies were under the fire escape, with anything that was left in the street or the courtyard too broken to move.

"*Si.* How we get out?"

"I think there another door at the bottom of the stairs," said Malik.

The stairwell at the bottom floor had a solid steel door, with a bar on it, and a red sign reading "Fire door. WARNING: Alarm will sound if door is opened." They pressed on it, setting off the alarm as they left the building.

The path across the street was still clear. They sprinted east, across Willis. Lucia and Maria came down the ladder and pushed the final segment down to the street. The four climbed to the roof.

Letitia had noticed the two crossing the street and had already pulled everyone up to the roof. As the two groups were getting back together, she heard Rosarita scolding Lucia and Maria, partly in English but with enough in Spanish that Letitia couldn't follow. Once again, she couldn't figure out why they kept talking about cuckoos.

She decided to just ask. "Why you keep talking about cuckoos? No birds 'round here, so why you keep talking about them?"

Rosarita looked blank for a second. "Ah ... *cuco.* My *abuela* ... my grandmother, she always talk to me about the *cucos.* She say they come to eat bad kids."

Jose piped up. "My mama always say the devil send the *cucos* after me if I don't clean my room."

Lucia and Maria just nodded agreement. They were afraid to talk any more, because they were afraid to get in any more trouble.

"*Cu coh.*" Letitia rolled the word around on her tongue for a bit. She liked it. "OK, they *cucos* then. 'Zombies' always sound like something out of a bad movie to me."

Letitia turned to Lucia and Maria. "Your mamas tell you about cucos too, huh? How they eat bad kids?"

They nodded.

"Well, let me tell you somethin', too. You two *been* bad kids. You do this again, I *feed* you to the cucos."

She looked around at everyone. "I mean it. Next one of you just sneak off, I ain't coming after. Lucia nearly die, we all nearly die, and all them puppies die anyway."

CHAPTER 17
ON THE ROOF

Letitia looked over the edge of the roof. The apartment fire alarm was still going, so everything that had come over to this side of the street was going back over to the apartment. The loud noise was bringing in even more zombies from everywhere around. It wasn't only *things* that could hear the alarms, either. Engine noises came down Willis Ave.

"Stay low," Letitia commanded. "Let's see what's going on."

The children all crouched and peered over the edge of the roof. A large pickup truck full of men was coming slowly down the street. It stopped right in the middle of the intersection, then the men started shooting.

It went on for twenty minutes but felt like hours. When the crowd was thin enough, one of the men got inside the apartment building and shut down the alarm. After that the gunfire slowed down and gunmen picked off stragglers.

"Should we go talk to them?" asked Jahayra.

"I'm thinking," said Letitia. "They ain't cops or nothin', are they? Anybody see any uniforms?"

Everyone shook their heads. No one had seen any kind of uniform. It was just men with guns.

"If they was policemen or somethin', I'd know. They just guys with guns, though. That don' sound good."

Everyone shook their heads again. They didn't live in the worst neighborhood in New York, but it wasn't one of the good ones, either. Every one of them had heard stories about people getting shot just because they were around when people started shooting each other.

"My mama, she always say that if I hear a gun, I should lay down flat," said Trevon. "If someone with a gun tell me to do something, she say I just do it. If I see one, I supposed to run away."

The others all started talking, but they were all saying the same things. Their mothers all lived in fear of drive-by shootings, and their mothers had all taught them what to do around people with guns. Lie flat. Hide in the bathtub. Get inside. Hide under a car. Not one of their mothers had taught them to walk up to a gunman and say "Hi. I'm hungry, scared, and think my mother's dead. Will you help me?"

" 'kay, then," said Letitia. "We wait up here till they gone."

They continued to peek nervously over the edge, watching as the men in the truck backed it up to the Pioneer Supermarket, just across 138ᵗʰ St. The men loaded the truck with food and drove slowly away. The sound of gunfire rang out periodically as the truck rolled out of sight.

"I'm hungry," complained Lucia.

Letitia glowered. "It your fault we ain't had no breakfast," she said. "We get food when we get down."

They took a look down 138ᵗʰ. It looked clear. They climbed down the ladder and crossed the street to the Pioneer Supermarket. The Pioneer was a bigger place than Sami's and still had a good supply of things to eat. They managed a decent lunch from bread and lunchmeat, fruit, and prepackaged pudding.

As they were eating, they heard a low trilling sound. Startled, they all stood up and gripped their stakes with both hands. Letitia smiled: they all looked ready, but no one was running around making noise or doing stupid things.

"What is that?" asked one of the children.

"Don' know. Any of you heard one of them things make a noise like that?"

Ten little heads shook back and forth.

"Me neither. Be careful, but let's look for it."

They searched the store carefully. Finally, hiding under one of the shelves, Lucia found a pair of small, fluffy animals. She and Maria pulled them out and showed them to the rest.

"*¡Es cuyes!* Guinea pigs!" said Lucia.

Letitia frowned. Still, look what happened with those stupid puppies. You can't keep a little kid from doing *everything*.

"You say your neighbor ate them things?"

"*Sí*, yes, she have cages on the roof and in the apartment. Every weekend, she go to swap meet, she sell them. She have a little barbecue, she cook them on sticks. Make good money, my mama said."

"If I let you keep 'em, you goin' to stay safe? If you gotta throw one at a cuco to stay safe, you able to do that?"

Lucia and Maria both nodded vigorously.

" 'kay, then. We get too hungry, though, I know where to find sticks."

Maria looked upset, but Lucia looked like she'd be happy either way. All of the other kids gathered excitedly around them, petting the new additions to the group.

Letitia looked at the little ones. They were a mess: dirty from running around on gravel roofs, their clothes starting to stink. Rinsing things in the sink just wasn't working out.

"There a Rite Aid down the street from here, ain't there?"

Jada nodded. "Yeah, two, maybe three streets down."

"They got clothes for kids there?"

Jada nodded again. "Yeah. My mama shop there sometimes."

They headed down 138th St. This street was mainly houses, so there weren't so many windows broken out. There were pounding sounds on some of the doors as they went past, but everything that had been out was back in the pile by the Pioneer Supermarket.

Jada had been right. Three blocks down, they found the Rite Aid, its windows all broken out.

"Careful!" said Letitia. "Check it out, just like we check out the houses. Don' want nothin' poppin' out at us."

Rosarita and Malik went back behind the counter and back into the rear room. The drug stockroom was smashed to bits, with things scattered all over.

Malik spotted a figure standing among the shelves. Dirty and ragged, it slumped there, facing away. He tugged on Rosarita's sleeve and pointed.

Rosarita gestured for Malik to be quiet. They waited a little bit, but nothing happened.

"Is just standing there," she whispered. "He no see us yet. We sneak up close, we get him before he knows we here."

They crept up quietly. Just as they got behind it, the figure turned. Each child stabbed reflexively into the nearest eye socket, before noticing the warm, pink flesh in the face and the fruity odor of cough syrup on their victim's breath.

Blood streamed from both eyes, and the figure dropped rapidly to the floor, his bottle of Histonex slipping from his fingers. The man lying on the floor had spent hours finding that last bottle of syrup in the wreckage. Now, with the parts of his brain that hadn't been disabled by hydrocodone slashed to bits by garden stakes, he didn't scream or struggle, managing nothing more than a gurgle.

Letitia heard the commotion and came running in, ax at the ready. Amidst the chaos, it took a moment for the sight of pooling blood to register in her brain. "What did you two *do*?" she asked. "That ain't no zombie or cuco or nothin'."

Malik stood silent, his head hung in shame.

"We thought he was a cuco," Rosarita blustered. "He no moving. He no doing nothing normal. Why he standing around in place like this? Is no our fault!"

Letitia walked over to the body and picked up the bottle. She recognized it from the days before her mother died, after her father had left, the days when she had to make sure her mother's needles were packed up and safely out of Jahayra's reach.

"My mom had boyfriends that drank this stuff. She used to drink it sometimes when she couldn't get her stuff." She paused. "Yeah, it makes you act dead and stupid," she finished.

Yelling at them wouldn't do any good. She had been afraid they would kill someone by accident, and she'd been right. But it *was* an accident, and she was glad that she wasn't going to have to deal with a junkie. What if he had been one of those things? She didn't want them to get hurt because they were too scared of hurting people. It didn't make any sense to be mad at them for killing a junkie if that meant that they might be too slow later.

Everyone was staring at her, waiting for to get mad.

"Guess it not really your fault," she said. "But you got to be more careful. That could'a been someone that could help us. Could'a been someone *nice*."

For just a moment, she felt the weight press down on her. Someone *nice*. Someone that *she* could follow around. That's what she wanted.

The rest of the children had gathered in a little clump behind Letitia. She turned around and shooed them back out. "We here to go shopping. Ain't nothing we can do back here."

Letitia supervised the shopping expedition. Since junkies didn't need tiny sneakers or t-shirts, the stuff that little kids needed was still there.

"How many of you can count to seven?" she asked.

Most kids proudly held out seven fingers and said "I can!" Trevon held out eight, but figured it out after Tiara pointed and laughed.

"OK, find clothes your size. Get seven pairs of underwear, seven t-shirts, and two pairs of jeans."

She found clothes for herself and changed right in the store, wadding up the stained and splattered jeans she had been wearing and throwing them in the trash.

She tucked a real notebook and some pens in her backpack. Rite Aid had a bunch of cheap games, too. Not great games, but good enough to keep kindergarteners entertained: coloring books, crayons, board games, all kinds of stuff. Jahayra found two boxes of fluorescent crayons and made a special point of giving one to Rosarita.

There was a tug on her arm again. "Is there any food for the *cuyes?*" Lucia asked. There was a little pet shelf with a few bags labeled *Rodent Food.* The pictures on them were of hamsters and mice, but that seemed close enough. They loaded up a big cart and pushed it back to their apartment over Sami's.

Malik was subdued when they played games that evening. Usually, he was just a little bit of a bully. He never really threatened the other children, but no one would dare tell him "no" when he wanted to roll the dice over or take another spin, either. This time, he lost every game quietly without a fuss.

CHAPTER 18
NOW I LAY ME DOWN TO SLEEP

"God,

"We sorry. We sorry we couldn't save the puppies.

"We sorry about the guy in the Rite Aid, too." Letitia glanced over at Rosarita, who made a nervous cross over her chest.

"We sorry about everything we did wrong.

"We tryin'. Honest. We really tryin'.

"Please stop making it so hard, and then we do better.

"Amen."

Rosarita fidgeted a bit more and crossed herself again. None of the preachers Letitia had ever watched did that, but she knew a lot of people that did. She hoped it didn't really make a difference, because she thought it looked kind of funny.

Before Letitia could get the story started, Kiara raised her hand.

"Letitia?"

"What's up, Kiara?"

"Are all of our mamas dead?"

Letitia groaned a bit inside. They really were going to make her say it. After finding Jorge and Diego's apartment empty and the attack at the railroad yard, no one had mentioned looking for moms again. She'd been glad. Since they didn't see anybody and nobody answered the phone, she was pretty sure that they were dead, but she didn't *know* that they were dead. She didn't want to run all over the Bronx fighting cucos looking for them either.

"Well, Jahayra's and mine be dead, but she been dead a long time. Jahayra can't even remember her. Yours? I don' really know.

"Everybody think their mama would have done what that note said? Run away to the park?"

Ten little pairs of eyes looked back and forth. Finally, eight heads nodded, Kiara's among them.

"OK, maybe they be all right, but we can't find them. I don' know what happened on Randall's Island, but if they ran away from that, they didn't come back here. Remember the bridges?"

They all nodded. They'd be quiet for tonight. Not forever, but for tonight.

Letitia looked hard at the remaining two, Jada and Jose.

"Jose, why you think your mama not go where the note say?"

"My mama, she no go anywhere with police."

That cinched it: Jose *was* a crack baby.

"Think she still be in your apartment? Even though she don't answer the phone?"

"No. She go out all the time. Sometime for days."

"OK, we be watching for her while we be doing other stuff, OK?"

Jose nodded. Letitia felt ashamed of herself. It was only a little harder to trick a crack baby than it was to trick a cuco.

"Jada? How 'bout your mama?"

"She in the apartment!" Jada insisted.

"Why?"

"She too fat to run away. She never leave the apartment. Can't get through the door."

Letitia couldn't argue with that, so she checked the address. It was on 137th St, right next to the Bruckner Expressway. She knew what they'd do tomorrow: see if they could rescue a fat lady.

CHAPTER 19
YO' MAMA IS SO FAT ...

They headed back down 137th St the next morning. The area next to the Bruckner was a mess here, too. There was a big column of smoke rising into the sky from across the river. Letitia wasn't sure what was on fire, but whatever it was, it was *big*.

Here on this side of the river, bulldozers had pushed cars off the highway into the streets below just like by the Willis Bridge, piling them three and four deep.

Jada took the keys from around her neck and opened the street-level door. Once inside, they proceeded up to the third floor. Jada unlocked that door as well.

"Careful," said Letitia, "we don' know what in there. Go slow." They started in, but as soon as they got to the little hall leading to the bedroom they came running back.

"You gotta go look, Letitia."

Letitia did. Jada had not been lying. Her mama was *fat*. A hundred "*Yo' mama is so fat ...*" jokes went through Letitia's head at once, but no one had ever said "*Yo' mama is so fat she'd die in an evacuation because she'd get stuck in the hall.*"

Jada's mom, a five-hundred-pound dead woman, was wedged in the hallway and still struggling to get through it. Letitia nearly ran like the little ones, but Jada's mom wasn't coming fast. There was no way to tell if she'd died from being wedged or become wedged after she died. It didn't matter much. Jada's mom could handle being squished tighter than a living person and didn't mind if things got ripped off. Part of her belly was stuck on a hallway closet doorknob. The doorknob made a ripping, gurgling sound as it slid through her body. The longer Letitia stood there, the more the woman vibrated and shook and the more things gurgled and ripped.

Jada stopped moving. Letitia had seen things like that on TV. Jada didn't cry, or scream, or run to her mother shouting "*Mama!*" or anything. She just stopped still. She stopped holding Tiara's hand, but, since Tiara didn't stop holding hers, her hand didn't go anywhere.

They all headed back to the street. Jada could still walk where she was pointed, but not much more. They sat in a little line on the curb. Tiara pulled a water bottle from her backpack and handed it to Jada. Jada looked numbly ahead, but took a swallow.

In a few minutes, she took another swallow. She looked at Letitia.

"You think it hurts?" she managed to ask.

Letitia thought for a moment.

"Don' know for sure. If she all the way dead, I be sure it don't. If she was all the way alive, I be sure it does. I don' know about halfway."

Jada sat still a bit.

"When I had a puppy that got run over, Uncle John hit it with a shovel till it was all the way dead. He said it what you had to do when something was halfway dead and you can't fix it. Finish it off."

Another pause.

"Can we fix her?"

That, Letitia knew the answer to. There wasn't anything she could do to fix Jada's mama. She didn't think anyone, anywhere, could fix any part of this mess, and Jada's mother was certainly a part of this mess.

"No."

"It just like we had to do with Jorge and Diego, ain't it?" Jada continued.

"Yeah."

The only thing left to decide was exactly who was going to do it. Jada thought it was her job, but didn't know if she could.

Finally, they decided that they would use Jada's stake, but Letitia would be the one that did it. They assembled in the hallway. Letitia took Jada's stake and ran quickly into the apartment.

Jada's mama had only moved a few inches and her arms were trapped against the walls of the hallway. Letitia got in front of her, pressed the stake into her eye socket, and twisted it. It felt weird. This whole time, she had always used her ax. The little ones had all gotten good at using the stakes. She hadn't, and parts of it disturbed her. That bit of resistance until the eyeball ruptured, then the easy slide into the brain. That *sflup* noise when you pulled it out.

She decided she'd stick with her ax.

CHAPTER 20
NORTH BROTHER ISLAND

Letitia thought again about that little island on the TV show. The Freeman's apartment had been near here. She'd been able to see the island from there, so if she could get high enough or closer to the river, she should be able to see it. She surveyed the big pile of cars and tried to figure out if she could get onto the expressway by climbing it.

She finally decided not to. It seemed like it would be fun, but she had to think of the little kids. She was getting tired of that, but didn't see any way around it. So, around the mountain it was. Or through it. It was kind of a combination. She picked her way through, turning round whenever she hit a dead end, picking a bit further, until she made it onto the east side of the highway. Once they reached the river at 138th St the islands were clearly visible.

She was relieved that the fire wasn't coming from the island, but was coming from five bright blue fuel tanks on the other side of the river instead. All the tanks were on fire, with flames and smoke pouring into the sky.

On the island, things looked just like they had on the show. They could see the old hospital and how the woods nearly covered everything. It'd be like camping. There wasn't any electricity or anything on the island, but the electricity won't last forever here, either. Sooner or later, the lights and power were going to go out. Winter was going to come, too. She either had to get south, or figure out a way to stay warm.

Letitia thought about that a bit. She knew birds flew south for the winter, and it was warmer there, but she didn't know how to get there if you couldn't fly. She didn't even know how to get past Randall's Island if you couldn't fly. That island looked safe enough, and she thought she could figure out how to stay warm faster than she could learn how to fly.

It was late. They picked their way back through the mountain of cars, Letitia leading the way. Just as they had dodged their way past one cuco, she noticed another approaching. They were trapped between two of them now, so there was no choice but to fight.

Letitia stepped forward and waited. Once the cuco was in reach she swung her ax as hard as she could. She was getting used to this now: the way the weight of the ax head felt as she swung the handle, the way she needed to shift her own weight to avoid getting overbalanced, the way her hands felt as she grasped the varnished wood of the handle. It still wasn't easy. Skulls are hard, so she rarely managed it in one blow. Usually she would cause enough damage with the first blow that a couple of the littler children could finish the job in safety.

This time was different. The cuco lurched forward just as she began the swing and she struck the skull with the handle of the ax, not the blade. The ax bounced. She lost her balance as the heavy piece of metal moved in the wrong direction and the handle slipped from her grasp.

The cold, waxy skin of the cuco's hands grasped her upper arms as it lifted her towards its mouth. She planted her feet firmly on its chest and pushed with all her might. A few kicks later she worked her way loose, but fell backwards and lay wedged into a gap in the line of wrecked cars, her feet poking up in the air, her face jammed into the grille of a crumpled Honda Accord.

Jahayra and Kiara rushed up from behind, prepared for the easy task of poking stakes into the eyes of a cuco that had its skull caved in or its jaw cut off, not one fresh and at full strength. It picked Jahayra up and drew her towards its mouth. She poked her stake between the rows of teeth, wedging it into the muscles at the back of its neck. The cuco kept trying to pull Jahayra into its mouth, but the stake blocked the way. It kept pulling on her, every pull pushing the stake further through its neck.

Kiara trembled. She knew that she had to get her stake into the eye socket to kill the brain. That's what Letitia had taught her, that's what she had practiced, but it had always been from behind fences or through grates. There weren't any fences or grates this time. The only thing she could think of to do was to climb the cuco, like she used to climb up on her uncle when he came to visit with a present and would tease her by holding it out of her reach.

She hooked her fingers into the cuco's belt and pulled herself up and in between its chest and her buddy. The cuco dropped its grip on Jahayra and grabbed onto Kiara just as Kiara managed to get her stake into the eye socket. The stake slid in like it was supposed to, into the meat of the brain, but the cuco didn't drop. She stirred the stake furiously, doing her best to cut the brain up. Doing this alone was harder: usually Jahayra was helping and they would just try to make their stakes meet in the middle. As she swirled the stake, she felt movement at her feet. Jada and Tiara were stabbing at the cuco's legs. It fell forward, collapsing on all of them, its own body weight driving the stakes home. She was sandwiched between the cold cement and the cold flesh of the cuco. Tears, blood, and snot mixed together in her nose, forcing her to breathe through her mouth as she gagged slightly on the liquids trickling down the back of her throat.

Letitia got loose from between the cars. Picking up her ax, she glared at the rest of the kids. "What you doin'? *Watchin*'? Get her out from there!"

Letitia picked up her ax as the children rolled the still cuco off of Kiara. Jahayra pulled on the stakes and got them loose so that she and Kiara were armed once more. She worked on getting Kiara's face clean and hugged her buddy until she could stop crying.

Letitia addressed the children that had held back. "That the way to do it," she said, gesturing at the four that had pressed the attack. "Keep stabbin' and swingin' till it dead. Kiara hurtin', but that the only reason Jahayra ain't *dead*. Standin' aroun' scared like you doin' just get you killed. Get *me* killed, too."

She walked over to Kiara and looked at her. There was still a little bit of snot and blood coming out of her nose, but the nosebleed had stopped. She hugged Kiara tightly. "Thanks. You did just what you supposed to do. Did it real good, too."

Kiara beamed.

She turned to Tiara and Jada. "You two done good, too." She was going to have to work out a treat for the four of them.

They got back to the apartment over Sami's just as the sun was setting. She was glad the electricity hadn't gone off yet. With the lights on and the dark outside, they could nearly forget what was going on outside. She was going to have to learn how to cook, though: candy bars and Flintstones vitamins *sounded* like it would be fun to eat every day, but it wasn't. The wrapped sandwiches from Sami's were pretty stale now, and the milk wasn't very good anymore. Potato chips seemed like they would last forever, and she remembered hearing jokes about how long Twinkies would last. Cooking from cans was easy enough: she'd made dinner for her and Jahayra from cans before. Maybe she'd learn to fish. She'd seen people fishing on TV. It looked easy enough.

After bathtime, they bundled together on the bed. Letitia made everybody bow their heads, then began:

"God, I sorry about today, too.

"I don't know if finishing Jada's mama was the right thing to do. I hope it was. If it wasn't, would you please figure out a way to tell me?

"Please take care of the rest of the kids' mamas, and don't let them be like that.

"Amen."

"Amen," came the hushed chorus.

Jada's hand came up.

"Yeah?" said Letitia.

"When someone get like that, do they still go to heaven? Even if they eat somebody?"

Letitia wished she didn't allow questions, because she didn't know the answer to that one. She did know what kind of answer Jada needed to hear, though.

"The preachers always be talking about souls, Jada. It a part of us you can't see, and it the part of us that goes to heaven when we die. I think that part of your mama went to heaven when she died and it was just her body that was left. I don't think it was really still her."

That quieted them for a bit. Letitia opened *The Little Engine That Could* and read it one more time.

As sleep came, Letitia wondered about Jada's question. She wondered if a preacher would really know the answer, either, or just give people the answer that made them feel better. She thought she knew the answer to *that* and wondered if that made her a preacher, too. She went to sleep with the low trilling of guinea pigs in her ears, still wondering.

CHAPTER 21
COLORING BOOK DAY

"We ain't goin' outside today," announced Letitia after breakfast. "We got enough food, you guys got your games and coloring books, so we just play inside."

Letitia needed a day to stop and think for a while, and there was no way to do that when they were outside going places. She pulled out the pen and little notebook she had grabbed from the Rite Aid. It made her feel much more adult. Big people didn't use crayons and construction paper, they used ballpoint pens and notebooks.

She started her list of things she had to figure out how to do:

1. Get to island
2. Cook on island
3. Fish
4. Stay warm this winter

After a few minutes, she wrote "fire" next to "Stay warm" and "Cook," and "boat" next to "Fish" and "Get to island." That felt better. It was easier to figure out two things than it was to figure out four things. She didn't really have to figure out "fire" yet, because the stove in the apartment still worked, and April in New York wasn't too cold with the eleven of them sharing a bed. Still, once they got to the island, they'd need it.

She thought about boats for a while. There were the great big boats she saw every day, but she had no idea how she would do anything with them. They were so big she didn't even know how to get on one. She'd seen little inflatable ones in that store Mr. Freeman bought her soccer uniform in. She couldn't remember its name, or exactly where it was, but she remembered it being by the ball fields in Hunts Point. She'd be able to find it. It was farther than they had ever gone, though, so she didn't want to try it today.

They went down to Sami's to get some more food and came back up the stairs with cans of chili. The little stove in the apartment was easy to use, and she managed to make a nice lunch and dinner. She checked the side of the cans. It only listed one vitamin on the label. She was pretty sure there were more kinds of vitamins than that so she made sure that everyone ate a Flintstones.

After dinner, they had guinea pig races. No one had figured out whether the guinea pigs were boys or girls, so they just named them "Brownie" and "Spot." They placed the two guinea pigs at one end of the kitchen and spread some of the rodent treats about five feet away. Brownie and Spot weren't great racers, but if you gave them enough time, one of them would find the food. The kids would make a big deal about being the winner, but there was no sign that Brownie and Spot cared at all.

CHAPTER 22
A TREASURE TROVE

The next day, they set out to look for the sporting goods store. Letitia planned on walking over to the ball fields, then searching around them until they found the store. She made sure that everyone packed a little extra food in their backpack because it was going to be a long, long day.

They crossed the Bruckner Expressway at Leggert. There were no mountains of cars this far from the bridge, just the occasional stack of two or three. They still had to pick their way through carefully, but it wasn't anywhere near as bad as it was further south. Once Leggert bent and became Randall, they were surprised to see activity about a mile down the street. There were carefully stacked piles of cars down there, five and six high, formed into walls. There were great big trucks parked next to the wall of cars and there were people on top of the trucks.

A cuco wandered into sight from in between a few of the cars and the people on the trucks opened fire with machine guns. The cuco was ripped to pieces in seconds.

Letitia didn't think it would be a good idea to run up to people with machine guns and shout "Hello!" but she was still curious. They carefully approached until she saw a sign reading "Hunts Point Food Distribution Center 1 Mile." That explained it. These people hadn't run away like everyone else. They had run to the food warehouses here and taken them over, kind of like how she and the kids lived right on top of Sami's. The adults had taken over *better* than she had, though. If someone took all the food from Sami's, there wasn't anything she could do about it. If someone tried to take the food from these people, they could do a lot about it. She thought about the big people at the Pioneer Supermarket and got a little nervous. What would happen when those people ran out of food? Would they come over and take everything out of Sami's? What would she do if they tried?

She sighed. These were still strangers, strangers with big guns, not policemen or firemen, so it wasn't safe.

They headed north, towards the baseball fields. Once they reached the fields, they began walking up and down each street, on the lookout for the sporting goods store. They walked for hours, up and down each street, finding nothing. Finally, Letitia decided to give up, but didn't tell the kids that.

" 'kay, we try on the other side of Bruckner. I must be wrong, it not right next to the field."

They walked up Tiffany. Letitia noticed that the car pile here was nearly absent. There were cars that had been pushed off, sure, but never more than one deep. She didn't know if that was because less had been pushed, or if it was because they had been taken to build the walls at the distribution center.

They turned onto Southern. There, in gold and green, was a giant sign: "Buchmans Sporting Goods." The windows were smashed out and things were a mess, but there were piles of stuff inside.

The first thing Letitia noticed inside was an entire display of small one- and two-man inflatable boats hanging from the ceiling on nylon strings. There was a big chart on the wall to help you choose which one you needed. The selection guide included things like "lake fishing," "river fishing," and "white water." "White water"? She had seen clear water, and blue water, and kind of murky green/brown water, but never white water. There wasn't any between here and the island, so she didn't worry about it.

She looked over the rest of the store. All the ammunition was gone, and most of the knives were gone, too. Nearly all the sharpeners were still there. She couldn't quite figure out why someone would steal a knife without a sharpener. There were a lot of small hatchets left. She picked one up and compared it to her ax. It was a lot lighter and felt like it would work. Might as well trade.

There was all kind of stuff here that she didn't even know about, but figured she could use. Water purifiers sounded handy. Little stoves that ran on gas would be useful. Sleeping bags to stay warm in the winter. Cots to sleep on. Tents. Bags of food with names like "beef jerky." Little heaters that ran on gas. Lanterns. Fishing rods. The list went on. She decided that the best thing for her to do was to take some of everything to the island and figure out how to use it later.

They had books, too, that would help her figure things out. *Golden's Guide to Fishing* had lots of pictures of how to fish. She spotted a copy of *Field Dressing and Butchering: Rabbits, Squirrels and Other Small Game* and looked through it. It didn't have any pages about guinea pigs, but how different could they be from squirrels?

She turned her attention back to the boats. They had two different kinds:

one that looked like a raft, and one that looked like a chair with a tube on either side. Putting all eleven of them in a raft would be a bad idea. The kids had learned a lot about being good and a lot about being quiet, but they were still little kids. If she crowded ten of them together in a raft, something would go wrong. Especially when all the little kids had sharp pointy stakes in their hands.

She looked again at the kind with the tubes on each side. The chairs were big enough that two little kids could fit, and each one could hold an oar. There were little boxes on top of the tubes that you could put pointy stakes in. If something went really, really wrong, only two of them would die.

She stopped thinking for a moment because "only two of them would die" made her shudder inside. Still, that was bad, but better than eleven of them dying.

She looked at the boats and puzzled over the chart. Was bigger better? What was a "rapid deflation valve" and did she want one? "Double-reinforced internal bladder"? Finally, she chose one of the smallest ones that still had good storage, because she figured small people needed smaller boats.

The eleven of them opened the box and puzzled over the instructions. The instructions were confusing: good pictures, but the writing was in about five languages. She hoped she didn't really need to read those parts in different languages to put it together. She could barely read the English. "*Please to be putting the red tube deliciously into the blue rod*" didn't even seem to be English. Still, she had a picture and a pile of parts, so she treated it like a jigsaw puzzle. An hour later, they had it together. She found a foot pump to inflate it with. Two little life jackets on two little kids, and they both fit into the seat. She could make this work.

Right now, it was too late to do any more. They walked back to Sami's. After prayers and story time, she got back up and got out her notebook. She put big check marks next to the first three items. She wasn't quite ready to put a check mark next to "get to island" yet, but she felt comfortable that she would get it puzzled out.

She looked at the list and wrote:

    5.   Get boats and stuff to river
    6.   Practice with boats
    7.   Guns?

CHAPTER 23
PRACTICE MAKES PERFECT

Getting to Buchmans was a lot easier once they knew where it was, Letitia decided. She stood inside the store with the rest of the children, trying to figure out how to carry the boat they had built yesterday. It was pretty light, but awkward. Finally, she put one kid on each end of each pontoon and they carried it that way. They looked kind of like cartoons she had seen of people carrying kings on a chair. She wasn't going to do this again: if this worked, they'd carry the kits to the river and inflate the boats there. She wasn't about to spend another hour with a foot pump on this one just to make it easier to carry, though.

They headed to Baretto Point Park. There was a big dock here for people to launch little fishing boats and things from. They could see the island clearly from here. The fires behind it were starting to go out.

Letitia looked out over the river. The water was nearly still. Wasn't the water in a river supposed to move? She thought that rivers were supposed to flow, but whoever named this the "East River" didn't know that. She tied one end of a long rope she had brought along to one of the handles on the boat and tied the other to a post on the dock. Malik and Rosarita went first: they were biggest, so if they couldn't manage it, no one could.

They had some trouble at first. Malik was stronger than Rosarita, so the boat went in a circle unless he held back a little bit. Whenever he did that, the rope would snag Rosarita and she would shout something. Letitia didn't need to know Spanish to understand that Rosarita wasn't saying nice things to Malik.

After an hour, they could make the boat go forward, backward and turn it on purpose, so Letitia gestured for them to come in. "Somebody else's turn, now." They had to paddle harder to get back, because the river was flowing now. Not fast, but it was clearly flowing towards Hunts Point.

Kiara and Jada went next. They were the same size and didn't turn so much, but they did have a hard time keeping the boat from heading straight to Hunts Point. It was a lot of work to keep from going with the river's flow and it seemed like that flow was getting stronger all the time.

Jose and Trevon couldn't manage the current. The boat went straight over towards Hunts Point and stayed there, the long rope taut and holding them in place. They rowed as hard as they could. The boat would move about a foot, but as soon as they pulled their oars out of the water, the rope would snap tight.

Letitia pulled on the rope, but she couldn't drag them in.

"Make like tug-of-war," she said to everyone. "Grab on to the rope and when they row, try to hold 'em."

Working together, they could build a foot of slack in the rope every time Trevon and Jose rowed. Once they got a couple feet of slack, Letitia would wrap the slack around the post. During the haul, it got easier and easier. Letitia noticed the river was slowing down. Finally, she told the exhausted group to stop and rest.

"Take a break. It look like the water stoppin' again. May get easy enough for them to do it by themselves."

They waited for a while and the river slowed down. Jose and Trevon finally had a chance to practice and came back in under their own power.

"Lunch time," said Letitia. "I want to watch this crazy river some more."

While they ate, the river slowed, stopped, then started flowing the other way. Letitia decided she knew less about rivers than she ever had before. Since it was slow now, Jahayra and Tiara got a chance to practice, but, by the time they came in, Letitia thought it was too strong to let Lucia and Maria go, especially since it was heading towards Randall's Island.

Letitia decided that it would be OK. All they had to do was wait for the slow period, give Lucia and Maria a chance to practice, and then they could make it to the island. They'd start while the water was turning around from going towards Randall's Island, because if it got too strong before they got there, they would get pulled towards Hunts Point. She may not trust the big people at Hunts Point, but she knew she didn't want to wind up on Randall's Island.

CHAPTER 24
THE NIGHT THE LIGHTS WENT OUT

" 'Can you help us?' the clown asked the big red freight—"

The lights suddenly went off. Letitia continued from memory, barely skipping a beat: "—engine. 'Of course not,' said the big red engine, 'I am much too important for the likes of you!'"

The little ones, their eyes already closed, didn't notice. After the final "I thought I could," she crept out of bed and went over to the window.

The lights were out everywhere. There had still been a scattered twinkling of lights at night and the street lamps had continued to work everywhere. Tonight, it was black outside, blacker than she had ever seen. The moon was down, and, when she looked upwards, there was a blurry white stripe of stars going clear across the sky that had never been there before. Someone would have talked about it if it was. She stared at the sky for a while before climbing back into bed.

There was still no electricity when they got up, which meant she couldn't toast her Pop-Tarts for breakfast. At least Sami's carried real Pop-Tarts, so it wasn't too bad. Most of the little kids liked the little snack donuts for breakfast, so not having any electricity didn't bother them at all, but with no electricity, there wasn't any reason to stay here anymore. They packed everything into their backpacks and the grocery cart and made their way to Buchmans.

Letitia called a halt when they got in sight of Buchmans. Things had been disturbed since they left: the side door was wide open and one more window had been broken out. They approached cautiously, staring through the windows first, then doing the full cop-show-style search when they went inside. An entire rack of portable generators was missing, but nothing else seemed to have been touched.

She set the kids to finding things she thought they would need. After a few hours, they had assembled a pile of sleeping bags, a big tent, lanterns, fishing poles, small knives, and packages of freeze-dried food. They built a raft to carry things in and five more pontoon boats, leaving them uninflated this time.

They headed for Baretto Point Park with all the new boats. Uninflated, they were much easier to handle, and each pair of children could handle one. Today was a bit more active than the day before and they had to dispatch three creatures during the walk. They all looked extremely fresh, so Letitia decided that they must have been doing something dangerous when the lights went out and gotten themselves killed in the dark.

The first boat was still there, bobbing happily in the water. They went to work with the foot pump and, a few hours later, they had assembled a fleet: six little pontoon boats and a big rubber raft sat tied to the dock.

Letitia looked at the river. It was aiming towards Randall's Island again. It seemed like it at least did the same thing at the same time every day, which meant that early in the morning would be a good time to take off.

They returned to Buchmans.

" 'kay, everybody. We sleepin' here tonight, we do it like we campin'. Get your sleepin' bag and put it in the room back there with all the boxes."

Letitia felt safe in the stockroom. There weren't any windows, so no one could see their lights. They closed the doors and slid the oars from the boats into the handles to keep them closed and locked as best they could. They ate granola and trail mix by the light of portable fluorescent lamps.

The school backpacks weren't holding up too well, but there was a big pile of good camping backpacks here. Letitia wanted to make sure the kids would have what they needed if they got lost or separated, too. She sat down with her notebook and made a list:

1. Flintstones vitamins
2. Flashlight
3. Extra batteries
4. Socks
5. Trail mix pouch (3)
6. Beef Jerky
7. Water bottle (2)
8. Blanket
9. Pillow
10. Pocket knife

She got a small backpack off the shelf and experimented. She packed, and repacked, and arranged, and rearranged, and finally crossed "Pillow" off the list. Hopefully, no one would be separated long enough to need a pillow. The rest fit pretty well, with enough room left over for a lunch and a coloring book or game. Or a guinea pig.

The backpacks came in six different colors, so she told them all to choose a color and bring one over. They ran over to the shelf. Lucia reached for a bright pink one.

Trevon looked at her. "That a stupid color! How you goin' to hide from one of them things if you wearin' somethin' that be glowin' in the dark?"

Letitia smiled. Trevon was smarter than she thought: she hadn't thought of that. Everyone settled on gray for the boys and khaki for the girls.

This was everybody's first camping trip, even if it was just pretend. Everyone chattered excitedly until bedtime. Letitia read *The Little Engine That Could* until they all fell asleep, each buddy pair sharing a sleeping bag, sharp stakes lying within easy reach on the floor.

CHAPTER 25
A FLOTILLA LAUNCHES

Letitia set out two spare rafts and inflated them. " 'kay, guys, stack those piles of stuff in here. We use 'em to carry things out." The rafts were quickly filled, and they set out, four children carrying each raft.

There was a low throbbing machine noise coming from Hunts Point. Letitia felt the hum coming up from the ground through her toes. Cucos were trickling in from everywhere, drawn by the noise, pooling up at the pile of cars by the Bruckner Expressway. Cucos would reach the cars and try to climb over. When they tripped and fell, other cucos would climb over them, get stuck someplace further up, where another would climb over them. It was like the messes at the railway and pet shop, just bigger. They could hear cucos that were trapped inside homes pounding on the doors, excited by the noise.

Letitia led the children on a detour to stay away from the car pile. There were no serious encounters until they reached the pier. There, staring at the bobbing orange boats, were several cucos.

"Come up behind me in case I need you," Letitia said to Rosarita and Malik, "but I goin' to try just pushin' 'em in the water." It worked: a good solid hit with the hatchet made each cuco lose its balance and fall in. She watched as the current quickly started them in the direction of Randall's Island. They didn't float at all, probably because they didn't breathe. They sank quickly, then half-walked, half-bounced along the muddy river bottom.

She watched the water flow. It was flowing slowly towards Randall's Island and getting slower. It was time to launch.

Rosarita and Malik were in front, still holding a rope that Letitia had tied to the dock. She tied each boat to the one ahead and behind. Then came the supply rafts, and then, last of all, came Letitia. She thought of going in the lead, but decided that she wanted to be where she could see what went on ahead.

Letitia looked ahead at the boats. She hoped the river would be nearly still when it came time to land. She had narrowed down the choices to two: there was a tall pier on the northwestern shore by the hospital that was built for boats to tie to, but a small beach on the northeastern shore looked much easier to land on.

"Rosarita, Malik, get to rowin'. Head for that beach we talk about."

Malik threw the rope over and began to paddle, the other rope that trailed behind him tugging gently on the boat behind. He smiled broadly. Aiming for the beach was easy, Rosarita was happy, and he hadn't done anything this fun for a long time, since before everything went wrong.

The water was barely moving when they reached the beach. He jumped out of the boat and helped Rosarita drag it up on the sand, then popped open the storage compartment and grabbed his stake, keeping lookout while everyone landed. One bush began to shake. He tugged on Rosarita's sleeve and pointed. They ran over, peeked into the bush, and quickly poked their stakes into the cuco's eyes.

"Letitia," Malik said, "look at this one. It all weird."

Letitia looked. It was limp and kind of flat, with bones poking out through the flesh. She poked it with a stick and the flesh tore off the bones just from poking it. She touched it. The flesh was slimy, soft and wet, and she poked right through the skin.

"Must be what happen to 'em when they stay underwater too long." She smiled. "If this all we got to worry about, we be fine."

CHAPTER 26
THE HOSPITAL

They dragged their boats and rafts up onto the beach and slightly into the brush. Letitia didn't think it was a good idea for it to be obvious they were there, but didn't want to spend all day trying to hide them, either.

They tramped through the woods towards the hospital, using the old roadway. It was covered in soil and leaves, with an occasional brick poking up and even a few spots where the layer of cobblestones was visible.

The main building came into sight, four stories tall, with a semicircular lobby open the entire height of the building. Large wings protruded northwest and southeast of the central lobby. Trees leaned against the building, breaking through the roof in spots. Vines with bright blue and purple berries climbed up the side of the building and through the window openings. There was even one window with a tree growing out of it.

Letitia was amazed when they walked inside. She had seen bad buildings before, but never one like this. Crumbling plaster lay inches deep on the floor. The vines not only reached inside, they *grew* inside, climbing the stairways and lobby walls. Sunlight flickered through the roof forty feet above them.

The ground floor was useless. The vines were thickest here, and, if anything wanted in, all it had to do was climb in a window.

"Look at them stairs!" Jahayra exclaimed, running over to the remains of a spiral stairway. Made of stone and brick, the vine-covered stairway led upwards. She looked upwards and saw clear to the roof. "You can see clear to the sky!"

"Careful with those! Don't you be runnin' up anywhere." Letitia looked up. How did the stairs get you to the top with those big holes?

"Stay down here. Let me climb up and see what going on." She stood on the first step. Nothing bad happened, so she took another. She slowly ascended the spiral. She got to the top step, a foot below the next floor, and looked down through a triangular hole. Splinters of rotten wood surrounded the edge of the opening, with rusty nails protruding into nowhere.

She pulled on a pillar. It felt solid. She held on tight while she stepped over the missing step onto the floor. The floor felt solid.

"Come up slow! Two at a time, no runnin'. The last step be gone," she instructed them. One pair at a time, the children climbed, grabbed the pillar, and stepped onto the second floor.

Letitia smiled. The little ones could do it, but there was no way a cuco would be smart enough to. She started to laugh.

"Why you laughin'?" Malik asked.

"Just thinkin' of a cuco trying to get up here. Bet he climb the stairs, step though the hole, climb the stairs, step through the hole. They so stupid, he probably do it forever."

She thought for a moment. "Clear up top be the safest, I think, so we look there first."

They climbed the stairs. When Letitia reached the top, she called back to the children waiting on the third floor. "Stop. Ain't no use everybody comin' up here."

The top floor was a forest. Sunlight streamed through the roof, plants grew out of the plaster, the doorways were piles of rotten wood, and moss grew everyplace there was a shadow. Living here would be the same as living outdoors. The roof wouldn't do much to keep them dry, and what was the point of a building where you couldn't stay dry?

Letitia came back down to the third floor. "We look around here, see if there a good place for us," she said as she started down one of the hallways. This floor had small rooms. Some had good windows, but most didn't. The ceilings all looked scary: exposed bricks and tiles, with roots coming through from the floor above.

She finally found a place on the second floor she thought was perfect, with bunk beds lining the walls. The mattresses were rotten and covered with plants and mold, but there were air mattresses at Buchmans. The walls were covered with graffiti: wild illustrations of monsters, needles with stuff dripping out the end, people killing each other, names and dates. One scrawl read "*Help. I am being held here against my will.*"

She liked the door to the room best of all. It was made out of steel, with a slot in it about the height of a person's eyes. It had a cage around it, with another steel door leading into the main room. There was something written on the door. Letitia wiped the crud free to get a better look, uncovering stenciled black letters: "HEROIN WITHDRAWAL WARD."

Heroin meant junkies. She knew what junkies were and remembered what her mama acted like the times she tried to stop using. She tried to imagine putting a hundred people like that in a room and shuddered.

Those doors and that cage would help with cucos as much as they helped with junkies, so if one got past the river, it still couldn't hurt them.

She looked around again. Steel doors, steel cages, windows with steel mesh that were twenty feet off the ground, staircase with great big holes in it — it was perfect. Letitia smiled. It was dirty, but she could make this place safe.

"Let's go get our stuff," she said, heading them back towards the beach.

They hid the small pontoon boats in the bushes and carried the supply boats into the lobby.

"You want us to carry *all* of this upstairs?" asked Jahayra. "*All* of it?"

"Don' make no sense, do it?" Letitia replied. "Let me think."

She looked over the boats. "We don' need everything to sleep. Get the mats, get the sleeping bags, lanterns. The rest stay down here."

They set the mats and sleeping bags on the floor of the recovery ward and had a dinner of trail mix and bottled water on the front steps.

Going to the bathroom was a bigger deal than she had thought of. They couldn't just break into a house here like they did in the city, and she hadn't thought through the idea that the water had been turned off for fifty years. The boys didn't have any problem peeing on a tree, but none of the girls had ever done it outside. It was awkward, uncomfortable, embarrassing, and more than a little bit messy. She had picked up wipes in the camping store, so she used them to clean up her little charges as best she could.

Bedtime was a bit more aromatic than usual. No baths today, no toilets to use, and all eleven of them together in the ward made for a bad smell. It quickly became Letitia's most important problem for the next day.

As she was just getting them settled for bedtime, the sound of distant gunfire disturbed their routine. They all ran to the windows. The night wasn't quite as black as it had been before. Over at Hunts Point, the lights were on. Whatever that hum was, it must have something to do with them figuring out how to make electricity.

"I can't believe how stupid those people be," said Letitia. "Makin' noise all day long, and now they the only thing cucos can see at night."

CHAPTER 27
SETTING UP CAMP

Trevon looked at the sheet of paper in his hand. Letitia had written down the words she was looking for: "JANITOR," "CUSTODIAN," "BROOM," "CLEANING SUPPLIES." He looked at the door again. "JANITORIAL," it said in big block letters.

"Think that close enough?" he asked Jose.

Jose looked at the paper and looked at the door. "Is very close, yes. We go ask Letitia, I think."

Letitia returned with them. "Yeah, that what we lookin' for. We see if anything be left." She pushed the door open. Dried-up bottles of cleaning supplies sat on rusty metal shelves. Some things had leaked, leaving a thick pasty mixture on the floor. Push brooms hung on hooks on the far wall. They were off the floor and out of the way of any leaks, so they still looked like they would work.

" 'kay, grab them brooms and we go back upstairs."

They all gathered in the recovery ward.

"I think it pretty safe here," Letitia said, "so some of you goin' to stay here and clean, the rest of us go get more stuff." It was the first time they had split up since leaving the school.

"Jahayra, Kiara, Tiara, and Jada, you comin' with me. Rest of you try to get this place lookin' better. Rosarita, Malik, you two in charge here."

Letitia tested the door before leaving. With a metal chair next to it, every kid she was leaving behind could poke a stake through the slot.

"Remember, you guys stay in here, keep the door locked as much as you can. Ain't time for playin' today, it a workin' day."

She left the room. "Now slide that thing like I show you." She waited until she heard the click and tried the door. It held tight.

They picked up the empty supply rafts from the lobby on the way back to the beach.

" We do it different today," Letitia said. "Everybody goin' to pull one raft."

She tied the boats up in pairs: one pontoon boat pulling one supply raft. The three pairs of boats set off towards Baretto Point.

The noise coming from Hunts Point was louder today. The cucos were thicker today than yesterday. The piles of cars next to the expressway were slowly getting covered in flesh, with cucos trapped in the spaces between.

"Do those piles of cars look taller to you guys?" asked Letitia.

The other children nodded.

"Look there," Jahayra said, pointing at a pile of cars that was trembling and starting to move. A bulldozer was pushing it around, belching smoke and making even more noise. "What they *doin'*?"

"Makin' them walls bigger, I think," Letitia answered. "Making lot of noise, too." That meant cucos, and that meant this place wouldn't be as safe. Gunshots rang out, adding to the noise.

"We got to be careful today. Be quiet as you can ... these guys makin' so much noise, if we quiet, cucos might not notice us."

It worked on the way to Buchmans. Cucos spotted them a few times, but each time all they needed to do was run. Once out of sight, the cuco would start walking towards the noise again.

Buchmans looked unchanged. Letitia grabbed a shopping cart, walked up and down the rows, and spotted a shelf full of buckets with toilet seats on top and *Luggable Loo* written on the side. "Luggable" and "loo" were silly sounding words, but the toilet seats and pictures made it clear what they were. Right next to them were boxes labeled *Double Doodie Toilet Waste Bags* with even more pictures on the side.

"*Doodie*," she snickered. "Didn't know they made *doodie* bags."

There were boxes next to them labeled *Solar Shower* and she grabbed a couple of those. Anything to keep the smell down.

She did the math. One bed for her, but the little ones liked to share, so they needed five between them. That meant six Single Bed Air Mattresses, six Single Bed Ground Pads and she was nearly done. There were little things left to get: disposable hand wipes, soap, towels ... She looked at her list and marked things off. The Luggable Loos were so big it took two carts to fit everything.

They pushed the two carts out and started down Tiffany, back to the boats. Letitia looked ahead. Bulldozers were busy shifting and moving the cars along the east side of Tiffany. Cucos were piling up, not able to make it past the more organized wall.

"That way," she said, pointing down Longwood. "We can get around the long way."

They took the jog down Longwood and started down Truxton. The wide street stretched out before them, with nothing but warehouses on each side. There were no cars on the street at all, just bulldozer tracks and little bits and pieces of cars littering the way. They walked quickly down the middle until Letitia spotted an opening in the middle of a big open area surrounded by corrugated tin walls with razor wire on top.

They left the carts on the street and went inside. The other sides of the area were surround by hurricane fence.

"You guys help me remember this place, 'kay? This a *great* place to run if we need to." The children all nodded.

Once they made it back to the ward, Letitia was impressed. The little ones hadn't gotten it *clean*, but they had tried. Nobody had goofed off. There was a big pile of trash and junk picked up and put in one corner and a big pile of dirt swept up into a big pile. There was a big pile of dirt all over the little ones, too. Most days they were all different colors, but today they were all the same shade of dust brown.

"You guys did pretty good here," she said. "That worth a treat." She handed out some candy she had picked up from the pile of stuff in the lobby.

Letitia looked for a place to set up the Luggable Loo. She found a little room close to the ward that had all the windows smashed out. The windows would keep it from smelling too bad, and there was a little shelf for toilet paper and hand wipes.

"You guys remember to close that lid when you done, and to use them wipes! Ain't no sink to wash your hands in around here."

She smiled again. Anything that kept her from having to wipe up after little kids that had fallen into a pile of leaves while they were trying to take a dump was a *good* thing. She could use disposing of a used Double Doodie Toilet Waste Bag as punishment, too.

With that, it was time for the Solar Showers and the Base Camp Water Filter. She filled them all with river water. As promised, the shower water was warm enough to use in an hour.

"Shower time!" she called out.

"But everybody see me naked!" Jada protested. "Mama told me never go runnin' around naked!"

"What you think I goin' to do, Jada? Build you a private shower? We got three showers, and they hanging on that tree over there. Everybody else naked, too, so you won't get in trouble or nothin'."

She got in the showers with everybody else. She didn't like looking at naked boys, but she didn't think they should be splitting up over something silly like this. The cheap camping towels were coarse and felt like they would rip apart, but they got everybody dry.

The water in the Base Camp Water Filter had run through now and looked clear. She had a taste. It tasted better than most tap water. She had everyone fill a water bottle and then refilled the filter.

By this time, the sun was getting pretty low on the horizon. The ground pads were laid on top of the bunk bed springs, then air mattresses, then sleeping bags. The fluorescent lantern came out, then it was dinner time, and then prayer time.

"God, thank you for this island. It little, but it the right size for us. It not as scary here, and we like that.

"Please take care of Mr. Buchman. I don't remember him from when I in his store before, but he the one that really own all this stuff. We be dead if he wasn't smart enough to have all this stuff. I hope he alive. If he is and he wants me to, I'll pay him back when I can.

"Can you please make the big people be quieter?

"Amen."

"Amen," came the replies, not as hushed as before. Everyone *did* feel safer here, and it was nice to not have to whisper all the time. Feeling a bit cozy and safe herself, Letitia allowed herself to read *The Little Engine That Could* all the way out loud. She played with the voices and had fun making the train noises with the whistles and the snorts and the chug-a-chugs. Everybody giggled and fell asleep.

CHAPTER 28
TEACH A MAN TO FISH

Letitia pored over her copy of *Golden's Guide to Fishing* and fiddled with the Mini Pocket Fishing Rod she had taken from Buchmans. The guide kept talking about flies, but then showed pictures of all these crazy feathered things. She didn't have any flies, she didn't have any crazy feathered things, but she could get a worm.

"Jose, Trevon! Think you can go find me a worm?"

Trevon nodded, then asked "How I goin' to dig in the dirt to find one?"

"There a little shovel in the pile of stuff in the lobby. Got a picture of a campfire on the box," replied Letitia. She was going to have to teach these kids to read someday. Not everything was going to have a picture on it.

A little later, Trevon and Jose came back with three worms.

They all went out to the big pier on the northwest corner of the island. Letitia went out on it first, stepping carefully on the cracked and weathered boards. Nothing broke.

" 'kay, come on out. Slow. Don't be jumpin' up and down or nothin'. Jahayra, bring that bucket of water along." It was actually the spare Luggable Loo, but the book didn't say your bucket couldn't have a toilet seat on it.

She puzzled over the instruction sheet and stared at the book some more. She tied her weight, bob, and hook onto the line. She poked the hook into one of the worms.

Casting was hard. The little weight would swing back around and she'd catch one of the kids on the shirt or shorts. She came really close to hooking Rosarita's ear. Finally, she gave up. She laid down flat on the edge of the pier and lowered the bait into the water. The book said to make the bait jump around, so she jerked on the rod.

The book didn't say anything about how long you should move it before you gave up. She was just starting to reel it back in when the line went really tight and pulled on her, nearly taking her off the dock. A big striped fish, eighteen inches long, flipped back and forth like, well, like a fish on a hook.

The book talked about "reeling the fish in" like it was easy. Letitia tried to crank the wheel and nearly lost hold of the rod.

"Malik, Rosarita! Help!"

They ran over. "Help me hold this thing!" Malik grabbed onto the handle and helped Letitia hold the rod still. Rosarita cranked the reel while everyone else watched. Finally, the fish was flopping back and forth on the pier.

They put the fish in the Loo. Everyone ringed around the bucket and looked at the fish excitedly.

"I never saw one for real before!" exclaimed Tiara.

Everyone nodded and talked excitedly. Some of them had been to the New York Aquarium, but none of them had been so close to a live fish before.

Letitia hadn't planned on catching one that was so big. That meant she would only need to catch one, though, and that was good. It looked like the picture of a "striped bass" in *Golden's Guide to Fishing*, but that didn't make any difference. No matter what kind of fish it was, the book said to start by cutting its belly open.

She pulled the fish out of the bucket by the hook and tried. The fish was half her size, and the book didn't say *anything* about what to do with a fish that was half your size. The pictures were all of these great big white men on great big boats. Not a little black girl in sight. She tried wrestling with it, but it flipped and bucked and jumped, nearly making her fall off the dock.

"Malik, use your stake on its head!" She sat as hard as she could on the body of the fish, and Malik pushed his stake through the head. The fish kept bucking. "Rosarita, get the tail!"

Rosarita drove her stake into the tail. Now that it was pinned on both sides, Letitia sawed the head off with a pocket knife. It stopped flipping around once that happened, so getting the tail off was easy.

She was leaning over the pier to throw the head and tail over into the water when she saw a body floating down the river, about twenty feet away. Red liquid oozed out of a hole in its head and its skin was red and sunburnt, so it wasn't a cuco. She recognized the bright orange jumpsuit from TV: something was going on on Rikers Island.

They watched as it floated past. It didn't look like it was going to wash up on shore and didn't look like it was going to pop back to life, so they got back to their fish and *Golden's Guide to Fishing*. It had instructions on how to cut the belly and remove the guts. Her knife slipped in easily and the guts came out easily. She threw them over the side, too. No people floated past this time.

Letitia emptied the water out of the bucket, put the fish in it, and headed back to the hospital. The InstaStart grill was easy: only one hose to hook up to one of the bottles of gas from Buchmans. The grill had looked huge at Buchmans, but it wasn't big enough for this fish. She sawed the fish in two and put one half on the grill. She wished she had cooked something that wasn't out of a can before. She didn't know how to tell when it was done and knew she was burning parts.

When she took it off the grill and stripped its meat from the bones, it was burnt in some spots, pink in others, but enough had become white and flaky that everyone could have some. Having a piece of fish to go with the trail mix was nice. It was the first warm food she'd had since the canned chili in the apartment.

She wasn't sure if fish had vitamins in it, so she still made sure everyone had some Flintstones. Today was a good day. She'd made a lot of mistakes, but nothing turned out too badly. She was glad she hadn't chosen Rikers Island to live on, that was for sure. She didn't know how the men there decided who to kill and who not to, but she didn't want to give them a chance to decide about her.

CHAPTER 29

THE NOTEBOOK

Life began to settle into a routine. The stockpile of camping food from Buchmans was enough to keep them going for a while once they added in a couple of fish each day. Most of the fish that Letitia hooked were small enough to handle, but every once in a while they'd hook something so large there was no choice but to cut the line. Letitia hated that, because replacing a fish hook would be hard someday. Nothing grew on the island that you could eat. That worried her.

It wasn't quite true that there was nothing to eat: the guinea pigs had escaped, and the children would spot them every once in a while. Either Brownie or Spot had turned out to be a girl and the other a boy, because after a few weeks they began to see little guinea pigs scattered about.

It was getting warmer, and life was feeling nearly like a vacation here. They spent their days exploring the nooks and crannies of the island. There were dozens of old buildings here. She had no idea what the large building with the twin smokestacks was, but most of the remaining buildings were cottages and sheds. Some were so old that all that was left was the floor, but a few still stood well enough to provide real shelter against the weather.

They made regular supply runs into the Bronx. Each time, she could see that the Hunts Point people were getting deeper into trouble, even though they didn't seem to understand that they were their own problem. The piles of cars would be a little higher and a little better organized each time. She could see sentries at different positions on the walls. Every once in a while, the Hunts Point people would go out with a great big fuel truck and steal gas from a station. Whenever they did that, it took them all day, they made a lot of noise pumping, and it wasn't safe to be anywhere near them.

The cucos kept coming from everywhere. They got thicker and thicker the closer you came to the car walls, with Tiffany Street being full of them, making Buchmans completely out of reach. The earliest arrivals had long since disintegrated under the pressure from later arrivals, and all the cracks and joints in the walls were being filled with rotting flesh. In some spots, plants and vines were beginning to grow in the decaying body parts. It reminded Letitia of the vines covering the buildings on the island.

Letitia took notes every time she went out. She had picked up a map book at one of the gas stations. She took notes all over it and took notes in her notebook, too. She had never thought of herself as someone that would do that kind of thing, but she just couldn't remember everything without it.

Her notebook was full of little entries that had been crossed out. "Batteries" would quickly become "~~batteries~~" on a scavenging run. Same with "~~socks~~," "~~soap~~," and other things they could find readily in stores. Two that seemed stuck were "garden" and "windows."

Today, Letitia was determined to cross "windows" out. The recovery ward didn't have too much trouble with water getting in from upstairs: the roof wasn't much, but the upper floors kept the water from getting to the second floor when it rained. When the wind blew, though, the water blew in through the steel mesh over the window openings. Most of the glass was long gone. She didn't think she would be able to fix the glass, but she had seen a lot of old cars with smashed windows that just used plastic wrap. She thought they could do that.

"Tiara, Jada!" Letitia shouted from the hospital steps. "You comin' with me today. We goin' to get stuff to fix up the windows."

Jada and Tiara ran up.

"Where we goin'?" asked Jada.

"Found a couple of hardware stores in the phone book. They should have window-fixin' stuff."

They got in their boats and began paddling, aiming for a little flat spot at the end of 132nd Street.

Letitia stepped out of her boat, tied it to a small tree, then helped the little ones to do the same. This wasn't anywhere near as nice as Baretto Point, but it wasn't right next to those crazy people, either. Even so, it was too close to Randall's Island to be completely safe.

Letitia walked up to the broken fence and pulled the wire section back. "Scoot, you two. Get on through so I can get through."

Greenhill Hardware was the closest hardware store, but it was so close to Hunts Point that it was already stripped clean, leaving nothing but useless junk. Well, maybe not *useless*. Letitia picked up a handful of auto air fresheners. *Something* had to help with that Luggable Loo.

Advantage Hardware was in better shape. She was able to pick up a big roll of plastic and a lot of duck tape. The Stanley 65-Piece General Homeowners Toolkit looked pretty interesting, so she grabbed a couple of those.

There was a big rack of books on one wall, all labeled *The Sunset Guide to This* or *The Sunset Guide to That*. *Basic Home Repair. Plumbing. Roofing.*

She leafed through them. They were full of more pictures of big happy white men doing big happy white man things, but they looked useful: fixing windows and roofs and walls and things.

Basic Home Repair had a section labeled *Things Every Homeowner Should Have For An Emergency.* "Dead people everywhere" was probably an emergency, she decided. A big roll of plastic sheeting, duck tape and a basic toolkit were on the list. She liked getting things right.

The *Western Garden Book of Edibles* looked like it could help scratch "garden" off the list, too, and it was right next to a giant rack of seed packets. She didn't grab any of the flower seeds, but she grabbed all of the ones with pictures of food. They spent an hour going through the store, and were able to find nearly everything from *Things Every Homeowner Should Have For An Emergency.* She could tell the list was from before, though: it didn't include sharp stakes or axes.

CHAPTER 30
WINDOW DAY

It had taken three trips to get everything across the river, but they had made it. The ladders were tricky. She was going to have to figure out something better than an inflatable raft for getting things across. Every once in a while she would see the men from Rikers going across in their big powerboats to get stuff. She knew that they must have seen the kids crossing in the little boats and worried about that. She guessed they just had enough to worry about without coming over. She wished she had a powerboat, too.

She had read the chapter *Emergency Window Repair* a dozen times. None of the windows in the book had steel gratings to keep junkies in on them. She guessed the happy white men didn't have junkies in the house. Or cucos in the yard.

She did just what the book said. Some of the things that one big happy white man could do took three little kids, but they managed. Two would hold the plastic in place while Letitia pounded the staples in with a hammer. Once it was all up, she trimmed it with scissors and sealed it up with duck tape. It wasn't pretty, but it would stay dry inside now.

She may not be a big white man, but she could be happy, too. And dry.

CHAPTER 31
HAIR AND SHARPENING STONES

Letitia sat on the front steps of the hospital, her legs slightly apart, with Tiara sitting in the gap on the step below and Jada watching them both. Letitia, armed with her Camping Utility Shears and a pick comb, looked down at Tiara's hair and poked at it with the pick. There was more in there than just twigs and bugs: it looked like someone had tied knots in someone else's hair and then tied that to Tiara's hair.

"What did your mama used to *do* to your hair?" Letitia asked.

"She always used all kinds of stuff. She rubbed it in and made me wait, and then she'd wash it out. Sometimes she bought hair and sewed it into my head."

"She *bought* hair?" Letitia poked harder at one spot and saw the threads that were tying one piece to another. "You mean some of this ain't even *yours*?"

Letitia made a few more stabs with the pick, but nothing smoothed out or knocked loose. The only things that changed were some little scabby blisters coming loose and some bugs running away and hiding.

"Tiara, there ain't nothin' I can do but cut most of this off," Letitia began. "I ain't got no chemicals or rollers or nothin' to make it look like it used to. Can't even get it clean, and that the big problem. That the reason you itch so bad."

Tears started forming in Tiara's eyes. "My mama always say my hair the prettiest thing 'bout me," she protested. "You can't just go cuttin' it off."

Jada wasn't much happier than Tiara. She usually kept her hair in a medium-length afro, about two inches deep. It was thicker now, so all sorts of things got stuck in it when she was outside.

"Do mine first," Jada said. "You know them ladies got hair only this long?" she asked, pinching her fingers together to about a half-inch apart. "Make mine like that. Then you do hers, we still look like buddies."

Letitia went to work on Jada. Jada's hair wasn't nearly as bad: at least it was all her hair with nobody else's mixed in.

Tiara sniffed a little bit, but sat back on the step in front of Letitia. Jada held her hand as Letitia went to work on the tangled, matted mess. Letitia cut the threads she could find, pulled the twigs out, cut more threads, and worked away until a short layer of natural hair was exposed.

It didn't make them look like twins, but Jada and Tiara certainly looked like they belonged together.

The rest of that afternoon was spent with the sharpening stones. Letitia had picked up a set of them at Buchmans because "sharpening" seemed like it would be important for axes and stakes. She sat on the steps and pulled one out of its box. How was a grey rock going to make something sharp? Wouldn't that make it dull? She looked at the little instruction sheet in the box. It kept talking about things like "17 degree angles" and "lapping," but the pictures were OK. She got the idea.

She called Jahayra over. Kiara followed along.

"Let me see your stake," said Letitia. "Goin' to try and see if it can be sharper."

"You goin' to make it sharper with a rock?" Jahayra shook her head. "That sound silly."

"Well, that what the box say. That what the piece of paper say. Can't hurt it, don' think."

Letitia did her best to copy the way the picture showed. She took one edge of one of the fins of the stake and rubbed it against the stone. The edge looked a little brighter, and she could see nicks and pockets. She rubbed until all the nicks and pockets went away, just like the paper said. Then, she turned it over and did the other side.

Letitia tested the edge with her finger. She didn't draw blood, but she could tell it was sharper. She began to work on the other fin.

An hour later the edges of Jahayra's garden stake were quite sharp. Everybody was in a circle watching. "Let me try now!" Kiara said. She banged her stake against the rock.

"That what you see me doin'?" asked Letitia. "Hold it like this," she said, guiding Kiara's hand. A few tries later, Kiara had the idea.

Letitia got the rest of the stones out of the pile and spent a few minutes with each kid. She got out her hatchet and began working on it while everyone else worked on stakes.

"Trevon doin' it wrong!" exclaimed Jada. "That ain't how Letitia show us!"

Letitia looked over. Jada was right. Trevon was holding his edge square to the rock, making it dull and flat. "That ain't how I showed you," she said, taking the stake and rock. "Watch! Like this." Letitia did her best to imitate the drawings. She handed it back and watched closely as Trevon tried again. "That better," she said.

By suppertime, every stake could cut paper.

CHAPTER 32
LAYING IN SUPPLIES

Letitia was working in her notebook when she saw Jahayra and Kiara running towards her. They were supposed to be out looking for cucos that had washed up on shore. Those were always so easy to take care of that she just let the little ones do it to keep them in practice.

She set the notebook down, picked up her hatchet, and went to meet them.

"Find somethin'? One of them still fresh or somethin'?"

"No," said Jahayra breathlessly. "It another one of them guys in an orange jumpsuit."

"He alive?"

"No. He got a bullet hole in his head, but you told us to look out for 'em."

She had, and went to look. It was the same as the ones they saw floating by now and then: big hole in his head, still brown, no blue in the skin. Once she satisfied herself that he wasn't going to come back, they pushed it back out in the water until she was sure it would float past.

Bodies floating up on shore made her nervous. All the noise around Hunts Point made her nervous. It seemed like everything was making her nervous.

After dinner, she talked to everybody. "Tomorrow, we all goin' back to the city. Next few days, we bring as much stuff back here as we can, so we don't have to go over anymore."

The next morning found them landing at the flat spot on 132nd St again. Things had changed again. 132nd St was clear. Clear of cars, clear of cucos, clear of everything. As they walked inland, the view down each street towards Hunts Point was the same: clear until 138th St, and then cars. Piles of smashed cars that clogged the whole street from building to building, and a sea of cucos trying to make it over the piles of cars.

Letitia tried not to cry. Every grocery store she knew about was on 137th St or 138th St. All the buildings here on 132nd St were things like sheet metal supplies and body shops, not places with food. She didn't let it show. The last thing she needed was a bunch of kindergarteners crying because she was crying.

"We goin' to keep walking up this way. See if maybe it get better."

They continued. Finally, at Brook Ave, the wall shifted, and by Willis Ave things were clear. They turned down Willis Ave, back towards Sami's.

Letitia looked inside Sami's. The shelves were nearly bare. There were only a few stray cans. The candy was gone, the drinks were gone, the little donuts were gone, the Pop-Tarts were gone.

They rolled their cart inside and took what was left. It didn't even cover the bottom of a grocery cart. The RDL Market, right across the street, was no better.

They walked up 138th St and checked each market in turn. It took three minimarkets before they filled the cart.

"OK, we go back, we put these by the boats, and come back for more."

CHAPTER 33
SLIM PICKINGS

Late in the afternoon on the second day found them in the Makey Deli and Grocery. Letitia looked at the cart. Pickings had been skimpy all day. They had visited fourteen stores, they were still on the first cart, and it wasn't even close to full.

The doorway to the back stock room was damaged: someone had broken the lock and forced their way in. Letitia pushed the door carefully open. Nothing came out. She peered into the dim light. There were some boxes still on the shelves.

"I be back in here lookin' around. You guys keep lookin' in here," she said, walking into the back room to take a closer look at the shelves.

There were boxes of Hefty 3-Compartment Foam Carryout Boxes and Dixie White Plastic Tea Spoons and Member's Mark Clear Plastic Cups. Dixie White Napkins and Member's Mark Condiment Cups. Boxes and boxes of stuff to put food in, but no food to put in them.

"Hey! That ours!" Jahayra's voice yelled from out front. Letitia ran through the door into the front of the store. A dirty-looking man had grabbed onto the cart and was trying to pull it out of the store. Kids were pulling on the other side. Rosarita and Malik held tightly onto their stakes and were beginning to walk towards the intruder. Letitia couldn't believe it: that guy had a gun as big as they were strapped to his backpack, and those two were going to wave stakes at him?

Letitia couldn't think of anything better to say than Jahayra had. "Hey! That ours!" she shouted.

"Mine now, kid," he said. "You think you can just walk into my neighborhood and take my food?"

"Who say it your food? Don' see your name on it nowhere. We found it, we have it, it ours!"

The kids continued to pull on the cart and make noise. The man kept yelling back. If this kept up, some cuco from somewhere was going to show up. She looked out the window: she hadn't expected one to show up this fast, but there one was, across the street and coming over, attracted by the shouting.

Letitia thought for a moment. He hadn't pulled that gun off his pack yet, but he was going to. She couldn't let that happen.

"Tell you what," she said. "You let me get those cans of peaches out of the bottom, we let you have the rest, OK?"

"Why you sayin' that, Letitia?" protested Jahayra. "We spend all day gettin' it, and you goin' to give it away?"

"Don' need nobody gettin' shot," replied Letitia. She kept a careful eye on the cuco approaching the door as she walked up to the cart. "Like I say, you let us get those peaches, you can have everything else. You don' want to shoot no little kid, do you?"

The man calmed down a little bit. Maybe he really *didn't* want to shoot a little kid. "Peaches? Where are there peaches in there?"

Letitia bent over a little bit like she was going to reach into the cart and then pushed as hard as she could. The man stumbled backwards, landing on his back, halfway out the door. The cuco quickly ripped his neck open and began to eat. The little ones noticed the cuco for the first time and backed away.

"Run into that back room!" Letitia shouted. Everyone ran, closing the door behind them.

"Quiet!" she said. "You know how dumb them things are. We quiet enough, it may forget we here."

The snuffling continued, but at least no one was bawling. Her heart pounded in her ears, and she couldn't stop shaking. It was hard enough looking at dead people, but watching somebody die was different. Killing someone was *very* different. Well, *she* hadn't really killed him, had she? All she had done was *pushed* him, it was that cuco that had killed him. She didn't even believe that lie herself. She'd gone from *Letitia Johnson, Girl Looter* to *Letitia Johnson, Killer* in twenty seconds.

She took deep breaths. She couldn't lose it now, not with a cuco in the next room, not with all the little ones with her. The kids were all on edge. They'd learned to fight cucos, they'd learned to ignore bodies, but this was the first time since the railroad yard they'd seen one feed.

The sounds of feeding stopped. "Get ready, and get back away from the door," Letitia said. "If it goin' to come, it be comin' now." She stood right past where the door would open, ready with her hatchet. The sound of footsteps approached, and the door bumped open. She swung at the cuco's knee. It wobbled and fell. She chopped over and over with the hatchet, first at the jaw, and then at the skull.

She stood. "That it for today," she said. "We get our cart, we go home."

They walked into the front room. Letitia grabbed the cart while the little ones held the door open. The dirty man's head was still there, snapping.

"You take care of that, Rosarita?"

Rosarita staked its eye sockets. Letitia nodded approvingly and scanned the room before rolling the cart out of there. She stooped and picked up the dead man's gun. If she was going to be a killer, she might as well have a gun.

CHAPTER 34
PRAYERS FOR LITTLE CRIMINALS

Prayer time was hard that night. Letitia said one prayer out loud, then another one silently to herself afterwards. The prayer that was out loud went like this:

> "God, thank you for helpin' us today.
> "Thank you for keepin' us safe.
> "Thank you for keepin' that man from shootin' anybody.
> "Thank you for the food we found.
> "Amen."

The prayer she said inside went like this:

> God, would you please stop doin' things like that?
> You could have made that man be someplace else.
> You didn't have to make me no killer.
> Don' do things like that no more.
> Amen.

CHAPTER 35
FISHING TRIP

Letitia walked out to the end of the pier with a bucket and her fishing rod. Trevon and Jose followed her, a small cup full of wriggling worms in Jose's hands.

Once Letitia was ready, Jose took the hook and jammed it through the worm, looping it back and forth. Jose liked this part of the job. He liked digging for the worms, he liked playing with the worms, and he liked putting the worms on the hooks.

Letitia laid on her belly and lowered the line into the water. She jerked and bobbed the bait, then felt it catch. Reeling it in, the line went taut. It didn't buck and jump like usual.

She kept reeling the line in, and a body surfaced from underwater. Another guy in an orange jumpsuit with most of his head blasted off. Gross. She wanted to cut the line, but stopped herself: hooks were hard to replace. She couldn't get to Buchmans anymore and didn't know where else to get one.

She walked to the side of the pier and pulled gently. The body followed the tugging. She slowly reeled it in as she walked back inland, dragging the body behind. It snagged itself in the shallow water.

" 'kay, Trevon, big job for you. Hold tight while I get the hook."

Trevon took the reel. Letitia walked around the pier and came down towards the shore. The body was worse than a mushy cuco: it smelled worse and it was all bloated. The hook was snagged in the cuff of its pants. She took off her shoes and waded out into the shallow water.

"Don' hold the string so tight!" she shouted upwards. "Ain't no way I can get the hook loose with you pullin' so hard!" The string slacked a bit, and she worked the hook loose. The worm was still on it: Jose had gotten really good at that. She pulled the body by the pants leg and it started to sink again.

She had just gotten up onto the pier and recast the line when the sound of powerboats started, followed by gunfire.

"Down flat!" she shouted. Jose and Trevon had beaten her to it. That was a rule they knew well. She turned her head towards Rikers. Both of their powerboats were out in the water. The one in front was going really fast and shooting at the one following it.

The boat that was behind slowed down and everybody stopped shooting. Letitia sat up and looked. Everybody in that boat looked dead. As the boat in the lead raced away, the people in the boat that was left behind started to stir and revive. It slowly idled its way downstream, carrying the cucos away.

Letitia continued to fish, waiting for the first boat to come back. It never did.

CHAPTER 36
FUN AND GAMES

Letitia got up early one morning, before the little ones started to crawl out of their sleeping bags. She grabbed a few empty boxes from the supply cupboard and drew scary looking faces on the outside. She set five boxes up on stakes on one end of the clearing, the eyes just a little over her own head.

"New game today," she said when everyone got up. "It got simple rules. Last team to get stakes in both eye holes loses. We go till there's only one team left. The winners, they get whatever they want for breakfast."

Letitia scratched a line in the dirt with a stick and ran to watch the five boxes.

"Go!" she shouted.

Ten pairs of legs pumped furiously as they ran towards the line of boxes, with Jose falling far behind.

She set everything back up. "Go!" she shouted again. It was closer this time, but Lucia fumbled her stake.

The last race was extremely close. Rosarita was clearly in the lead, with Jahayra close behind. Malik and Tiara ended in nearly a dead heat. Letitia finally decided that Kiara had gotten hers in a bit ahead of Malik, making Jahayra and Kiara the winners.

"Again!" everyone shouted.

"Breakfast first," said Letitia. Jahayra and Kiara took their time looking over the stock of supplies and finally decided on yoghurt-covered cranberry granola bars for breakfast.

They spent the morning playing. They all agreed that they could give Jose a head start to make it more fair, so he and Trevon even came in second a couple of times.

The breakfast race became a daily tradition, with the losers having to sharpen everyone's stakes and the winners getting a treat.

CHAPTER 37
SHOOTING PRACTICE

A few days later, Letitia waited until all the little ones were taking their naps and opened the storage closet. There, hidden underneath a pile of junk, was the gun she had picked up at Makey's. She picked it up and closed the closet again. No need for the little ones to know where she kept it.

This was the only gun she had ever seen close up. They always had guns on cop shows, but this looked different: two barrels instead of one, and it had a row of shells clipped on one side. It was *big*. If she stood it on the floor, it came up to her waist. It wasn't a pistol, or a rifle like in Mr. Freeman's movies. It looked kind of like the guns that Elmer Fudd used, but it was too short.

She looked at it closely. They always talked about the "safety" on TV, and that lever on the side must be it. No markings? How do you know whether it's on or off?

She got a used box and set it up on a post on the pier. She walked away twenty feet, held the gun in her hands and spread her legs, just like the cops always did when they shouted things like "Let her go! We've got you surrounded!" She used the sight just like she did on that game machine she played once.

She pulled the trigger. Nothing happened. She flipped the safety and tried again.

It felt like the gun picked her up by her hands, threw her backwards, and then pounded her forearms with her hatchet. Her hands stung. Her ears rang from the noise. Her shoulders hurt. Her butt hurt from landing on it.

The box sat on the post, silently laughing at her. Nothing had happened to the box.

She walked back to the hospital to put the gun back in its hiding place. Maybe she'd find the *Sunset Guide to Shooting Things* on a trip to the city someday, full of pictures of big happy white men shooting each other. Until then, she wasn't going to try this again.

CHAPTER 38
AS YE SOW, SO SHALL YE REAP

Letitia looked over the plot of land. They had gone over it with her EZ-Stash Folding Camp Shovel, turning the dirt and pulling the weeds. It was right where the *Western Garden Book of Edibles* said it should be: a little high, so water wouldn't make a pond when it rained, with one end that got morning shade, one end that got afternoon shade, and a spot in the middle that didn't get shade at all. The book said that May was a good time of the year to be planting a garden, and that was the part she wasn't certain about. If she was counting right, it was late May, but it might be June.

The seeds came in packets, packets with a big picture on the outside of what grew from the seeds inside, which made it easier to figure out what to plant. Letitia didn't want any of those nasty leafy things like they had in the community garden to eat, so she tried to make sure that she recognized everything and it would taste good.

She went up and down the garden and punched holes in the ground with a camping stake. Lucia put fish guts in each hole and then Maria put a seed in. The fish guts were Lucia's idea. The book talked all about fertilizer, but she didn't have any of that. Lucia reminded her of the Thanksgiving story the teachers told, with the Indians showing the Pilgrims to put bits of fish in with every seed. Letitia thought of the Pilgrims as being the old-fashioned version of the big happy white men in the Sunset books.

She planted some carrots, because the book talked about planting carrots all summer long. Halloween was her favorite holiday, so she put down some pumpkins. She planted watermelons and potatoes. She was surprised by how many types there were of some things: Orange Hybrid Krush Watermelons and Rattlesnake Watermelons and Tweety Hybrid Canary Melons and Connecticut Field Pumpkins and Magic Max Pumpkins and it just kept going. She planted a few of every different type, because she figured that gave her more chances to get it right. Some of the things she planted would take a long time: cherry trees, apple trees, plum trees. She planted all the trees away from the garden, but still in a nice row. She figured if she was still here by the time they grew, she would really be missing fruit by then.

While the three of them were planting, the other children were gathering wood. One of the Sunset books had all kinds of pictures of big happy white men cooking things on barbecues. The book made it look easy and it had instructions on how to build a fire pit. They made one with bricks and a grille from one of the collapsed cottages. She didn't have to worry about running out of gas bottles anymore, but now they had to gather wood every few days.

She was just deciding between a Connecticut Field pumpkin and a Magic Max pumpkin seed when everyone came running out of the woods at full speed. Jahayra ran up to her.

"It one of them men in the orange jumpsuits. This one be alive!"

"Real alive, or cuco alive?" asked Letitia.

"Real alive."

"OK, get in the lobby. We watch from there, see what he do."

They concealed themselves by the lobby door. Letitia watched as a thin, hungry-looking damp man in an orange jumpsuit came into the clearing. He must have swum here from Rikers. Rikers had been very quiet since the boats took off down the river. No more bodies in orange jumpsuits had been washing up. She'd thought it was empty.

Letitia finally went out to face him. The kids hung back, but didn't hide. She didn't need to have him able to reach them, but she didn't need him thinking she was alone.

"Where are your parents?" he asked.

"Other end of the island," lied Letitia. "They be back real soon."

"Where's the food?"

"None left," lied Letitia. "That's what they lookin' for."

The stranger approached Letitia and crouched down.

"One more time, kid, where the hell is the food?"

"None left," she lied one more time.

He grabbed her by the neck and stood up, holding her face in front of his, her legs dangling in the air. She started to kick and struggle, trying to suck air into her lungs. How was she supposed to answer when she couldn't breathe? She kicked harder, aiming for his face.

" Where's the damn foo—," he started. He stopped when he felt a stabbing pain in one calf and then the other, as Rosarita and Malik's pocket knives cut large wounds into each leg. Dropping to his knees in pain, he lost hold of Letitia.

It was only moments before a pair of garden stakes went in and out of his eye sockets.

Letitia caught her breath. The blood pouring out of the man's legs and eye sockets didn't seem like it would stop spreading. It made a small pond on the ground in front of the hospital. Cucos didn't bleed this way. This felt a lot more like killing something.

Rosarita and Malik were standing there, waiting for her to do something. Malik looked like he was afraid someone would hit him. Rosarita looked ready to bite. Everybody else was waiting for her to say something to them. Letitia felt all the eyes on her.

She didn't know what to say at first. She remembered when all this started and the only thing she had wanted was to find an adult that would help her and take these kids off her hands. Now, if she never saw another adult again, she'd be happy. Seemed like all any adult wanted was to steal food.

She walked over to Rosarita and gave her a hug, and then gave Malik one.

"That time, it the right thing to do. He not just some junkie, he tryin' to hurt me and steal our food." They stood taller and prouder. The other children started to move again, giving the heroes hugs and trying not to look at the dead man.

It took all of them to drag the body to the pier and push it over. Everyone was messy, smeared and stained with blood. They used the solar showers when they were done and then had a late dinner.

Everyone was quiet that night. When prayer time came, it seemed like they were all too scared to talk.

"God," Letitia began, "we sorry. Nobody knew nothin' else to do.

"If someone comes again, will you make sure that he nice? I promise we won't kill people that be nice to us.

"Amen."

"Amen," came the chorus, muffled once more, as if the children were afraid someone would hear.

Letitia lay in the dark after story time, trying to make sense of the day. On the one hand, she was very glad that everyone was OK and that the kids had been able to take care of her when she needed it.

On the other hand, she decided that she had better always be nice to Rosarita and Malik.

CHAPTER 39
BARBEQUE

Letitia sniffed the air. Pork ribs? Where had the little ones gotten pork? When had they learned to cook? She went over to the fire pit. Cold. Nobody had been cooking here.

She climbed up on the roof to look around. Black smoke was rising from Sound View Park, just the other side of Hunts Point, across the Bronx River.

The Hunts Pointers were using some kind of gas bomb. She didn't know how they were throwing them, because they were flying a long way, crossing the river and landing right in the middle of the crowd of cucos. The cucos didn't do much to avoid the fire. They wouldn't walk right into it, but they didn't run, either. Even the cucos that were on fire just walked around until they were too burnt to move. The Hunts Pointers threw some bombs deep and some bombs shallow, spreading the fire all over.

They had hundreds of them on fire right now, and the way the others moved made her think there were more lying on the ground. Still, it looked like there were millions of cucos over there. When she looked that way, she could see clear to Ferry Point, but she couldn't see the end of the crowd. The whole piece of land between the water and the interstate was just cucos, doing the same thing the cucos on this side of Hunts Point were doing: trying to get to the generators.

Staring at that every day could drive you crazy. Letitia wasn't sure that setting them on fire was a good idea, but you'd have to do *something*.

She hated not knowing more than she did. She, Maria, and Lucia went to the shed and got two of the paddle boats. She told Rosarita and Malik they were in charge.

"If somebody come while I gone, hide. Just hide. No need to be killin' nobody."

Rosarita and Malik looked disappointed. Letitia hoped that they would obey. She didn't like killing live people, even if they weren't *good* live people.

The two boats set out on the journey. The first destination was South Brother Island. She took the boats around it and peered into the woods. Someone *could* hide in there, but she didn't see any sign of footprints on the beach. There were a couple of waterlogged cucos on the shore, but they were in no condition to be a threat. They dealt with a few of those every day, and these weren't any different.

Next, it was across the strait to Rikers Island. She didn't want to land, she just wanted to get a better view. She wanted to know if there were living people still there, or if it was just an island of cucos.

They started south, towards the Rikers Island Bridge. The center was bombed out, making it impossible for anyone to cross on foot or by car. There weren't piles of cars near the roadways here, though. There weren't very many cars in the lot at the foot of the bridge, either. Hundreds of empty spots and only a handful of cars.

One of the runways at LaGuardia poked out into the water, coming within a few hundred feet of the shore of Rikers Island. The runway was another sea of cucos, all looking towards Hunts Point. It wasn't as bad as Sound View Park or by the car wall, but she wouldn't want to try to get through there for any reason.

"We goin' further up the river now," Letitia said. "See that park over there?" She pointed at a grassy area across the river from Sound View Park. "We go there, see what we can see."

The view from there showed that the entire spit was covered in zombies. The Hunts Pointers had started a big fire, but it was just a little fire compared to the whole crowd.

They came back to Rikers and completed the circle. That island was empty. The parking lots were empty. The roadways were empty. No people, no cucos. Just empty.

Letitia put it together in her head. All the cars were gone. They weren't in piles. They weren't in the lots. That meant that everyone had driven off. How did they get all the prisoners out? There's no way they had enough cars.

That meant all the prisoners were still in their cells. Most of them were probably cucos now. If she ever went on the island, she didn't want to open the door to any of the prisons.

So who was on the boats? She thought about that for a while. Maybe it was just the prisoners that were out of their cells for some reason when the evacuation came. Maybe it was the escape artists. She'd never know now.

Thinking about the men that were left in the cells made her sad. She had a hard time not thinking about them. Then she thought about how the kids had killed the one that got loose, and that made her even sadder.

CHAPTER 40
TO MILLS ROCK AND BACK AGAIN

Letitia smiled as the morning races went on. The last race was Lucia and Maria against Rosarita and Malik. Lucia was way out in front and got her stake into the eye hole before anyone else was even close. Then came Rosarita, then Maria, so Lucia and Maria won. Malik was close, though, and he had more power than anybody. It would be nice if she had a game that trained them to push hard instead of just in the right place.

Lucia and Maria's prize wasn't just breakfast: they got to come along while she went looking at things today. She was able to keep a pretty good eye on the Hunts Point people from the roof. Things were getting better for them. They used those bombs every day, and it looked like they were doing some good. That crowd of cucos was still huge, but it seemed thinner.

She couldn't see past the car wall to the south anymore. They had stacked the cars high and tall, higher than the buildings in spots, coming down to the shore of the East River right along the railroad tracks. The buildings, cars, and storage tanks kept her from getting a very good look at Randall's Island, and she didn't like that. She'd wake up at night sometimes because of dreams about Randall's Island.

She waited until the current was flowing its hardest towards Randall's Island and took off, once again accompanied by Maria and Lucia. The current would help them get there, and, when it turned around, it would help them get back. This still really confused her. *Golden's Guide to Fishing* had a big chapter on river fishing. It talked like rivers flowed the same way all the time, but this one sure didn't.

Randall's Island was still a mess. It didn't seem as bad as Sound View Park, but there were a *lot* of cucos there. As they went by, the cucos gathered on shore. She couldn't tell how many there were and knew she couldn't count that high. With the binoculars, she could see the remains of tents and big army trucks. There were trucks with big red crosses on them and trucks with big mounted machine guns on them. You could see that a lot of the cucos had been hit by the guns, because they were only half there, the bottom part ripped away by bullets and the upper part just walking around on the hands. She'd figured that much out about them: every piece of them that was hooked to the brain was still kind of alive, and every part that wasn't hooked to the brain wasn't. She was glad about that last part. She had seen a movie once about a hand that walked around on its own and didn't want to have to fight off things like that, too.

When they reached the FDR Bridge, she made everybody stop. She could see another small island there where the river narrowed. It wasn't any bigger than South Brother Island. She saw a small group of people on the beach on the northern tip. These, she could count. Six. There weren't any buildings on the island, but they had tents. She couldn't see a boat from here, but that didn't mean they didn't have one.

She decided that she wasn't going to talk to them today. It was nice to know that there were some big people that were smart enough to stay quiet, though. She figured she'd come back down when she had to.

CHAPTER 41
DAYS OF SUMMER

May became June, and June became July. Letitia didn't even smell burnt cuco flesh anymore. Not because it wasn't there, but because it was *always* there. Hunts Point had successfully fought to a standstill on both sides. Sound View Park looked like charcoal. There were still always cucos in it, but not so thick that the shelling was an all-day affair anymore. Every morning, she would hear *thwump... thwump... thwump... thwump* for a half-hour or so, but that was enough to keep the numbers down. She couldn't see past the walls, but they didn't seem to be getting higher anymore. She didn't know how they were getting their tanker truck in and out, but they managed somehow. The hum of the generators continued.

She continued making occasional reconnaissance trips. The people on the little island (her map told her it was called *Mills Rock*) seemed to be OK. She thought that maybe they had spotted her once, but they didn't chase her back up the river. She saw occasional signs of people in Queens, near Astoria, but there didn't seem to be many people there. The cucos weren't very thick on the Queens side. She figured everyone had run south and the cucos had followed them there.

She had made a few trips to Rikers Island, too. It was empty. She still hadn't figured out who the people with the boats *were*, but they were all gone now. She had walked around the island a few times. She was surprised to find out that it wasn't just a prison. They had a barbershop, a grocery store, a car repair shop, clinics, everything.

The garden continued to grow. The carrots had been first to be ready, but now some of the melons were starting to ripen. They still had a big pile of trail mix and freeze-dried food. She worried about winter when they wouldn't have the garden and didn't know how easy it would be to fish. She was pretty sure that there would still *be* fish, though. *Golden's Guide to Fishing* had a whole chapter on ice fishing, with pictures of people standing around holes in the ice and fishing. She'd seen ice in the East River, but never seen it ice over. If people could fish *through* ice, then they should be able to fish *by* ice.

Right now, though, the water was warm enough to swim in. During the part of the day where the water didn't flow too hard, the kids would swim off the north beach. They were learning how to do stuff that they never had a chance to before, and some of it was fun. Gardening was fun when you got used to it. Climbing trees was neat, and playing hide-and-seek in the old buildings could pass the time.

Other parts weren't fun. She hated washing clothes, but she hated smelling bad. Swishing the clothes around in a bucket of soapy water and then rinsing the clothes in the river worked, but took a long time.

Shower time remained a communal affair. She'd fill the shower bags and hang them in trees. When the water was warm, the little ones would all get spritzed, rubbed down with soap, and spritzed again.

She understood why everyone's mama spent so much time on hair. Tiara was far from the only one that had trouble: it seemed like some of their hair just turned into an explosion of knots and frizz as it got longer. She finally decided that the solution she had used on Tiara was the only answer. Every couple of weeks, it was scissors time. All eleven of them had the same hairdo: a layer of fuzz about a half-inch deep. Any thinner than that and the girls looked funny, any thicker and it became hard to deal with.

Letitia tried to be fair with everyone, but still had to punish them every once in a while. Sometimes it would be no fruit for dinner, or having to sit while everyone else had play time. If someone was really bad, they got the worst punishment she had available: emptying the Luggable Loo.

CHAPTER 42
EMERGENCY 911

Late one afternoon, Letitia heard a loud yell from the woods. She grabbed her hatchet and ran towards the sound just as Jahayra was running out to find her.

"Kiara's hurt real bad!" Jahayra managed to get the words out while bawling.

"Her leg's stuck, and I can't get her loose!"

Jahayra led Letitia over. Everyone assembled around Kiara. Her left leg had slipped into some kind of drainage hole, and her right leg stretched out in an awkward position. The streets were covered with dirt, but they were still there, complete with gutters and cobblestones and sewers and drains. The section she had stepped onto had collapsed. Letitia tried to put her arms around Kiara and pull her up, but Kiara screamed and cried so loudly that she had to stop.

Letitia stopped and looked. That right leg had to hurt, bent like that. She pulled and moved it into a better position. "Jada, Tiara! Go get them camp shovels." They ran off.

She started to scrape the dirt around Kiara's left leg with her hands. The cobblestone and remains of a grating came into view. When the shovels came, Letitia and Malik started to dig while Jahayra held onto Kiara's hand. Things shifted and crumbled under Letitia's feet. Whatever Kiara had fallen into, it was big. When they got the dirt scraped off the street, Letitia worked her ax into a joint between two cobblestones and wobbled one free. Once she got the first one loose, the rest came up pretty quickly. Kiara's leg still disappeared down further into the ground.

They kept digging and it became obvious what was wrong. Kiara had stepped onto a rotten storm grate, and her leg was dangling down into the storm sewer. The rusty steel pressed into both sides of her leg, wedging her into the grate. Every time they tried to pull her loose, the grate pushed itself deeper into the leg.

Letitia managed to work the grating loose from the street, and they pulled Kiara up with the grate still wedged into her leg. There was blood everywhere. Kiara didn't seem to be all the way awake anymore.

Letitia knew that Kiara was probably going to die if she couldn't get help.

She didn't want to go to Hunts Point. She just didn't trust crazy people with gas bombs and machine guns and big trucks. That left Mills Rock.

"Rosarita, Malik. Go get one of the flat rafts!"

When they returned, she slid Kiara into it.

" 'kay, we all got to work together. No more crying or nothin'. Grab a handle. We got to carry this to the water."

They carried Kiara, complete with grating, and set the raft in the water at the beach. Jahayra hung on to Kiara as tightly as she could.

"How we going to pay?" asked Rosarita.

"What?" asked Letitia.

"If you no can pay, nobody help you. My mama, all the time she say so. Lots of times we couldn't go to the hospital. No money, no hospital."

Letitia thought. They didn't have money, but they had stuff. Stuff that the people on Mills Rock didn't have and might want. The other supply raft was quickly filled with melons and carrots, a carton of trail mix packets, and three of the precious propane gas canisters.

The group set off, Letitia towing Kiara and Jahayra, with Rosarita and Malik towing the supply raft. The current wasn't going the right way, but it wasn't going the wrong way too strongly, either. They paddled furiously, down the East River. They were so worried about Kiara that passing Randall's Island didn't even phase them.

As they approached the little cove on the north side of Mills Rock, Letitia started to shout. She didn't care if it got everything on Randall's Island excited, she needed the people to know she was coming. She turned to the followers. "Stay on your boats. Be ready to run."

Four adults stood watching on the beach as the cove was suddenly full of scared kids, little pontoon boats, two rafts, a pile of fruit and vegetables, and an unconscious, bleeding little girl.

"Please don't hurt us," said Letitia. "She need help, and it ain't nothin' I can help with."

CHAPTER 43
HELPLESS

"John, help me with this!" Marie said as she waded into the river. Side by side, she and John pulled the boat up onto the rocky beach, a boat with a tiny girl with a very sharp stake hovering over an unconscious little girl and a growing pool of blood inside.

The larger girl spoke again, her voice running right on the edge of panic. "She fell and hurt her leg, and I think she's dyin'!" She pointed at the raft full of melons and trail mix. "We can pay you!" The look on her face mixed panic and hope. The littler ones were either crying or on the edge of tears.

Alex came and crouched beside Marie. "Don't worry about paying us," said Alex to the largest girl. "Let's get a look at her."

Alex and John didn't take the injured girl out of the boat. They stretched the boat out on the beach and moved her as little as they could as they examined the leg and the grating. Streaks of blood, rust, and dirt ran down her legs, now wet with splashed-up river water.

"Jesus," Alex said, "I don't know what we can do about this. Marie, run get Catalina and the first aid kit."

Marie had already left without him noticing. Far ahead of him, she was already running back from their camp to the shore, a little white box with a blue cross on the outside in hand. Catalina accompanied her.

He opened it and shook his head.

"It would be like trying to put out a fire with a squirt gun," he said. "Once we take that grate off, we're going to need some serious bandages. I don't even have any idea *how* to get that grate loose without ripping up her leg even worse."

Catalina looked it over. "You're right, Alex. The grating is what's plugging the hole. Once we take it out, we're going to need to plug the hole up fast, and that little roll of gauze isn't going to last a minute."

Letitia wanted to scream with frustration. All of her Sunset books, her *Golden's Guide to Fishing*, the story of the Pilgrims, everything had these big white guys running around fixing everything. TV shows always had big white guys doing everything, too. The first time in her life she needed a big white guy to do something for her, all they could do was stand around talking about how they couldn't do anything. Yelling at them wasn't going to help, either.

"What do you need?" she asked.

They listed stuff. Bandages. Antiseptic something-or-other. Antibiotics. The list went on. None of it was in the pile she had picked up at Buchmans.

"They got that stuff in a clinic?" she asked.

They nodded.

"Most of it."

"Then get your boat and let's go!"

"Hold your horses, honey," Alex said. "Go where? It's not exactly like we can just go to the neighborhood free clinic anymore. There's a hospital on Roosevelt Island, but they won't deal with you unless you bring a lot more than you have in that raft."

"Rikers," she said. "It empty. I know where the clinic is."

"How the hell do you know Rikers is empty?"

"We live right next door. I can see it. Was on it just last week. I think there a bunch of cucos in the jail cells, but you can walk around on the island. I know right where the clinic is. I wrote it down in my notebook."

"You kids live next to Rikers? By the crazies at Hunts Point? And you grow cantaloupes?" Like most New Yorkers, he didn't know about the Brother islands. He wouldn't admit it, but the melons had him pretty excited. He hadn't seen a piece of fresh fruit in months.

He was actually pointing at a Tweety Hybrid Canary Melon, but Letitia didn't think it was important to point that out.

"Kind of, yeah. Please come and get the stuff you need. Please?"

The adults were uneasy, Letitia could tell. Still, the sight of Kiara was enough that they couldn't say no. Sometimes, there were things you just had to fix if you could, and, for these people, Kiara was one of those things.

CHAPTER 44

THE CLINIC

John, Alex, and Catalina boarded a six-man aluminum rowboat. All the kids kept to their own boats. The adults talked for a while about whether they should put Kiara in the big boat, leave her in the raft while they got supplies, or bring her along in the raft. They finally decided to bring her along in the raft.

Letitia directed everyone to the old ferry slip on the north point of the island that the powerboats had used.

John and Alex each grabbed an end of the raft. Jahayra leapt from the raft and held onto one corner, but John and Alex really handled the weight. Letitia and Catalina ran ahead to the public clinic, a small facility normally used to provide care for visitors to Rikers. Letitia's hatchet got through the glass door quickly, getting them inside.

Catalina went into the examining rooms and tried to get her bearings. Most of this wasn't much different from the things she had used as a veterinary assistant. She said a brief prayer and got to work, setting an examination table into position.

Alex and John came in, Alex cradling Kiara in his arms, John stabilizing the grille, and laid her down. Jahayra took position at the foot of the table, two sharp stakes clutched firmly in her hands.

Catalina went off in search of supplies, Letitia close behind. Catalina would point at cabinets, and Letitia's hatchet would make short work of the locks and latches.

Catalina managed to secure an IV, a supply of antibiotics, gauze, and basic wound-cleaning and dressing supplies. She set up the drip and started to clean around the grating. She looked carefully and saw that the grating had embedded itself deeply into the thigh, probably an inch or more. She wiggled it. The flow of blood along the edge increased.

"I can't just rip this thing loose," she said, "it'd be worse than it already is. We need to cut it apart."

"Would a hacksaw do it?" asked Letitia.

John and Alex talked with each other. A pneumatic saw would be better, but they thought they could get through with a hacksaw.

"Rosarita! Malik! Go home. Get the big Stanley toolkit!" She stopped for a second. "Grab a few water bottles. More trail mix, too." Each of her kids had a water bottle permanently inside their backpack. She had noticed that none of the adults were smart enough to wear backpacks.

Catalina continued to clean things while they waited. Twenty minutes later, a Stanley 65-Piece General Homeowners Toolkit arrived. The hacksaw hadn't been touched and there were five spare blades included.

John and Alex were visibly impressed with the toolkit and took position. Catalina held one side of the leg still, Letitia grabbed the other, John gripped the grille, and Alex began to work. The metal was old and corroded, but still remarkably strong. It took the better part of twenty minutes for Alex to cut through the pair of slats that would allow them to pull the grille apart.

Catalina was prepared with the bandaging material. As John and Alex separated the grate, she was relieved to see that the blood wasn't spurting through the new hole, so no arteries were involved. She quickly cleaned and packed the wound with gauze.

Catalina knew that she should transfuse blood, but she didn't dare. Everything she had done so far was something that she had helped Dr. Martinez with before. Maybe it was a bulldog that had stepped on a nail, or a cat that had gotten tangled in barbed wire, but it was familiar stuff. Blood transfusions were out of her league and she knew it. She satisfied herself with adding a glucose drip. Blood pressure was low, but there, and Kiara's little heart was still beating. She thought she had saved the day, but there was no way to tell yet.

CHAPTER 45
SNACK TIME

Catalina came out into the room and explained the situation to everyone. "I've done what I can. The bleeding has stopped. I've gotten the dirt and junk out of the wound. I'm giving her water and glucose to try and replace some of the lost blood. I've got antibiotics going in her to keep the infection from spreading, and some sedatives to help her stay asleep. Right now, all we can do is wait. I'll stop the sedatives in an hour or so, and, after that, she should wake up. We'll know then."

Letitia was uncomfortable around the three grownups. It had been a long time since she had seen any of them close up that weren't trying to steal her food and it was weird to see people that were so big.

She handed water bottles and packages of trail mix to them. All the kids got out their water bottles, and Letitia handed out packages of trail mix all around. Rosarita and Malik had brought back a couple of the canary melons to go with it. Letitia cut them into slices and handed them around. She left the room to hand one to Jahayra, who was still standing guard over Kiara.

When she came back, the adults were all greedily nibbling on the rinds of the canary melons, trying to get the last bit of fruit out.

"OK, kids, you guys have a story to tell. Where are you from? Where on earth are you getting fresh fruit? Where are your parents?"

Letitia opened up and recounted the story of her little band. She didn't leave too much out and didn't exaggerate too much, either. She was proud of how they lived, and she was happy to realize that in a lot of ways, she and the other kids had done better than the adults. *They* didn't have fresh fruit. *They* didn't have a 65-piece Stanley toolkit. *They* didn't have a heroin ward to sleep in at night.

Nope, she had done well and was happy to get a chance to brag about it.

CHAPTER 46
WHAT HAPPENED, ANYWAY?

As they waited for Kiara to wake up, Alex and Letitia talked.

"You know where everybody is?" asked Letitia.

"Well, I think Catalina and John are looking through the supply cabinets, and ..."

"Not them," Letitia interrupted. "Everybody! Ever since I left the school, it just been the cucos. A few crazy people with guns. You the first grownup I talk to since Mrs. Robinson, and that was about social studies."

"You mean you've been living on your own the whole time? Three months? I figured you just left some parts out."

"Nope. Told you everything."

Alex shook his head. "Wow. So you don't know anything about what happened?"

"No."

"Somebody made a bioweapon ... that's a kind of special disease ... that does this to you when you die. They spent a couple of weeks spraying it in the subways. Here, Boston, Washington ... all up and down the East Coast. We all had it without knowing it. All you had to do was get close to someone that had been riding the subway that day. You've got it. I've got it. When we die, we'll turn into one of those things.

"I heard a few news reports before it went wild. People in emergency rooms going crazy and needing to be shot, things like that. No one really understood what was happening.

"Then, one morning, they triggered it. Poison gas in the subways. The news said the gas got at least 200,000 people in New York in about five minutes. That meant 200,000 zombies came up out of the tunnels all at once and started after everybody they saw. They hit every place with a subway system, all at about the same time. Things blew up fast.

"It spread like wildfire. If you've already got the virus and you get a piece of an active zombie in you, it's like it's supercharged. I've heard people claim it only takes 15 minutes to die from a scratch or bite.

"At first, the government tried evacuation and camps. They didn't realize that we all had the disease. You've seen Randall's Island, haven't you?

"Of course you have ... went right by it today, didn't we?

"That was one of the first camps the army set up. We all escaped from there. There were camps all over, but that one was ours. They searched everyone carefully coming in, checked everyone out, made sure we all looked healthy.

"It only took one guy with a gun. He went crazy and started shooting people. They'd come back in a few minutes and start chasing and eating. The army would shoot back, people would get caught in the crossfire, and it just grew so fast no one could stop it.

"We jumped in the river and swam for it. We got to Mills Rock. Some of the others are on Roosevelt Island. We heard gunfire for about a day, and then it became what you see.

"We had a radio for a while. At first, there were instructions about where to go: that we should try to get to these places they had set up. They'd get all the living people out of an area and then blow the bridges and tunnels. They put all of Manhattan in New Jersey, and then all of New Jersey in Delaware. They kept running and evacuating.

"They were using the rivers as barriers, because the zombies have such a hard time with rivers, but they kept bringing infected people with them so it just started all over again anyway. I don't think there's a bridge still up within five hundred miles of here.

"Then, they lost Virginia Beach. They were taking everyone from Baltimore and Washington down to Virginia Beach, and it got loose there. They stopped telling us to try to get out and started warning us to stay where we were.

"The last we heard, armies from every country in the world were here to help. There's an army line from Lake Erie down south to the Gulf of Mexico. If you are on this side of the line and try to make it across, they'll shoot you. In the head. They've learned that lesson, at least."

Letitia tried to absorb that. She decided it was all kind of too big to think about. She asked some local questions:

"What is it over at Hunts Point that they so crazy over?"

Alex chuckled. "That one's easy. Food. The Hunts Point Food Distribution Center is the biggest food distribution center in the world. You could have fed everyone in New York City for a few days with the pile of food there. If they manage to keep the freezers going, they'll never run out."

Letitia felt good that she had been about right. She hadn't realized just how much food was involved, but she had known what was happening.

"How about here? Why didn't they let the men here out?"

"What do you mean, honey?"

Letitia talked about how all the cars here were gone, with none of the piles there were in other locations. She told the story of the men in orange jumpsuits floating down the river and the big boat battle. She left out the part about the kids killing the hungry one that made it to their island. She didn't think that would help make friends.

"No one else?"

Letitia shook her head.

"I don't know how many people would have been here. Ten thousand? Fifteen thousand? Something like that," Alex said. "You mean they're all still in their cells?"

"I don' know for sure," Letitia said. "I think so."

CHAPTER 47
OVERNIGHT CAMP

Catalina watched as John and Alex rowed back to Mills Rock, complete with a newly-built first aid kit. This day had hammered home just how unprepared they were for a medical emergency. She was going to stay with the kids at least until Kiara was better.

Letitia wasn't sure if she liked that. It was nice to have an adult around, but did Catalina think she had to *obey* her? That didn't seem good. Still, having just one adult around was better than having a bunch of them around. She didn't even want to think about what Rosarita and Malik would do if John or Alex decided that someone needed a spanking.

She made the kids go out to the slip, grab all of their boats, and stash them in a small storage shed near the slip. She wasn't certain if the people at Hunts Point were watching, or even knew they were there, but there was no reason to advertise that they weren't home and leave their boats lying around to be stolen, too. It'd be nice if there was a way to lock things.

One thing that was nice was having running water. It was brown at first, but there was still running water. The toilets worked, a novelty that all of them appreciated.

The clinic had a number of small beds, just the right size for a pair of kids. Buddy pair by buddy pair, they climbed into bed. Jahayra curled up on pillows laid out on the floor by Kiara's bed.

The topic for prayer time wasn't a surprise that night.

"Bow your heads, everyone," Letitia began. Catalina smiled and complied, curious as to what kind of prayer this child would lead.

"God,

"Please help Kiara. I'm sorry I didn't have a good first aid kit so I couldn't help her faster. I promise I'll make a good one now.

"Thank you for making John and Alex and Catalina be good people. I told you we wouldn't kill anybody that be nice to us.

"Amen."

"Amen," came the chorus.

Catalina didn't quite know what to make of the last part, but she didn't think about it much right then, because Letitia started to talk again.

"*A little railroad engine was employed about a station yard for such*

work as it was built for, pulling a few cars on and off the switches ..."
Letitia began in a soothing voice. Catalina relaxed, lulled to sleep by the story of the little engine that just kept trying.

CHAPTER 48
LATE NIGHT AWAKENINGS

Jahayra shook Letitia awake. Letitia didn't know what time it was, but she never did anymore.

"Kiara awake!" said Jahayra.

Letitia gave Catalina a shake and they all went to see. Catalina had to borrow a flashlight from Malik. That was another thing about these people that bugged Letitia: they didn't carry anything. Didn't they know that bad things could happen any minute and you might *need* stuff?

Kiara panicked at first. She didn't understand where she was or where this woman examining her had come from, so her first reaction was to frantically try to grab her stake from Jahayra's hand. It took some reassurance to get her to calm down, and she still cringed as Catalina touched her.

Catalina gave a quick check: blood pressure and pulse seemed good. Kiara was reasonably lucid and seemed to understand where she was once people explained it to her.

Kiara clutched Jahayra's hand throughout the examination. Jahayra's face seemed visibly relaxed now that Kiara was awake.

Catalina unwrapped the bandages around the leg. Things seemed clean, with no signs of infection. The scars would be nasty ones, though. The stitches and steri-strips looked like they would hold, but the wounds were pretty deep. The best way to make sure nothing would pull loose was to keep Kiara from wiggling around too much, and the best way to do that with a five-year-old is sedation.

"OK, hon, it looks like things are going pretty well. I'm going to add something to the drip to help you sleep, and we'll see you in the morning."

Catalina was happy there was a dosing schedule on the outside of the packages. She guessed that Kiara was about the size of a year-old St. Bernard, but wouldn't have wanted to try to guess dosages based on that.

As Catalina adjusted the drip, Jahayra moved her pillow up onto the examination bed and started to snuggle in next to Kiara. Catalina thought for a moment about putting a stop to it, but she could see how much it calmed both buddies. She rearranged the drip tube so that Jahayra could lay down without snagging it and pulled a cover up over the pair.

It was hard to tell whether the sedatives did more for Kiara than Kiara's safety did for Jahayra. Both were asleep before Catalina had the lights off.

CHAPTER 49
NEW ARRIVALS

The next morning, John and Alex returned, bringing along Marie and a couple that Letitia didn't recognize. Letitia thought about the public service ads on TV when she saw them: all happy, smiling, and different colors. The new man was black, one of the women Latina, and the other Asian of some kind. The TV ads always showed groups like this right before they talked about how important it was for everyone to work together for the community. She hadn't thought there really were groups like it in real life. They especially didn't try so hard for "red" that they had anyone around that looked like Marie, either. Letitia wondered if it hurt to be so red all the time.

They did introductions all around. The new man was Levon, the women Amanda and Li.

Marie was anxious to see how Kiara was doing. Letitia listened to her talk about finding Kiara and winced. Marie talked like pulling the boat in and fetching that tiny first aid kit were acts of heroism. In her view, if Kiara was alive, it was because of her. Letitia decided not to correct her. She was trying to make *friends* with these people, after all.

Everyone went in to Kiara's recovery room. Kiara had been awake for a while, but was napping again. Catalina was trying to manage the sedative dose so that she wouldn't be energetic until the wounds were a little better healed. Jahayra was sitting on the bed, with a coloring book lying flat out on the mattress, two sharp stakes holding it open. Catalina had tried to move the stakes out of the recovery room, and Jahayra had made it extremely clear that that was against the rules. They had compromised once at keeping them set against the wall by the door, but as soon as Catalina would leave the room, Jahayra would fetch them back.

They all "ooh"ed and "aah"ed over Kiara and her "brave little guard." Marie patted Jahayra on the head. Letitia decided to give Jahayra a treat later: it *must* have been tempting to use one of the stakes. Show-and-tell needed to be over. "Catalina? Think maybe we should get everyone out of here? Let Kiara sleep?"

Catalina nodded and shooed everyone out of the room. Letitia quickly became the new center of attention and had to repeat the story of the little band's survival for the new people. Yesterday, she had felt proud, but today she felt vaguely annoyed. These people acted like they were in charge now.

Still, she did notice that John and Levon were packing small revolvers now, and the rest at least had a large knife holstered at their belts. They weren't *completely* clueless about the need to carry things. They still weren't carrying food or water, though. They must be expecting her to feed them.

"No need for us to just sit in the waiting room," Alex said. "Is there anything to see here? Anything useful to do?"

"I looked around some," said Letitia. "Want to see the map I made?"

"Sure," said Alex.

"Isn't that cute? She made a map!" Marie said. Letitia winced again. Did she look too little or too stupid to draw a map?

Alex was a little different, though. Maybe it was because they had had an extra day to get used to each other, maybe it was because he really was different, but he wasn't so irritating. She laid out her notebook pages before him. There was a map she had copied from a sign, with useful things marked on it: the grocery, the clinic, sheds that looked like there might be tools and things inside, pretty much anything she wanted go back and look at again. Hiding spots were marked down, too: storm drains, culverts, ledges, any place where she had thought a little kid could hide and a cuco couldn't fit or reach. The ten jails were marked, but Letitia didn't have much interest in breaking into jails. LaGuardia was marked as well, with a large "C" for "cuco."

Alex noticed the big "C" and asked what it meant.

"Cuco," said Letitia. "That what we call them things."

"I heard you say that before," said Alex, "but why?"

"It some kind of monster that the Spanish grandmas talk about. The devil send them to eat bad kids. I like it better than 'zombie.' 'sides, may be true. I always tried to be a good kid, and they ain't eat me yet."

Catalina wasn't carrying any kind of weapon that she could see, Kiara was still too weak to get out of bed, and Jahayra couldn't handle much on her own. Letitia called Rosarita and Malik over.

"I'm leaving you two here. Make sure nothing get in and guard everyone. Remember what I say about killing people?"

Rosarita and Malik fidgeted a bit.

"Remember?" Letitia continued insistently.

"We don't kill nobody unless we sure they be dangerous," said Rosarita and Malik in unison, obviously reciting a rule.

They didn't sound like their hearts were in it, but that would have to do.

Letitia heard muffled laughter from the adults, but decided not to say anything. If they didn't think Rosarita and Malik would kill them, that might come in handy some day.

CHAPTER 50
OUT AND ABOUT

Alex insisted that the first thing he wanted to see was LaGuardia. Everything else sounded interesting, but that sounded dangerous. Letitia liked that: Alex seemed to understand what kinds of things were important. He and Catalina seemed useful. The rest of these guys...

She didn't let the thought finish. They set off towards the southeast corner of the island. Alex and Letitia at the front, followed by the adults, followed by eight small children, still holding hands, still holding sharp stakes.

Every once in a while, Marie or Levon would break off from the group to look at something. Each time they broke off, one pair of children would follow them and another would run ahead and tell Letitia. Letitia would stop, then the whole group would stop. She would refuse to start again until they were all back in place.

Levon found this quite amusing. "Quite a military operation you have going here, kid," he said with a broad grin on his face.

Alex bristled for Letitia. "They're *alive*, man. Months and months of this shit and they're still alive! If this had happened to us when we were this age, we'd have been zombie kibble in ten minutes. She wants to do things this way, we'll do things this way."

Levon at least had the sense to look a little chastised. Letitia's view that Alex was worth keeping around became firmly cemented in place.

They arrived at the southwest corner of the island. Two hundred feet away, LaGuardia's runway was full of cucos, still staring at Hunts Point. They stood shoulder to shoulder, a continuous mass of flesh. Occasionally one would fall in the river. The fallen ones seemed to head towards Hunts Point, following the sound. There were a few on the beach, but they were in pretty bad shape.

"Jose, Trevon! Go take care of them mushy ones." Jose and Trevon ran off and took care of them pretty quickly.

"They look pretty good at that," said Alex. "Don't they get scared?"

"Of the mushy ones?" Letitia snorted. "Not the mushy ones. They scared of the ones that can hurt you, but that don' stop 'em. Jose be pretty little, but he can kill a regular one if he have to."

They worked their way back to the clinic. Having the adults along was useful because they recognized things that Letitia didn't. Letitia wasn't happy to recognize the diesel fuel tanks next to buildings that had emergency generators. Alex pointed one out and asked Letitia to mark it down.

"Why they got a tank of diesel?" asked Letitia.

"There's probably a generator inside the building. If there's still fuel in the tank, we could probably get electricity going," answered Alex.

"You mean like them people at Hunts Point?"

"Yeah, they've probably got the same kind of thing."

"We ain't goin' to be doin' that, then," said Letitia.

CHAPTER 51
ME AND MY SHADOW

While people were out exploring, Catalina took the dressings off to examine Kiara's wounds. Jahayra watched intently. Catalina was extremely satisfied with the progress: there was no streaking, pus, or other sign of infection. She began to carefully wipe the wounds with a sterile sponge and prepare to replace some of the steri-strips that had come loose.

Jahayra asked if she could help. Catalina opened another small sponge, dipped it in antiseptic, and handed it to Jahayra.

"Careful, now... don't press on the wounds. Just lightly dab at it and get the dried blood off. If you notice anything come loose, let me know."

Catalina watched them both, looking for signs of discomfort on Kiara's face. Jahayra was following instructions closely, carefully and softly cleaning Kiara's wounded leg. Kiara was smiling as she watched the process, and it was obvious that she found Jahayra's attentions comforting.

"You two are really good friends, aren't you?" she asked.

"We *buddies*!" the two answered in chorus.

"Is that so different from being friends?"

"Way different," said Jahayra.

"You don't have to be friends to be buddies," said Kiara. "Lucia and Maria never be friends, but they buddies now."

"Yeah, Rosarita and Malik didn't like *nobody*," Jahayra chimed in. "Letitia told them they were buddies, so they buddies."

"Then what does it mean?"

"Well," said one, "if I got to use both hands, she hold my stake. Makes sure that nothing hurts me."

"And," said the other, "if we go somewhere, she always be holding my hand so that she know where I be."

"When we sleep, she be right by me so that I don't get scared in the dark."

"If a job too big for me, she help me and make sure it get done."

"Wow!" said Catalina, in a tone of voice that would have made Letitia squirm under the weight of the condescension. "That all sounds pretty special. What's the most important thing about being a buddy?"

Kiara and Jahayra thought for a moment, their brows wrinkled in concentration. Suddenly, Kiara's face relaxed.

"If I have to kill somethin'," Kiara said, "she always help so we be sure it all the way dead."

CHAPTER 52
ORGANIZING

That afternoon, Letitia asked Catalina to go through the clinic supply room and help her organize a first aid kit. At first, Catalina grabbed a small box and put in a few tubes of Bacitracin, some bandages, tape, and some wound-cleaning supplies.

Letitia looked at this dubiously. "If this all I had when Kiara got hurt, it good enough to fix it?" she asked pointedly. Catalina started to protest, but got interrupted.

"I mean, we goin' back home as soon as Kiara's OK. I goin' to need something like this for myself."

"You mean you won't be staying with us?"

Catalina had assumed that the children were eager to stay with the adults and thought maybe she should be forceful. Letitia had certainly demonstrated that she could take care of the other children, though. It was hard not to think of Letitia as just a small child, probably because she *was* a small child. "Just" didn't seem to apply.

"No," Letitia answered. "We goin' home tomorrow. Unless you say Kiara still got to be here."

They started over. Catalina grabbed a couple of much larger cases. This time, the first thing she put in it was a copy of one of the books they had in stacks around the clinic: *A Practical Guide to First Aid for the Corrections Officer.* Not her first choice in first aid manuals, but, not too surprisingly, the first aid manual of choice on Rikers Island. Catalina suspected that the clinic gave refresher courses, given the large stacks.

Letitia picked up another copy and flicked through it. More big men saving the day, but not everyone was white, and nobody looked happy. It was at least a little better than the Sunset books.

Next came the same basic selection of bandages. These were followed by steri-strips, more Bacitracin, rubbing alcohol, and packaged sterilizing wipes.

After that, Catalina looked sternly at Letitia. "Some of the things I'm going to put in this red box are things that I don't want you to use on your own unless you absolutely have to, understand? If you can find me first, I want you to do that."

Letitia nodded. She was happy to have someone help with frightening stuff that she didn't understand. With that, Catalina put in a selection of basic antibiotics and painkillers. She took the time to look up dosages, calculate them for a small child, and help Letitia write them down in her notebook. She put in a small supply of basic splinting supplies, gloves, scalpels, tweezers, thermometers ... pretty much anything she could imagine using that she didn't think Letitia could accidentally kill anyone with.

When they were done, Letitia had three cases of medical supplies, neatly stacked side by side.

Catalina left the clinic to find Alex. He was sitting in the lobby with the rest of the adults. "You know," Catalina said, "Letitia says she's going back to her island tomorrow. She doesn't plan on staying with us."

That notion hadn't occurred to anyone. "You can't seriously be thinking about that!" exclaimed Marie. She was adamant that they had a responsibility to take care of these children. Levon sided with Marie, and Li sided with Levon.

John and Catalina both felt like they needed to keep an eye on the kids, but had seen them in action enough to feel like it would be OK to just check in on them once in a while.

Alex closed the discussion.

"This isn't our choice. I like John and Catalina's idea that we should keep an eye on them, but I'd *rather* keep an eye on them from a bit of a distance. This isn't a bunch of Cub Scouts and Brownies out on a camping trip, these children have gone *feral*. Living with them would be like living with a wolf pack. I don't *want* to go to bed worrying about whether I've gotten an armed kindergartener mad at me. You heard the two big ones with that '*we only supposed to kill them if they dangerous*' stuff. You think that came up during a heated game of hopscotch or something? No way. Those two have learned to kill. They probably had to. I don't want to think very hard about exactly *why* they had to, but I'm pretty sure they did.

"We've all been talking about moving here, and I think that's what we should do. We'll live here, they'll live on North Brother Island. We can see them every day. We can trade things for cantaloupes if you want. We'll watch over them. But don't be surprised if they do just as much watching over us."

Letitia was eavesdropping and was glad to hear that it sounded like Alex had it right again. She wasn't quite sure what "feral" meant, but if Alex said it, it was probably true.

CHAPTER 53
TYPHOID MARY

The morning the children moved back, Catalina examined Kiara's leg carefully.

"It's healing nicely," she reassured Kiara. "You should be fine in a few days." She turned and addressed Letitia and Jahayra. "As long as you clean it like I showed you every day, use the Bacitracin, and make sure you come get me if you see any pus, there's no reason she can't be at home. Just make sure she doesn't run around too much."

" 'kay then, time for us to get ready to go home," Letitia said. She looked at Jahayra. "You get it easy today. Stay in here, keep your buddy company till we ready."

Letitia gathered the children and headed for the storage shed with the boats. It took far more time to load and unload boats than it did to travel. All the children's boats were pulled out of a storage shed on Rikers, paddled for five minutes, then reloaded into storage on North Brother.

Letitia noticed the aluminum rowboat lying on the beach. "Ain't you goin' to put that up?"

"Ought to be fine there," replied Alex. "We'll need it later today. I don't think anybody's going to steal it." Letitia shook her head in disgust. How can they be so careless with something they need? They think she's going to give them rides home if something happen to it?

"First thing we got to do is get Kiara into bed. Then we show you around, check for any new cucos that wash up," Letitia said. She started towards the hospital, the children following her closely.

The adults followed behind. Alex commented as they walked. "This place is amazing. Look at that ... see how the path we're on is so perfectly flat and wide? I bet if we dug through the dirt, we'd find the old road still down there."

They emerged from the woods in the clearing in front of the hospital. The semicircular lobby, four stories in height, rose high above them. The steep stone stairs, still covered in brush and vines, ushered them into the dark interior.

"They live here?" asked Marie. "It looks like a place out of a horror movie."

"Yeah, but it's safe enough," said Alex. "Lots of places to hide and not much of anything to hide from. Damn good choice for a kid, I think."

The kids climbed the stairway, nimbly negotiating the missing top platform. Kiara winced at the stretch, but made it across the gap. The adults followed.

"You have got to be kidding me!" Marie objected at the top. "You think this is safe?"

"It safe from cucos," said Letitia. "We all do fine with it." She led them to the Heroin Recovery Ward.

"Still think they aren't safe, Marie?" Alex asked. "Look at this place. Steel doors, steel gratings, steel bars on the windows, eye slots, cages ... It's like an anti-zombie fortress!"

Letitia was glad she had made the kids clean up the ward. She had always wondered why everybody always cleaned for company, but now she understood: it just felt better to show people where you lived when it was clean and nice.

They hadn't done anything to clean the walls. The graffiti drew John's eye. "Poor bastards," he murmured. He walked slowly along, reading the pleas of the various addicts that had suffered in this room over the years, studying the illustrations of internal horror that spilled out onto the decaying wall. "If we ever find a working camera," he said, "I'm going to want to come back here and do a complete study of this room. You could have gotten a Pulitzer with this."

He studied the image over Kiara's bed. An eyedropper? A syringe? A sword? He couldn't quite tell. It was signed: "*Willie Cortez, April 26, 1962*." Long dead, so no way to find out.

Kiara was safely laid out in bed, with Jahayra next to her. As Letitia shut them in, Jahayra pretended to read a story from her coloring book: "*There was this train full of toys, see. And it was really sad, 'cause it was broken...*"

Letitia took them on a quick tour of the building. The wood stove was another source of praise and acclamation, as was the shower area. The Luggable Loo hadn't been emptied for a week, so it did not create the same positive impression.

Leaving the building, everyone walked towards the pier, passing the clearing where the garden had been planted. "Now we know where the melons are coming from," said Alex. The adults were quite impressed with the garden. All the melon vines were producing fruit, the carrots were doing well, and there were new potatoes to be had. All the trees had sprouted, but were still only seedlings.

Once at the pier, Letitia started to walk around the island, alert for any noises or sounds in the bushes. John couldn't stop talking about how much he missed having a camera. He stopped outside one of the cottages that was in relatively good condition.

"You could nearly still live in this one," he said.

"Yeah, that the one we took the stove grating from," said Letitia. John brushed the debris from a plaque set in the ground in front of the cottage.

MARY MALLON ("TYPHOID MARY") WAS
QUARANTINED IN THIS HOME TWICE,
ONCE FROM 1907-1910,
AND AGAIN FROM
1915-1937, WHEN SHE DIED.

Alex laughed out loud. "I guess it fits, you know. It's still a quarantine zone, it's just inside a bigger quarantine zone."

Letitia looked insulted. Even after Alex explained, she still wasn't sure she wasn't insulted.

They continued on their journey around the island, killing a few soggy cucos along the way. None of them presented a major threat.

"Time to go catch some lunch," announced Letitia. These people had eaten way too much of the trail mix and other stuff, but there was no harm in feeding them fish. Or melons. She was amazed at how many melons were growing in the garden, and there was nothing to do but eat them.

She took the pocket fishing rod down to the pier. As always, she baited the hook and lay down to slowly lower the bait into the water.

"Do you want to learn how to cast? It's faster," said John.

Letitia nodded. She'd tried figuring it out a few times, but it was one of those things you couldn't learn from a book. John took the rod, and, after a few false starts from dealing with the tiny rod, successfully cast the bait out on the water and rapidly reeled it back in. Letitia took the rod and attempted to imitate the motion. As before, her first couple casts resulted in the hook wildly swinging around.

John crouched behind her and gently guided her arm. A few more shots with him coaching and she successfully cast the bait. As she reeled it back in, a bass struck. It was a large one.

"Rosarita! Malik! Got another big one!" She had forgotten John was there. Rosarita and Malik ran up. Together, the three of them reeled it in. John stood by and watched, prepared to help if necessary, but sensing that this was something the kids had down.

They dressed it with their standard approach. John was both amused and impressed at how slick they were at this now. Letitia dropped the fish on the pier and stepped on it with one foot. Rosarita rapidly pierced the head with one stake, Malik pierced the tail with another. Letitia rapidly gutted the fish, removed the head and tail, and retrieved the hook. He figured it took no more than thirty seconds from the time the fish was up on the pier.

Fish in hand, they returned to the hospital. Tiara and Jada rapidly filleted the fish while Maria and Lucia got the fire started. Twenty minutes later, everyone was sitting down to a meal of fish and melon, with purified water to drink.

The events of the day went a long way towards calming Levon, Marie, and Li down about "abandoning" the children.

"You know," said Marie as they steered their boat back to Rikers, "they've actually done a much better job than we have."

Alex could only nod.

CHAPTER 54
NEIGHBORS

The two groups rapidly established a neighborly routine. At first, Catalina came over every morning to check on Kiara and make sure that everything was progressing smoothly. Letitia and the kids would go over periodically to help Alex and John go through the island facilities and take inventory.

Initially, Letitia insisted that the kids maintain their defensive line formation whenever they were on Rikers, but, in time, both groups relaxed. Letitia began to permit buddy pairs to go off on their own, even when adults were present. The adults tried a few times to assert authority over the children, but found it quickly undermined. In the end, they decided to think of Letitia as the children's mother and take any issues they had to her. They all had trouble with it, but couldn't see any alternative that didn't risk bloodshed.

For her part, Letitia decided that the adults weren't going to do anything to hurt them on purpose. She didn't like Marie or Li, but they didn't seem dangerous, just scatterbrained. Catalina was clearly useful. Levon was kind of a jerk, but didn't cause trouble.

Letitia's bond with Alex did grow tighter, but not in a way that most would have anticipated. Alex described it to Catalina once as the kind of relationship he might have with a well-trained attack dog. He was fond of her, wanted to help take care of her, but he wouldn't do anything that she might treat as a threat. He knew that if it came down to a choice between him or the kids, Letitia would use his testicles as bait to distract the zombies while the kids got away.

Letitia was actually fonder of Alex than Alex realized. She'd use Li or Marie as bait without much hesitation, but she'd try to help Alex get away.

CHAPTER 55
THE NEWS

One of the cars left in one of the lots had a Sirius radio antenna on it. It didn't register on anyone the first few times they saw it, but ultimately Levon realized that they could probably get some news on it. He didn't think anyone would have turned off the satellites aimed at the East Coast yet. He smashed his way in and, with a few hours of work, managed to cut the wire harness and splice it together well enough to get the radio to turn on.

Everyone gathered around, eager to hear some news from the outside world. The defensive line had fallen back to the main rivers. Nearly everything east of the Mississippi and Illinois rivers had collapsed. There were holdouts in some areas around Mobile and Cincinnati. Small towns along the Ohio and Wabash were still managing to trade goods with each other and keep some level of functioning government, but they were islands. The western portion of the country had made it clear: no one and nothing was permitted to cross the water.

The lead story of the day was from Eppley International Airport in Omaha, where a retired airline pilot from Indianapolis had managed to land during the night with a hundred passengers, all demanding asylum. The consequent military action had damaged two runways, resulting in flight cancellations.

CHAPTER 56
DORMITORY DAYS

John and Alex stood at the entry gate to the Anna M. Kross Center. Most of the facilities on Rikers weren't traditional jail cells at all, but dormitories, lined with bunk beds. The Anna M. Kross Center concerned Alex the most. The tourist brochure described it as a low-security facility, and it looked no more secure than the average fraternity row, with forty low buildings holding approximately sixty inmates each. He liked the idea of dealing with sixty zombies at a time better than trying to deal with two thousand at once, but it was still a lot for six people to deal with. Three people, actually, as everyone but Alex, John, and Levon were on North Brother Island for safety.

"You sure we need to do this?" John asked.

"Sooner or later," said Alex. "You can hear them inside there, and they're going to break out sometime. I don't want to be asleep when they do it."

Each of the men had a pistol, but their primary weapons were large trenching spikes, liberated from one of the maintenance shops. Levon waited at the dock with the aluminum boat, ready to evacuate at a moment's notice. John and Alex approached one of the dorms. Alex held back as John attacked the doorway with the spike and a small sledge. After a few minutes, he successfully sprung the door off its hinges. The zombies inside burst forth and John made a break for the gate. They closed and latched it, moving to the fence about twenty feet from the opening.

Only twelve zombies emerged. A couple had obviously been doing most of the pounding: their forearms were limp and weak, the bones inside splintered during several months of futilely striking steel. The rest, though, were remarkably intact, undecayed after long months indoors. Intact or not, the hurricane fence provided the same set of easy kills it always did.

"Twelve?" asked Alex. "All that buildup, and only twelve? Where are the rest?"

They went in. Bed frames were stacked up haphazardly into barricades. A few zombies roamed back and forth inside of cages built out of beds.

"These guys mainly starved to death, I think. They must have tried to lock the dying ones up," John said. "Or maybe I've got it backwards. Maybe they built those cages to hide in and died when they starved. They would have been too weak to kill them once starvation set in."

Alex looked he was going to be sick. "This wasn't fast at all, man. I think these guys were alive in here for weeks."

John and Alex walked through, their trenching spikes rapidly taking care of the numerous skulls lying about the floor. They undid the bed-frame cages one by one, taking care of the occupants one by one. They found one intact zombie inside a closet: when the end came, the resurrected corpse didn't understand how to twist the knob to get out.

Alex and John sat on a porch and wept before moving on to the next unit. It was a long, hard week, but, at the end, the dormitories were free of the undead. They assembled the pile of nearly 2000 inmates into two heaps: one with flesh and one without. They doused the fleshy remains with gasoline and set them ablaze, trying not to think about the 12,000 left to go.

CHAPTER 57

A PRAYER FOR THE PRISONERS (SILENT)

God

I saw the pile of bones today. That was a big pile. I didn't think you could make one that big out of bones. I didn't think anyone could make a pile so big out of bones.

Why did they leave those people here to die?

Why did they leave *us* here to die?

Will there be somebody that make a pile of us when we die?

If we just supposed to die, please figure out a way to tell me.

I think you want us to live, but some days, I'm not sure.

Amen

CHAPTER 58
WHERE THERE'S SMOKE...

Letitia was out inspecting the pumpkin crop. They still didn't look much like pumpkins. They were small, not much bigger than her fist, and still green. There was a little bit of yellow in a few of them. Maybe next week there'd be some orange. She reached down to pull a small weed when the ground trembled under her feet, followed by a massive *thwump*, just like the gas bombs the Hunts Pointers used, but much, much larger. The wind blew for a moment, then stopped.

Dense black smoke was rising from Hunts Point. All the little ones were doing what they were supposed to: running for the Heroin Recovery Ward. She followed.

"Stay in there till I come get you! I'll be up on the roof!" she yelled through the door.

She climbed to the roof with her binoculars. The smoke was climbing from the center of the car wall. She could see pieces of the big fuel truck scattered around, its metal tank charred and torn to bits. However they got that big fuel truck in and out, something had gone wrong today. Really wrong.

Big parts of the wall were falling over, and the bulldozers were running around trying to get them put back up. They must be going too fast, because things would stand up and then slide right back down.

Letitia went down to talk to the little ones. "Somethin' going on over at the crazy people's place. Don' think anything goin' to happen to hurt us. Come up to the roof if you want, or stay in here. Don' go wanderin' around."

She returned to the roof. All the little ones followed, some too curious not to watch, the rest too scared to be alone.

All the cucos that she could normally see south of Hunts Point were moving, heading towards the holes in the walls. The gunfire got louder, and the bulldozers kept trying to work faster. There were cucos in the main compound now.

The battle raged on for hours. The main compound was completely overrun. People were climbing the semi-trucks, but every time they did that, the cucos would pile up. It looked like trying to shoot the cucos that were coming at the trucks just made the piles grow faster, because it was easier for the cucos to climb on top of dead cucos than on top of moving ones.

Someone started using the gasoline bombs inside the compound, making things worse. Flaming cucos would make other cucos catch fire, and then buildings. There were more big *thwump* sounds as more storage tanks exploded. All the boats at the dock were on fire.

The little ones were frantic.

"Are you *sure* the fire can't get here?"

"Are you sure?"

"Are the people over there getting hurt?"

Letitia made reassuring sounds as best she could while she tried to keep track of what was going on.

One group made it out to the docks at Baretto Point Park, a couple dozen adults against thousands of the creatures. Only a few cucos at a time could get on the dock, but the people couldn't win. All they had were axes and clubs. Swinging that kind of thing is hard, even for an adult. They couldn't do it forever.

She couldn't make herself stand by.

"Back into the ward!" she told the little ones. "I goin' to see if I can't get a few of 'em away from there. They may be crazy, but there ain't no need for all of 'em to die."

She put all the children in the ward and instructed Rosarita and Malik to watch them. She tied two supply rafts to her pontoon boat and took off for Baretto Point Park.

As she paddled over, she saw them fighting. Sometimes things would stop for a moment, but she decided that those must be the times that someone was being eaten.

By the time she got there, there were only a dozen people left. She had a hard time making herself heard over the noise.

"Jump!" she shouted. "I got boats! You can get away!"

The entire group had been so focused on the attacking horde that they hadn't noticed her approach. When they looked down, they saw what looked like a little angel from heaven as Letitia paddled against the current, holding the boats in place.

They leapt as a group, clambering their way into the boats from the water, capsizing them multiple times in their panic. Finally, they were all seated.

"Grab the paddles," Letitia said, "I ain't goin' to *drag* you."

CHAPTER 59
BACK ACROSS THE RIVER

As Letitia aimed back across, she realized that she hadn't completely thought this through. She couldn't stand by and watch these people get eaten, but she didn't have a way to feed them, or a place to put them, or think that having them mix with the little ones was a great idea. She saw Alex and John approaching in their aluminum rowboat, carrying another small group.

"Look, there more of you guys over there," she said. "We go meet up."

They swung over towards Rikers and the aluminum boat.

"See you caught some pretty big fish there, kid. Any idea what you're going to do with them?" asked Alex.

"Not really. Couldn't watch 'em get eaten, but I ain't got no spot for 'em."

A voice spoke up from one of the boats.

"We'll do anything you need us to. Just get us away from that," he said.

Alex nodded. "That" was the right word. It wasn't really even a "there" anymore. The flames had spread through the entire compound, and, as it spread to the wall of cars, the residual gas in the tanks of the vehicles began to go up. Most of the time they just burst into flames, but every once in a while the tank would have just the right mix of air and fuel to go up explosively, raining shrapnel all over the area. The original diesel fire was still raging and the ash from burning tires was spreading a thick black layer of grime all over everything. Fortunately, the wind was blowing to the northwest. Otherwise, the islands would have been covered in black smoke.

"Don't worry," Alex said, "we've got a place. We've been cleaning out one of the dormitories. It's not done yet, but it's got beds and toilets. Showers, even. Lots of clean orange jumpsuits for everyone."

They came up to the ferry slip, and all of Letitia's passengers got off. She made sure the paddles were securely back in place and headed home.

She went back, got some help storing the boats, then returned to the roof with everyone. That fire was not going to go out soon. The car wall was on fire now for nearly a mile, and not a minute went by without the *fwooosh* of another gas tank going up.

She gathered everyone around her.

"We be more careful, now, 'cause there new people over at Rikers. I don' think they *bad* people, but I don' know that for sure. For a while, we just mainly goin' to stay over here and mind our own business."

CHAPTER 60
SETTLING IN

Alex and John escorted the refugees to one of the dorms in the Anna M. Kross center. Li and Marie had turned these buildings into a private project. Neither wanted to be around on the days that the inhabitants were cleaned out, but neither could sleep well thinking of being next to the bloodstained rooms. Cleaning them wasn't too hard: the floors were tile, the paint was full-gloss paint where there was paint at all, and there were floor drains in every room. All the features that made it easy to wash up after drunks and junkies made it easier to wash up after zombie massacres.

They had given this dorm special attention because Marie still entertained the notion that Letitia and the children would come over to Rikers Island if there was a nice place for them. The mattresses had been sorted and only the least bloodstained had been kept. The hot water was from an LPG heater, not electric, so the bathrooms not only worked, but people could take hot showers. That was another of Marie's motivations for cleaning up the dorms: she hated the cold showers in the clinic and didn't feel comfortable in the children's open shower arrangement.

After an hour, everyone had gotten a chance to wash off the grime of battle and change into clean clothes. "We've got every style and color you want, as long as you want an orange jumpsuit" was the joke that had been beaten into the ground over the last month. Alex hauled it out once more for a fresh audience.

While the newcomers were getting settled, John rowed over to North Brother Island. Tiara and Jada ran to shore to meet him, then escorted him to Letitia. John wondered for a moment what would happen if he refused to go where they pointed him, but decided the day had been exciting enough without testing his limits.

"Catalina and Marie sent me over to invite you to dinner tonight," he said to Letitia. "They decided that the best way to welcome the new people is a fancy dinner, and they want to be sure that everyone's there."

Letitia mulled it over for a bit, then decided that going to the dinner was the best way to meet the new arrivals. If there *was* any trouble, there would be people she trusted there to help.

"We goin' to have dinner over with the new people tonight," she told the group. "Go pick about ten of those bright orange melons," flashing her hands to show all ten fingers, "and one of the little buckets of carrots." She couldn't believe how many melons grew on those Hybrid Orange Krush vines. She wasn't going to mind giving them away, especially if the adults shared food back. They were pretty good about sharing now that they found that big supply room. They had all kinds of powdered food: it wasn't great (except for the pancake mix), but fish and trail mix got old.

They boated across to Rikers, put the boats in the shed, and walked over to the dining hall. It was lit, as usual, by battery-powered fluorescent lamps. The newcomers, just arriving, were surprised by this.

"Don't you have electricity?" asked one of the women.

Alex looked at her quizzically.

"After what just happened, you have to ask why we don't run our generators? Didn't you guys ever figure out that that's *why* you had such a problem with the zombies? We've got a small one in a basement that we use to charge batteries and things, but we never run it for more than an hour at a time."

"Cliff may have figured it out, but he never told any of us."

"Yeah, Cliff was like that," chimed in another voice from the back.

"Grab some food first, and then tell us about Cliff."

CHAPTER 61

CLIFF

Chris, a tall, lanky man in his mid-thirties, began the tale:

"Cliff was the guy that had the idea. He was always big on conspiracy theories. Remember the bit about swine flu vaccine bein' some secret weapon to wipe out blacks? Cliff was down with that. The CIA distributing crack in Harlem to wipe out blacks? Cliff believed that, too..."

"Don't forget Church's Fried Chicken!" came an interruption from the end of the table.

"Yeah, Church's Fried Chicken, even. Supposedly the Klan was messin' with the recipe and puttin' in stuff that only sterilized black people. There wasn't nothing that happened in the last twenty years that wasn't a plot to wipe out the black man, if you listened to Cliff.

"The day the government put out the evacuation notice, Cliff was all 'If every white man on the planet is running this way, I'm running *that* way.' Usually, I just laugh at Cliff, but this time, I listened for a bit.

"Man had a point, you know what I mean? Here we are, sitting next to the biggest pile of food in the world, world's coming to an end, and there's a bunch of people telling us to run away from the food and go live in a tent with people pointing a gun at us?

"There were a bunch of us that had worked at the distribution center for years. We knew how to run things, we had the keys, the passwords, combinations, everything you would need to keep the place going. Cliff, he and some of his friends had been collecting guns. Don't think he ever would have been crazy enough to use 'em in the old days, but with this hitting the fan, using them didn't seem crazy at all.

"Always pissed me off, anyway, spending my days working with all this fancy food that I couldn't afford to eat." Chris paused for a moment, grabbed a few bites of fish, and continued.

"Anyways, we just grabbed our families and headed for the warehouses.

"It worked out pretty good at first. We just pulled up a line of trucks around the warehouse and posted guards on top of 'em. Anyone we liked came up, we let 'em in. Anyone we didn't like ran pretty quick once you aimed an AK-47 at him.

"Army didn't even bother us. They saw we didn't want to come and didn't want nothing to do with us. It was weird watching them with all those cars, though.

"Everyone was running towards the bridges, trying to get south. Traffic jam for miles. Was like nobody could *read*, man. All the evacuation notices told 'em to walk, and here they all are, in their cars. Loaders coming up the interstate would just get the shovel under the front of the car, flip the damn thing over the edge of the highway.

"Meant business, too. Saw one guy in a BMW, just wouldn't get out of the car. Army guy yelling at him to get out, he's just yellin' right back about how there's no way he's getting out of his brand new Beemer so that some guy with a bulldozer can throw it off the highway. Finally, the guy with the loader just picked it up and threw it over the side, driver and all. Airbags saved him, but boy he was pissed. Last I saw, he was walkin' south, though.

"After it was all over, we just stole the loaders. The operators got evacuated in helicopters, and we just went and grabbed 'em. Used 'em to build walls out of all those cars.

"It did start to go crazy after the power went out. I never hooked it up in my brain with the generators, though. You say it was the generators that were doin' it?"

Letitia snorted milk through her nose.

"Generators the things that made that humming sound?" she asked.

"Guess so."

"That it, then. Easy to get around till you turned them on. Every cuco in town kept walking towards that hum. That why they were all aiming at you and not at us. They were even getting across the water at Randall's Island to try to get you."

Chris thought for a bit.

"That'd be easier to see from the outside. We didn't know that it was different other places.

"Anyway," he continued, "that was when it got harder.

"We used the loaders to build bigger walls, and they just kept coming. At first, we'd just build the walls taller and go on runs where we'd just aim into a big mob of 'em with a loader and try to squash 'em flat. Then, we got the idea of building these kind of pens: walls ten or twelve cars high on each side. Zombies would pile up over the wall, fall in the middle, and get stuck. We'd drop a Molotov cocktail in every once in a while, burn 'em out."

"A what?" Letitia interrupted.

"Molotov cocktail. Named after some Russian dude. Bottle of gasoline with a rag stuffed in one end. You light the rag and throw it."

"That what you was using in that park?"

"Yeah."

Letitia got out her notebook and wrote it down. Chris raised an eyebrow, but continued.

"It was the fuel truck that was the worst. All those warehouses took a lot of power, and we had to get fresh fuel every week. That meant that we'd have to get a bunch of guys on top of the wall to shoot anything that got too close. We'd take the loaders and punch a hole through the wall for the truck to drive through, build the wall back, and tear it down again when the truck came back. Guys with guns riding on the truck to kill anything that attacked. One loader would go out in front to clear a path for the truck, too. Always an all-day affair. Started to be two days, once we'd stolen all the diesel from the gas stations that were close.

"Cliff had the idea that we could pump it across from the old Con Ed plant in over by Bowery Bay, but I guess you guys all know how well that worked out. We lost a bunch of guys and a bunch of boats on that thing. Never did figure out what they did to set it off, but there was no putting it out. We didn't even know how to try. There we were, getting one truck of fuel at a time, and all that stuff had just burnt up. Made you sick inside.

"We tried to convince Cliff that we didn't need all the food, but he wouldn't hear it. We had an entire warehouse full of frozen Chinese dumplings. Weren't bad, but how many Chinese dumplings can a hundred people eat? Lot of weirder stuff than that. Baby asparagus. Lox. Octopus. Most of us figured that we could just let half the food go, only have to get fuel every other week, maybe shrink back the walls and have an easier time of it.

"Cliff just wouldn't hear of it. He was convinced that we were going to need every single speck of that food. He had most of the guns, and we just weren't going to cross him.

"One guy did try to take him out, though. After it was over, Cliff tied up his family and then gutshot him. Made us watch while the dude ate his wife and kids ..."

Chris stopped for a moment. He didn't eat while pausing.

"Anyway, this morning, people just screwed up. They were moving a wall to let the fuel truck back in and accidentally opened up a wall that had some burning zombies inside it. Enough managed to rush the truck to set it off. You saw what happened after that."

CHAPTER 62
DESSERT

Marie was proud of tonight's meal. Experimenting with the powdered eggs and powdered milk from the food supplies and the melons from the garden, she had managed to make a passable melon pie that made for a good change of pace. That should help make the newcomers feel welcome.

She sat at a table with Chris and his obviously pregnant wife, Angela. Pedro, Magdalena, Roberto, and Angelica rounded out the set at the table. Marie's mother had always taught her not to ask about a pregnancy unless the baby was crowning, so she was grateful when Angela volunteered that she was seven months along.

"I had just figured out I was pregnant when everything happened," Angela said. "I hadn't even figured out how to tell Chris yet, and I wasn't about to tell Cliff."

"Did they give you any problems about it?"

"No, not really," Angela replied. "You could tell Cliff wasn't happy about it, but he wasn't going to do anything about it. At least not yet."

"It was worrying me, too," Chris said, "but where were we going to go? I just couldn't see being on the run with her pregnant and all. I hope this place will be a bit friendlier towards her."

"Of course!" Marie bubbled. "It'll be nice to have a regular kid around." She couldn't help but glance over at Letitia.

"What did that kid call those things, anyway?" Chris asked.

"*Cuco*," said Marie. "That's what all the kids call them. Alex does sometimes, too, but I think he's just an overgrown kid. It's some kind of Spanish word."

"Means 'ass', doesn't it?" This time, Chris directed his question at Magdalena.

Magdalena laughed. "*Cuco*, not *culo*," she said. "A cuco is kind of like, well ..." She stopped for a second. "I guess 'boogeyman' would be the best English word. It's a story people use to scare little kids.

"A cuco is one of the devil's helpers. They watch little kids and eat the ones that misbehave. My mama even used to have a lullaby about them: *Duérmete niño, duérmete ya ... Que viene el Cuco y te comerá.* That means 'Go to sleep, little baby, or the cuco will eat you.' Some lullaby, huh?

"Anyway, they're supposed to live on roofs and hide in shadows. If you're *really* naughty, they will eat you right where you are. If you are just a little bad, they kidnap you first and *then* eat you. It fits. I can understand why they call them that.

"What's up with those kids, anyway?" Magdalena asked. "Whose are they?"

"Foundlings, kind of. They showed up on the beach one day when one of the girls got badly hurt, back when we lived on Mills Rock. They've been living on their own ever since things fell apart. The big one's name is Letitia. I never can keep track of most of the rest. The biggest boy is Malik, and the biggest girl is Rosarita. The one that limps a little is Kiara ... she's the one that got hurt. I just smile and nod at the rest."

"Be careful around them. Those little stakes they have sitting next to their plates are *sharp*, and they know how to use them. Letitia makes them practice with them and swats them if they ever drop them. Always in pairs, too."

"Living on their own? You mean they don't live with you?"

"Nope. They stay on the island next door. Creepy place: an abandoned drug recovery center. They've cleaned it up, though, and have a spot where they live. Nice, big garden, too: that's where the melons for this pie came from."

"You mean you have fresh melons? This isn't from a can?" Angelica looked excited.

"Sure."

"I haven't seen a fresh piece of fruit for five months!"

Everyone at the table agreed excitedly. Marie went to the kitchen and sliced a few of the remaining melons, bringing a plate to each table. The newcomers ate greedily.

So much for her pie, thought Marie.

CHAPTER 63
THE PILE GROWS

The newcomers were a great help when it came to clearing the jails. Hunts Point being one of the poorest neighborhoods in New York City, several of them had spent time on Rikers Island. That came in handy in terms of knowing how to get in and out of some of the jails and knowing which ones had cells and which ones had dorms.

It took about two days to clean each dorm to their satisfaction. Of course, there was no end in sight. Every few days, John and Alex led the charge on a new low-security installation. The results were always the same: unless there were cells to separate the inmates from each other, they would kill a handful of zombies and recover numerous skeletons, the bones gnawed clean by hungry zombies.

This had become another compulsion. They didn't have the energy or facilities to bury them and didn't feel right just throwing them in the river. They couldn't even just leave the places closed, knowing what was inside.

Instead, the pile of bones grew. The pile left Catalina numb. She didn't help with the zombies, nor did she help with the mops and the bleach. She would come to the bones for an hour each morning and pray over them, but wouldn't tell anyone what she was praying for.

The high-security section of the Otis Bantum Center was unapproachable. Someone, probably the group that had been here before, had operated the remote security locks on the wing after everyone had died, opening all the cells. The view through the door to the wing was a sea of zombies: thousands, by Alex's count.

One morning, while clearing a dorm, Alex heard a loud "*¡Madre de Dios!*"

Pedro, a large, burly man, had frozen. A smaller snarling zombie stood in front of him, trying furiously to get through the fence. Juan, another newcomer, rapidly drove a spike through its head. Juan and Pedro walked away from the fence, Pedro still shaking, having a hard time holding back tears. Alex walked over.

"Are you hurt?"

"No, not hurt. That was his Uncle Luis," said Juan. "I remember his uncle. A very nice man. When we were little, Luis and my father would sit on the porch and play music. My father played the cuatro, and Luis would sing and strum the guitar. Always songs about women."

He took a look at Luis.

"I don't think Luis will be chasing women no more."

Luis's body was kept separate from the rest. Three piles of bones held 7000 people that week, but Luis was not among them. They used the trenching spikes and shovels to dig a grave in the soft soil on the beach facing towards Hunts Point. His body was laid to rest, a small marker of stones over his head.

Despite all the death around them, it was the first funeral any of them had attended in months.

CHAPTER 64
NEW SKILLS

"Mawltoff cocktails," said Letitia. "I need to learn how to make Mawltoff cocktails."

"Mawltoff?" Chris asked. "Oh, *Molotov*. Mol-o-toff."

He was taken aback. He still wasn't used to Letitia. She was still keeping mainly to her own island and wasn't a frequent sight around Rikers. The armed guard of kindergarteners that accompanied her wherever she went freaked him out.

Letitia hadn't grown completely comfortable around the newcomers. Until she did, she kept everyone together. She wouldn't leave them alone on North Brother Island and didn't let them roam on Rikers unless they were with Alex or Catalina. Today, they were with her, forming the little twenty-legged caterpillar, replete with garden stakes for spikes, that they had in the early days.

"Why on earth do you want to learn how to make Molotov cocktails?"

"We not big like you guys. You get in trouble, you grab a shovel, or shoot a gun, or just kick 'em until they fall over. We got to get way up close and jab 'em in the eyes. That scary. That how Jorge and Diego died. Don' want to do that when I don' have to."

"You know you can't just throw 'em anywhere, don't you? You can't just set one off in your living room or someplace like that."

"I know. Don't spend much time in a livin' room no more, though."

Chris decided that he just wasn't the one to judge. They trooped over to Alex.

"Alex, do you think it's a good idea to teach Letitia how to make Molotov cocktails?"

Alex paused. He paused so hard it seemed that his heart had stopped.

"Why would you *want* to teach her how to do that?"

"Not my idea. She's asking for lessons."

Alex and Letitia conferred for a bit. He decided that now that she had the idea, she was going to try. The idea of the kids *experimenting* with matches and gasoline scared Alex more than the idea of teaching them how.

"You know, Chris," said Alex, "I've been wondering how you got them to go so far. We could see you throwing them at Sound View Park, and I don't think you were doing that by hand."

"Catapults. They've got a place with spare tire tubes for the big trucks around here, don't they? Big rigs still use inner tubes. That's what we used."

The project was on. It took a few days, but they were able to cobble together a working catapult design using a hand dolly as a frame, a section of inner tube as a spring, a shallow frying pan as a tray, and a two-by-four as a throwing arm. They tested it with soda cans at first and found they were able to get a 500-foot range.

Letitia watched and made sure that her needs weren't getting forgotten. They put a step plate on the throwing arm so that it could be depressed by a five-year-old child standing on it. Jose was the tester: if Jose could manage it, anybody could. The release bar could be locked by a child kicking it one way and popped out by a child kicking it the other.

Letitia was still skeptical, because she didn't think she was going to haul one of these around wherever she went. Still, she had learned that if you wanted these guys to do anything, you let them think they were doing what they wanted. She just had to make sure she understood how the fire part worked.

They drained some gas out of one of the vehicles still parked on the island and filled some small bottles. First, they ranged the catapult so that it was dropping soda cans down into the middle of the mob on the LaGuardia runway. The mob there hadn't dissipated. They were no longer being drawn to Hunts Point, but they weren't drawn anywhere else, either. When people were in sight, they got excited. When no one was in sight, they just stood there.

Chris and Alex took a few runs without lighting the fuses and got their range adjusted.

Finally, time for the big test. The first one was spectacular. Since they had already wet the crowd down with gasoline from the test shots, the first live round was like firing five at once. Twenty zombies in the middle of the crowd went up.

Subsequent rounds weren't as exciting, but they were still effective. All of them took practice shots and learned how to run it. Each learned how to fill the bottle, stuff the rag, and light it without getting burnt. In the process, the mob on the runway was thinning out. Where there had been tens of thousands, there were now merely thousands. The best part was that there really wasn't much of anywhere for the fire to spread: the massive expanse of runway was proving to be an excellent practice field.

"But how you do this without the big machine?" asked Letitia.

"Well, same thing, but you just throw them. Can't get them anywhere near as far that way, so you don't want to do that," said Alex.

What Alex wanted and what Letitia wanted were quite different. She had figured out a couple of days ago that everyone had forgotten that the whole idea was for the kids to be able to do something when they got in real trouble without having to get so close.

Letitia managed to get some full, sealed bottles of gasoline and some of the greased rags into her backpack. That night, the kits were laid out: one half of each buddy pair got a small bottle of gasoline, tightly sealed, placed in a small locking plastic bag. The other half of each pair got a butane lighter from the camping supplies and a small rag, again sealed in a locking plastic bag.

Letitia always made sure the kids got some time to play every day, and game time got a new game. Throwing a water bottle into a bucket became a contest, with the one that could hit the bucket from the farthest away being the winner. Every time a bottle hit the bucket, a little voice cried out "I thought I could!"

CHAPTER 65
THE NURSERY

John, Alex, and Levon headed towards the open door of the Rose M. Singer Center. All the zombies that had come out were women, the first they had encountered here.

Levon's gut felt like it was going to let loose. This zombie-killing stuff was hard enough when it was men, but stabbing a stake in a woman's head went against everything he thought of himself doing.

He couldn't let that stop him, though. A lady zombie could still bite you or eat you, and he wasn't going to let anything threaten Li.

After sweeping the main room, they turned towards a pile blocking a pair of doors. It was an impromptu, disordered heap: mop handles through the door handles, overturned desks, file cabinets. If a zombie was capable of puzzling its way through a problem, it wouldn't have done anything to slow it down. As it was, it had been effective.

Alex and John pushed the final file cabinet out of the way, and Levon read the sign on the door. Stenciled letters spelled out "NURSERY."

They pulled the mop handles loose and pushed the doors open.

The cribs were full of zombies. Little baby zombies. No teeth yet, so they couldn't bite. No muscle strength, so they couldn't pull themselves out with their arms. Most couldn't even stand and simply lay on their backs, flailing dead limbs back and forth.

Levon's gut trembled some more and then stopped, like something that had been pushed too hard and broken, unable to tremble any more.

"I got this," he said. "You two go check the rest of the place out."

He stopped at the first crib and gently picked up the baby inside. He laid it face down on the pillow and hammered his spike through the soft spot at the top of the skull. He turned the baby face up, the hole resting on the pillow.

He visited nineteen more cribs. Nineteen babies went still.

Levon left the nursery and went to a small grassy spot in front of the building. Using his trenching spike he laid out a grid of twenty marks.

Alex and John watched. "You want help with that?" Alex asked.

Levon barely heard him. "No," he answered flatly, "this is something I've got to do on my own."

He dug holes on each of the marks. When dinner time came, he refused to stop and worked until the sun set, taking a break only for a small meal that Li brought him.

On the morning of the third day, he was done. He went looking for Catalina. He found her in the infirmary, helping with a small cut on Jada's arm.

"I'm done now," he said. "I need some help with the praying part."

Catalina finished the bandage and followed Levon to the yard. Letitia and the kids followed, curious to see what was going on.

Levon walked into the center and brought back a baby, wrapped in a blanket, its head still supported by a pillow. He placed it in the first hole.

Catalina bowed her head and crossed herself. All of the children bowed their heads as well.

"Lord,

"Bless this infant, for he has done no wrong, and committed no sins.

"Into your hands, we commend his spirit.

"Amen."

"Amen," came the murmured echo from the children.

Levon filled the hole with dirt.

Twenty times, Levon placed.

Twenty times, Catalina prayed.

Twenty times, Levon sprinkled.

Twenty times, the children echoed.

And on the evening of the third day, Levon rested.

CHAPTER 66
A PRAYER FOR BABIES

God
We watched Levon and Catalina bury all those babies today.
Please don't do that to them again.
Amen

CHAPTER 67
A LAZY AFTERNOON

Levon refused to get up the next morning. No one pushed him. Everyone was worried he would snap and decided that if he needed to sleep late to get over things, that wouldn't be a problem.

Letitia and the little ones were over that morning for catapult practice. Chris and Alex had built several more, one of which was supposed to go back over to North Brother Island to help defend it.

"Take a look here," Alex said, "I made a few changes. There's a little scoop in the tray now, so it should be easier to get the bottle into the right place. I worked on this lever part, too, so it should be easier to set the spring."

Letitia saw the scoop. The "lever part" looked just like it used to, but when she latched the spring in place, she could feel the difference. Whatever Alex had changed, it made things better.

They spent the morning homing in on LaGuardia. The kids all got practice in assembling the little bombs and casting them far, far away.

Lunchtime came, and everyone took a break for pancakes. Levon still wasn't there.

The children and Alex returned to catapult practice. Alex was amazed to see how fast they could get it done. One buddy pair would handle the mechanism, the other the bomb manufacture. One child would stand on the step plate, and the other would kick the latch in place. The other pair would hand the first an assembled bomb. The first child would set it on the throw plate and light it, then his buddy would kick the latch out. At full speed, they could fire a bomb every twenty seconds.

Letitia started to call out targets: "OK, get the woman in the red dress." "Hit that guy with those green pants." The kids had to work harder at that because they had to set the stop to adjust how far the bomb would fly. It wasn't as fast, but they were getting better, coming within a few feet of the target every time.

When the screaming started, it took a moment for people to hear it over the *fwoosh* of the bombs and the noise of the latches and kicking. By the time Alex had located the source of the sound, Letitia and the kids were already fifty feet ahead of him. He caught up just as Letitia's ax was breaking Levon's legs, Magdalena still desperately trying to wriggle free from his grasp. Jahayra and Kiara had stakes in each of Levon's eyes as soon as he sagged down on his mangled limbs. Magdalena's arm was bleeding profusely, the flesh from a small hole in her forearm now hanging loosely from Levon's mouth.

"Where's Li?" he heard Marie shout. He hoped he didn't know the answer and sprinted along the blood trail to the dorm. Li's head lay there, still silently snarling at them, her eyes staring at the rest of her remains. Rosarita and Malik didn't hesitate, reaming her eye sockets with those little stakes they carried everywhere. The *sflup* sounds made his stomach flip.

The dorm was a mess. The blood from Levon's sliced wrists and Li's blood mixed together in a pool on the floor. No way to tell when one started and the other began.

Meanwhile, Marie and Catalina were trying to save Magdalena. Marie made a quick tourniquet from her shirt to slow down the bleeding. Catalina looked at the wound. The tourniquet was holding things back well enough that the blood was no longer pumping out. That it had been pumping was bad enough, because it meant the bite had nicked an artery. Even if the worst didn't happen, it was going to be hard to stop the bleeding without losing the arm. They led her back to the clinic.

Alex entered the clinic. When Catalina headed to the supply cabinet, he stopped her for a moment.

"I know you need to make her feel comfortable, but get her sedated, and be prepared. You know what's going to happen," he said.

"Do you think it's really as fast as they say?" Catalina asked.

"I don't know. Some people say fifteen minutes, others say an hour, but no one says it's slow."

Magdalena's pulse was irregular by the time Catalina returned to the room. She gave Magdalena a quick shot of local anesthetic. She followed it with a light dose of Brevital, just enough to keep her from thrashing and fighting.

"You aren't going to let me turn into one of them, are you?" Magdalena was frantic.

"We aren't sure what's going to happen, Magdalena. I'll take care of you no matter what happens. You relax, now. Let me take care of you." Magdalena's face relaxed as the Brevital kicked in.

The wound was a ragged crater about an inch deep and two inches across, so there was no hope of suturing it. Catalina cleaned it, packed it with gauze and bandaged it. Blood oozed when the tourniquet was released, but didn't gush or spurt.

The flesh at the edge of the bandage began to turn blue. The bluing spread rapidly up the arm and across the torso, and Magdalena passed out once the bluing reached her neck. All traces of pain left her features as it rose rapidly up her face. Her eyes snapped open. Alex pressed his trenching spike into her eye socket, and Magdalena relaxed one final time.

CHAPTER 68
THE BURIAL

Some wanted to throw Levon on the pile with the zombies they pulled out of the jails, but Catalina wouldn't have it.

"Levon died when those babies died. It just took four days for him to figure it out."

John and Alex dug three graves, right next to Luis. They placed the three bodies in the graves and went to stand with the small crowd.

Catalina crossed herself.

"God

"Bless these three.

"They have done wrong, but they were good people.

"We will miss Magdalena, for she was good, and strong. She helped those that needed help, and was grateful when help was received.

"We will miss Li, for she brought brightness to our lives. She helped those that needed help, and was grateful when help was received.

"We will miss Levon, for he too brought brightness to our lives. He helped those that needed help, and was grateful when help was received.

"Forgive Levon his final day. He was broken, as all is broken around us.

"Please grant us the strength to avoid his path.

"Amen."

CHAPTER 69
A PRAYER FOR CATALINA

God
Please don't do *that* to Catalina again, either.
Please stop.
We just want everything to stop.
Amen

CHAPTER 70
THE GREAT GUINEA PIG ROUNDUP

As September hit, the temperature began drop at night. Jada and Tiara were the first to notice that the guinea pigs were having trouble with it. They found nests of them clustered together to stay warm and found a few lying dead. They picked up a dead one and brought it to Letitia.

Letitia looked at it. "So, it dead. Don' look like it comin' back or nothin'. What you want me to do? You think it need a funeral or somethin'?"

She stopped for a moment, then grinned. "Talk to Lucia. She say she like to eat 'em. Maybe she eat it for lunch."

"I think it just too cold for them," said Jada. Tiara nodded. "Can't we bring them inside?"

"Inside? That many? Brownie and Spot had *lots* of babies. Grandbabies, too, maybe. Where you goin' to put 'em? "

"We got a lot of room where we sleep, don't we?"

"You want to let 'em loose in the room where we sleep?" Yuck. Guinea pig crap everywhere. It stunk bad enough over Sami's when it was just two of them.

Still, even though she joked about Lucia eating them, that's why they were here. Keeping these things alive was the only way she knew to get fresh meat. She played along.

"How you keep 'em from messing the place up? Don' want it so when I walk anywhere I got little bits of guinea pig poo all over my shoes."

Letitia could see their little heads working.

" Can we ask Alex? Maybe he got somethin' over on the big island that'll hold 'em."

"Sure, go ask him. *After* you got your chores done, though."

Jada and Tiara worked their chores as quickly as they could that day. It wasn't too much work today: they had won the morning games, so the other kids had to do the really nasty stuff. All they had to do was weed their section of the garden and gather wood for the cooking grate.

They took their little boat over to Rikers and walked into the dorm. Catalina was there, taking care of her chores. She was surprised to see the two of them by themselves. Letitia by herself wasn't too rare of a sight, but the little ones tended to be an all-or-nothing proposition.

"We lookin' for Alex. You seen him?" asked Tiara.

"Haven't seen him for a little bit. Why do you need him?"

"The guinea pigs are gettin' sick. We think that they too cold at night. Letitia say we can't bring 'em inside unless we can keep 'em from messing up the place. We thought maybe Alex could help us build somethin', or maybe you guys already got somethin'?" Tiara looked hopeful.

Guinea pigs were something Catalina actually knew something about. It felt good for her experience as a veterinary assistant to be useful for something to do with animals instead of stitching up people.

"You're right. It's getting too cold outside for guinea pigs. How many do you have?"

Jada and Tiara consulted with each other. Math not being one of the skills that six-year-olds excel at, this was actually quite a conundrum. After a bit, they gave up.

"We can't count that high. Lots. We see new ones every day."

"Well, I hope it's not *too* many, but I think I've got something that will work." Catalina led them over to one of the kitchens and showed them a wall lined with wire pantry bins.

"Think those will do it?"

Jada and Tiara smiled. Catalina melted a little bit inside. It felt good to see the children so happy. She worked with them to get the bins off the wall. The bins stacked nicely, so the children were able to handle a stack of ten.

"Thanks!" The two gave Catalina a little hug and hurried off with their treasure.

Getting that many bins into their little boat and leaving room for themselves was a bit of a struggle, but they finally arrived at home, the proud owners of ten wire pantry bins. They set the bins by the entryway and got Letitia.

" 'kay, they should work. Now, you just got to catch 'em all."

This became the afternoon's work for the entire group. Dealing with the young ones was tougher than dealing with Brownie and Spot had been since the young ones had never gotten used to people. Still, it turned out to be a matter of coaxing with food. They still had some rodent treats. One by one, the herd was captured.

Jada and Tiara couldn't count that high, but Letitia could. Forty-one. The bins sat on the floor along one wall of the sleeping area, propped up on bricks stolen from one of the collapsed cottages. Letitia solved the poo problem with plastic trays sitting under the cages. Jada and Tiara took over the task of feeding them and keeping things clean.

Eight new arrivals came during the first week and four more the next. Letitia felt pushed. Still, she had to do something. There was such a thing as too many guinea pigs living in your bedroom. After breakfast one morning, she talked to Lucia.

"You sure your neighbor ate those things?"

"*Si*, yes, it was those things, the *cuyes*. I had them once. Is good food. *Saboroso* ... delicious."

Tiara and Jada got angry. "*Eat* them?" Tiara protested. "They *pets*, not food."

"Why you need fifty pets?" asked Letitia. "We got twelve more now than when we started. Twelve more next week, more after that ... Ain't got room for so many pets."

She stopped for a moment.

" 'sides, the reason I said we could bring them in the first place was 'cause Lucia said they was food."

"But we got plenty of food!"

"Sure, but it in boxes. You see anybody makin' more boxes of food? When they run out of boxes over in Rikers, we got to go into the city. Any time we go in the city, there be cucos everywhere. Remember that guy with the gun? Someday, one of you die tryin' to get a box of food.

"Things like the fish, the guinea pigs, the melons, they ain't just food. They food that keep growin' so that we can eat without fightin' anybody. Every day we eat food like that another day that nobody die."

Tiara and Jada continued to fuss.

"OK. Everybody gets to choose one. Don' care how you figure out which ones, but choose 'em. They your pets. I promise you we ain't never goin' to eat 'em.

"The rest, every week we count the new babies, and that how many big ones we cook. That way, we always have some."

It was a lot easier to talk like that than to actually do it. That afternoon, Letitia got out the copy of *Field Dressing and Butchering: Rabbits, Squirrels and Other Small Game* that she had picked up at Buchmans. She looked at the pictures of the cute little bunnies and squirrels being gutted and felt a little sick inside. She closed her eyes and thought of Jorge and Diego, then forced herself to picture Jahayra's head like that, snapping and chattering after the cucos had eaten the rest of her. "Every day we eat somethin' like this a day that nobody die," she said to herself quietly, and forced herself to look at the pictures again.

She studied the pictures and tried to convince herself it was no different than what she did to fish every day. Same two eyes, same guts, just warm and fuzzy instead of cold and scaly. The only really different part she could see from the book was the way you had to cut the skin off before you cooked it.

After the children had each picked a pet, she had Tiara and Jada bring her a bin of three guinea pigs. She pulled one out and looked at it. She sat it down on the big flat rock she used for fish and pulled out her knife.

She couldn't do it. She just couldn't look at the guinea pig and cut its throat.

Rosarita piped up. "Is no so big a deal, Letícia. I do it."

Rosarita took the knife and efficiently sliced the throats of the three animals. Letitia noticed that as tough as Rosarita tried to be, she didn't actually *look*, either. She'd face the pig away, place the blade against the throat, close her eyes, then draw the blade.

Once they were dead, Letitia didn't find the next parts too hard. She skinned and gutted them. This really wasn't too different than the way she dealt with fish, she decided: once the head was off, it stopped looking so *cute*.

The book had different recipes for rabbits and squirrels. Most involved cooking it by poking a stick through it and roasting it, but she decided that wouldn't work the first time. Even if it wasted some meat, she filleted the small animals and cut the flesh into small strips, just so it wouldn't look so much like what it was.

Dinner time came and every child's plate had a small pile of roast guinea pig flesh on the plate. Most stared at the plates. Lucia giggled.

"Is no big deal. Taste *good!*" she declared, and began to eat. The other children watched nervously until, one by one, they took small bites.

Letitia hadn't realized how tired she was of fish. She wasn't sure that she would have liked guinea pig before this all happened, but she was sure that she liked it now.

After dinner, she called Tiara and Jada over.

"Been thinkin'. I think this make you two guinea pig ranchers. That your job now: you make sure everything stay clean, make sure they be healthy, keep 'em fed. Other kids'll do your other chores."

CHAPTER 71
THEOLOGY

"Thank God we've got more than enough bandages," Catalina said as she repaired a small cut on Letitia's leg. "I don't know why they needed quite so many here, but we'll never run out."

" 'Thank God'?" asked Letitia. "What make you still be thankin' *him*?"

"What do you mean?" asked Catalina.

"I mean, I pray in front of the little ones 'cause it make 'em feel better. Ain't you old enough to know better?"

Catalina looked a little stunned. "I don't think you can 'know better' than to thank God, Letitia."

"I do. Look around. Dead people that want to eat you. Everybody dead. Piles of bones so big you can't climb 'em. Dead babies. Islands full of dead people. Prisons full of dead prisoners. Dead *everything*.

"If God some great big powerful guy that do all this great big powerful stuff and make everything, then he hates us. He doin' all this stuff to us. It him that make dead people walk around, it him that lock me in a bathroom for two days listenin' to little kids get eaten, it him that made everybody's mamas run away, it him that set all those people in Hunts Point on fire, it him that do *all* this stuff.

"If I could reach him, I'd hit him with my ax. Kill him if I could. Maybe all this would stop."

Catalina said an extra prayer for Letitia that night. She couldn't shake the feeling that Letitia would be very angry if she knew.

CHAPTER 72
COLD SNAP

In early October, the first real cold snap occurred. Temperatures dropped near freezing overnight. The children didn't find it too bad while they were asleep, as the body heat from each buddy pair helped them stay warm. Tiara and Jada worried about the guinea pigs and got Letitia's permission to put the cages under the blankets with the children. It made the cold night fun and exciting, with the cage under the blankets forming a little tent in each bed.

Getting out of bed was a major chore. They grumbled and complained all the way through breakfast. It had been hard for Letitia to get them excited about the regular "stab the box" race this morning, and none of them wanted to get too far from the cooking fires.

Letitia decided it was time to go back to the Bronx and find some warmer clothes. In May, she had selected t-shirts and tennis shoes. Now, she needed jackets, sweaters, and boots.

Letitia went over to Rikers and found Alex and Chris.

"We got to go over to the city to get some warmer clothes. Think you two can come along to help?"

"Sure," Alex said. Chris nodded.

"That sounds like a good break," Marie said, "I'll come too."

Letitia frowned. Alex and Chris were her idea of help. Alex seemed smart. She didn't know Chris very well yet, but he hadn't done anything stupid, either. What could Marie do to help?

"Why you want to come along? There ain't be nothin' to cook on the trip," she said.

Marie was obviously irritated. "I think you'll find that I'm at least as useful as a five-year-old, Letitia."

Letitia had her doubts, but could see she was getting nowhere. Adults were like that sometimes, and there just wasn't much she could do about it.

They went back to North Brother and picked up the children.

"Look to me like that spot by the Coca-Cola plant the best place to go," said Letitia. "Our old place by Baretto Park is all burnt up."

"Where are you talking about?" asked Alex. Letitia handed him the binoculars and pointed at the little beach.

"That where the people that used to live here always used to get in and out of their boats."

The crossing was uneventful. They tied the boats together to a post and got onto the beach. Letitia had a quick discussion with Rosarita and Malik.

"I'm going to leave you here with the boats. Stay out of sight, 'kay?"

"OK," said Rosarita and Malik, looking a little glum.

"If someone try to steal the boats, try to just get them out on the water. Stay where we can see you when we get back, 'kay?"

"OK," said Rosarita and Malik, not looking much more pleased.

"If you can't get the boats on the water, it all right if you go ahead and kill them."

"OK!" said Rosarita and Malik, more cheerfully this time.

Chris started to object, but Alex interrupted him.

"No, she's right. We can't let anyone steal the boats."

Marie was livid.

"You're going to leave a couple of five-year-old kids by themselves on a riverbank and tell them to kill anybody that gives them trouble? Are you *serious*?"

"Don't really see what else to do, Marie. You'd rather I sent seven of them alone into a burnt-out city armed with garden stakes? Just so they can find a Foot Locker?"

Marie just wouldn't have it. Finally, Marie said that she would stay here. Rosarita and Malik protested. Letitia seized the opportunity to be rid of her and told Rosarita and Malik to be quiet.

There was a drainage culvert here, with a small fence at the top. They climbed up. As they walked towards the city, Letitia tried to comfort Alex. "Don't worry," she said. "Rosarita and Malik will take care of her."

CHAPTER 73
THIRD AVENUE

They headed for the shopping district on Third Avenue. The ecology that was establishing itself in man's absence was all above street level. Anything that lived on the street had been fair game for the cucos which meant that the dogs were gone. Feral cats, on the other hand, were everywhere. They perched on windowsills and rooftops, occasionally swooping down to street level chasing a small rodent. The bird population was thriving as well: flitting about, chasing insects, eating seeds, and getting chased by the cats. The only life at street level was the grass and weeds. Every crack in the sidewalk was a miniature forest, with the roots cracking the sidewalks and roadways further apart. In fifty years, the Bronx would be as covered with vines and trees as North Brother Island.

Chris and Alex were amazed to watch the pattern as the kids moved their way down the street. Left to themselves, they would have just strolled along. With the kids, it was like having their own portable war movie. The lead pair would move forward to an intersection or obstacle, scanning as they went. When they got there, they would signal the group to catch up. Every time there was anything they couldn't see around, it was treated as a military objective.

Flames from the car wall had done a lot of damage here. The brick and concrete wasn't badly damaged, but the roofs of many of the buildings were burnt away, and the interiors were gutted. The I Am Park was scorched, the grass and trees burnt away during the long nights of fire. By the time they got to Third Avenue, things were looking relatively intact. Heavily looted, but not burnt.

The Kids Foot Locker was untouched. As usual, no one seemed to want to bother to loot the stores that kids needed. Everyone had fun trying on the selection of boots and shoes. At this age, six months was a *long* time to wear the same size of shoes.

Everybody got a pair of low boots in their size and one pair one size bigger. Letitia guessed for Rosarita and Malik. The nearby V.I.M. store had a good range of warmer clothes, including some light jackets. There had been a clearance sale in progress in April, with most of the coats marked 75% off. The remnants of the sale were enough to choose from.

Loaded with clothes, they began heading back to the dock.

CHAPTER 74

ON THE BEACH

Marie, Rosarita, and Malik stayed by the boats. Rosarita and Malik played along the river's edge. Five months had done a lot to clean up the East River, so there were all kinds of interesting things to look at and play with: mainly small fish and crabs, but Malik had found a small diamondback terrapin. He would pick it up, carry it away from shore, then watch as it crawled its way back towards the water, where he would pick it up again and repeat the cycle. Like most small boys, this was a game that could entertain him for hours.

Rosarita wasn't such a big turtle fan. There were lots of pretty rocks along the shore to keep her entertained, and she began sorting through them, making a pile of them, sorting out the ones that met her personal standards of beauty from the ones that did not.

Marie smiled as she watched them. She tended to think of them as a tribe of savages, but, at times like these, you could see they were still little kids. She remembered playing with her brother by a lake near her grandfather's house and playing much the same games. It may have been frogs instead of turtles and shells instead of rocks, but it still had a cozy, familiar feel to it.

Cozy and familiar, that is, until you noticed the sharpened stakes and the way they hung so close to each other. She didn't ever see them get ten feet from each other. When they were apart, you could tell that each knew precisely where the other one was.

"See, Jim, I knew I saw boats! And look here!" came a voice from behind Marie. She stood up and immediately felt a pair of hands clutch her from behind.

Rosarita and Malik instantly sprang to alert. There were at least a dozen men at the fence along the end of 149th Street. The one down below had Marie firmly in his grasp, one hand wrapped tightly around her waist. They weren't sure what to do. They knew that if Letitia had a choice between losing the boats and losing Marie, Letitia would lose Marie. They leapt for the boats and began to loosen the ties so they could get out on the water.

The men didn't seem interested in the boats, though. The man with a grip on Marie had taken her shirt off and was starting to work on her pants. Malik was confused. These men were *big*. A lot bigger than Marie. Her shirt was too small for them. Her pants would be, too. Why were they trying to steal her clothes?

A man in a bright green shirt came down and grabbed Marie's arms. Marie kept crying and saying that the men could do what they wanted as long as they didn't hurt the kids.

"They can do what they want? She say it OK to take her clothes?" Rosarita asked Malik. The men didn't even look like they were thinking about the kids, much less wanting to hurt them.

"I dunno. I wish Letitia was here. She know what to do."

At this point, Marie's pants were off, but the men didn't try to take them. They just threw them in the river. The crowd started to yell.

"Leave some of that for me!"

"Don't use her all up!"

"Jesus, look at her!"

The first man had his pants off now too, and the man in the green shirt was holding Marie down. The first man started to lay down on top of Marie. She was crying harder now, and kicking.

"I think we gotta stop 'em," Malik said. "I'm sure they hurtin' her now."

Rosarita nodded. They opened their backpacks, and in twenty seconds the dozen men on the street were in flames, the Molotov cocktail having burst immediately in front of them. Malik clipped the top of the small fence with the second bottle. It burst quite spectacularly, with flaming gasoline spraying directly into the faces of several of the men.

"That enough?" asked Malik.

"One more," said Rosarita. "They not all burning yet." She was satisfied after the third.

Rosarita and Malik ran towards Marie. The man on Marie turned to face the new noise, so they staked his eye sockets. The other one began to run for the top.

Rosarita and Malik each grabbed one of Marie's hands and tugged on her until she stumbled her way towards the boats. They pushed her into a supply raft, leapt into their pontoon boat, and cast off. They began to paddle off. When they got out in the water, they began to steadily row against the current, holding the boats in place until Letitia came back.

"We in trouble with Letitia again?" asked Malik.

"*Es posible,*" Rosarita replied, "I no understand Letícia sometimes." She looked at Marie, curled up in a ball in the raft, naked and sobbing. "I no think so. I no understand what they doing, but it must have been very bad, or she no cry that way."

CHAPTER 75
THE MAN IN THE GREEN SHIRT

As the shopping expedition approached the shore, they saw a man in a bright green shirt standing on top of a small stack of cars, with several charred cucos trying to climb the stack to reach him. They couldn't get him, but, at the same time, there was no way for him to get down. Some of the cucos appeared to be nearly whole, but there were shreds of bodies lying around, and blood everywhere.

Neither Alex or Chris was a great shot. They took aim and fired, but all they did was get the cucos' attention. Letitia looked at them with disdain.

"Stop shooting!" she scolded, sounding much like Mrs. Robinson always had when kids were chattering in the back of the room. She had seen what happened when the Hunts Point guys tried to shoot cucos during the fuel runs. The first thing the shots did was bring more cucos.

She found what she was looking for: a basement apartment entrance with a security fence around it. She pointed at it, and all the kids ran for it. It took Chris and Alex a moment, but they got the idea. They all huddled in the stairway, and, as always, the cucos began to press their faces up against the bars, making them easy targets for the stakes.

"Don't *ever* shoot them in a place like this," said Letitia. "Think we should try to save that guy?" she asked.

Chris and Alex both thought they should. Letitia climbed up on Alex's shoulders and jumped out of the enclosure. She ran towards the cucos, waving her arms. A few broke off from the mob, so she ran back to the basement entrance. After she jumped inside, the children would stake the eye sockets. She repeated until there were only two left.

"I don't think we should let that guy go until we know what's happened here," Alex said. Chris nodded agreement. They walked towards the stack and drove spikes through the skulls of the remaining two cucos. The man began to run. Chris and Alex each grabbed an elbow.

"Hey, calm down! We're not gonna hurt you or anything!" said Chris.

The man still struggled. Alex and Chris tightened their grips.

They walked that way towards the culvert, each on one side of the man, holding his arms firmly, forcing him to walk. His constant struggle reinforced Alex's feeling that something was up.

Lucia and Maria went ahead as advance scouts. Rosarita and Malik came to shore as soon as they spotted them. By the time the main group was to the culvert, they were retying the boats.

Marie looked up and saw the man in the green shirt. She held out her hand to Rosarita.

"Give me that stake, please," she said.

Rosarita looked over at Malik. Malik nodded, so she did. They still didn't quite know what was going on, but they knew that this was the first time that Marie had stopped crying in hours.

"What the hell is going on?" Alex's brain was frantically trying to decipher the scene in front of him: the corpse with its eyes reamed out lying on the ground, the angry nude woman climbing the hill, the smell of gasoline, the burnt remnants of clothing, and the increasingly frantic man next to him.

Marie took Rosarita's stake, placed it against the man's throat, and pressed upwards with all her might. The man lay slack in Chris and Alex's grip.

"Tomorrow," she said, "you are going to teach the kids how to shoot."

CHAPTER 76
SPECIAL TREATMENT

When they got back to Rikers Island, all the adults huddled together away from the children. Letitia couldn't really make any sense of the story she got from Rosarita and Malik, but she could tell that none of the adults were mad at them for killing those men. No one was mad at Marie, either, and she was running around naked and killing people.

When the adults were done talking and Marie wasn't naked anymore, they were invited for dinner. Before dinner, everyone gave Rosarita and Malik great big hugs. They weren't sure how to take the special attention, but Letitia told them just to smile and be happy.

When dessert came, Rosarita and Malik got served first and got the biggest slices of pie.

Letitia couldn't take it anymore. She drew Catalina aside.

"Catalina, what happened today?" she asked.

"Some bad men tried to hurt Marie," Catalina said, hoping it would be enough, but knowing it wouldn't be.

"I know *that*," said Letitia, "but it still don' make no sense. Why they try to steal her pants? Why she cry so hard? Why it all right to *kill* people for tryin' to steal pants? Why it all right for Marie to drive a stake through that man's head? I keep tryin' to tell Rosarita and Malik that it no good to keep killin' people. This time, you give 'em *pie* because they did. I tryin' to figure out how to stop 'em, and you giving 'em *pie*. I just don' understand why you doin' that."

Catalina looked a little sad, the kind of sad where you can't help but smile at the same time. She reached over and gave Letitia a hug. Letitia tensed, but tried to relax.

"Honey, please don't even try to understand," she said.

Letitia gave up.

CHAPTER 77
A PRAYER FOR MARIE

God

Thank you for letting us find new boots and clothes. It's good to be warm again.

Please take care of Marie.

Catalina says I'm too young to know what happened, but I don't understand how I can be too young for anything anymore?

Whatever it was, please don't let it happen to us, too.

I hope Rosarita and Malik did the right thing. I told them that they did, so I hope that good with you.

Amen

CHAPTER 78
PLUMBING

Letitia was insistent. "We ain't givin' the little ones no guns," Letitia said. "Just ain't goin' to happen."

Marie resisted. "If you had guns, you wouldn't be setting people on fire. If they'd been able to point guns at them yesterday, none of that would have happened."

Alex shook his head. "I'm not sure about that. If they had guns yesterday, they may have just gotten shot instead. The only reason it turned out well yesterday was because they surprised them." Surprised *him* too, he thought. The way the kids didn't seem to understand that they should feel bad about killing those men shook him in a way he tried not to think about.

"Look," Letitia said, "it just don't work, anyway. I *got* a gun. Tried to use it one time, nearly broke my arm and knocked me on my butt. One of the little ones try it, just goin' to knock 'em around, kill somebody by accident."

Marie was insistent. Alex told her the story of dealing with the zombies on 149th Street. He pointed out just how well Rosarita and Malik had done with the level of armament they normally carried. She finally relented. Still, though, she wanted some kind of major rewards bestowed on the kids.

"If you really want to do somethin' special," Letitia said, "figure out how we can have heat. Winter coming. You guys don't want to run electricity, and I *can't* run electricity. You goin' to need heat too."

Alex actually had been thinking about this. It was still mid-October, so it was only a bit cool. Everyone had to snuggle with someone at night, but that wasn't a big deal. They had a decent supply of diesel. As long as they didn't try to heat entire buildings, they should be able to get by with steam heat.

"There are radiators in the room you sleep in, aren't there?"

"You mean them metal things hooked to the wall? Yeah, but they don't work."

"They won't work by themselves. They need hot water. But if there are radiators in there, there must be a boiler. That place is old enough, it might be a coal boiler, and we could get that working with wood."

Alex, Chris and John took the boat over to North Brother Island to see what they could do.

"Have you noticed any rooms that have big machines in them? Big piles of black rocks?"

"Naw, nothin' like that," answered Letitia. "But I don' go around on the first floor much. So full of vines and bushes you can't get nowhere, and there ain't nothin' to *get*, anyway."

"Let's just look for the cellar," said John. "If it's coal-fired, they had to load the coal into the cellar from an outside door, and the boiler will be right by that."

They took a couple of Letitia's spare hatchets and started to work their way around the building. An hour of hacking and cutting later, they were back at the front of the building.

"No coal doors? How on earth did they heat this place?"

"We're really stupid, you know that?" said Alex. "Look at the roof. No smokestack anywhere. Can't be a coal boiler for a place this size without a smokestack."

"Only place with a smokestack is that place over by the pier," Chris replied.

The three walked over to the large squat building by the pier, a building with twin smokestacks rising five stories above the roof. They walked up the stairway and entered a room dominated by enormous water tanks, a series of pumps, and a boiler. Large pipes ran off the boiler and plunged into a basement.

"There's the answer. Steam tunnels. If you want to use this to heat the hospital, you're going to have to heat the whole island."

"We've got to rethink this. The kids don't need anything fancy. We don't even know how to do anything fancy. I say that we just grab one of the hot water tanks from Rikers and set it over a fire pit. Hook it to the pipes and they'll have heat."

"I don't want to do anything like that inside. No way. If we do that, we set it outside and run the pipes."

They argued for hours. Finally, Chris said "Let's just go shopping. We went right by a heating supply shop yesterday, so let's go see what they've got."

CHAPTER 79
MATERNITY WARD

Catalina had never expected being a veterinary assistant would lead to becoming a doctor, but she was doing her best to take the transition in stride. Kiara was doing well, and everyone seemed to expect Catalina to perform similar miracles with everyone. She did her best to live up to that. It helped that nobody was getting seriously ill. The worst that happened to people was a scrape or cut from doing the work around the island. She would clean the wounds, bandage them up, and send them on their way. There was the occasional bout of indigestion or diarrhea, but nothing serious.

Angela was a different question. She was nearly eight months pregnant now, which meant that she could deliver any day. Catalina had only assisted with a pregnant horse. Once. She felt no more prepared to deliver a baby than she did to go to the moon. Didn't matter much: she was going to have to try.

Angela came in for her checkup that morning. Catalina did everything she knew how to do: took Angela's temperature, verified that the cervix wasn't dilated (it wasn't, to her relief), and that she could hear the baby's heartbeat (she could, to her relief).

"The baby is still kicking?"

"Oh, certainly," Angela said, "there are days that I feel like I'm growing a football team."

"Any bleeding?"

"No, none at all," she replied.

"Abnormal discharge?" Catalina continued straight down the list, and got reassuring answers to each one.

At the end, Catalina closed her notebook and made reassuring noises. Angela visibly relaxed.

Catalina felt like she had done her job. She understood the value of reassuring noises. She just wished that someone would make them at *her*.

CHAPTER 80
BE PREPARED

Marie didn't insist on coming this time. There was more than a bit of arguing about whether the kids should come at all, but Letitia made it pretty clear that the issue was not whether the children would be safe, it was whether Alex, Chris, and John would be safe without them.

"How you get by without learning how to fight cucos, anyway?" Letitia asked.

"Well, that's not quite fair," said Chris. "I learned how to fight them. It was just always from on top of a semi with an assault rifle. What's your excuse, Alex?"

"Same kind of thing, really. The army evacuated us, and they did the fighting for us. When we swam off to Mills Rock, there weren't any of them there. When we needed supplies, we'd go down to Roosevelt Island and get some of them to go with us. It was always a group of a dozen guys, and some of them had some pretty big guns. I mainly just carried stuff and let other guys fight."

Chris looked down at Letitia. "Are you guys *always* armed?"

"Yeah."

"What are you packing right now?"

"Got my hatchet on my belt. Got a smaller one in my backpack. Got a bottle of gasoline and a rag. Got a lighter in my pocket. Got a hunting knife in my backpack and a pocket knife in my pocket."

"What do you do at night?"

"I use my backpack as a pillow. Everyone does."

"How about the little kids?"

"Everybody got a stake. One buddy carry the fire, the other carry the gasoline. Everybody got a pocket knife and a hunting knife."

They contemplated that for a moment. The realization that dinner with the kids meant that they were surrounded by incendiary weaponry didn't set well.

They made the journey back to 149th Street.

"This time," Letitia said to Rosarita and Malik, "run first. Ain't nobody here to save. I don' want there be no more dead people when I get back."

Rosarita and Malik seemed highly displeased.

The trip to Automatic Heating Supply supplied just what they needed. They had tankless boilers, which were nothing more than twisted manifolds of copper tubing that you could set straight into a fire. They had pressure-relief valves. They had big coils of plastic tubing and fitting adapters.

On the way back, they stopped at Bruckner Building Supply to pick up some missing pieces. Letitia hadn't been in here before, and her eyes lit up when she saw the supply of gardening tools. There was a thing called a Mini Planter Pick that she had never known she needed until she saw one. It was the size of a hammer, with a large straight point on one side and a curved point on the other. She held the grip firmly and took some practice swings in the air.

She looked around and saw some large bags of fertilizer. After a few full power swings, driving the point as deep as she could into the bag, she was satisfied. She removed the hatchet from her belt, slid it into her backpack, and hung the pick on her belt with care.

CHAPTER 81
ONE IS THE LONELIEST NUMBER

Angela came in for her checkup. She sat down on the exam table, smiling, but obviously tired.

"This kid never seems to sleep anymore, Catalina," she said. "All night long, it's kick, kick, kick. Are you sure it's not triplets taking turns?"

"I'm sure," Catalina said, smiling. "The only heartbeats in there are yours and one baby's."

She took her stethoscope out, placing it on Angela's belly. She heard the distinct sounds of the baby moving and shifting in the womb. It even seemed to fight back against the pressure of the stethoscope, as babies often press back in response to pressure. Try as she might, she could only hear one heartbeat. Angela's.

She did her best to look unconcerned, and continued. Angela's temperature was normal, and her cervix was just barely dilated, less than a centimeter. Angela seemed fine, and the baby was certainly active.

She checked one more time with the stethoscope and made soothing noises at Angela while she felt her own inside curl into a tight ball at the thought of the dead thing Angela was carrying inside her. Today, Catalina needed someone to make soothing noises at her more than ever before.

She went over to where John and Alex were installing the radiators they had liberated from North Brother Island.

"I think we have a real problem on our hands," Catalina began.

They looked at her expectantly. Usually, the "problem" had to do with clogged plumbing or some other mundane thing, but they could sense this was more.

"Angela's baby is dead, but it's still in there. Moving."

"Is Angela all right?" was John's first question.

"I checked everything I know how to check, and I *think* so. I think it's just like the babies in the nursery. There aren't any teeth, so it can't bite. No nails, so it can't scratch. It's no stronger than a fetus would be, so it can't do much. It doesn't sleep anymore, and Angela's noticing that."

"Do you think she can deliver it?" Alex asked.

"That's what I really don't know. If it was a regular stillbirth, she'd deliver it in a couple of weeks. She's due in about four weeks, anyway, so that isn't much different."

"Jesus ...What do you think we should do?" asked Alex.

"I think we need to take a trip down to Roosevelt Island. They may still have a real doctor there, and I'd love to talk to a real doctor. If not, they've got a much better medical supply than we've got. If I have to do this, I'm going to want to have it under control by inducing labor. This is going to be crazy enough without it happening at 2AM and taking three days."

"What do we tell Chris and Angela?"

"Just that I want to go and get some better supplies. There's no reason for them to be panicking until I'm able to do something about it."

They tried not to make a big production of it. Letitia noticed them going silently down the river. There was something that made her uncomfortable. She liked these people enough, but they just didn't seem careful enough. They were keeping something secret, too.

"Jahayra, Kiara, come over here," she called.

They ran over.

"You two watch over the big dock today. Take a game or somethin', but I want to know as soon as you see a boat come back up the river."

Letitia decided to go up to the roof. She had some things to think about and plans to make. She could do them from there.

CHAPTER 82
ROOSEVELT ISLAND

Catalina and Alex were struck by the increasing density of zombies as they moved south. LaGuardia was nearly cleared off, Hunts Point was burnt flat, and the Bronx area had been cleared out by the fires. Not so as they approached Roosevelt Island.

The theory that generators drew zombies appeared to be well-founded. Alex wouldn't swear it was the hum, like Letitia did, but the shores next to Roosevelt Island were teeming with the undead. On Rikers, you could nearly forget why you were there. The only daily reminders were the piles of bones. Catalina still prayed over each pile every morning, but she thought of them as the dead, not as the undead. Here, it was clearly the land of the undead. Zombies lined the shore, agitated by the pair's presence as they glided by in the aluminum rowboat.

Roosevelt Island itself was clear. Electric lights dotted the hospital facility, and people were moving freely around the island. Alex thought it was just as likely the light and activity that drew zombies as the hum, himself. He didn't want to run experiments.

There was a small beach in Lighthouse Park. They landed their boat on the beach and were immediately confronted by a couple of armed men.

"Take it easy," said Alex. "We're just here to talk. We used to work with you guys every once in a while when we lived on Mills Rock. Jim still in charge here?"

"Yeah, Jim's still in charge here. We'll take you to him," said the taller of the two guards. "We'll be needing those guns first, though."

Alex thought about resisting, but decided that they really didn't have a right to. Their island, their rules. He wouldn't much like it if a stranger was packing heat on Rikers.

They were marched into the lobby of the Coler Goldwater campus. It looked strangely cheery and normal: bright electric lights, electric heat, the hum of vending machines.

Jim had moved into the main administrative office. He even had a secretary. She buzzed them in.

"Hello," Jim said. He turned to the guards and chatted a bit. "You can wait outside for now," he said, finally.

"You said that you used to work with us?" he continued.

"Well, mainly doing some foraging runs. We always lived up on Mills Rock."

"Aah, I remember now. The group with the little blonde? And the Chinese girl?"

"Yeah, that would be Marie and Li. Li's dead now, though."

"Sorry to hear that. What happened?"

They went through a brief history of what had transpired since they had moved to Rikers, complete with the clearing of the dormitories and trying to get the basics of life established.

"What brings us down here today," Alex went on, "is medical. One of the women is pregnant, and the baby has died inside her. We could use some better medical supplies, or maybe even a doctor to talk with. We have stuff we could trade, if you want."

"Trade?" Jim asked.

"Oh, yeah. Rikers fed its inmates a lot of freeze-dried and powdered stuff, so we've got food. Diesel generators all over that we don't run, so we've got fuel to trade as well."

Jim looked very interested. "Diesel? We can always use diesel."

Alex nodded.

"Wait here a bit. I'll go see if we've got a doctor that wants to come up and help with this," Jim said as he left the office.

CHAPTER 83

BEING USEFUL

The sound of powerboats had already caught Letitia's ear when Kiara and Jahayra came running up the stairs to the roof.

"Quick. Go get everybody! Now!" Letitia told them. She used her binoculars to look at the boats. There were lots of men on those boats, and none of them looked friendly. They were all dressed in riot gear: black pants, black gloves, thick long-sleeved black shirts, and helmets with faceplates. Kevlar vests went over the black shirts, while shin guards and arm guards completed their armor. They pulled into the ferry slip and started to tie off.

Pedro and Juan ran out to see what was happening. They raised their hands over their heads as the lead man aimed a gun at them. A couple of other men ran over and began to frisk them.

Letitia had seen enough. "Get the bombs going! Hit the boats!" she shouted at the kids coming up the stairs.

Letitia kept the catapult aimed at the ferry slip, and they had tested it a few times at night with soda cans. The first couple of Molotov cocktails missed, but they had the range dialed in with the third. A rain of fire from above came down on the boats, and no one knew where to return fire.

She wished that she had let Marie force people into giving them shooting lessons. There was no way to get rid of the three that had gotten off the boat without getting rid of Pedro and Juan, too. She wasn't as used to killing people as Rosarita and Malik and didn't want to be.

Letitia had learned one lesson from the attack on Marie: using gas bombs on live people left cucos. She was just going to have to believe that the adults weren't completely helpless and concentrate on what she could do best. She kept an eye on the boat, and, whenever anything got up, she sent over another volley to knock it back down.

She'd take care of those thirty. The adults were going to have to handle the last three.

CHAPTER 84
RESISTANCE

Marie was just getting ready to start dinner when she heard the boats. Curious, she started to head out the door when she head the *fwoomp* of the Molotovs going off. She noticed it was coming from the wrong direction: at the pier instead of the runway. She grabbed three of the sharpest knives she had and motioned Angelica and Angela towards the food service refrigerator. It was empty and dark, but had a nice secure metal door. They closed the door and hid in the dark, waiting.

John and Chris were still working on the radiators when they heard the powerboats. "Hey, that was quick," said John. "Catalina and Alex are back already..."

He was relieved, because he was having a really hard time talking to Chris without letting on that there was something wrong with Angela. The feeling of relief quickly evaporated when the sound of the Molotovs started. They started to run towards the docks.

"You come in from that way, I'll hook around this way. Let's see what the hell is going on!"

Chris jogged over towards the north. They weren't as good at the military rhythm as the kids, but they weren't idiots, either, despite anything Letitia might think. By the time they got near the docks, most of the initial action was over. The boats were in flames, sinking slowly into the river. Three strangers were shouting at Juan and Pedro while they held guns on them.

"Tell me where those bombs are coming from, Pedro, or you'll get this in the gut!" the large one said, gesturing towards them with his gun. The man's tone made it clear that he had no clue that Pedro's name actually *was* "Pedro."

Pedro genuinely had no clue. He had never been on North Brother Island and couldn't conceive that they were being firebombed by five-year-olds.

"I don't know. I really don't!" he protested.

It was a lot harder to be brave than he had thought it would be. He'd always thought guys in the movies that gave it all up instantly were silly little cowards. Now, faced with a bunch of guys with helmets and guns, with explosions going off everywhere and the smell of burning flesh in his nose, it was everything he could do to hold onto his bowels.

He may be a coward, he thought, but he wasn't going to do that. He wasn't going to shit his pants with these men watching.

"I really, really, really don't know. If I did, I'd tell you, but I don't."

John saw a few figures begin to rise from the boats. He was trying to figure out if they were alive or dead, when suddenly it didn't matter. A fresh Molotov fell from the sky and set them all back ablaze.

The leader squeezed off a burst, nearly reflexively. Pedro no longer had any choice about his bowels, as they were lying in several pieces around him. The leader turned to Juan. "Where the fuck are those coming from?"

Chris saw that he had a clear shot at the back of the leaders head: a small area the helmet didn't come down to and the flak vest didn't rise up to. He steadied his arm and tried to remember everything he'd been taught.

Brace.

Sight.

Don't hold your breath.

Squeeze, don't pull.

The shot went true. The leader's brains splattered forward, coating the interior of the face shield, just as Pedro rose up and lunged for one of the guards; his teeth clamping down ineffectively on the thick black riot gear. The guard pressed his gun to Pedro's temple and fired. He was worried about gasoline bombs and worried about phantom shooters, but he wasn't worried about zombies.

John circled around to join Chris.

"Come on ... there's nothing we can do to save Juan. If we rush him, they're going to shoot him. If we leave them alone, maybe they'll just drop him. They're not in a rush to start shooting."

Chris and John headed back towards the Kross Center, intercepting those they met along the way, sending them to South Brother Island instead of North Brother Island, since it was a much easier swim and wouldn't draw attention to the kids.

"Where are Angela and Marie?" Chris asked.

"They should be in the kitchen, shouldn't they? This time of day?"

They worked their way over there. This was a spot where they had an advantage: the attackers had no idea where people might be on the island, and Rikers had a lot of places to hide. That meant a lot of places for the attackers to look, most of them wrong.

CHAPTER 85
ON THE ROOF

Letitia saw John sneak up and knew someone was near him because it hadn't been John that shot the guard. When they started to run for it, she guessed it was Chris. The swimming had confused her, because she couldn't believe they were trying to swim here. It was a long way, and she didn't want anyone following them here. She was relieved when she saw they were going to the other island.

"Rosarita! Malik!" Letitia called out. "Get a bunch of the bombs out of the storage room and get over to the little island. It look like the adults goin' there. Get the bombs to them on the island. When you done with that, use your boat to help get people out of the water."

At least she was sure Rosarita and Malik wouldn't freeze up. If they had to use those things, they would. Rosarita and Malik grabbed a couple of small boxes out of the storage room, put a dozen bottles in them, then headed for their boat.

The tower of smoke from the boats reached high into the sky. Dense and black, it cast a dark shadow straight across the East River, right across Hunts Point.

The guards still hadn't done anything to Juan. Maybe they had figured out she hadn't thrown a bomb at them because it would hurt him. When the next round of stirring occurred on the boat she decided to leave the cucos alone and see if Juan could run away during a fight.

CHAPTER 86
COLD STORAGE

Chris and John made it to the kitchen. None of the women were in sight. They looked for hiding places and spotted the stainless steel doors of the refrigerator at about the same time. John opened the door. Marie leapt out, checking her knife blow in the nick of time.

Angela and Angelica were in the corner, with Angela reclining into a pillow made out of clothing.

Chris ran over to Angela. "You're all right, aren't you?"

"Tired and scared, but all right. Baby's just kicking so hard all the time that I'm worn out. Needed to rest. What's going on?"

"Couple of guys with guns on the island," Chris replied. "It was some kind of invasion, but the kids got most of it stopped with the gasoline bombs. We're getting everyone to swim over to the little island while we get it taken care of."

"Swim to a different island? Are you *kidding* me?"

"You still float, hon. We may have to get you some help, but you're not staying here while this is going on."

John interrupted. "Nobody in sight. Let's make a run for it, and get them off the island. Have you seen Raul and Nate yet?"

"No sign of 'em. We've got to hope they can take care of themselves right now. Let's get these three safe." Chris helped Angela to her feet.

The five of them scurried to shore, Angela doing her best not to slow them down. The East River was cold in late October, but not deadly, as long as they kept moving. Marie and Angelica plunged in and headed for South Brother Island. John and Chris each hooked an arm into one of Angela's and began to swim, Angela lying on her back as the two men pulled her through the cold water.

About halfway to the island, a rope suddenly appeared in front of them, attached to the little pontoon boat holding Rosarita and Malik. They hitched the rope around Angela's waist and focused on keeping her above water and calm while Rosarita and Malik rowed the trio to shore.

Getting to shore, John took a quick roll call. Raul and Nate were still missing, as were George and LuAnn.

"Where are the rest of you kids?" John asked.

"Up on the hospital roof," Rosarita answered. "Letícia told us to bring you some bombs and help anybody out of the water."

John smiled. The Molotovs would come in handy.

"Everybody, stay here. Get into the brush and stay low. Most of you have guns, and you know how to use the Molotovs. It's not going to do anyone any good for all of us to be staring at an assault rifle. Chris, come with me: I'm going to the roof to see what's going on."

CHAPTER 87
THE CONTAINER YARD

Raul and Nate were in the container yard when everything started. There were hundreds of shipping containers on Rikers, holding all kinds of things that were in the midst of being shipped on or off the island, and, in some cases, just acting as warehouse space. One of the tedious jobs was going through the containers one by one and building an inventory.

The explosion came just as they were sorting through a container which proved, in the end, to contain nothing but computer paper. It had never occurred to either of them that anyone would ever need 2560 cubic feet of computer paper, but there it was.

"Maybe we could have a big paper airplane contest," Raul joked, "or the kids could use it to run that heater Chris built for them." Then came the noise of the gasoline bombs. They ran towards the dock.

"Stop!" said Nate when he got his first look. "Those are semi-autos. We can't go up against those."

As they ran back towards LaGuardia, they ran into George and LuAnn coming the other direction.

"You don't want to go up there unarmed," Nate said, "I don't know what's going on exactly, but Pedro's dead, and they've got Juan. They're all dressed up in riot gear, and they've got automatics."

George and LuAnn joined them. George actually *had* a fully-automatic pistol, the only one on the island. That didn't mean he liked two-against-one odds, or that he had an infinite supply of ammunition. A full-auto wasn't much good against something that could only get killed with a precise head shot, and he hadn't planned on using the thing to shoot people.

When they got back to the catapults, they found only a handful of filled bottles next to a pile of empties and a gas can with a couple of gallons in it. They gathered the supplies and ran back to the containers. There was a small stepladder leaning against one. They climbed on top of a container and started to fill bottles.

CHAPTER 88
CORNER OFFICE WITH A VIEW

Alex was kicking himself. Jim had only been out of the office ten minutes when the boats took off. He had tried to tell himself that they were going after something on the shore, but the riot gear didn't seem to fit that. When he saw the column of smoke rising from the north, he knew. He could see from Catalina's face that she understood what it meant as well.

He shouldn't have been so trusting. "Hey, we have lots of valuable stuff! There's only a few of us to defend a huge stockpile of everything you need!" just wasn't the smartest thing he'd ever said. He continued to forget that the zombies were the easy enemies.

They were on the ground floor, in an office with floor-to-ceiling windows. They hadn't taken the spikes he and Catalina carried, but those were the only weapons he had left. He didn't think they were going to let him out the front door, but he didn't see any guards around the windows.

"Catalina," he said, "we're going to have to run for it. I think we should be able to get out the window. I don't think we should even try to get out the front door."

"What made Jim turn like this?" she asked.

"Too many people needing too much stuff too much of the time. They must be running out, or he wouldn't have taken off so quickly. C'mon, let's see what the spikes can do against these windows."

He swung hard, putting his full weight into it. The safety glass shattered and a small hole appeared, but the glass stayed in its frame. The two of them worked on the hole, pushed their way out, and ran north.

It was clear that no one had even thought of them as important. They weren't being tricked so much as ignored. There were no squadrons of armed guards in their way. The guard at the top of Blackwell Lighthouse was the sole exception, constantly shouting things like "Stop! Or I'll shoot!"

"What now?" Catalina asked.

"I think he's shouting that loudly because he's scared to pull the trigger," Alex said. "Guys that really want to shoot you just shoot. I'll move up closer, and we'll see what happens."

Alex walked ahead, leaving Catalina in the entryway to a small building. Alex was nearly right: the guard didn't shoot until Alex was ten feet from the boat. When he did, he shot the boat.

Alex ran back. "What now?" Alex asked.

"We've got to get back," Catalina said. "Who knows how many people are hurt?"

"The only way back is through that," Alex said, gesturing at the horde lining the shore.

"Not really," she said. "Look over towards Astoria. They aren't as thick over there on the point. It's the lights and noise that are attracting them, and that's pulling them south. It's only five or six hundred feet. It's our best hope."

Alex wanted to argue with her, but he couldn't. There wasn't another way home. They strapped their spikes to their belts and dove in.

The current was on their side, pushing them north at about 4 knots. Cold and shaking, they made it to Astoria before getting out of the water. They desperately wanted to stand by a fire, but that wasn't going to happen. They were going to have to warm up on the run.

They took one more look over towards Roosevelt Island. Three large rowboats were on the way north, holding maybe twenty people. Maybe they were out of powerboats. Maybe they were trying to be stealthy.

Alex hoped they were out of powerboats. He and Catalina turned northwards and took off at a brisk walk. LaGuardia was four miles away, and then another small swim to be home.

CHAPTER 89

BACK ON THE ROOF

Letitia didn't see anything else she could do. She had done too good of a job on the boats. A few of the crew members did resurrect, but they were too charred and damaged to be a serious threat to the invaders. The two men in riot gear took them out with a couple of shots. Juan hadn't managed to do anything to save himself. She couldn't think of anything he *could* do.

John and Chris came up the stairs.

"What can you see?" John asked.

"Look for your own self," she said, handing him the binoculars. "They got Juan. I can't throw a bomb at 'em without hurtin' Juan."

Chris's little pistol wasn't going to do anything at this range.

"You said you have a gun? What kind?" Chris asked.

"Don' know what kind it be," said Letitia. "Big one."

"Can you get it?"

Letitia hesitated. The gun wasn't much use, but it was the only one she had. Even if all she could do was point it and look scary, that might be important.

"I go get it, but it still mine. You give it back when we done."

Chris nodded, and Letitia ran to retrieve it from its hiding spot. In a few moments, she was back. Chris found himself looking at a sawed-off tactical shotgun. No wonder she'd said it hurt to use it. That thing must pack a real kick.

He'd been hoping for a rifle. A shotgun was useless at this range. He couldn't hit anything with a pistol at this range, either, and neither could John. Chris had managed that one shot, but that was at fifty-foot range. This was at what? A thousand feet, maybe? No way were either of them going to be able to hit a small spot on the back of a head with a revolver from here.

As they watched, one of the men pulled Juan's arm behind his back and started marching him. They were aiming into the center of the island.

CHAPTER 90
ESCAPE ATTEMPT

Arnie was scared. He wasn't a storm trooper or prison guard, he was a cashier at Costco. A Costco cashier, yet here he was, dressed in riot gear, holding a rifle, surrounded by things burning up and exploding. At least the explosions had stopped. He still hadn't figured out where the hell those gas bombs were coming from, but he had a feeling that whoever was throwing them was still watching.

Nick wasn't doing any better. He didn't want to kill anybody. He didn't want to shoot this poor Mexican guy that was gibbering in terror in front of him. He just wanted to get off this island before someone set him on fire. All of his friends were burnt into black chunks of ash, and he didn't want to get like that.

"OK, what's your name?" Arnie said, gesturing at Juan with his gun.

"Juan. Juan Mendoza."

"OK, Juan, I'll make you a deal. You figure out a way for Nick and me to get out of this alive, and I'll let you get out of this alive. Sound like a deal?"

That was the best deal Juan had heard of in a long time. He was excited. He had decided ten minutes ago that he was going to die and had never been happier to be given a chance to be wrong.

"Can you swim?" Juan asked.

"Yeah," said Arnie, "but you can't expect me to swim home."

"No, no, no ... LaGuardia is *real* close to the back of the island. Couple hundred feet, maybe. You get down there, swim across, walk home. Or at least close."

Nick wasn't really sure they'd go home. He didn't like doing crap like this and had a feeling that things were going to hit the fan pretty soon, too. Still, *not here* sounded great.

He got a good grip on Juan and said "No funny business, now. Take us there."

Juan began leading them towards the center of the island. When they got to Hillside, he turned them left, trying to keep to the coastline. He didn't want to run right down the center and run the risk of meeting everyone. Fewer people they meet, fewer people they shoot, he figured.

It was Nate that spotted the trio first. "Hey!" he whispered loudly, pointing west. The three of them had made it pretty far down the west coast of the island. "That's Juan, isn't it?"

"I think so. Can't quite tell from here. Where are they going?" George replied.

"Don't know, but it can't be good. If they stick to the road, we should be able to head them off right by that other container stack. You know, right where the road branches in that funky intersection?"

George nodded. The five of them took off at a run.

Juan was getting talkative. "See what I mean? You can see the runway from here. If we just keep walking, we'll get to the beach in a couple of minutes."

Arnie and Nick were starting to feel kind of relieved. It didn't look like anything was going to happen. Maybe they were going to get away.

Everything was good until Arnie felt the sharp pain in his leg. George, shielded behind one of the containers, had managed to squeeze off a good shot. Arnie fell, letting Juan loose. The shin guards may be able to deflect the bullet, but it still hurt like hell. He was going to have one enormous bruise.

"Do that again, and Juan gets it. And it won't be in the leg!" Nick shouted.

Juan had started to run back the way they had come, away from the containers, away from the crazy men, just away from everything. He was just building up hope when Nick's gunfire spattered around him. He stopped, raised his arms, and turned around.

"We had a deal, Juan. Tell your friends!" Arnie shouted at him.

"He's right, guys!" shouted Juan. "They just want to run away. I was helping them get away. They said they'd let me go."

"Helping them get away? To where?"

"The runway!" Juan shouted in reply.

The four defenders huddled. Never in the history of warfare had there been two sides that were less inclined to shoot at each other. They reached a decision.

"OK, we'll go along. As long as they don't shoot at you or us, we'll let them by. We've got bombs, though: if they hurt you, they're dead. Fast."

Nick and Arnie had seen what those bombs could do and didn't want to screw around with them.

Nick shouted back "That's a deal! We don't want anything to do with those bombs. Let us get away and we'll let Juan go."

They trooped towards the runway. The noise had attracted some attention, and there was a mob. Arnie and Nick couldn't figure out how they were going to swim in full riot gear.

Negotiation ensued.

"You guys got friends coming?" George asked.

Arnie said "Probably. We didn't all come. Didn't think you guys were going to be able to do anything against us. I'll bet the rest will be here in a bit."

"OK, then, here's the deal. You give us the rifles and riot gear, and we'll give you some spikes. We'll throw a few bombs at the runway, and you guys can make a run for it."

Nick and Arnie looked at the Molotovs. Everybody else looked at the automatic rifles.

"Set things down on three?" Arnie asked.

" OK. One ... two .... three," George counted off. Everyone sat everything down. Nick and Arnie began to strip off. Nick wished this wasn't the day he had put on silk boxers, but there they were. Arnie's leg was a purple mess, but he could still walk.

LuAnn was over at the catapults and let three rounds go at the mob. Satisfied that the crowd was thin enough that they could make it, Nick and Arnie dove in.

LuAnn and Nate picked up the pair of automatic rifles and ammo clips. Juan got Nate's pistol, and, along with George, strapped on the leg guards and arm guards.

"What about the helmets?" George asked.

"Don't think it's a good idea," said Juan. "Someone sees two guys with helmets, they're going to think it's those guys, not us."

George thought about it.

"Yep. Friendly fire kills you just as dead, doesn't it?"

With that, they began the march north.

CHAPTER 91
BETWEEN BROTHERS

Three rowboats slipped up the river towards Rikers Island, aiming for the column of black smoke that pinpointed the location of their comrades. Their course up the river took them directly between the two Brother islands.

Enrique was the first to spot them.

"Shhh ... get ready, everyone. When they get close enough, throw the bombs into the boats. Wait for my signal."

The group waited patiently, bottles filled, rags stuffed, lighters at the ready.

Enrique murmured "Ready ... set .... go!"

Six bombs arced in the air. Rosarita's and Malik's hit their targets, smashing down on the lead boat. The remainder were of mixed effect. Some overshot, some undershot, one skipping off the deck.

Enrique murmured "Again ... ready ... set ... go!" Enrique lit his bomb, stood, and had the back of his skull blown away before he could release it.

Angela watched the bits of Enrique's skull fly backwards and ran for the water as she saw the bomb slip from his still-standing corpse, the flaming gasoline landing on three more bottles. The sky flared bright orange as she lay in the water, afloat, the flaming island in between her and the remaining rowboat. The sound of automatic weapons fire filled her ears as she felt a couple of splashes and saw Rosarita and Malik treading water beside her. She heard several more bombs cook off. Anyone that hadn't made it into the water was dead. She didn't know precisely how many that was, but figured it was most.

The part of the second volley of bombs that had made it off had fared better against their targets. Two of the three boats were now in flames. Some of the attackers were in the water now, too. Their heavy riot gear wasn't serving well in this environment. Bogged down, overweighted, they flailed in the water. They stripped off and began to swim to Rikers, one rowboat continuing in the lead.

CHAPTER 92
ASTORIA

Astoria seemed largely deserted. Catalina had been right: all the lights and noise were drawing the hordes southwest, and here, next to Hell Gate and the strait between the mainland and Rikers Island, there wasn't anything to draw them in and nowhere on the north for them to come from. They had occasional encounters, but Alex followed Letitia's example: if he could just walk another way, that's what he did.

As they approached the fence around LaGuardia's Avis lot, the noise of a brief car honk from inside the lot surprised them. They climbed the fence to find two damp men, clad in underwear and boots, depressing the lock button on a key fob, trying to locate the car it belonged to. Alex and Catalina walked over, hands exposed, lifted shoulder height: not surrendering, but making it very clear that they weren't aiming a gun at anyone.

"What are you up to?" asked Alex.

The two seemed very surprised to see anyone. "Looking for a car we can drive out of here," said the one in the silk boxers.

"Drive? Where do you think you are going to go?" Catalina seemed amused.

"As far from here as we can get. I bet we can get all the way out to the Hamptons in a car. Should be a lot better than here."

"Where are you from?" asked Alex.

"That's enough questions," said the man with the key fob. "What are *you* doing here?"

"Trying to get back to Rikers."

"*Back* to Rikers? I wouldn't be going there right now," Arnie blurted. "It's gonna get messy real fast."

Nick gave him a look.

"You two from Roosevelt? What's happening on Rikers?" asked Alex.

"*Were* from Roosevelt, you mean," answered Nick. "I don't want anything more to do with those guys. Neither does Arnie. We been talking. We're just gonna take one of these cars and drive. Drive someplace where we can find a cabin or something, fish, live. No more of this crap."

"What's happening on Rikers?"

"Last we saw, the guys on Rikers had wiped out Jim's best forces. Set 'em on fire. We ran away. Traded our guns for help getting off, and we're done."

If Alex had a gun, he might have done something. He didn't, though, and neither did these guys. None of them seemed in the mood for clubbing each other with spikes.

"Everyone on the island OK?"

"Last we saw, the only dead people were from Roosevelt. Don't know how long that's gonna last, though. Jim's not the kind to sit back and let people burn his boats and kill his men."

The last Catalina and Alex saw them, they were still trying to chase down that honking car.

It took some work, but since they didn't have to worry about TSA agents shooting them, getting to the runway was tedious, not hard. They had to walk along the fence until they found the openings. Large sections of fence were knocked down, with ruined cars poking through the hurricane mesh. A disturbingly large number of those cars were bullet-riddled, with others showing signs of even heavier artillery.

The runways themselves were pocked with bomb craters, systematically placed every thousand feet or so on every runway. No one was going to escape quarantine by flying out of here. Columns of smoke rose from Rikers Island and South Brother Island: black, greasy smoke from Rikers as the powerboats continued to smolder, and grey from South Brother Island as the trees and underbrush burnt to the ground.

They dove in the East River and swam for home.

CHAPTER 93
CONFLAGRATION

Angela, Rosarita, and Malik continued to float in the East River, just off the shore of South Brother Island. The heat from the fire warmed their faces even as the cold water began to make them feel numb. They kicked their way towards the western shore, keeping the island in between them and the boats aiming for Rikers Island. Eventually reaching the north side, they found the pontoon boat still tied. It was discolored in spots, but the cold of the water and the direction of the wind had protected it from serious damage.

Once again, Angela lay on her back, treading water, as the two children tied the tow rope under her arms. They rowed north to the larger island, pulling Angela behind. Two derelict rowboats were drifting. The current was nearing a reversal point and, with the water so nearly still, they weren't going much of anywhere. A couple figures on the boats moved, but it wasn't clear whether they were living people in the midst of dying or dead people in the midst of living.

They moved up the west side of the island, tying off at the large pier on the northwest side, well out of sight of anyone or anything on Rikers.

Chris and John, in the meantime, had rushed down the center of the island and leapt into the water, swimming as rapidly as they could to the south. They swam several times around the small island, and, determining that there were no survivors, began to swim towards Rikers.

The lead rowboat was just getting near shore when it came into Letitia's sight. It wasn't aiming for the ferry slip, but, instead, to a small beach a little west of it. The men on the ship were pretty certain that wiping out South Brother Island had taken out the source of the fire bombing, but weren't about to show up at precisely the same spot. Letitia began to take sight and range. The beach in front of them burst into flames briefly as she overshot.

The flames drew the attention of LuAnn and George, who were just approaching from the south.

"What do you think that was?" LuAnn asked.

"Looks like they're trying a new spot," George replied. They ran west down Hillside Avenue towards South Brother Island, where they got a clear view of Letitia's attempts to range a moving target. The guys in the boat weren't stupid, either, steering south and moving rapidly, trying to be a little confusing. They gave up when the third try dropped within a few feet of the boat, ditching the boat and jumping over the side.

LuAnn had been queasy about shooting people that were running away, but showed no real qualms about people that were on the attack. She sprayed the area next to the boat with her shiny new automatic rifle. Letitia polished the boat off with a final bomb.

Armed men, fleeing the wreckage around South Brother Island, started to come up on shore. George responded with a burst, and everyone still in the water scattered.

They began to pick off figures one by one. Hitting swimmers wasn't easy, but that's what an automatic is for. No real need to aim, or even see the target: just release a cloud of bullets in the general direction and cross your fingers.

CHAPTER 94
FLOTSAM AND JETSAM

Alex and Catalina, attracted by the sounds of gunfire, ran and quickly caught up with the small group on the beach.

"What the hell is going on?" asked Alex.

"Don't really know everything," said George. "Big group of armed guys with guns came. People fought them off, then another group came. Things went *really* wrong over there," as he gestured towards South Brother Island, "and now we've been dealing with these guys coming up on the beach."

"Where is everybody else?"

"I think most of them were on the little island."

The current was still floating bodies up on the beach. Nothing had been in the water long enough to deteriorate, so most of the dead were still moving. Juan was taking care of those, one pistol shot to the head as each one staggered to its feet.

When Chris and John washed up, they didn't try to rise. Neither of them was quite dead. Not yet, anyway. Chris was still feebly paddling, but John was completely unconscious. George and Alex waded in and dragged them to shore.

Chris had been hit in the leg and was bleeding profusely. John was in far worse shape. He'd been hit in the gut several times. Catalina did a quick triage and focused her attentions on Chris. It didn't look like the bullet had hit an artery, and the bone was intact. She ripped some material from her shirt and made a hasty bandage. She held it tight for a bit and saw that the bleeding slowed. Chris was conscious and looked like he could make it.

"Alex, hold pressure on that for me while I look at John," she said.

Opening John's shirt, she saw that it was as bad as she had feared. At least five shots had hit him in the abdomen and exposed intestines worked their way through the openings. There was no way she could put him back together again.

"Come on, help me get these two someplace warm and clean. Let's get back to the clinic."

Juan stayed behind to take care of any lingering problems that might wash up. Alex got Chris into a fireman's carry and began walking towards the clinic.

"How do we even carry him?" George asked, looking down at John.

Nate shook his head. "I'm not sure how to do it without hurting him worse."

Finally, George slipped his arms under the small of John's back, while LuAnn cradled his head and Nate lifted the legs. The three of them stood up and slowly shuffled towards the clinic. All seemed to go well until John began to get restless. His eyes opened and his teeth sank into the side of LuAnn's neck, ripping through tendons and arteries.

Catalina used her spike on John, and, after a moment, on LuAnn as well. She carried LuAnn's remains, leaving George and Nate to deal with John on their own.

CHAPTER 95

IN THE CLINIC

Catalina decided that Chris was going to be all right. She had managed to pull the bullet out of his leg with a pair of surgical tweezers without doing much more damage in the process, cleaned and bandaged the wound, and set up an antibiotic drip.

Alex, George, and Nate had laid John and LuAnn out in an examination room, white sheets pulled over the bodies. They waited for Catalina in the lobby.

"He going to be OK?" Alex asked.

"I think so. He didn't lose too much blood, and I got the bullet out. Bone isn't broken, and it missed the arteries. He's going to limp for a while, but shouldn't be too much worse."

Alex turned to the three men. "What were you doing out there? Just shooting at everything in the water?"

"Don't blame us!" George protested. "It was a mess out there! Things blowing up, guys with rifles, boats on fire ... how were we supposed to know they were out there?"

"By looking, maybe? Not just shooting everything in sight with your rifles? Who knows how many others were trying to get away from that fire?"

Alex was angry, sad, and disgusted. He hadn't known John before all this, but he had come to rely on the man. Not as smart as he could have been, but steady and reliable. The kind of guy that when things were all messed up, he would at least *try* to make them better. Not the kind of idiot that would shoot people that were swimming for their lives.

"We met a couple of guys on the way here, told us a story about trading their guns so that they could be allowed to run away. Those the guns?" He gestured at the weapons they were carrying.

"Yeah," George said. "I just couldn't kill a guy that wanted to run away."

"I'll tell you what," Alex said. "Give me that gun, and I'll let you run away, too. Head out for LaGuardia and go. There's cars in the Avis lot there: you should be able to get somewhere."

He clenched his hands together tightly. He wasn't sure if he would punch these people, shoot them, or drive a spike into their eyes, but he knew he would do something if he let his own hands loose.

They looked at Alex and started to protest. Juan shut them up.

"He's right. Any of you going to be able to look Marie or Angela in the eye?" The other two men just stared at the floor. Juan turned back to Alex. "Let us grab a bag of food, and we'll go."

Alex nodded.

By the time Rosarita and Malik showed up in the lobby, they were gone.

CHAPTER 96
WHAT NEXT?

"Letícia told us come bring you a boat," Rosarita said.

"We supposed to see if they need help, too!" protested Malik.

"*Olvidé* ... I forgot, she say to ask if help necessary."

"No, we're all right right now," said Alex. "Who's over there with you guys?"

"Just the fat lady," Rosarita said. "We found her floating in the water after the big fire. Is in the bed of Letícia, next to the radiator."

"Is she all right?"

"Think so," said Malik. "Real cold, though. That why she next to the radiator."

"No one else? No one at all?"

"Nope. Aren't they here?"

"Just us. And Chris. How about the little island?"

"No one on it no more. We checked. Everything there be on fire," Malik replied.

The enormity of the loss sunk in. Alex and Catalina just held each other in silence. Rosarita and Malik fidgeted. Finally, Alex let Catalina go.

"You need to stay here and watch Chris. You two, stay with her. I'll go over and talk to Letitia a bit."

He turned to Rosarita and Malik. "Where's the boat?"

"Not the usual place. It at the little dock, the one that be closer to our island."

Alex took the boat over to North Brother Island. His first stop was the heroin recovery ward. As promised, Angela was there, lying in Letitia's bed. Exhaustion had driven her to sleep. She didn't have a fever and her breathing was steady. Alex put his hand on her belly, and what was left of the child within quickly responded by kicking that spot. He permitted himself a few tears before climbing the stairs to the roof. He found Letitia there, still scanning the river with her binoculars.

"All clear?" he asked.

Letitia nodded. "No more boats since them last three. Saw you carrying John and Chris. They all right?"

"Chris is hurt. John's dead."

"Couldn't believe it when those guys just started shooting everyone in the water. Where did you go? Where did these bad guys in the boats come from?"

Alex suddenly realized that Letitia had no idea what was going on. She'd been up here guessing what to do based on what she could see, and, so far as he could tell, hadn't slipped up at all. Many were dead, but probably the only reason they weren't all dead was because of this little girl. She may be like an attack dog, but she was on his side.

He explained quickly. He didn't explain exactly why he and Catalina had gone to the hospital in the first place, but did his best on all the other points.

Letitia listened patiently. She stood there, waiting, and finally gave up.

"What about the people still on that island? Maybe think you should find out what they up to?"

Alex couldn't argue with that. He didn't like thinking about it much. If they didn't have boats, they would have a hard time getting off the island. Alex and Catalina had gotten off without much of a problem with the surrounding horde, but thirty or forty of them would attract attention. And who was going to be left, anyway? Women and kids? Or more fighters? Were they marching towards him right now? Should he go down and try to get them first?

These were the kind of things he liked to talk over with John. He usually wound up making the decision, but John would keep him on track.

He took the supply raft and paddled down the river.

CHAPTER 97
GOSSIP

He was hailed as he passed by Mills Rock. A tall blond man stood on the shore.

"What the hell is going on up there?" the blond asked.

"The guys from Roosevelt attacked us. What have you seen down here?"

"Less than you, probably. One big group of boats went by, then there was the big fire. Another group came by, stole our boat and headed up after the first group. Heard a lot of shooting, and saw a lot of fires. You guys all right?"

Alex thought about lying, but answered truthfully. "Most of us are dead or ran away."

"How about the kids we see every once in a while?"

"They stayed hidden. They're OK. You guys going to be able to make it without a boat?" Alex wasn't sure what he would do if they weren't, but he had to ask.

"Shouldn't be too big of a deal for a few days. Even then, we should be able to get to shore and get a replacement from somewhere in Queens. Zombies aren't too thick over in Astoria, and we can swim there when the tide turns around."

Alex agreed. "Yeah, walked through there yesterday without any real trouble. It's down towards Roosevelt that it gets bad."

The blond looked a bit aggravated. "Yeah. Pisses me off, too, 'cause there's a nice Costco right across from them. We could live twenty years on the stuff in one Costco, but there's no way inside.

"They won't last long, though. They're just about out of fuel. That's why they tried to get yours. The guys on Governors Island have everything south of them locked up tight."

"Governors?"

"Yeah. Big military-looking camp. Survivalists. Quiet guys, don't attract much attention, but they hoard. Got a mountain of stuff, and they aren't going to let go of it. They've got enough to keep themselves happy for a while. They don't go out looking for more, but they won't let anybody anywhere near anything that's theirs.

"Can't get much further south, though. That's where the British Royal Navy blockade is."

Alex continued down a bit, until he had Roosevelt Island in sight. He didn't want to get too close to the guard in the lighthouse, but, from what he could see, there weren't any boats at the docks and nothing was aiming north. Combined with what he had learned, that was going to have to do for tonight.

He turned back north and paddled home.

CHAPTER 98
SPEEDING THROUGH THE NIGHT

Alex's first stop was the clinic. Catalina, Rosarita, and Malik were in the waiting area, playing a game of Chinese Checkers. It was one of the games from the original raid on the Rite Aid, so many months ago. Rosarita and Malik played as a team, arguing and discussing each move. Alex smiled. It seemed homey and nice, a contrast to the events of the day.

"How's Chris doing?" he asked.

"He'll be OK. I don't even think he'll wind up with a limp. I've put some sedatives in his IV so he'll stay asleep, but he should be able to walk in the morning.

"What's going on everywhere else?"

Alex gave her a brief rundown. "Do we have anything that will keep me awake in the medicine cabinet? I don't want to leave the river unguarded, and Letitia can't stay up on the roof forever."

Catalina thought for a bit. "I think there's some. Not much, though: it's not the kind of thing they keep around in a clinic like this."

She checked her inventory and finally found a small bottle of stimulants. "It's not real strong. I think they used it when someone had overdosed on a depressant. You'll make it through a night if you take one every few hours."

He gave her a hug and returned to North Brother Island. Letitia was still on the roof, watching the river.

"Time for you to take a break, kid," Alex said. "I don't think anyone's coming, but I'll spend the night up here and keep watch."

"All night?"

"Yeah, all night. I've got some things to help me stay awake. I'll be OK. Where are you going to sleep with Angela still in your bed?" Alex asked.

"Rosarita and Malik still in the clinic. I just steal their bed for the night."

When Letitia got to the ward, all the children were waiting for her. All of them were excited, and all of them were tired. Letitia knew the answer to this, the same answer that generations and generations of parents have learned: familiar rituals. She took a spot on Rosarita and Malik's bed. She bowed her head. All the children bowed their heads. Angela, looking on from her spot on Letitia's bed, sat up and bowed her head. Letitia began to speak:

"God,

"Thank you for keeping all of us safe.

"I know some of the big people died today.

"Please take care of them now.

"We will miss them.

"Please take care of Angela, and Chris, and Alex, and Catalina.

"We like them.

"They help us when we need help.

"Please help them to stay alive.

"Amen."

With that, she opened the old familiar book, with the old familiar pictures and the old familiar story. Once again, the children heard the tale of the little tiny train that did what the bigger trains could not, simply because he thought he could.

When storytime was over, she went to Angela and held her tight while she cried. She may be bigger than the little kids, Letitia thought, but she isn't really any different. Just harder to get your arms around.

CHAPTER 99
REGROUPING

Catalina's predictions proved sound. Chris was up and walking the next morning. Letitia put Jahayra and Kiara on lookout duty and accompanied Alex and Angela back over to Rikers.

Catalina felt lost. Her days usually began by praying before each pile of bones. When that was over, she'd help Marie set out breakfast. Then, she'd check anyone that she was taking care of. There was always somebody, even if the problem wasn't any more severe than a sprained muscle or a scrape. Those little rituals marked the time and gave her a feeling of comfort, a sense of knowing what her place was. Today, she still had the bones and she was caring for Chris, but there was no Marie, and not many people to be serving any kind of breakfast.

Each morning, she walked to each of the piles, knelt and prayed. It wasn't a long prayer, or even complex. She believed in getting straight to the point, even with God.

> God
> Please take care of the souls that once used these bones.
> I don't know who they were.
> I don't know what they did to get here.
> I do know they were your children.
> Please take care of them, since we could not.
> Amen

Today, she walked over to the west coast. She looked out over the blackened remnants of South Brother Island. She looked at the bodies of the invaders littering the beach. She knelt and tried to pray. No words came. She stared at the little island, the water washing up against the shore, the black ash mixing with the sand. Charred corpses, some still moving slightly, laid in the remains of the vegetation.

She cried, then decided that was prayer enough.

CHAPTER 100
BREAKFAST

Catalina headed to the kitchen and opened a fresh can of pancake mix. The can claimed it had a 30-year shelf life. Some days she mused over whether she would outlive the pancake mix or not. Other days, she mused over whether she *wanted* to outlive the pancake mix or not.

Today, she drove any such thoughts from her mind and mixed the white powder with water, dribbled it out on the gas-fired griddle, and made a stack of twenty pancakes. It would give her day one bright spot: the kids loved pancakes for breakfast. Whenever she wanted to bribe the tribe into doing something for her, she found that giving them a can of pancake mix worked wonders to get them motivated.

Rosarita and Malik dug in with relish. Letitia was more subdued, and the adults were somber. Catalina could barely look at Angela.

Alex laid out his thoughts.

"I don't think those people are going to be a threat today. They don't have any more boats. There weren't that many of them in the first place, so there can't be many left. This had to be nearly all of the trained fighters they had, so they won't be able to attack again."

Chris thought a bit. "How about the guns they used?"

"Most of them are at the bottom of the river. I've picked up the dozen or so they left on the beaches," replied Alex.

"Why they come here in the first place?" Letitia asked.

"Food and fuel, probably," Alex answered. "They're trapped, just like the people on Hunts Point were."

"But why they need it so bad? Can't they fish like we do? We don' use any fuel, and you guys barely do."

There wasn't an easy answer to that. Certainly having a real hospital was handy, but no group that size needed to keep a whole hospital running for themselves.

"Can't really say. I know I like electricity, but we've learned to live without it for most things."

Bad answers generate more questions, and that answer was no exception.

"What are they going to do when they run out?" Letitia asked. "Can they take care of themselves?"

"No idea," Alex replied. He didn't like where this was headed at all.

"Seem to me if you make it so they got to steal from you, there goin' to be trouble," Letitia declared. Alex couldn't argue.

"OK, we'll figure out a way to talk with them."

First, though, came the burning and burials. They made a large funeral pyre for the remains of the strangers. Chris and the children tended the fire, keeping it burning, while the others rowed over to South Brother Island.

The island was still smoldering. The trunks of the larger trees were black chunks of burning coal, while the lighter underbrush was completely gone. There was no need for zombie disposal here, as the fire had done a thorough job of cremating the remains. They stacked the remains in the boat, then swam back, pushing the boat before them.

They carried the boat over to the beach where Luis, Li, and Levon lay buried. The remains were too intermingled to attempt to separate, so they settled for one large grave and laid the pieces of eight bodies inside.

As usual, Catalina led the service, saying the words over them.

CHAPTER 101
PREPARING FOR A VISIT

Alex didn't like this. He didn't like it one bit. Catalina and Chris were both adamant that Letitia had a point. If the people on Roosevelt still had weapons and a desire to steal, they either had to face it or run away. If they didn't have weapons, the ones that were left might need help and might do something desperate. One way or the other, they had to go talk.

He decided to play it safe. He knew that the Astoria area was reasonably clear. They'd boat to Whitey Ford Field and walk from there. There were some pretty tall buildings near Roosevelt: he'd leave Chris and Catalina on the roof armed with a gun and a catapult, then advance under a white flag.

First, though, he had to figure out what to do with Angela. He didn't *want* to take Chris along. There was no way that anyone could convince him to take someone in her ninth month along, and no one tried. He figured the best thing was for her to stay on North Brother Island with the kids for a while.

Letitia had no problem taking care of Angela.

"No problem. I'll take her. Catalina too. I be sending Kiara and Jahayra along with you."

"What?" Alex was dismayed. "Why should they come along?"

Alex had never seen a nine-year-old roll her eyes with contempt for him before. He didn't particularly want to see it again.

"You guys just blew yourselves up. We just buried ten of you, and it because you don't *practice*. Used to be there were always big people telling me to practice stuff. 'Practice your cursive.' 'Practice this song.' 'Practice your multiplication tables.' Practicing those things didn't do no good, but practice is *important*. That the only thing I learned in school that I still use. Kiara and Jahayra come in first or second with bottle tossing *every day*. When we play stab the bag, they always be second or third. They the fastest with the catapult. The *fastest*. That because they *practice*.

"Catalina staying here because I need Catalina. She the only one know how to fix things when we get hurt. I need her for that. Chris knows how to shoot a gun. Kiara and Jahayra, they know how to run a catapult. Chris, Kiara, Jahayra, they what *you* need for your trip."

He couldn't argue. He didn't like this either, but he couldn't argue.

They loaded up the boat they salvaged from the attack, laying one of the catapults in it. As they were loading up, Chris asked Letitia a question. "You talked about how fast Kiara and Jahayra are with the catapult. How did you get it aimed at the slip so fast in the first place?"

"What do you mean?" Letitia asked.

"I mean, there's no sign of you having missed. It looks like your first shot was right on target."

" Missed twice," Letitia replied, giving Chris the same look that had crushed Alex so. "But we was close. We always keep it aimed at you."

CHAPTER 102
SETTING UP HOUSE

Alex decided that if he had to be accompanied by armed children, he couldn't do much better than Jahayra and Kiara. If Letitia was a bulldog, Rosarita and Malik were Doberman Pinschers: you always had the impression that they were refraining from attack because a more entertaining opportunity might show up later. Jahayra and Kiara still seemed like children. You knew that if you gave them a set of Barbie dolls that they would still know how to play with them, and, more importantly, would *want* to play with them.

"How old are you, anyway?" he asked Jahayra.

"I think I six," she said. "My birthday in August. It way past August, ain't it?"

"Way past," Chris agreed. "It's October ... October 17th, I think."

"What goin' to happen with school? They still let me go to first grade when this over? Even though I didn't finish kindergarten?"

"I'm sure that no one will make you take kindergarten again," Chris said. He didn't add that he didn't think the question would ever come up.

"October?" Kiara asked. "That mean Halloween coming, don't it?"

"I guess it does," said Alex.

"Cool. I know those pumpkins in the garden be turning orange. We can have jack-o-lanterns."

They came ashore at Whitey Ford Field. As before, Astoria was pretty clear, so they could have simply avoided any of the dead that were there. Alex knew he was going to be in and out, though, so he didn't just let a pile of followers build up. As they went, they took care of any problems they encountered. He was also pretty proud of his catapult design. Using a dolly as the frame had been *smart*. He was able roll it one-handed.

Reaching the entry to the building closest to Blackwell Lighthouse, he smashed a small side window with a spike. Jahayra and Kiara were able to slide in and open the door from the inside. Six flights of stairs, and they arrived at the top floor.

Having no respect for property or fear of the police made things simple. Chris took his spike, ripped the drywall away next to the door frame, then pounded through the other side. Jahayra popped in and opened the door from the inside.

The view out the apartment window was straight over the north tip of Roosevelt Island, including the Blackwell Lighthouse. Chris used the scope of his automatic rifle and spotted the guard, high up in the tower. No other guns, and still no boats.

They set the catapult up in one of the other windows and sighted the beach area. The apartment pantry yielded a couple of cans that were roughly the same size as the bottles, which allowed them to set a rough range. Jahayra and Kiara did, indeed, know what they were doing, Alex noted: their first shot was a bit short, but, on the second shot, a soup can hit directly on the beach. No one seemed to notice.

"OK, remember, if I twirl my flag over my head, I want Chris to shoot the tower with the gun just to let them know he's here. If I drop the flag, hit everybody you can see with everything you've got. Except me."

With that, Alex walked back to the park and got inside the boat. He tied a big white flag to the bow and began to paddle towards Roosevelt Island.

CHAPTER 103
UNDER A FLAG OF TRUCE

Alex paddled his way south, aiming for the beach at the very tip of Roosevelt Island. He knew the guard was there, so that was the best way to get some sign of whether they would honor a white flag or not.

No shots came as he hit the beach. He got out, dragged the boat ashore, and stood next to his flag. He had liberated one of the automatic pistols from the invaders, but kept it in its holster. He hoped he sent the message of "willing to talk peace, but able to take care of himself."

"Hey!" came a voice from atop the guard tower. "Aren't you one of the guys that was here yesterday?"

"Yes, I am. I'm here to find out how we can put a stop to this. I need to speak to Jim."

"That won't do you much good. Jim's not in charge anymore."

"Then let me speak to whoever is in charge."

"Already radioed them. They should be here in a couple of minutes."

Alex waited patiently on the beach. He pointedly signaled OK in several directions, trying both to signal Chris and the kids and give the impression that he was being covered by multiple gunmen.

After a few minutes, a tall red-headed woman, flanked by two men, one black, one Hispanic, appeared from behind Blackwell Lighthouse. They conferred for a bit and the two men stopped. Their weapons were clearly visible, but, like Alex's, clearly holstered. She appeared to be unarmed, holding only a couple of folding beach chairs.

She walked forward, stopping a few feet in front of Alex. Now that she was closer, Alex recognized her as the woman that had been Jim's secretary yesterday afternoon.

She held out her hand. "Siobhan. Siobhan Roache. And you?"

"Alex. Alex Moss," Alex replied. "I see you have a couple of guards watching over you. It's only fair to warn you I've got a couple of guards you can't see."

"I figured as much," Siobhan said. "I also figured that if they could shoot me here, they could shoot me by the lighthouse, too. Care to sit?" She gestured with the two chairs and unfolded them.

"I'll start out by telling you that Jim's gone," she said. "After that fool stunt yesterday, we kicked him out."

"Kicked him out?"

"Gave him a fair chance. We've got one boat left. We used it to carry him down to Walkabout Bay. If he's smart, he'll make it. I don't really expect it, but he's got a better chance than we do, right now. How much damage did he do up on Rikers?"

"A lot. Most of us are dead. All of your people are dead. This boat is the only one of yours that's left, and, since you shot ours to bits," Alex said, pointing at the remains of his boat, still up on the beach, "we're keeping it."

"I was afraid of that. Jim kept insisting that no one would trade with us, that no one would give us anything, that we'd all *starve* unless he did shit like that. I kept trying to tell him that with a few good doctors and this hospital, everyone would be happy to give us food and fuel if we'd just help them stay well.

"Yesterday, I realized that Jim had lost most of our boats, most of our husbands and sons, most of our weapons, all for something that you had come here trying to give us. If you've ever seen twenty angry widows and grieving mothers, you know how easy it was to get rid of him. It was harder to convince people to give him a chance: most just wanted to shoot him or make him swim for it.

"Anyway, what's it going to take to get this to stop? We don't have much fuel or food left: Jim was right about that part. I do have a hospital, I do have doctors."

"How many of you are left?" Alex asked.

"About forty. Mainly women and kids. A few of Jim's guards that changed sides."

"Well, for a start," Alex said, "I need a doctor to come up to us. We'll see later if we can trust you enough to bring people here. Aside from that, we won't shoot you if you don't shoot us."

"I think I can go along with that," Siobhan said. "What kind of doctor?"

"OB-GYN," Alex replied. "We've got a situation."

Siobhan walked back to her guards. After a brief discussion, the guards went back to the hospital.

"They're bringing back Alyce," Siobhan said. "She's in family medicine, but this isn't the old days. We don't have hundreds of specialists."

As promised, Alyce showed up a bit later. Alex laid out the problem: a baby with no heartbeat that never slept. Alyce and Siobhan both turned a little pale.

"Catalina could have made a mistake," Alex pointed out, "but I don't really think so. She's only a veterinary assistant, but she's been doing pretty well with everything else."

"How are you set up?" Alyce asked.

"Not too bad," Alex replied. "Rikers has a hospital and a good set of clinics, we just don't have real doctors."

Alyce went to the hospital and packed a kit. She didn't figure that Rikers would have a lot of call for Pitocin, so she grabbed a few vials. She was on Catalina's side: better to induce this thing and get it over with instead of letting nature take its course.

CHAPTER 104
A BOAT RIDE HOME

Alex and Alyce paddled the boat northwards, stopping at Whitey Ford Park. They waited there, and in a bit, Chris, Jahayra, and Kiara showed up.

"What adorable little girls!" Alyce exclaimed.

"They're good kids. Make sure that you don't do anything they think is threatening, though. They're armed, and I don't have any real control over them."

Jahayra and Kiara looked at Alyce intently. They couldn't have told you exactly what they were looking for, but, after a few moments, they nodded at each other as if to agree that it wasn't there. They loaded their case of bombs into the boat and helped secure the catapult.

Alyce couldn't help but notice Chris's limp and the slight bloodstain on his pants from leakage through his bandage. "Is that a serious wound?" she asked him.

"Bullet wound. Catalina dug the bullet out, but it's still pretty fresh. Hurts bad, too."

"I'll take a look at that while I'm up there, too, then. Anything else?"

"I think everyone's pretty much all right. Kiara's the only one of the kids to ever get badly hurt, and I think she's pretty well patched up."

"How many kids are there?" Alyce asked.

"Eleven," said Jahayra. "Used to be thirteen."

"More than that!" said Kiara. "There was twenty-five of us in our class!"

"I wasn't counting the ones that got eaten the first day," Jahayra said, "just the ones that Letitia got out of the school."

"Letitia?"

"She my big sister."

"She takes care of you, does she?" Alyce continued.

"She take care of *everybody*," said Jahayra, "even the big people."

Alyce gave a look over at Alex and Chris. They shrugged.

North Brother Island loomed ahead, to the extent that such a tiny place can loom. They landed the boat in the small cove and dragged it ashore.

"I thought you lived on Rikers," Alyce said.

"We do," said Alex, "but Letitia feels more comfortable keeping the kids over here. We help them when they need it, but they pretty much take care of themselves. They were the heroes yesterday. We'd all be dead if wasn't for them."

Alyce just decided to go with the flow. She was getting more and more confused, but this wasn't really her problem. They walked up to the old hospital. Catalina walked out to greet them.

"We've got a truce," Alex said. "I'll give you the details later, but for now, they've lent us a doctor until we can deal with Angela's situation. She in the heroin ward?"

That look flashed across Alyce's face again.

"She's trying to nap. Poor thing never gets any real sleep anymore."

"I'm not surprised, based on what you told me," Alyce said. Now it was Chris's turn to look confused.

"Based on what they told you? What exactly did they tell you?"

Alyce covered for herself fast. "Just that the baby is extremely active," she said. "Let's get a quick look at her."

Alyce could see how exhausted Angela was as soon as she walked in the room. No "glow" here, just the sallow look of a desperately tired, sleep-deprived woman that had something kicking her twenty-four hours a day. She did a quick check and came to two conclusions. The first was that Catalina was probably right and the second was that it would be OK to move her to the clinic. These people might treat these children like adults, but there were conversations that she wanted to have in private, away from a group of children.

It was approaching late afternoon by the time they got Angela over to the clinic. While they were getting Angela comfortable in a bed, Alyce took the time to review Catalina's notes. She was impressed: for a veterinary assistant, she seemed to have a pretty good grasp of what was going on. She called Catalina over. They walked outside of the room for a bit.

"Catalina, it looks to me like the last time you heard a heartbeat was three days ago. How was it then?"

"What do you mean 'How was it'?" Catalina asked. "It was a heartbeat. Fast, but steady."

"No fluttering? No skipping? Loud and strong?"

"Yes, it sounded perfect. It was perfect all the way along."

"She says she was due in early November?"

"Yes."

"OK, that's just a few weeks away, so we can assume the baby is the size of a thirty-six-week fetus. Too big for a simple D&C or anything like that. I think you were right: if it's dead, I should induce labor and then deal with what comes out after it's out."

With that, Alyce went into the room. She checked Angela's temperature and other vitals. Angela may be tired, but she wasn't ill. She tried again with the baby. It kicked. It responded to pressure. It seemed to be in position for birth. But, no matter how hard she tried, she couldn't detect a heartbeat.

"Catalina, go get John and Chris. I need to talk to all of you."

Catalina fetched them. They had been trying to figure out if they could rig one of the radiators to work through the night and had decided that they probably could. They came.

"Chris, Angela," Alyce began, "my news isn't very good. Catalina's notes show that your baby was doing fine up until a few days ago."

The sound of the word "was" brought both of them to attention.

"When she checked the baby yesterday, she couldn't find a heartbeat. I've checked, and I agree. That baby's heart isn't beating. I'm afraid it's dead."

"It can't be dead! It's still kicking ..." Angela's voice trailed off as she realized why. Chris looked like he was going to die right then.

"You mean, it's one of those *things* now?" he asked.

"I can't be 100% sure *what* it is. I've never seen this before. There's no one I can ask. There are no books about it. All I can tell you is that it isn't a living, healthy baby, and I think it's best that we do something about it."

"What kind of 'something'?"

"Well, we have several choices. First, we can just wait. This is really just a stillbirth, and there are stillbirths every day. Usually, the mother gives birth about two weeks after the baby dies.

"Our second choice is to treat it as a late term abortion. That's surgical, and involves me actively killing whatever's in there, and then waiting for Angela's system to flush it out, as it were. That's risky, especially without a real hospital.

"Our third choice, and the one I think is probably best, is for me to induce labor. We'll try to get Angela's body to deliver it normally, and deal with whatever comes out when it comes out."

" I think we need some time to talk about this," Chris said, holding Angela's hand tightly. He gestured towards the door.

Alex and Catalina looked awkward, then left the room, Alyce following close behind.

"Got any coffee?" Alyce asked.

"Sure. We've got a gas stove, and we rigged up a filter system." Alex was actually quite proud of the setup. He'd built it out of tubing, plumbing, and some of the clinic's glassware. Heated water from the stove was poured onto the grounds, and coffee slowly dripped out an IV tube into a glass urn. He was always happy to show off how he could build something out of things that were meant for completely different purposes, and it helped him not to think about the conversation that must be going on in the clinic room.

He was just pouring out a cup for Catalina when he heard the shots.

At least Chris had been more considerate than LeVon. Both bullets had gone cleanly through the skull. Neither of them would be coming back.

CHAPTER 105
CLEANING UP THE MESS

Alex and Catalina brought a cot into the room and stretched Chris out on it. They gently covered him with a sheet. Turning to Angela, they saw Alyce donning surgical gloves.

"Catalina, I'll handle this," Alyce said, "but I need you to get me some supplies. Sponges, scalpels. The biggest pair of surgical shears you can find. Sutures."

It hadn't dawned on Alex or Catalina that Chris had only killed the living, not the dead. The child was still in there, still kicking and struggling. With no muscle tension to resist the undead child, Angela's belly moved vigorously as the child within sought an escape.

Catalina went out and came back with the supplies. She and Alex left the room.

Alyce didn't waste any time, as she didn't want this process to last any longer than it had to. She had learned the trick in med school of being able to lock part of herself away when she had to. That was what let her help mangled children instead of crying over their wounds, how she was able to help a mother that was coping with a stillbirth. She found the part of herself that was about to break down and locked it away.

Stripping Angela, she made a simple, vertical incision through the wall of the abdomen, the kind of old-fashioned caesarean section that Julius himself had been delivered by. She carefully sliced open the uterus.

The child didn't look that different from any other. Tiny fingers clenched, tiny toes wiggled. Its arms and legs flailed. The eyes scrunched and then opened.

She lay the child out on the table, holding it still with one hand. She used her stethoscope one final time. No heartbeat, no breath sounds, despite all the vigorous motion.

She held the child's eyelids open and carefully pressed one blade of the shear through the right eye. She wiggled it back and forth until the child stopped moving.

She placed surgical packing in the eye socket, closed the eyelids, then placed a few quick, nearly invisible sutures to hold the eyelids closed. She washed the child in the sink and wrapped it in a sheet.

She turned her attention to Angela. She couldn't do much about the head but wash it. Fortunately, it was a clean wound: it was such a high speed rifle that the entry and exit wounds were both small. She cleaned the worst of the gore off and combed Angela's hair to disguise the holes. Using larger sutures, she patiently sewed the belly wound back up. Nothing pretty, but strong and sturdy, enough to ensure the body would stay together. She redressed Angela, laid her on the table, making a small nest with her arms. She laid the child there.

Chris was messier. She couldn't fix him to be presentable, but settled for getting the blood wiped off. She poked her head out the door. "Catalina, could you bring me a mop?"

A few minutes later, a janitorial bucket and mop arrived. Alyce gave the room a good scrub, making it at least presentable. She sat for a moment.

The moment stretched. Alyce felt a numbness seep into her, a deep, dark blackness that masked the pain. Finally, she stood, opened the door, and walked out of the room.

"I've done all that I think I can. I'd like to go home now."

Tomorrow, she could find the piece of herself she had locked away and let it out to have a good cry.

CHAPTER 106
NOW IT'S TIME TO SAY "GOODNIGHT"

This was the second night in a row that there had been extra people in the room. When Alex and Catalina came back from returning Alyce, neither of them could think of a reason to go back to Rikers that night. They were lying in one of the beds, and Letitia was snuggled in with Jahayra and Kiara.

The room wouldn't settle. It was full of wriggling children, and the wriggling wouldn't stop. They all had questions.

"So the fat lady was fat because there was a baby inside?" asked Jose.

"Yes."

"Like the guinea pigs?"

"Yes, like the guinea pigs."

"And that baby's dead?"

"Yes."

"Why did they kill the baby?"

"They didn't kill the baby, it was dead."

"Then why is the lady dead?"

"Angela and Chris were so sad about the baby being dead, they killed themselves."

"But why is the baby dead, then?"

And so on. It took hours, but finally she got them all quiet. Letitia bowed her head.

"God,

"I'm sorry, but I don't understand.

"Don't you like babies? I thought everybody liked babies.

"Please be nice to Alex and Catalina. They're the only big people we have left.

"Amen."

"Amen," came the soft chorus.

Letitia pulled the book out and began to read. Even Catalina and Alex found the message of the little train soothing.

CHAPTER 107
A FUNERAL

Alex was getting very tired of digging holes on this beach. At least the soil was soft and moist, so it was not too strenuous, just tedious. And depressing. He couldn't help but wonder about who would dig the last hole on this beach and who would go in it. He realized that he didn't want to be the one doing the digging when that happened. If this was a contest as to who could live the longest, he didn't want to win.

He could picture it being Letitia, though. There was a ruthlessness in her that he could never duplicate. Again, he wasn't sure he wanted to. It wasn't the natural-born-killer vibe he got from Rosarita and Malik either: she didn't want to hurt people, but didn't care much if she had to. Her home-grown theology served her well. They'd discussed it once, and she was blunt: God did it. If he was this big guy in the sky that was all powerful, it was him that had decided this was going to happen. If she wound up in a situation where she had to set twenty living men on fire to save herself, that was God's fault, not hers. She wasn't going to worry much about it.

Standing in a pit that was already four feet deep, he wished that he found the same comfort in that thought. If he went down that path, he had to conclude that God hated him, Catalina, and everyone he had ever loved. He wasn't even certain whether a God that would do that had saved him so far because he hated him the least or hated him the most.

He lost himself in the digging. Two more feet. That's all he needed.

When he was done, he walked to the clinic. He and Catalina placed each body in a gurney and carried them one by one to the hole. He took the time to arrange them, with Chris lying on his back, Angela curled up under his right arm, the baby lying on his chest, facing Angela.

They all stood before the hole. Catalina knelt.

"Lord

"Bless these parents. Please forgive them for what they have done.

"It was a hard, hard path you set in front of them, and they were not strong enough.

"Please take their souls into your care, and mend them.

"Please grant us the strength to avoid their path.

"Bless this infant, for he has done no wrong, and committed no sins.

"Into your hands, we commend his spirit.

"Amen."

"Amen," came the murmured chorus.

Alex filled the hole, then went into the dormitory, laid down, and did not rise until the next day.

CHAPTER 108
REMODELING

Catalina was adamant that she no longer wanted to live on Rikers Island. Letitia was dubious about having Catalina and Alex share the recovery ward, and Alex was quite dubious about sharing his life with the kids.

They compromised on a small cottage, near the site of Mary Mallon's. It was still in fair shape. With a tar paper roof, some brickwork, and a replaster, it appeared like it could be quite liveable.

Letitia was enthusiastic about this project. Her *Sunset Guide to Home Repair* had pictures of big happy white men doing all this stuff, but she would like to learn how with somebody else's house. She also kind of hoped that the project would make Alex back into a big *happy* white man. The funk he had sunk into was deep and nothing seemed to shake him out of it.

They made trip after trip to Bruckner Building Supply, bringing back item after item. Alex rigged up some harnesses so the children could drag loading dollies behind them. They looked like little mule teams hauling loads.

Letitia followed Alex around like a shadow and refused to be told she wasn't big enough to help with any task. She enlisted the little ones in mortar stirring, finding unbroken bricks from other buildings, all the tasks that they could do. She would clamber on the roof, replacing boards, nailing shingles, caulking joints, all the jobs she could handle. Alex was quite impressed.

The were done just in time for Halloween. The ruins of the Rite Aid yielded an array of makeup, and Catalina spent the whole day painting faces. It was a happy day of happy makeup: no one wanted to be a monster or a witch, instead it was a parade of clowns and cats and dogs.

They took the biggest pumpkin from the garden, made a jack-o-lantern out of it, placing one of the flourescent lanterns inside. It sat on the porch of the little cottage. Each pair of buddies came to the door, holding a bag and shouting "Trick-or-treat!" Alex or Catalina would respond by placing a small treat in the bag: usually some of the infinite-seeming supply of trail mix, but some dried fruit or bottled drinks.

As Catalina and Alex went to bed in their new home, it seemed like the scariest night of the year was the safest day in five months.

CHAPTER 109
ROUTE PLANNING

One morning, over breakfast, Letitia dragged out her atlas and carried it over to Alex.

"South. Where is 'south' and how do you get there?" she asked.

Alex was a little confused. He gestured southward and said "That way. What more do you need to know?"

"Everyone say that birds go south for the winter, and that food grow there all year round. Someday, other men goin' to come up and take all the food out of the warehouses on Rikers. We can't stay here when that happen. We'll need to run. 'South' sounds like a nice place.

"So where's south?"

"Can't we deal with that when it happens?"

Letitia gave him that look again, that look that made him feel like he couldn't quite graduate from a school for village idiots.

"If a bunch of men come and steal all the food, you probably get killed. I need to ask now."

That little streak of ruthlessness came out again. He understood why she planned around him dying, but she didn't sound all that broken up over the idea. Still, she had a point.

They pored over the atlas. Letitia got out her notebook and took notes.

"Well," Alex began, "your best bet is probably to follow I-95 south. You won't be able to get lost, because there will always be signs that point you there."

He showed her what the interstate signs looked like.

"How would you do it? Walk?"

"I can't drive," Letitia answered. She gave that look again. He was getting very tired of that look.

"How would you carry anything?"

"I figured those dollies you helped us with when we were getting stuff from Bruckner's."

Alex could see how that would work. He hoped it never got to the point where little children were running for their lives while hauling their possessions on furniture dollies, but nothing else he had hoped for was happening, while a lot of things he had hoped wouldn't happen had.

"So where I-95 from here?" she asked.

That was a tricky question. He sat down and looked at the map.

"Big problem is that the British Navy still has us blocked off. You can't take your boats past Governors Island without getting shot. That means you have to go north first."

He studied the map some more.

"Here you go. Down around Randall's Island, then back up the river here. You can come up here and get out at Spuyten Duivel, cross the river, then get on I-95 at Fort Lee."

Letitia stared intently at the map. She asked a few questions and took more notes.

" 'kay, then, how far I have to go?"

"To get to a place where it's warm all year and food grows all the time? You'd have to get to Jacksonville." Alex quickly looked at the mileage chart on the back page of the atlas. "955 miles. It would take about three months, walking and carrying boats and stuff. They've probably bombed every bridge, so you'd need to carry boats to get across the rivers."

He looked at her sadly. She planned so hard and planned for everything. He was sure that set of notebooks had a plan for everything she could think of ever happening to anyone. The title at the top of this page was "ALEX AND CATALINA DEAD, BAD MEN ON RIKERS." He didn't really want to see the table of contents.

"Promise me something, honey," he started. "This is for when you are desperate. Don't take off running because you have a fight with me or Catalina. If you try to make a run like that, some of you are going to die. Maybe all of you. Try to make friends with the people on Roosevelt. Try to make friends with whoever killed me and Catalina, for Christ's sake. But don't run like that unless you absolutely have to."

Letitia listened intently. He thought he had gotten through.

"Remember the day Marie said you should teach us how to shoot? I think it time, now," she said.

"I thought you said guns were no good against zombies."

"I ain't worried about no cucos. Nobody getting killed by no cucos. The only thing killin' people around here is people with guns killin' people because they *scared* of cucos. Or running out of food. Or even just scared of running out of food."

CHAPTER 110
THE SECRET PAGES

There was one section in Letitia's notebook that no one was allowed to see. She usually tried to be by herself when she wrote in the books, but didn't make a fuss if someone looked over her shoulder. With the kids it didn't matter much anyway: once it got much beyond names and three-letter words, none of the little ones could read. Rosarita could struggle her way through simple Spanish, but written English baffled her. Letitia actually tried to work on some sections when Alex or Catalina were around because it was nice to be able to ask them questions about things she didn't know.

The section labeled "Mistakes" was different: she'd make sure Alex and Catalina weren't around when she was writing. She didn't like to admit she made mistakes and didn't think the adults would like to know what she thought her mistakes had been.

Most of them were simple, things like "*Should have left the school earlier while the army was outside to help.*" Others got written in, crossed out, and replaced multiple times. "*Should have saved the puppies the first day*" became "*Shouldn't have tried to save Lucia*" and finally became "*Don't make them cheat.*"

The worst problem with the section was the line that kept showing up, getting crossed out, and showing back up again: "*Should have run away with Jahayra when I had the chance.*"

CHAPTER III
WAREHOUSING

Early in November, after the morning supply run to Rikers, Alex started examining a large storage room on the second floor. Letitia poked her head in.

"What you looking for?" she asked.

"I was thinking," Alex said. "This room stays plenty dry. I could bring some of the shelves over from Rikers, and we could build a big storage room here. We could bring most of the food over from Rikers, and then we wouldn't have to go get it every day."

"No," said Letitia. "I won't let you do that."

This was the first time Letitia had made it clear that she thought he needed her permission to do things, and that rankled.

"Won't *let* me? Why won't you *let* me?" he replied.

"Because people that steal stuff shoot the people that get in the way. We stay here and the stuff stays over *there*, nobody shoots us. If we live over there, people shoot us. If we bring the stuff here, people shoot us. So, we stay *here*, and the stuff stays *there*."

She had that look again. He had to admit she was right.

"How about the storeroom you've got?"

"I got to have *some*," she said. "There's enough here to give us a chance to run away if we got to. No more."

CHAPTER 112
TARGET PRACTICE

Letitia changed her mind about guns. The attack on Rikers still shook her. The kids played their games to practice killing cucos, but they needed to get better at killing people, too. They wouldn't always be hundreds of feet away and they couldn't carry catapults. Alex reluctantly agreed.

"You're going to need small guns, though. That big tactical shotgun thing you've got is useless to you."

"What kind do I need to look for?"

"All these kids are going to be able to handle are .22s. Little bullets, little guns, not much kick."

Small-caliber revolvers were like children's sneakers: looters concentrated on larger sizes. It took dedicated searching, but Letitia managed to scavenge eleven small .22s from gun shops. Most of the bigger stuff was long gone, but she could always find a .22 somewhere. It was as big of a gun as any of the kids could handle, so she was happy to take it.

Ammunition was no trouble at all. Shops stripped of larger calibers would have cases of .22 bullets left over.

Target practice became another part of the daily rituals. Each child became quite fast and accurate. As with all their skills, Letitia hammered in the concept of practice.

Stopping power was the major concern. A .22 to the head was actually less likely to stop a zombie than a garden stake. They finally decided on teaching the buddies to shoot in patterns: one buddy would always aim for the head, the other for the chest. The chest shot wouldn't do much against a zombie, but Letitia didn't plan on using the guns against cucos.

CHAPTER 113
SCOUTING TRIPS

Letitia continued to make scouting runs every few days. She would get in the lead boat and get one or two buddy pairs to follow her out. It always reminded Catalina of ducks: mama duck floating out ahead, baby ducks following in a line behind.

Letitia felt safer knowing where everything was and what was changing. Mills Rock was deserted. The cold weather had made them seek refuge in other places. Most had settled down on Roosevelt Island, but a couple of the men had fallen in with the Governors Island crowd.

Roosevelt Island was doing better. They had cut back their electricity use. They had set up a trade program with Governors Island and, to the north, groups on City Island and Hart Island. Letitia was wary of all these groups, but would wave and exchange gossip. Sometimes, Alex would come along. He and Catalina were lonely for adult company, and these trips helped. Lonely as she was, Catalina stayed on the island most of the time. She rarely left, not even venturing to Rikers for the supply runs.

Governors Island was still unfriendly. They were actually unfriendly with the Roosevelt group, and it was obvious that the relationship between the two was a relationship based on *need* rather than *want*. Letitia wasn't welcome to scout the area: they fired warning shots at times.

One day, Letitia announced that they were going to go look at Fort Lee.

"Fort Lee?" asked Alex, having forgotten about the page titled "ALEX AND CATALINA DEAD, BAD MEN ON RIKERS."

"That where you said I-95 started. I feel better if I know what it like."

Alex insisted on accompanying her on this trip. Catalina wouldn't hear of being left alone while Alex went somewhere completely new, and that meant that Letitia felt like they had to take all the kids. It was the first time the full flotilla had gone anywhere in a while.

They took the southern route around Randall's Island, remembering quite well how narrow the waterway became at the north side. Randall's was still the single densest collection of cucos they saw.

"It's strange," Alex said, "I would be expecting them to rot, or fall apart, or *something*, but they don't. It's like they'll keep going forever."

The shore was full of essentially undecayed bodies. Unlike the zombies in the movies, they weren't some constantly decaying gore fest. Whatever wounds had killed them were still there, they had a pale blue-grey cast on top of their original skin color, but it was like they had been frozen in time. The only thing that damaged them was when their stupidity led them to damage themselves by accident. The evidence of that was all over: bodies damaged in an effort to get through narrow gaps, crushed when something interested a group and they piled in front of an obstacle. Aside from that, they were unchanged. In a perverse sense, they were immortal.

The bridges over the Harlem River were all the same. Bomb strikes had taken out the center section of each bridge, dropping rubble and steelwork into the water. The small boats were able to pick a path through with ease. The image on the shore was always the same: piles of cars bulldozed off the bridges, lying in heaps at the base.

Reaching the Hudson, they turned south. The remnants of the George Washington Bridge came into sight.

"Jesus Christ," said Alex. The GWB wasn't a small bridge like the ones across the Harlem River, so no single bomb punching a hole in the center was enough to take it out. Multiple bomb strikes had dropped the upper deck onto the lower deck, then more bomb strikes had smashed the rubble until the lower deck collapsed. All that was left were the suspension towers at each end.

The flotilla landed at the boat ramp at the base of the bridge.

"Lucia, Maria, you guard the boats," Letitia said.

Lucia and Maria didn't look happy, but they had lost "stab the bag" this morning and were prepared to take an unpleasant chore in consequence. All the boats were tied together, and Lucia and Maria were assigned the job of taking the boats out if someone approached on shore. They had taken well to firearms training, too: there was no need to worry about them defending themselves.

They walked up the winding road from the boat ramp. "That's what I was looking for," Letitia said. She pointed at a building inconspicuously nestled away in the woods. They went over to investigate.

A large sign on the outside read "Fort Lee Historic Park Visitor Center." The brick building was unlocked and apparently undamaged. There was nothing here of interest to looters, and no survivors had much time for random vandalism or American history. Upon walking inside, they were greeted with the sight of historic panoramas and displays, all devoted to the heroic exploits of Washington's army.

"Why was this 'what you were looking for'?" asked Alex.

"We arguing about where to keep stuff, and this be a great place to keep stuff," said Letitia. "No one know it here, so no one steal stuff. If we got to run, we got stuff. There ain't a bunch of cucos around, so it pretty safe."

Alex had to admit she had a point. A cache of supplies hidden somewhere might come in handy someday.

He decided he needed to get a notebook, too. Maybe that was the secret.

CHAPTER 114
I-95

They continued up the roadway. This area was a mass of on-ramps and exit-ramps, but clear of much of the car wreckage that marked the New York side of the river. Apparently any car that managed to make it this far had been allowed to drive on, at least for a while. They eventually located an on-ramp that allowed them onto the southbound lanes.

In many ways, Alex found it spookier than much of New York. There were cars parked on the shoulders, but the traffic lanes were clear here. The long line of toll booths marked "NEW JERSEY TURNPIKE" were empty, but, like the visitor center, immaculate. No one was looting for quarters and dimes. The long stretch of pavement lay before them like a concrete river, flowing south.

"I really think this has to be your last resort, you know," said Alex.

"I know. Don't mean I shouldn't think about it, though."

Alex stopped and tried to guess what was down I-95. Most of the rural areas of the country hadn't really been hit by the zombie apocalypse *per se*. The big cities with subways, sure, but the little towns? Small towns had been hit by quarantines, evacuations, and bombed-out bridges. The virus had spread far enough that the world had cut them off, but it would be starvation that got them here, not zombies. The kids might stand a chance if they had to run.

Hell, it might be better if they all ran now.

When they got home, Alex got the atlas back out and helped Letitia work out a path around Newark, Baltimore, Washington, and Norfolk.

CHAPTER 115
ANOTHER NOTEBOOK PAGE

THINGS TO HIDE BY THE BRIDGE

1. Dollies for carrying things
2. Water
3. Camp stove
4. Rifle
5. Gasoline
6. bottles
7. matches
8. trail mix
9. beef jerky
10. granola bars
11. sleeping bags
12. Vitamins

CHAPTER 116
THANKSGIVING

They decided to make a big deal out of Thanksgiving. There weren't any turkeys to be found here, so a handful of woodcocks that Alex managed to shoot would have to do. They decided to prepare the meal over in the kitchen at Rikers, as Catalina wasn't in any mood to try to cook a bird over an open fire grate and the thought of Thanksgiving softened her stance against spending a lot of time on Rikers. For her part, Letitia was willing to risk being between food and bad people for one day.

It was another happy day. Catalina taught them all how to make bread, and the children had fun kneading the dough. Catalina had never made pumpkin pie from actual pumpkins before and was pleased to see how well it turned out. She was glad the prison library had books. There weren't a lot of cookbooks here, but there were enough.

The children thought the woodcocks were funny, like bite-size turkeys. The fresh bread and pumpkin pie were enough to make that Thanksgiving feel like a feast despite the miniature turkey substitutes.

After Thanksgiving cleanup, Letitia pressed Catalina for help with food planning. This led to a little library trip the next day, Letitia armed with her notebook, Catalina along to help interpret the results.

Catalina was pleased to find that Letitia had been making the children take the Flintstones.

"I was worried about them dying from not getting their vitamins. We went a day without nothing but candy, and I know candy don' have no vitamins."

"Don't worry about something like that happening fast," Catalina said. "You'd need months to die from not getting your vitamins."

Catalina stopped for a moment.

"Honey, what's bringing this up now? Are you still worried about what to bring if you had to run?"

Letitia nodded.

"Yeah. When this happened, we in our own neighborhood. I knew how to find things. Now I trying to figure out what to pack that they can carry if we had to go a long way, and I just don't know what to bring."

"You know I think this is silly, don't you?" asked Catalina.

"I know. I don't. People goin' to come take this stuff someday, and they ain't going to want to take care of us when they do."

Catalina couldn't tell her she was wrong, even though she *hoped* she was wrong.

"All right, that's our problem then. Food that little people can carry on those little dollies that will keep them alive while they look for more food."

It took a day of research, but they came up with the answer. Peanut butter. One tub of institutional peanut butter would keep two six-year-olds fed for six days. Conveniently enough, Rikers had a *lot* of peanut butter, and it didn't need to be refrigerated.

CHAPTER 117
CHRISTMAS

When Letitia did her scouting run on December 22nd, the guard in Blackwell Lighthouse called out for her to stop.

"Why?" Letitia called back.

"I've got something for you from Siobhan," came the answer.

Letitia, Kiara, and Jahayra came ashore, and the guard came down with an envelope. Bright red, it said "To Alex, Catalina, and the children" on the outside in flowing cursive. Letitia opened it. It was a party invitation. Letitia smiled, even though she didn't think Santa Claus was going to risk cucos to get her a present.

Letitia took it to Alex and Catalina as soon as she got back.

"Should we go?" she asked. "You think Santa will be there?"

"I don't know about Santa, Letitia. The army and navy have us locked up here pretty tight, and they might not even let Santa through. But I'd like to go," said Alex. Catalina nodded.

"What's 'potluck' mean?" Jahayra asked, studying the invitation.

"That means that everybody brings some food, and everyone shares."

There was an extra small note, addressed to Catalina, which read "*Please bring a list of the children's clothing sizes. We have a selection, but we want to be able to get the boxes labeled right — Siobhan.*"

Catalina scoured the storerooms for festive foods. Tiara and Jada volunteered some extra guinea pigs, but Catalina vetoed that. There weren't enough of them to go around, for one thing, and, for another thing, she still hated the idea of eating guinea pigs. She did, but she did her best to not think about where the little slices of meat came from.

The powdered milk, powdered eggs, and flour were still holding out, so pastries were the order of the day. Fresh fruit was beyond impossible, but there were canned pie-fillings. Most of those were actually cans that Marie had insisted on bringing back on supply runs. Catalina's throat caught for a moment looking at them, but pressed on.

They spent the twenty-fourth in the kitchen, rolling out pie crusts, cutting them into shapes, and filling them. All the children pitched in with filling the crusts, arranging them on the cooking trays and putting them in the ovens. She wasn't as good at this as Marie had been, but she felt quite proud of the accomplishment. She loved the opportunities to do things with the children where she felt like they were children again.

Letitia made it haircut day and took extra time getting all the knots and frizz out of each of the children's hair. She'd stuck with the half-inch length for everyone. She'd experimented once with letting the Hispanic kids' hair grow out a bit. Softer and straighter, it didn't present the same trouble as the black kids' hair. After a couple of weeks, though, all the kids demanded to be cut the same way. They liked looking like they were all a part of one big family, and to them, the hair was just a part of it.

The party began Christmas morning. Everyone was fitted out in their best clothes, which basically meant the least-stained shirt and least-stained pants. They boarded the boats and floated down to the tinsel-laden dock at Roosevelt.

The locals had put on quite an effort. They had searched the storerooms of the hospital and schools for Christmas decorations and had even managed to find a Santa costume in the pile. Guests from as far north as Glen Island were there. The people on Governors Island had, as expected, politely but firmly refused the invitation. There were some quite accomplished duck hunters on City Island and they brought several ducks ready for roasting.

The little ones clustered around Letitia, feeling both like they were the center of attention and like they were clearly out of place. They weren't the only children there, as there were one or two children from each of the other islands. The others had survived because of the luck of being with a parent when things went bad. Carefully protected by the parent and cherished by each little community, each of them had become pampered and spoiled. Most of them were actually a little chubbier and softer now than they had been eight months ago.

All of the children stood in line to climb on Santa's lap. Each would dutifully hand his stake to his buddy and climb on Santa's lap, the buddy standing at Santa's feet during the process.

Santa, more generally known as Ralph Odom, former head of accounting for the hospital, was taken aback by the crew. He was glad to see that the children were handing away those sharpened stakes before climbing on his lap, but still noted the presence of the .22 strapped to each child's belt. He'd played Santa before, but never to children that were packing heat. Alyce and Siobhan had been extremely insistent that he be nice with these children. He thought that was a fairly easy position for them to take, as they weren't the one surrounded by armed kids. Still, he tried. He managed to take some comfort in the sight of the remaining buddy standing at his feet, dutifully wielding both stakes to ward off any would-be attackers.

"Ho ho ho, merry Christmas!" he began. "And what's your name, little boy?"

"Jose," the tiny boy in his lap replied.

"Have you been a good boy this year?"

"Dunno," replied Jose. Jose vividly remembered getting yelled at loudly for accidentally killing a goldfish one year, and he just wasn't sure where all the people he had helped kill this year fit in.

Alarm bells ran loudly in Ralph's head, but he persisted. "Why?" he asked.

Jose got about halfway through his explanation when Ralph decided those alarm bells had gone off for very good reasons. "Well, Santa's sure that you've been as good as anybody could be this year," he said, as he grabbed two boxes labeled "Jose" from the stack beside him. When Trevon climbed on his lap, Ralph decided that the only question for the rest of the crew would be "What's your name?"

One of the boxes that each child received contained a practical Christmas: rugged corduroy pants, socks, underwear, a long-sleeved shirt, and a light sweater. The other box contained a collection of fun. Siobhan had thought long and hard about what a child should get for Christmas and ultimately came down on the side of things that you could play with over and over for hours. Each of the packages had a Lego set, modeling clay, crayons and paper. It had been a little bit like traveling in a time machine for her, as she remembered being overwhelmed last Christmas trying to choose between piles of little electronic things that she didn't really understand for her grandchildren. She wished she could see them again, but, as they lived in Denver, that wasn't likely. At least they were probably still all right: the last news reports she had heard, everything west of the Missouri was still holding up.

CHAPTER 118
THE CHILDREN'S TABLE

When dinner time came, all the children were segregated at one long table. As they sat down, each dutifully lay his stake in front of him, just on the opposite side of the plate. There was a small scuffle as some of the children from the other islands attempted to sit between members of a buddy pair, but that was quickly sorted out.

Wendy, a City Island girl a few years older than Letitia, was frankly terrified. Wendy had been a fifth-grader at PS 175 and would have been terrified by Letitia and the little ones before anything had happened. She had heard stories about the "other" schools her entire life. Now it seemed like the worst parts of all those stories had come true and were sitting down to dinner with her, wearing guns and brandishing sharp stakes.

Still, her father had told her to be nice and attempt to get along. She cast a nervous glance at the nearest adult's table, and there he was. "Remember," he'd said, "these kids didn't have all the advantages growing up that you did, and they've had a hard time of it since the trouble started. They'll act a bit differently from what you are used to, but they won't be dangerous."

" 'Won't be dangerous', huh?" she thought as she looked around. The little scuffle between Johnny and those two little girls sure looked like it could have gotten dangerous. Johnny scooted over a chair fast, though. Now, he was stuck between the one bigger girl ("Rosarita"? Something like that) and the tiny boy. He looked nervous, too.

The big black girl, Letitia, was closest to her age. Wendy decided to try to talk with her.

"So where did you live before all this?" Wendy asked.

"Mott Haven," answered Letitia. "We all went to PS 43."

"How'd you wind up with all these little kids?"

"That one's my sister," said Letitia, pointing at Jahayra. "Rest of these kids was in her class."

"I was in class when my dad heard the news," said Wendy. "He came and got me out of school."

"You lucky," Letitia replied. "Nobody came got us."

"Nobody came to get you? How did you get out?"

"Didn't for a few days," Letitia replied. "We hid in a bathroom until the mess was over. Been on our own since then."

"On your own? Where are your parents?"

"Dead, I think. I know mine are. We had to kill Jada's mom. If any of the rest of 'em are alive, they ran away, probably. No one came looking for us."

Johnny was listening to this exchange and turned even paler than he normally was at the sound of "We had to kill Jada's mom." Wendy gave him a little kick under the table.

"What's it like where you live now?" Wendy asked.

Jose piped up. "I like it!" he said proudly.

"You do?" Wendy asked.

"Sure! Always, other people they laughed at me because I so small. They say I stink because Mama would forget to wash my clothes or give me a bath. When I hungry, sometimes there no food, sometimes there nobody to feed me."

Jose's voice got faster and faster. He didn't usually talk much, but once he got going it didn't seem like he would ever stop. Or breathe.

"Now, Trevon, he no let anyone laugh at me. It no matter that I small, if I do good in the games. That is what *everybody* say when I do good. Is always food, is always someone to watch me, is always shower to get clean. Letitia, she cuts my hair, she teach me to tie my boots, she teach me how to shoot, how to stab things, and she read us a story every night."

"I just as good as everybody now, and she takes just as good of care of me as she does of anybody else."

"How about those adults that live with you?"

"Oh, they help Letitia, but Letitia, she the boss."

Wendy and Johnny mulled that over and were happy to see a big plate of food get set in front of them. It gave them a chance to think.

"You said something about games. What kind of games do you play, Jose?" Wendy finally asked, thinking it would be safe. After hearing the answer, she and Johnny decided it was best just to eat quietly.

CHAPTER 119
ICE FISHING

Letitia was glad to see that she had been right about one thing: there were still fish in the river even when there was ice on it. The river was never covered by ice like the pictures in the book, but there was enough ice to make fishing tougher than usual.

She'd finally gotten the hang of casting and was usually able to do it without injuring herself or anyone around her. Today, she'd been particularly successful and was feeling proud of herself. Her cast had been beautiful, arcing over the pier and into the water. She began to troll it back and felt the fish strike. The fish she snagged was a monster and she was worried about getting pulled in. Even with three of them on the pole, they couldn't succeed in reeling it in.

"Quick!" she said to Jahayra. "Run, get Alex." Kiara and Jahayra scurried off, and, in a few minutes, Alex came running over to take the pole. He slowly reeled the fish in and landed it on the deck. He guessed it had to be a fifty-pound bass, large enough to be dinner for several nights.

Alex decided that this would be an opportunity to try smoking a fish. He'd been thinking about if for a few days, and this seemed to be his chance to give it a try. After carving off enough for tonight's meal and setting it on ice, he cut the remainder into small strips and rubbed them in salt. He put a tray full of fine pieces of wood on top of his water-heating fire, set the slices of fish on a small grating above that, then set a board on rocks above that, trapping the smoke in a layer under it. He played with it most of the day, fiddling with one part or another until he felt it was going right.

He was disappointed in the group's reaction. He had always liked smoked fish and was expecting everyone to enjoy what he thought was a treat. When he put out pieces with lunch the next day, the children's reactions ranged from being unimpressed to being disgusted.

"Why would you *do* this to a fish?" was Letitia's question.

"You don't have to refrigerate it. It'll stay safe to eat for weeks," was the reply. She didn't seem overly impressed, but he saw her making drawings of his smoker in her notebook later that day.

CHAPTER 120
SPRINGTIME IN NEW YORK CITY

Letitia checked her list of things to bring back. Number one was a few tarps. It had been raining so hard and long that the rain was getting through the roof, the fourth floor, the third floor, and dripping into the recovery ward. Alex seemed to think he could make that better if he had tarps. He wasn't feeling well today and wasn't up to a big trip.

Tarps would be hard to handle, so all the kids were along. The flotilla set out, paddling its way across the East River. Most of the ice was gone, and the sound of returning ducks was in the air.

It was a wet April for New York, and the city was starting to turn green in ways that it never did before. Grass grew out of the flesh pressed into the remnants of the car wall. Small vines, weeds, and even the occasional wildflower grew out of any zombie bits lying on the ground.

They arrived at Buchmans. Letitia felt a little homesick, remembering how bright and cheery the sporting goods store had seemed. The inflatable boats still hung from the ceiling, but looked funny with most of the air gone. Unreadable mushy boxes sat on the shelves, destroyed by the rain that came in through the windows.

The tarps were just where she remembered, and there was a set of little pup tents that should come in handy if they ever had to make that trip south. She picked them up to add to her cache at Fort Lee, placing them on the dolly. Jada and Tiara had dolly duty today, the result of getting into a fight with Jahayra and Kiara over whose turn it was to wash dishes. Strapped to the furniture dolly, they pulled it behind them wherever the children went.

Kids Foot Locker and V.I.M. had some fresh shoes and clothes for everyone. The children headed back for the island, looking for an apartment building to pilfer as they went. Food stores weren't worth it anymore: everything had been taken or ruined by weather. Apartment buildings, on the other hand, still had canned goods and things in the kitchens.

Letitia stopped in front of one promising-looking building. None of the windows were broken, and that meant the kitchens would be dry. She swung her hatchet next to the doorknob until she had broken through the wood.

She looked carefully through the hole. Nothing was moving. She reached in and opened the door from the inside.

"Rosarita, Malik, stay here with Jada, Tiara, and the cart. Everybody else, come help."

A kitchen on the second floor was untouched and full, with an entire closet full of canned food, and one special treat: two unopened tubs of Hershey's Cocoa. Not the little bitty cans, either, the big tubs. Letitia smiled broadly. She loved hot chocolate, the little ones loved hot chocolate, Alex and Catalina loved hot chocolate. She looked forward to sharing it with the adults that night. She never really knew how to let them know how much she appreciated them.

They headed back towards the Coca-Cola plant. Its dock was best for a day like today, when they needed to load the dolly in and out of the boat. Outboard motors buzzed in the background. Letitia pulled out her binoculars, looking for them. Small boats were docked at the ferry slip at Rikers.

"We ain't goin' the usual way," she said. "Somethin' goin' on. We go over to the little beach under the pier. That way, nobody on Rikers see us."

The pier was a harder place to come ashore. The current along here was stronger, and there were some spots right at the beach that the little ones couldn't handle. Letitia got her boat ashore, dragged it inland, then came back to the beach. "Throw me your rope," she gestured at Lucia. Lucia threw it, and Letitia wrapped it around a small post, helping to keep the boat from being swept downstream. One by one, she helped the little ones ashore.

"Quiet now! Stick together! We don' know if anybody here that ain't supposed to be here." They carefully approached Alex and Catalina's cottage. It *looked* normal. Letitia crept up and peered through a window. Alex was lying in bed, flushed and sweating. Catalina was nowhere to be seen.

Letitia opened the door and went in. Alex looked a lot worse than when they'd left this morning. She reached out and shook him awake.

"Hey! You gotta get up! Somethin' going on next door at Rikers. All kind of boats and things."

Alex sat up and nearly fell right back over. He wobbled.

"Boats at Rikers? ... Men? ... Where's Catalina?"

"Ain't seen Catalina. How long you been like this? You just had a runny nose when I left."

"Yeah, it hit me really hard right after you went. I've been in bed ever since." Alex got ready to stand, planting his feet on the floor. He stood, the color leaving his face as soon as he did. He swayed a bit again, but stayed standing.

"You sit back down. We go look for her and come let you know when we find her.

"Rosarita, Malik: you stay here with Alex. Rest of you, we go find Catalina."

Letitia led the troop off on the search. Catalina wasn't anywhere to be found: not in the supply room, not by the garden, not by the water filters, nowhere. The aluminum rowboat was gone.

Letitia climbed to the roof with her binoculars. The boats on the island weren't Governors Island boats, and the men didn't look like Governors Island people: no army clothes, regular guns instead of big army guns. They looked more like the people from the Pioneer Supermarket they had hidden from that day by the pet shop. Scattered all over, too: she wasn't going to be able to just hit them with bombs.

One of the big boats shifted a little bit on the water, revealing the aluminum rowboat tied up to the dock. Catalina was over there by herself with those men.

Letitia stopped by the utility closet on the way back to the cottage. She pulled the big gun out from under the pile and headed back to the cabin. Rosarita grinned when she saw the gun. "Is for me?" she asked.

"No, it ain't for you. Too big for me, way too big for you."

Letitia turned to Alex. "Think you may need this. You ain't strong enough today to be swingin' your spike or nothin'."

Alex took the gun in his hands. "Did you find Catalina?"

"I think Catalina be on Rikers. The metal boat over there, I can't find her nowhere over here."

"She must have gone over to get something. Got caught by surprise." Alex stood up again.

"I've got to get over there to help her," he said, wobbling a bit, but still standing.

"What you goin' to do to help her?" asked Letitia. "Puke all over 'em?"

Alex collapsed back onto the bed. "You're right. I can't be the hero when I can't even walk ten feet."

"Think you well enough to use that gun if you need to?"

"Yeah, I've got enough strength for that. Why?"

"I take Rosarita and Malik, we go over, see if we can find her, see if she OK. I think you need to be in the ward with the little kids. You can't be fightin' nothin' today."

Alex looked like he was going to argue and then shook his head. "You're right," he said, "I'm useless this way. Let's see if I can get over there."

He sat up on the edge of the bed. He sat a moment, gathering his strength before standing up. Letitia held on to him, giving him support.

"Let's go," he said in a weak voice. "We need to try to get there before I fall over."

They made their way to the hospital, Letitia leading, with Rosarita and Malik in the rear. Alex was in the middle, protected by the children and their sharp stakes.

Alex made his way slowly up the entry steps to the lobby, reaching the spiral stairway leading upwards. He grasped onto the handrail for support and climbed upwards, stopping at the missing landing. He tried to swing across the gap, but fell back. He couldn't make it.

"Go get my harness for my dolly," Letitia instructed Jaharya and Kiara. They ran off and came back. Letitia fastened it around Alex and tied the other end around the railing on the next flight. "There. That way, you won' fall if you slip." Using the rope and the railing for support, Alex made it to the second floor.

Alex settled into a bed, then examined the short-barreled tactical shotgun. Three shells left in the clip and two loaded: enough to handle anything that might come to the door. "At least I don't have to aim it," he said, setting it back against the wall.

"I don' want none of you *touchin'* that thing while I gone!" Letitia told the little ones. "It too big for you."

"C'mon," she said, gesturing at Rosarita and Malik, "we need to go see what happenin'."

CHAPTER 121

SNEAK ATTACK

Letitia, Rosarita, and Malik boarded their boats. "We go around the little island and come up on that little beach on the side," Letitia said.

"You mean that one next to that funny-looking building? The one that look like a ball made out of triangles?" asked Malik.

"Yeah, that the one I mean. Nobody see us if we put our boats there."

They paddled their way around the western shores of North Brother Island and its little brother, then aimed for the little beach on Rikers. Low rock walls rose up from the beach, coming up a little over Letitia's head. Water dribbled out of a large concrete storm drain onto the sand.

"You think that pipe big enough for the boats?" Malik asked.

Letitia hadn't thought of that. "You right!" she said. "That even better. We put the boats in there, ain't nobody goin' to see 'em. Nobody know we here at all."

The boats fit easily into the large pipe. The three children climbed up the rocks and peeked around. Nobody in sight.

" 'kay, we sneak over to the storeroom. We see if Catalina there."

They climbed the wall and ran to a storage container sitting by the side of the road. The roadway here was lined with little buildings and storage containers. They moved southward, moving the same way they did when they were in the city: hugging the low buildings for protection, peering carefully around corners, and running across the gaps between buildings. Letitia took the lead, with the others coming behind.

Letitia looked around the corner of a storage container. "We at the gate now. I don' see nothin'. Go back, see if you see anything from the other end."

Rosarita and Malik were only gone a minute. "Don't see nothin' from there neither," Malik said. "Where you think they be?"

"If they stealin' stuff, they goin' to be by the big warehouse. That where Catalina should be, too, but I don' see nobody. C'mon. Let's go."

There was room for four trucks to unload at the back of the warehouse, and three of the spots had trucks parked in them. The fourth spot was empty. Letitia led them through the empty spot and up a little concrete stairway. "We go in the back way, maybe no one see us." She turned the knob and pulled open the door. There was no one in sight in the loading dock office. "C'mon, you two. Inside."

Letitia turned to make sure no one was coming up behind them when she heard the shots. Rosarita and Malik came running back out the door, revolvers drawn.

"We get him?" Malik asked.

"*Si*, we hit him. I no think he dead, though!" Rosarita replied.

"You two shoot somebody *already*?" Letitia felt her heart pumping. "Why you need to go doin' that?"

"He point a gun at us! That door in the back open, and he come through, he point it at us!"

Malik nodded. "That what happened. He surprise us."

Letitia looked back into the office. There was blood on the floor, but the room was empty. "Yeah, you hit him, but he gone. Probably gettin' his friends. Everybody be goin' to be chasin' us." Why did she bring these two? She made herself calm down. She brought them *because* they would shoot if they had to. Hadn't worked out too well, though. The door in the back of the office opened.

"Run!" she said, pointing back the way they had come. She slammed the outside door shut. The three children ran out of the loading dock and towards a group of dumpsters lined up beside a fence. They reached one just as they heard the office door open again, letting angry voices through.

Crouched behind the dumpster, Letitia whispered commands. "Don't you two be movin'. We stay quiet, maybe they won't find us here."

The voices got closer.

"You say it was little kids? Little kids with guns?" a deep voice asked.

"That's what Ralph said. Little black kid and a spic girl," a medium voice said. "Said he surprised 'em in the office and they started shooting at him."

A walkie-talkie came on. "You find anything yet?"

"Don't see a damn thing," deep voice replied.

"Keep looking," the walkie-talkie said. "Lots of stuff to load up, and I don't want anybody taking potshots at me while we're loading the boats."

Footsteps walked away, heading towards the road. Letitia started to calm down and then got anxious again.

Those men were between them and their boats.

CHAPTER 122

IN THE DORMITORY

Someone pounded loudly on the door to the dormitory. "Dave!" a voice shouted through the door. "Put it back in your pants and get out here! We got trouble!"

Catalina no longer felt the greasy man's weight pressing her into the mattress. The foul odor of his rotten teeth stopped filling her nose, but her mouth was still full of the flavor of tears and blood.

Her eyes still closed, she heard a zipper zipping. "What kind of trouble?" she heard.

"Ralph's been shot. Two little kids with guns. George says we've got to find 'em. Now. No more fun with the broad till we find them."

Catalina's eyes popped open. Alex had let the kids come over? No, you couldn't blame Alex. Even if he tried to stop her, if Letitia had decided to do it, there was probably no stopping her. She lay still, waiting for "Dave" to leave the room. The door opened, then closed, and she was alone.

Her wrists were tied over her head, the sleeves of her sweater wrapped and tied around them. Craning her head back, she saw that the sweater was looped around the frame of the bunk above her. Inching her way back, she sat up, the sleeves slackening until she could bring her wrists together and untie the knots.

She sat up and tried to stand up. That felt like a mistake. Her legs were bruised, her insides felt like they'd been smashed, fluid dripped out of her. She wiped her leg with her hand, then wiped off the mixture of blood and semen on the sheets of the bed. She used the sheets to wipe herself as clean as she could and took a quick moment to vomit in the trash can.

She wanted to find a shower and stay in there for weeks until she washed away every trace of the men, until she had washed away every trace of her skin that had ever had a trace of the men on it, but she couldn't lose time. Some of the children were here. Maybe they were trapped, maybe they were looking for her, but they were definitely going to get hurt if these men found them. Besides, they were armed, and she wasn't. She needed them as much as they needed her.

She put her sweater back on. There was no sign of her pants, or shoes, or underwear. She pulled the sweater down to cover herself as well as she could and went to the door. The lock was still broken from when they had cleared the place. She slowly pulled it open a crack and listened. Nothing. She poked her head out the doorway. The hallway leading to the guard station was clear.

If someone was looking for her, they would have gone to the supply warehouse. That's where they would expect to find her, so that's where she needed to go. She walked to the guard station, through the central area, and back towards the main loading entrance.

The loading entrance led to a long sidewalk, fenced with hurricane fence and razor wire. There was nowhere to hide here, but it was the only way back to the warehouse. She listened for the sound of men. Nothing. She sprinted down the long sidewalk, her bare feet slapping against cold cement.

A small rock flew out of nowhere, bouncing in front of her on the sidewalk. She was trying to see where it came from when another one came flying at her. She kept running until she saw a small dark hand holding a small rock reach out from behind a dumpster across from the loading dock ahead. Letitia!

CHAPTER 123
UNLEASHING THE HORDE

"She see us now," Letitia said. "Here she come." Catalina was coming straight for them, reaching the end of the sidewalk she was on and turning towards the driveway they were in. She looked bad. Letitia could see blood and bruises everywhere.

"Hey! The chick's getting away!" someone shouted in the distance.

"Unless she's got a gun, I don't give a rat's ass," another voice answered him. "We find the kids that shot Ralph, *then* we go looking for pussy. Got it?"

Catalina crouched behind the dumpster. Letitia took in the blood smears on her legs and face, the bruises, the swelling.

"You goin' to be all right?" Letitia asked.

"Think so," Catalina answered.

"You lose your pants? This another one of them things like with Marie? You goin' to give these two *pie* for killing people again?"

"They won't be in trouble with *me* for it. They can kill all of these bastards they like."

Rosarita, clutching a bottle of gas in her hand, brightened at the sound of that.

"Where's your boat?" Catalina continued.

"Down by that funny ball-shape building. But there all kinds of these guys lookin' for us over there."

"Funny ball-shaped building? ... Oh, you mean the geodesic dome. Did you hide them?"

"Yeah, hid 'em inside the big pipe. Don' that pipe got to go somewhere? That what I been tryin' to figure out." She held out the map she had drawn last summer. "If we get in the pipe, nobody see us get our boats."

"It should hook to a grating, but that's not going to work. This is a prison. They aren't just going to make handy doors and hatches for prisoners to climb into pipes and escape."

Letitia's face dropped. "I guess you right."

"There they are!" a voice shouted.

Letitia pointed west. "That way! I got an idea!"

"Hit 'em once," she said to Rosarita, "then run!"

"¡*Fuego!*" said Rosarita. Malik clicked his lighter, Rosarita stood and lobbed the bottle underhand. It burst on the ground by the men running into the driveway, splashing them all with burning gas.

"Where are we heading?" Catalina asked as they ran, the screams fading in the distance behind them.

"Those big buildings over there." Letitia pointed at the Otis Bantum Center. "Remember the one part Alex wouldn't open 'cause it all full? We open it, nobody be worried about us no more."

"Are you crazy?"

"You got a better idea?"

They continued their dash, reaching the entry to the courtyard, then making their way past the smashed locks on the main entrance. They paused for a moment and took a breath. The central lobby rose five stories above them. Balconies ran along the lobby on each floor, and smashed doorways led off of each lobby.

Catalina started again. "You're just going to let the zombies out? Alex said there were thousands in here!"

"What you want to do instead? There twenty of them guys after us. They got guns. They mad. We give 'em somethin' else to fight, then we figure out how to get past 'em."

As Letitia talked, pounding noises started from one of the hallways on the second floor. She pointed. "That where they be, up there.

"You think anybody saw us come in here?" Letitia continued.

"I don't think so," Catalina answered. "They must have seen which way we ran, though, so we haven't got too long before they come through the door."

"I think the way this work," said Letitia, "is for you guys to stay down here and find some chairs and things to hold the front doors open with. I go knock that door down. When there a bunch of cucos down here, we open the doors to outside, and run real fast."

"Run real fast where?" Malik asked.

"How I suppose to know? We get outside, we look for men with guns, we run the other way."

Catalina shook her head. "We need a better plan than that. Think we can reach the roof?"

"Maybe. Never looked," replied Letitia.

"Go take a look. I can't get up and down these stairs too many times."

Letitia climbed the stairs. The emergency exit door at the top led to a large roof divided into three pieces: a large central square with machinery on it, and two wings, each about four feet lower than the center.

Letitia returned. "The roof easy to get to. Hard part goin' to be the doors down here. If they closed, cucos be too dumb to open 'em. Think them chairs work to hold 'em open?"

Catalina looked around. "No, but those desks should do it."

" 'kay, then. We get 'em close. I get the door up there open, you open these, and we run to the roof."

Catalina nodded. Letitia climbed up to the second floor. The door to the closed-off wing had big metal hinges, big enough that tip of her rock pick could fit inside. She tapped the pins upward until they were all about loose. She turned towards the entrance. The desks were close to the doors, ready for a push.

"Open the doors!"

She tapped on the pins, knocking them all loose. The door began to swing out backwards under the pressure, but didn't pop loose. The other three were already on the stairs going up, and men were already coming in the front door.

She pounded the lock mechanism with her pick. It finally weakened enough that the door came loose, letting the flood loose. She ran for the top of the stairs. Lying flat at the top of the stairs, she fired two quick shots, injuring two of the men. Their screams made sure the cucos chased them, not her. She opened the door and followed her friends to the roof.

CHAPTER 124
TACTICAL SUPPORT

Alex heard gunfire and wobbled his way to his feet.

"Get that harness ready for me. I need to get up on the roof and see what's going on." He started towards the central stairway. By the time he got there, Tiara and Jada had untangled the harness. He grabbed on and made it to the first step leading upwards.

"Move it up a floor," he said. "Get it ready for me to make the next jump."

Tiara and Jada untied it and ran up a floor, tying it in place again. Alex pulled on it and it seemed secure. He swung onto the third floor. The doors to the roofs of the two wings were here. He climbed out on the eastern roof. Kiara and Jahayra were already there, watching anxiously.

"What have you seen?"

"Can't see nothin'," Jahayra answered. "Big puff of black smoke over there," she said, pointing towards the warehouse, "but it all gone now. Heard some shots."

Alex peered anxiously towards the island. There weren't any more shots. Hopefully, that meant that everyone had gotten away, not that everyone was dead. The Otis Bantum Center blocked his view of everything interesting. Everyone must be by the warehouse, but he just couldn't see it.

A door opened at the top of the Otis Bantum building and four figures ran out the door.

"You kids got binoculars?" he asked.

"Letitia, she carry 'em *all* the time," answered Jahayra. "She don't think it *important* for nobody *else* to see nothin'." Alex could tell he had picked an old scab.

That had to be Catalina and the kids, though. Why were they on the roof? And why on the Otis Bantum Center? He'd thought about burning that place out. Why on earth would they go inside it?

Shots began to ring out on the ground.

"You two still the best with the catapult?" he asked.

Jahayra and Kiara beamed with pride. "We always the best with the catapult! Every time we play!"

"OK, then, show me how many times you can hit those boats at the pier," he said. If things were bad enough that they had opened the prison to get rid of the invaders, he needed to be sure the invaders didn't just run over here.

Four shots later, the three boats docked at the ferry slip were on fire.

CHAPTER 125
ROOF OF THE
OTIS BANTUM CENTER

They stood on the square central section of the Otis Bantum roof. Two wings spread out west and south of the center section, large flat planes about four feet lower than the section they were on.

"At least nobody can shoot us up here," Catalina said.

"Least not till they climb up on a different roof," Letitia said. "They bad men. That don't mean they *stupid* men."

She peered over the roof edge, looking down at the main entrance. A swarm of cucos was coming out of the entrance. The men were across the narrow roadway, firing.

"Maybe I wrong. Maybe they be stupid," she said. "Look at that. No spikes or nothin', just those little guns."

She looked over at Catalina. "These things only hold six bullets. Think them guns they got be the same?"

Catalina looked down. "No, those look a lot bigger. I don't know how many those hold, but I'll bet it's a lot more."

Letitia looked down again. "Can't hold way more, though. Ain't those army kind of guns that the Hunts Point people had. Just little things."

There was a rapid series of *thwump* noises. Black smoke began to rise from the ferry slip. They turned towards the noise and could barely make out Alex and the children on the hospital roof.

"Alex figured out that we were in trouble," Catalina said.

"Look like it," Letitia said, casually tossing a Molotov down at the men below.

Catalina shuddered. She wanted to hurt these men, but she would at least *feel* something about it. Letitia took care of things like this the way she would spray ant spray on an anthill.

Down below, the invaders were rolling on the ground, too busy trying to put out their burning clothing to defend themselves from the horde. The horde advanced, overrunning the men's position.

"What you two got in them backpacks?" Letitia asked.

Rosarita and Malik sat down and went through them. Two water bottles, three granola bars and two boxes of bullets each, one more gas bomb, and a selection of knives and spikes. Letitia had a rockpick, a couple more granola bars, a few water bottles, a coil of rope, one more bomb and another two boxes of bullets.

" 'kay, that's ..." Letitia paused a moment. "Six boxes, twenty-four bullets each ... one hundred and forty-four bullets?" She looked at Catalina, who nodded. "And two bombs. Alex said there about two thousand cucos in there?" She looked at Catalina again, who nodded again.

"Ain't enough, is it?"

"Not to just fight our way out, no."

"Should have left more of those guys alive." A quick glance over the roof edge showed four of the invaders still fighting in the street. That didn't mean that some of them hadn't run someplace else: they couldn't *all* be stupid.

"Think this rope be long enough to get down from here?" She held the small coil up.

"No way to tell but to test it," replied Catalina. "Hand me that rock pick." She tied a knot around the pick and let the weight drag the rope down the sloped face of the building. It reached the bottom of a window on the second floor.

"We could drop from there," Catalina said, "but it's a one-way trip. There'd be no way for us to grab it again and come back up." She pulled the rope back up.

"Can I keep this a while?" she asked, grasping the rock pick.

"For a while."

"Might as well sit and wait for a bit. Let them four guys do what they can, then see what left." She pulled a granola bar out of her backpack and held it out to Catalina. "Hungry?"

The four of them were sitting on the edge of the central roof, drinking water and eating granola bars, when a shot rang out from behind them. Rosarita flew forward from the ledge, landing face down in the tar and gravel, large red stains spreading from her right shoulder.

The other three flattened out right beside her. No more shots came. Catalina crawled over to the injured girl. Letitia ran back to the ledge, peering over it from below. No one in sight. She hoisted herself over the ledge and ran over to the gap between the elevator tower and the air conditioning units. The building next door had four men on the roof.

She ran back. "They doin' the same thing we doin' ... hidin' on a roof. Long as we don't stand up, they can't shoot us no more."

She looked down at Rosarita. Her shirt was off and Catalina was wrapping torn strips from it around her shoulder. Her head lay in Malik's lap. Both of them cried as they held hands.

"How bad she hurt?"

"Not too badly," Catalina replied. "The bullet went right through. I don't think it hit a bone."

"Move your fingers, honey," she said to Rosarita. Rosarita continued to cry, but wiggled her fingers. Catalina watched approvingly.

"That's all I can do up here. She'll be OK. Where'd you say those men are?"

"Over on the next building. It just as high as we are, so as long as we stay over here and don't stand up, we be OK."

"Same four as were down on the ground?"

"Don't think so. Can't you hear 'em still shootin'?" Letitia crawled over to the edge and looked over.

"Three of 'em still down there. Don' know whether the missin' one is one of the guys over on the roof.

"Still think we should just sit here for a while. Guys down there goin' to run out of bullets. Guys on the roof goin' to run out, too. Then it time for us to do somethin'."

Twenty minutes later, Letitia went back by the elevator tower. The men were lying at the edge of their roof shooting rifles down into the crowd of cucos. They seemed to have completely forgotten about Letitia and the others.

The buildings were about fifty feet apart. She might be able to shoot them from here. She knew that Malik could. She crept back to the lower level. Rosarita was resting her head in Malik's lap, with Catalina crouching nearby, unable to rest her naked lower body comfortably on the graveled tar roof.

"Malik, you got to come with me for a few minutes. You a better shot than me."

"No," said Malik. "Rosarita be hurt bad. You said I always got to take care of my buddy." He clenched Rosarita's hand more tightly.

"Yeah, I did. Which you think she need more? You holdin' her hand, or you shootin' a guy that goin' to shoot her again if he get a chance?"

Rosarita opened her eyes. "*Sí*, Malik. Go get him. You go shoot him for me."

Letitia and Malik walked back to the ledge. Malik was completely safe: his head didn't come over the edge. Letitia crouched slightly. She pointed.

"See that crack there? You squeeze in there, you able to see all four of 'em. Don' try to shoot 'em in the head. They layin' down, so you can see their backs. You just hit 'em fast and run back here. Don' worry if you don' get all four."

Malik crept forward. Letitia was right: the men were all lying down, and they were all looking down. He could do this easily. He pulled his revolver, carefully sighted one man's back, and fired. As soon as his bullet hit, the other three began to look for him. He got two more in the stomach, then ran back.

"Couldn't get 'em all," he said. "Hit three, right here and here." He gestured at his lower back and his belly.

Letitia nodded approvingly. "That probably be enough. The one you didn't hit probably shoot 'em in the head so they don't eat him." Three shots rang out in quick succession.

"See. Told you so."

CHAPTER 126
NOISEMAKERS

As the sun began to set, the sound of children shouting started north of them. It took a moment for words to become clear.

"Ugly face? Poop butt?" Catalina asked.

"They think it funny," Letitia said. "They must be trying to get the cucos to come over."

"Why?"

"Trying to let us get away, probably. Alex must be helpin' 'em. No way they thought of it by themselves. This goin' to be slow. We spent all day in a pet store doin' that once. We got time to figure out how to get down."

"Can't we just go back down the stairs?"

"Don' think so. There a bunch of 'em still in the buildin'. See how they still comin' out the door?"

"I know I could climb down the rope," Catalina said. "That was my favorite thing in gym class. How about you two?"

Malik and Letitia nodded uneasily. "Yeah, think so," Letitia said. "Don' think Rosarita can."

"No, not with that shoulder. We'd have to lower her." Catalina paused. "She wouldn't be able to drop at the bottom, though."

"There a little building over on the other side. Bet the rope able to reach it," Letitia replied.

"How are you going to get down over there? Isn't there still a man with a gun over there?"

"He ain't shootin' no more," Letitia said. "He just sittin' there."

"He might have saved a few bullets. I know *I* would."

"How big a thing we need to land her on?"

"Ten feet, maybe?"

"So, about thirty cucos? Forty, maybe?"

"What are you thinking about?"

"Make a pile of 'em, climb down onto the pile."

"Are you crazy? How are you going to make a pile of zombies?"

"It kind of hard *not* to make a pile of 'em, ain't it? All you got to do is let 'em see you when you up high.

"Put that rope around me and let me down. I shoot 'em when they under me. We get a pile pretty quick."

Catalina started to argue, but couldn't think of another answer.

"Where?"

"Over in that corner, by the fence. Enough of 'em over there, but not too many."

"I'm doing this," said Catalina. "I know you kids can get down, but I'm not sure you can get back *up.*"

Catalina tied the rope carefully around herself and wrapped the rope around one of the lamp fixtures, enough to drop about twenty feet. She began to climb down the building. Letitia had been right about one thing: the motion down the side of the building and the sight of fresh meat was enough to attract attention. A zombie came over to the edge of the fence. She shot it in the head and it collapsed. The next zombie that came stepped on it, and she shot again. And again.

The rope was cutting into her around the shoulders, but it was holding her weight for her, letting her dangle in the air out of anything's reach. She emptied the pistol, then reloaded, emptied it and reloaded again. The pile was high enough that zombies were clearing the fence now. The pile began to build inside the fence.

Two more boxes of bullets and the pile was up to the second floor.

Now, it was time to get back up. She turned in the loop of rope and pressed against the slick, sloping, cold marble face of the building with her bare feet. She pushed upwards and wrapped a loop of rope around her upper arm. When she hit the wall again, she was a couple inches higher. She pushed again and wrapped again. She reached a window ledge that gave her enough stability to move the rope from her arm to her waist, and moved up another floor.

She reached the top, grasping the edge of the roof with her fingers. Letitia and Malik pulled on the rope, and Catalina spread her arms out on the roof to pull herself up. She looked behind. She had certainly built a pile, but zombies swarmed around the base.

"Get over here away from the edge!" Letitia said. "They follow the noise if they don't see you."

Thwump noises continued over by the pier. The shouting and cheering grew louder. A column of greasy black smoke began to rise, barely visible in the moonlight. Letitia crept back over to the edge. The base of the pile was clear now, and the cucos were all heading towards the dock again.

"You two saw how she did that, right?"

Rosarita and Malik nodded.

"I go first, then Rosarita, then Malik, then Catalina. Catalina goin' to help you two with the rope."

Letitia lowered herself down, copying Catalina as best she could, holding her weight with the rope wrapped around her arms, unwrapping as she went down. She set down on the pile of bodies. It shifted a bit, but it held.

She let the rope loose and looked around. No one had spotted her. The rope slid back up into the darkness. Looking up, she saw Rosarita coming down. She was tied up tight, and Catalina was lowering her down on the rope, doing all the work for her. Letitia helped get her loose and sent the rope back up.

"We just stay here, wait for Malik."

Malik came climbing down. The pile was shifting more under the extra weight, and they were starting to attract some attention.

"Rosarita, you wait for Catalina. Malik, you come on down with me."

They clambered down the pile of bodies into the street.

A few cucos noticed them. "Quiet, now. No guns. We do this the hard way," said Letitia. She readied her hatchet, ready to swing. The first few reached them, and she swung. As each cuco staggered, Malik ran his stake into the eye socket. It wasn't as fast as when Rosarita helped, but they managed to keep the base clear.

Catalina came scaling down the wall. It was easier the second time, her feet guiding her downward as she unreeled the rope. It stopped being easier when her feet found purchase on top of the pile of bodies: the sensation of cold dead flesh against her bare feet made her squirm.

"C'mon," she said to Rosarita, "let's get down from here." Catalina climbed down to the ground, forcing herself to seek handholds in the pile of corpses. Once Rosarita was close enough to reach, she grabbed her by the hips and set her on the ground.

"We're down," she said to Letitia.

" 'kay, then. Run for it."

The four ran south, away from the horde, away from the Otis Bantum Center, towards their boats. The boats were still there, tucked away in the drainage pipe.

"You able to row one of these things, ain't you?" Letitia asked.

"Don't see why not."

" 'kay, then, we put Rosarita and Malik in the flat raft and I haul 'em. You take the other boat. We go meet up with the rest."

The boats headed northward on the dark nighttime waters of the East River. As they approached, they could see three boats bobbing in the water, the children inside taking turns yelling. Letitia took her turn to yell.

"We got her! Time to go home!"

CHAPTER 127
BACK HOME

Alex, Kiara, and Jahayra saw the boats coming home. The kids started to run downstairs.

"Hey, you two!" Alex yelled. "Don't forget I need some help!" He felt better than he had earlier, but not so much that he wanted to tackle those stairs. They came back and helped him past the missing landings.

They walked slowly to the beach. The boats were just arriving, and Letitia was already dragging her boat ashore. Catalina came up behind her. Even in the dark, Catalina's bruising was obvious. Alex ran to her, and Catalina collapsed against him, sobbing. He sobbed with her: he was supposed to be able to protect her, to take care of her, and he had failed. He felt very small and very weak, and being sick had nothing to do with that.

By the time he was done crying, Catalina's tears had slowed down.

"What happened?"

"I don't want to talk about it. Not now, maybe not ever. The kids came and got me, and everyone that did this is dead.

"I'm going to try to forget."

He stood beside her, keeping his arm around her waist. He looked down at Rosarita. "She going to be OK?"

"Think so. I'm going to clean that out before we go to bed and get some Cipro in her, but she should be all right. Looks like the bullet went straight through."

Alex bent down and put his arms around Letitia. She stiffened. It took a moment, but she relaxed and accepted the hug. She wiggled out of it quickly.

"We got to get somethin' to eat." Letitia paused a little bit, trying to remember something. "And I forgot! We found hot chocolate!" She smiled. She felt awkward getting hugs, but that didn't mean she didn't want to share a moment of closeness.

After breakfast the next morning, Letitia went up to the roof with her binoculars. There were still cucos *everywhere* on Rikers. Alex had to have been wrong about how many there were. She only saw one living person: one man, trapped on the roof of the building next to the Otis Bantum Center, sitting there with his three dead friends.

She came back down and rounded up the little ones.

"We got a new chore for the losers now." Lucia and Maria, today's losers, stared anxiously at her. "You get to go take your boat out by the end of the pier and shout. Everybody else get to have target practice with the real bombs today."

Lucia and Maria went out in their boats. Everyone else assembled on the roof, taking turns flinging the bombs at the crowd of cucos. By the time Letitia checked on the man on the roof again, he was gone.

CHAPTER 128
HUNTING PARTY

"We got a problem," Letitia said. "There still one guy left over there."

Alex sighed.

"That's not going to work, is it?"

"Don' think so. Can't go over there to get food when a guy with a gun runnin' around. You still too sick yesterday to do nothin', but you better today. We got to do *somethin'*. Can't just go get stuff from the pile at Fort Lee forever, neither. We goin' to do that, we should just move south now."

"I'm glad you didn't do that the other day."

Letitia glared at him. "You ain't *dead*, are you? Ain't goin' to just leave you behind. Catalina neither.

"You the first big people that ever stay with me 'cause you want to. Nobody pay you or *nothin'*. Ain't goin' to just let you die, even when you stupid."

Letitia paused.

"Still think we should go south. Too many guys with guns tryin' to steal stuff around here."

"A thousand miles is a long way. Longer than you can imagine. I think you're dreaming, too: it won't be any better anywhere else. Probably worse, because there'll be more people left."

Letitia shook her head. "Anyway, got to do somethin', and I can't do it alone. Rosarita the best one to help me with this stuff, and she can't do nothin' with her arm all tied up. I got to go find this guy and kill him, and I can't do that with just Malik."

"Find him and kill him? Just like that?"

"You got a better idea? You goin' to give him another chance to hurt Catalina?"

That did it for Alex. Letitia's matter-of-fact way of dealing with this bothered him, but he could focus on Catalina, who still cried when she thought he wasn't watching. He hoped he could think about that hard enough to make him pull the trigger when the time came.

"What kind of gun does he have?"

"A rifle, I think. Big long thing, skinny pipe on it. Telescope thing on top. They were doin' pretty good shootin' cucos with 'em."

"Yeah, that's a rifle. He'd be able to shoot us from a lot farther away than we could shoot him."

"So we got to surprise him?"

"Maybe trap him. You still have spare reels of fishing line?"

"A few."

Alex experimented for a few hours and eventually devised a working tripwire that would trigger the tactical shotgun. He'd made it so far without ever having to kill anybody, and he didn't trust himself to be able to shoot when the time came. This way he didn't have to worry about whether he had the guts to pull the trigger.

Late that night, he rowed over to Rikers and went into the warehouse, set the tripwire into place, then curled up behind a counter to sleep.

CHAPTER 129
PANCAKES FOR BREAKFAST

The life of a guinea pig rancher was a hard one. Jada and Tiara got up early every morning to clean the cages, dispose of any animals that had died, and feed the rest. Now that it was spring, the cages were lined up in the lobby, not the recovery ward. The guinea pigs liked the sun, and it kept the smell in the bedroom from being so bad.

Tiara put the last guinea pig back in the cage. "You think we can get Letitia to make us pancakes for breakfast?"

"Hope so," replied Jada. "Don' like that oatmeal she keep givin' us. Think maybe we out of pancakes? That why she keep feedin' us oatmeal?"

They ran to the shelves to check. No pancake mix anywhere.

"Think we can go get some out of the warehouse?" Jada asked.

"You goin' to get us in big trouble," Tiara said. "Letitia said we ain't supposed to go over there by ourselves. Got to have her or a big person with us."

"Letitia be asleep. We can do it. We tell her we found a box in the wrong place. She never know."

The two buddies fought, but Jada finally prevailed. They took their little boat over to the dock and picked their way through the field of burnt corpses on their way to the warehouse.

Alex woke immediately to the sound of the shotgun blast and rushed to the door to take care of the invader. Jada's legs lay on the ground, propping the door open. Her upper body was scattered in a ten-foot-wide arc through the doorway, with a small interruption in the spray of meat and blood marking where Tiara had been standing. The two intermingled buddies lay at his feet.

He stood in shock, unable to move. When Tiara took her first bite, Alex didn't even struggle. After all, he decided, he'd been right: God did hate him the most.

CHAPTER 130
A JOURNEY OF A THOUSAND MILES
BEGINS WITH A SINGLE STEP

Letitia unzipped a sleeping bag and laid it out on the floor next to hers. She took Catalina's hand, led her over to the bag, laid her down and zipped her in. Catalina shifted to her side and pulled her knees up tight against her chest. Letitia knew she would stay that way until morning.

The children snuggled down for the night in the living room of the abandoned suburban home. Pair by pair, they laid their stakes on each side of their sleeping bags, squeezed in next to each other, and zipped themselves in. Despite the children being exhausted from the long hike down I-95, whispered conversations filled the room as they waited for story time.

Letitia reached into her backpack. The book was tattered and frayed, the blur of colors on the faded cover only representing a train if you knew it was supposed to. Still, the book was a soothing presence in her hands.

She opened the cover, and began:

"A little railroad engine was employed about a station yard for such work as it was built for, pulling a few cars on and off the switches ..."

For just a moment, Letitia thought she saw Catalina smile.

ABOUT THE AUTHOR

Kevin Wayne Williams has been an engineer for much of his life, beginning with GTE in 1980. He rose through the ranks and eventually became an executive in Silicon Valley. In 2004, tired of it all, he fled the country with his wife, Kathy. They opened a hotel on Bonaire, a small Dutch island north of Venezuela. In 2009, for reasons he still doesn't quite understand, they returned to the United States.

He has since resumed his engineering career, but writes novels to help dull the pain.

Made in the USA
Middletown, DE
25 October 2022

13482944R00179